D1712429

THE MOOSICIANS

BY STEVE BEHLING
AND JEFF CROWTHER

Andrews McMeel
PUBLISHING®

Andrews McMeel Publishing
a division of Andrews McMeel Universal
1130 Walnut Street, Kansas City, Missouri 64106

www.andrewsmcmeel.com

24 25 26 27 28 SDB 10 9 8 7 6 5 4 3 2 1

Paperback ISBN: 978-1-5248-8114-6
Hardcover ISBN: 978-1-5248-9376-7

Library of Congress Control Number: 2024934507

Made by:
RR Donnelley (Guangdong) Printing Solutions Company Ltd
Address and location of manufacturer:
No. 2, Minzhu Road, Daning, Humen Town,
Dongguan City, Guangdong Province, China 523930
1st Printing — 5/27/2024

Editor: Erinn Pascal
Art Director: Julie Barnes
Production Editor: Jennifer Straub
Production Manager: Julie Skalla

CHAPTER 1

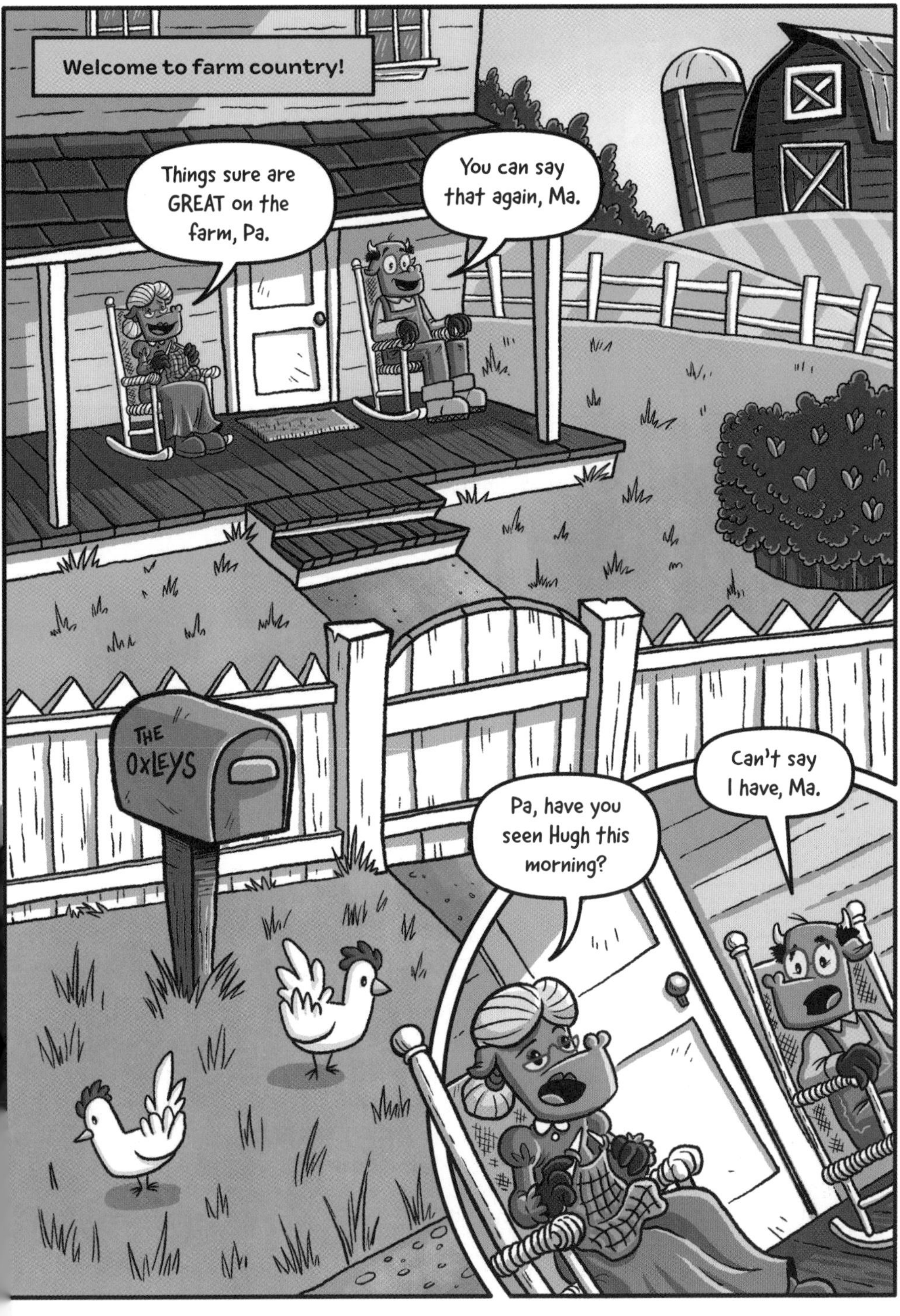

Welcome to farm country!
Things sure are GREAT on the farm, Pa.
You can say that again, Ma.
THE OXLEYS
Pa, have you seen Hugh this morning?
Can't say I have, Ma.

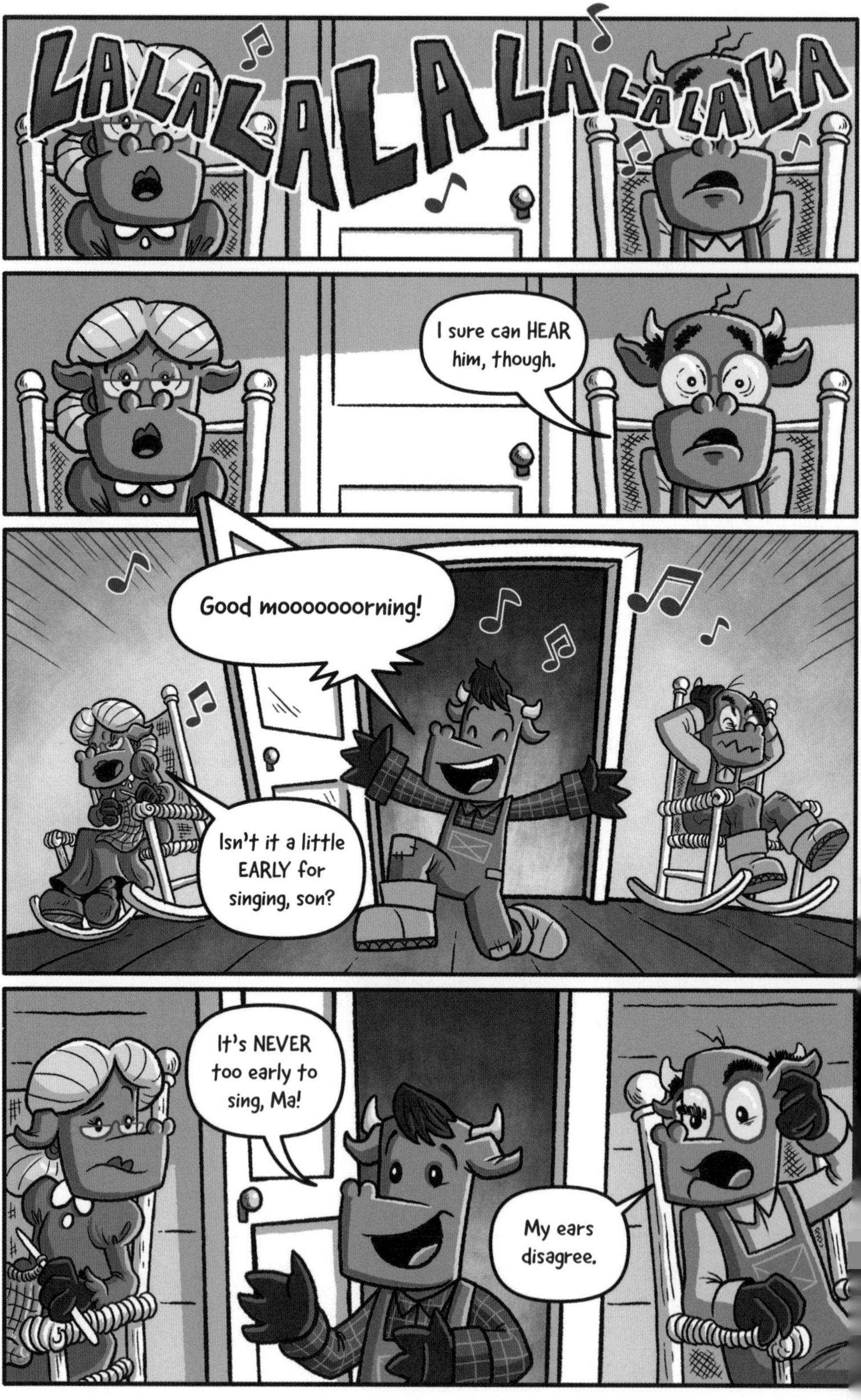
LALALALALALALALALA
I sure can HEAR him, though.
Good moooooorning!
Isn't it a little EARLY for singing, son?
It's NEVER too early to sing, Ma!
My ears disagree.

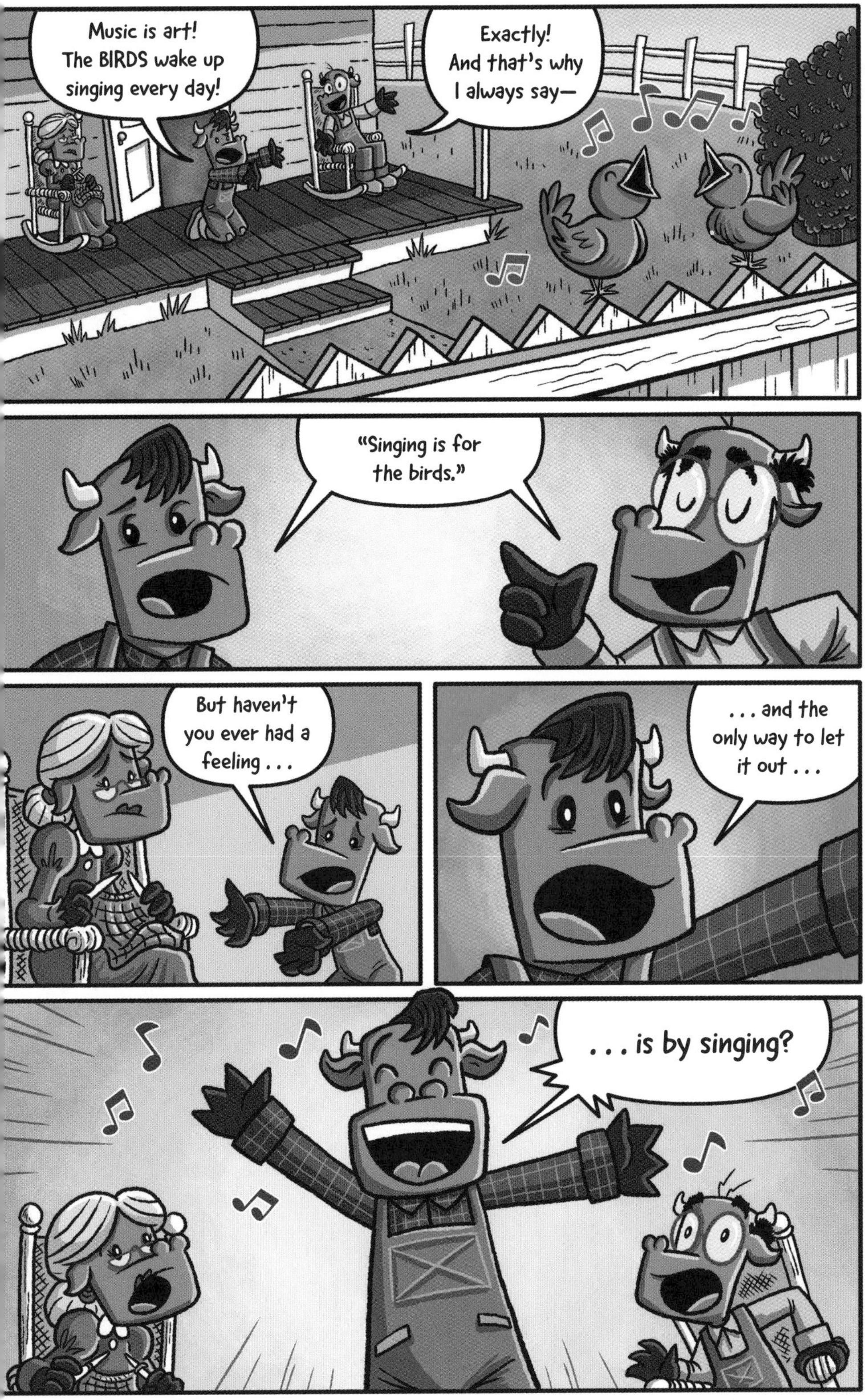
Music is art! The BIRDS wake up singing every day!
Exactly! And that's why I always say—
"Singing is for the birds."
But haven't you ever had a feeling . . .
. . . and the only way to let it out . . .
. . . is by singing?

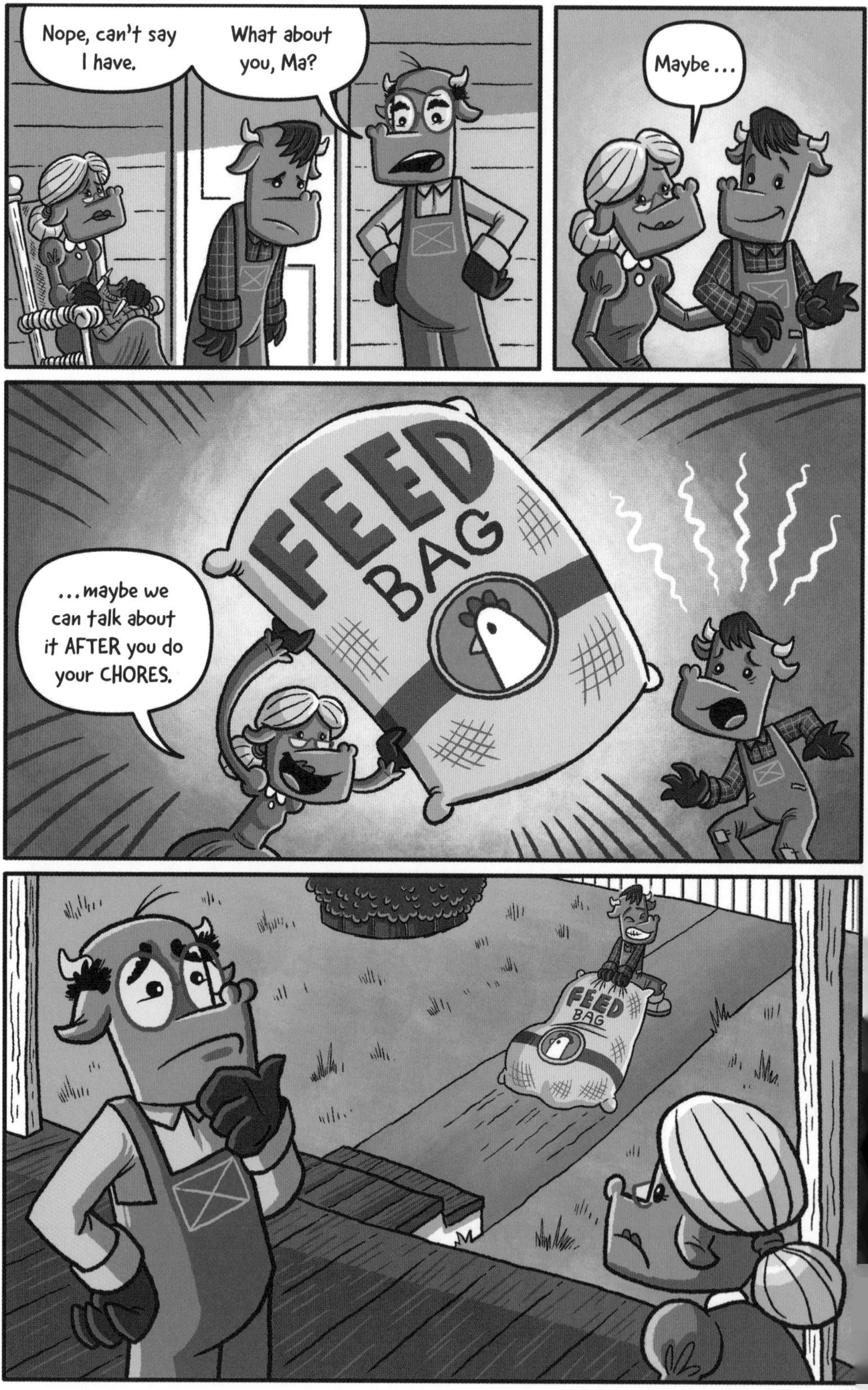
Nope, can't say I have.
What about you, Ma?
Maybe . . .
FEED BAG
. . . maybe we can talk about it AFTER you do your CHORES.
FEED BAG

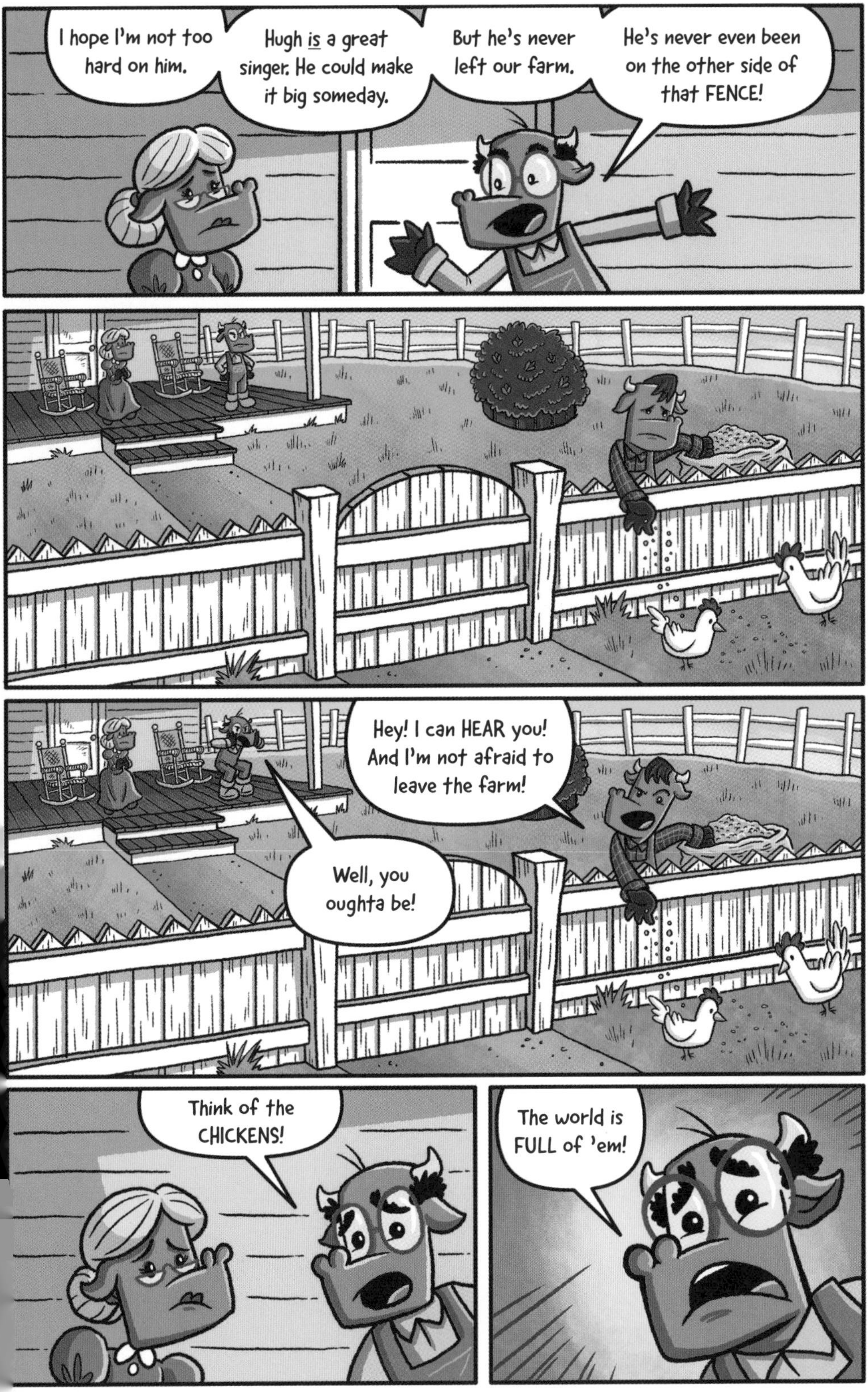
I hope I'm not too hard on him.
Hugh is a great singer. He could make it big someday.
But he's never left our farm.
He's never even been on the other side of that FENCE!
Hey! I can HEAR you! And I'm not afraid to leave the farm!
Well, you oughta be!
Think of the CHICKENS!
The world is FULL of 'em!

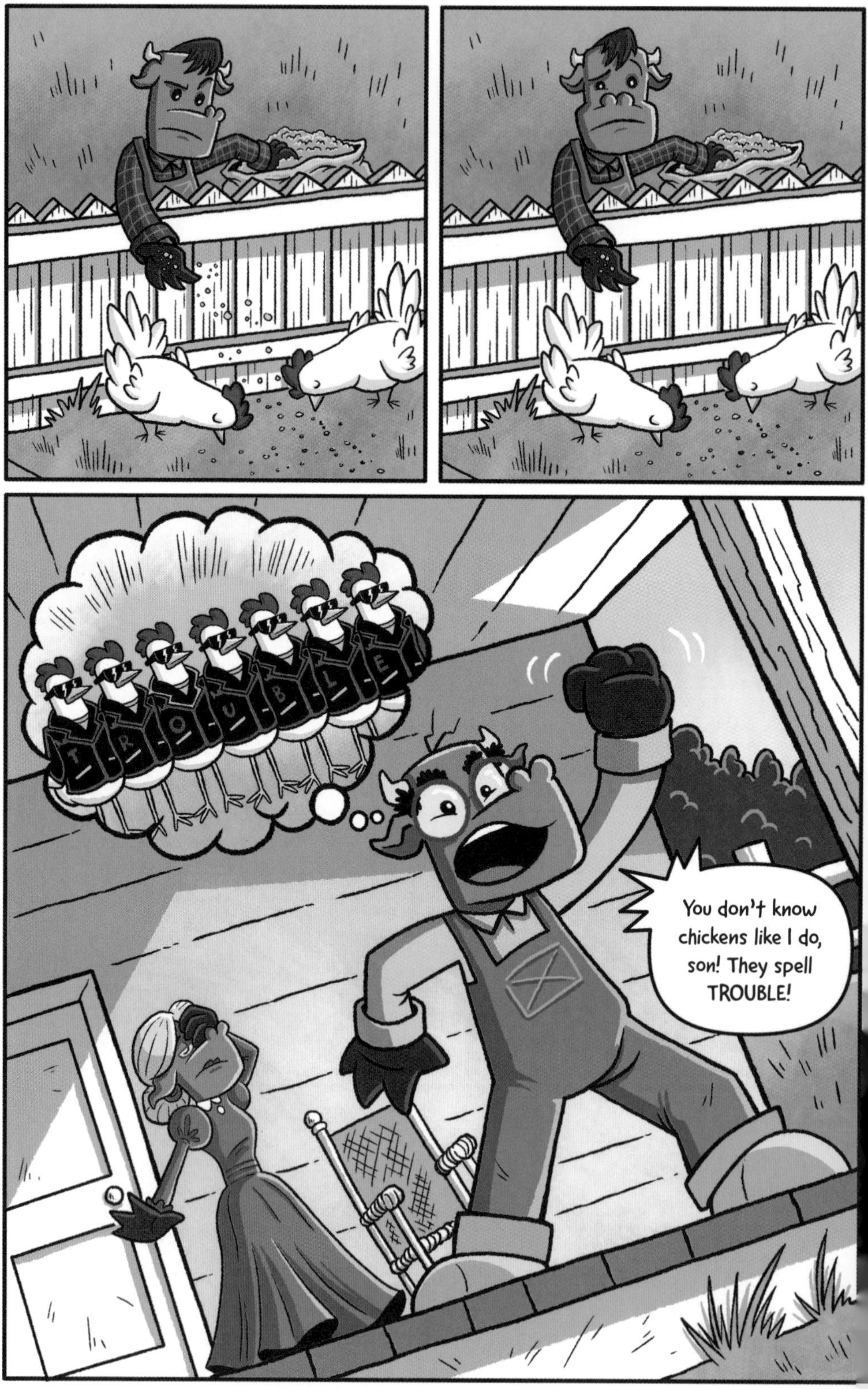
T-R-O-U-B-L-E
You don't know chickens like I do, son! They spell TROUBLE!

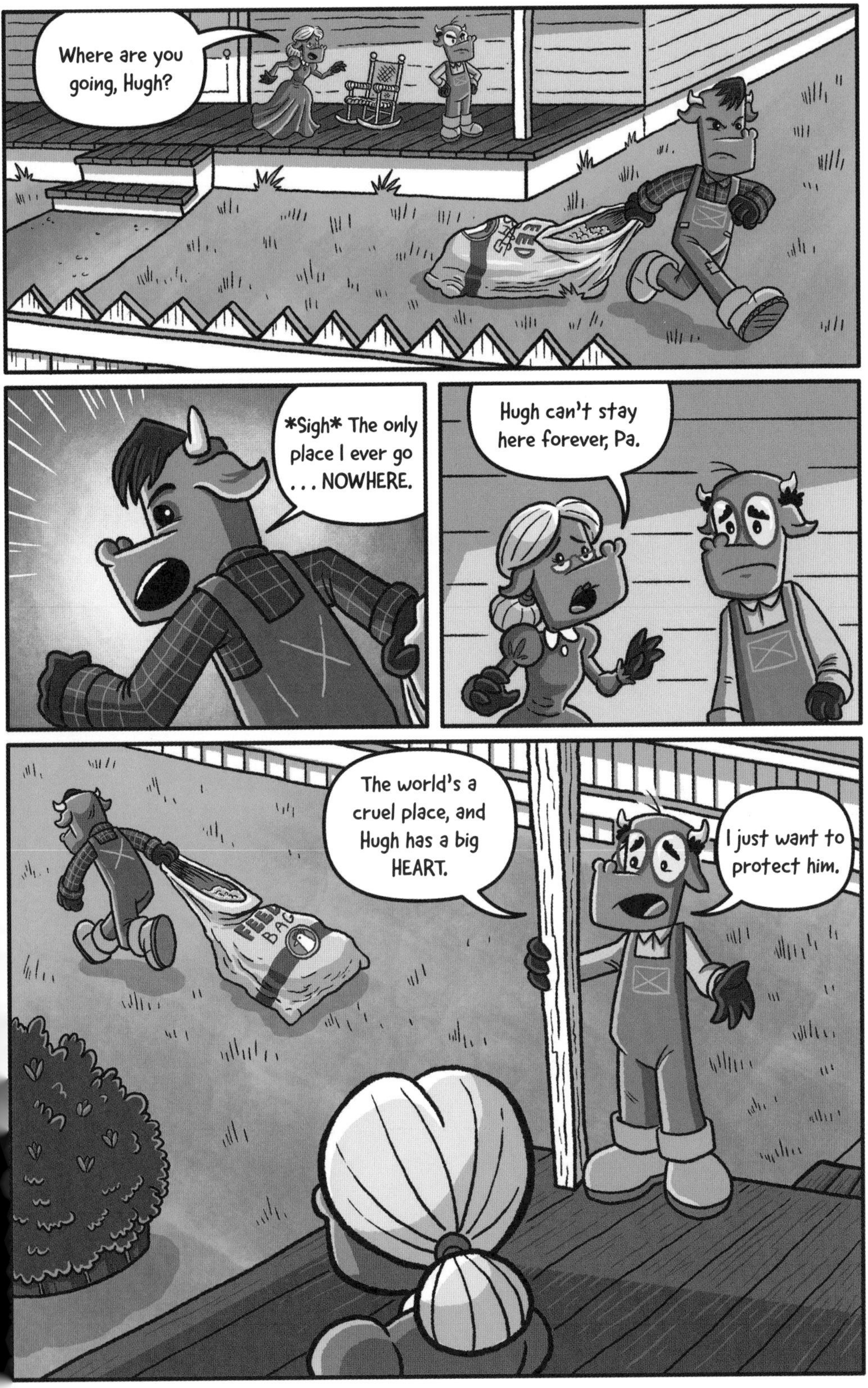
Where are you going, Hugh?
Sigh The only place I ever go . . . NOWHERE.
Hugh can't stay here forever, Pa.
The world's a cruel place, and Hugh has a big HEART.
I just want to protect him.

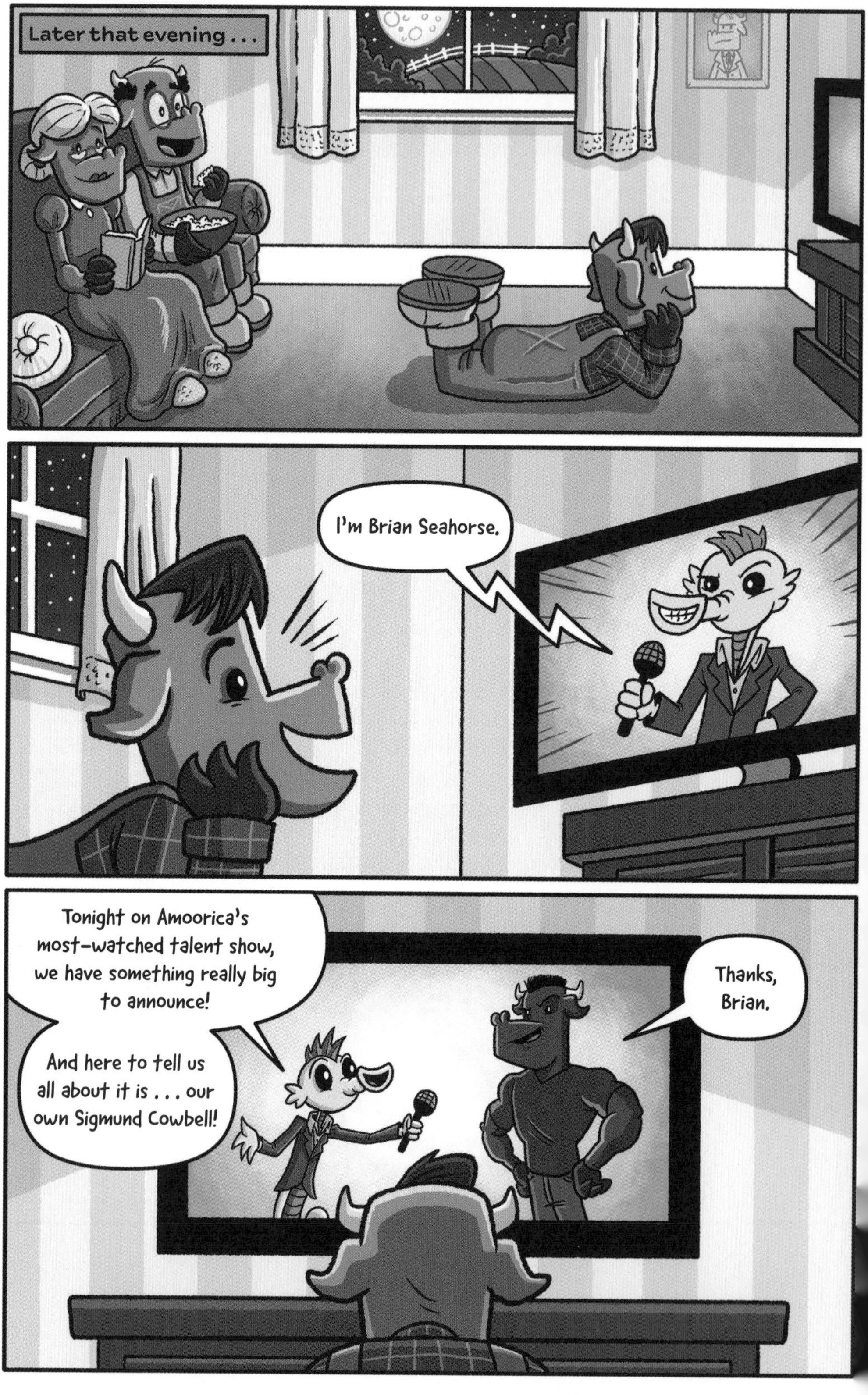

Later that evening . . .
I'm Brian Seahorse.
Tonight on Amoorica's most-watched talent show, we have something really big to announce!
And here to tell us all about it is . . . our own Sigmund Cowbell!
Thanks, Brian.

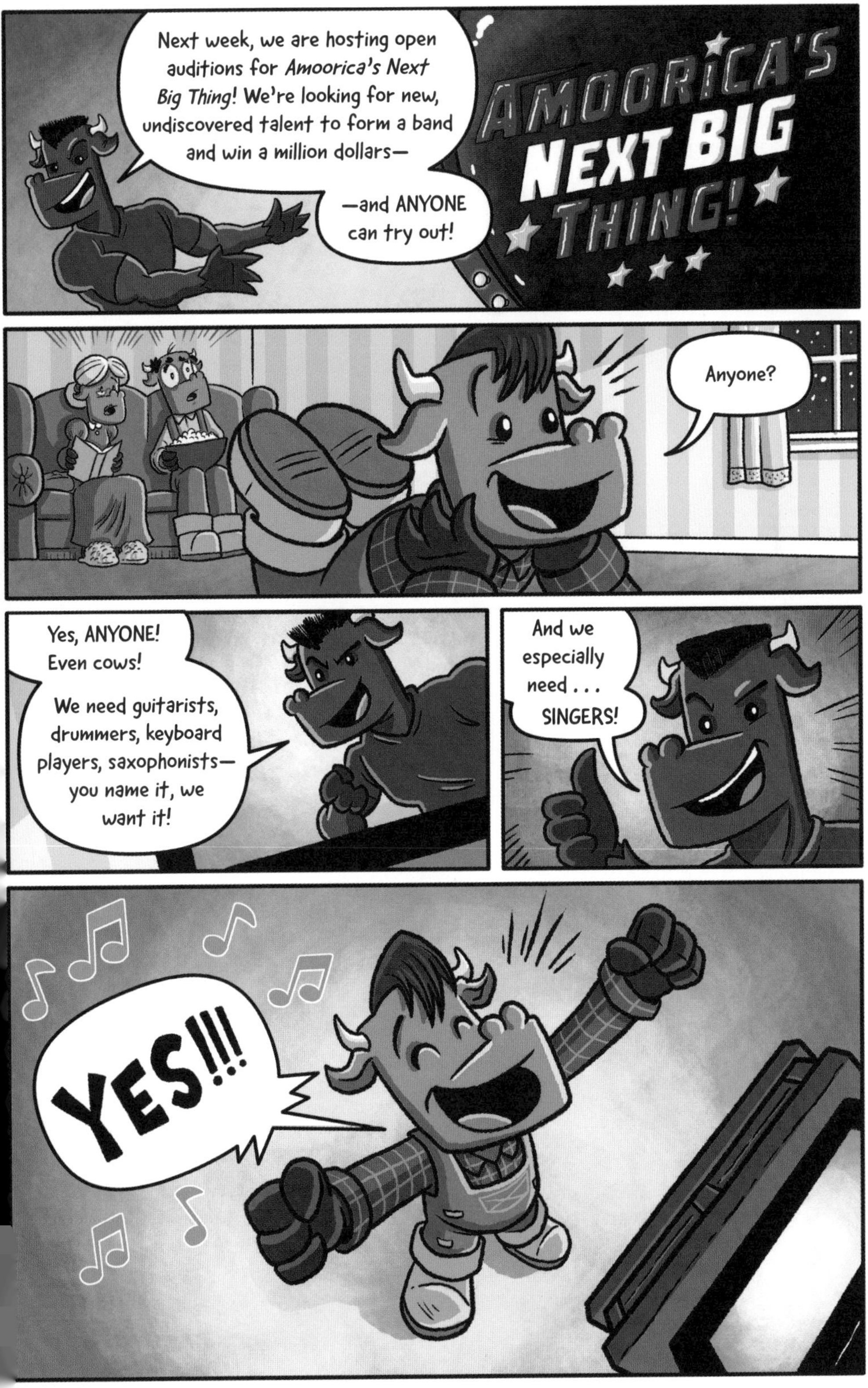
Next week, we are hosting open auditions for *Amoorica's Next Big Thing*! We're looking for new, undiscovered talent to form a band and win a million dollars—
—and ANYONE can try out!
AMOORICA'S NEXT BIG THING!
Anyone?
Yes, ANYONE! Even cows!
We need guitarists, drummers, keyboard players, saxophonists—you name it, we want it!
And we especially need . . . SINGERS!
YES!!!

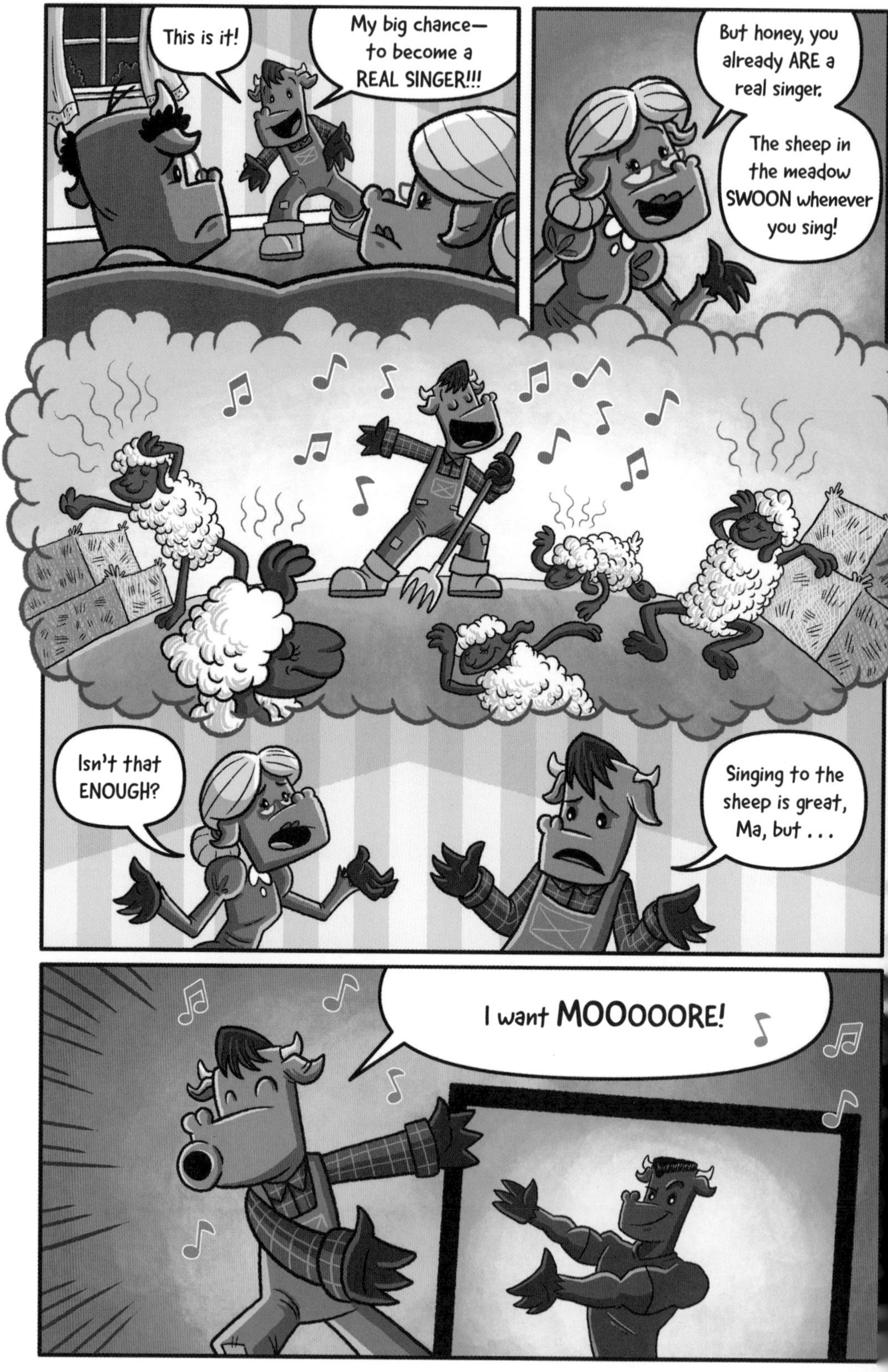
This is it!
My big chance— to become a REAL SINGER!!!
But honey, you already ARE a real singer.
The sheep in the meadow SWOON whenever you sing!
Isn't that ENOUGH?
Singing to the sheep is great, Ma, but . . .
I want MOOOOORE!

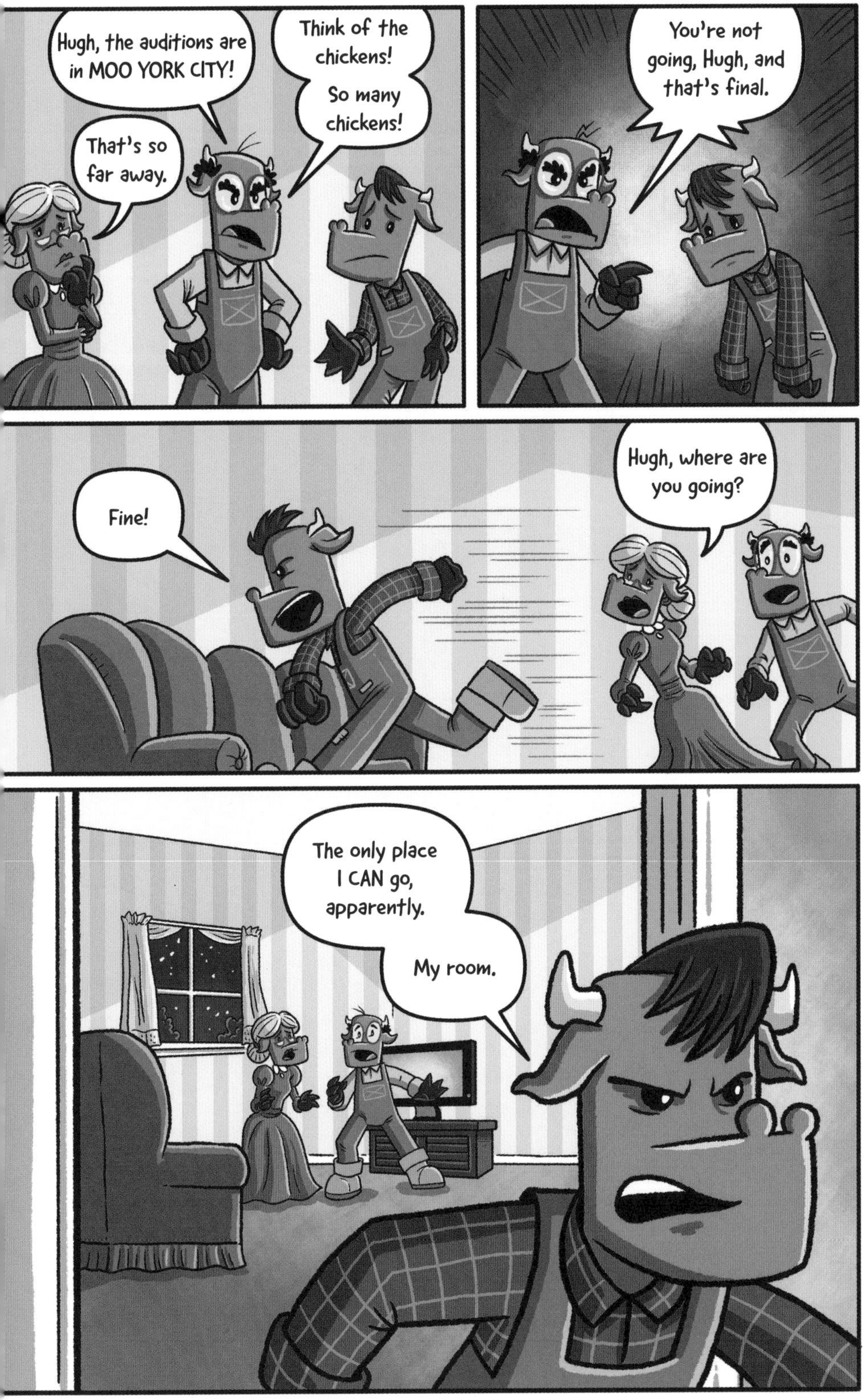
Hugh, the auditions are in MOO YORK CITY!
That's so far away.
Think of the chickens!
So many chickens!
You're not going, Hugh, and that's final.
Fine!
Hugh, where are you going?
The only place I CAN go, apparently.
My room.

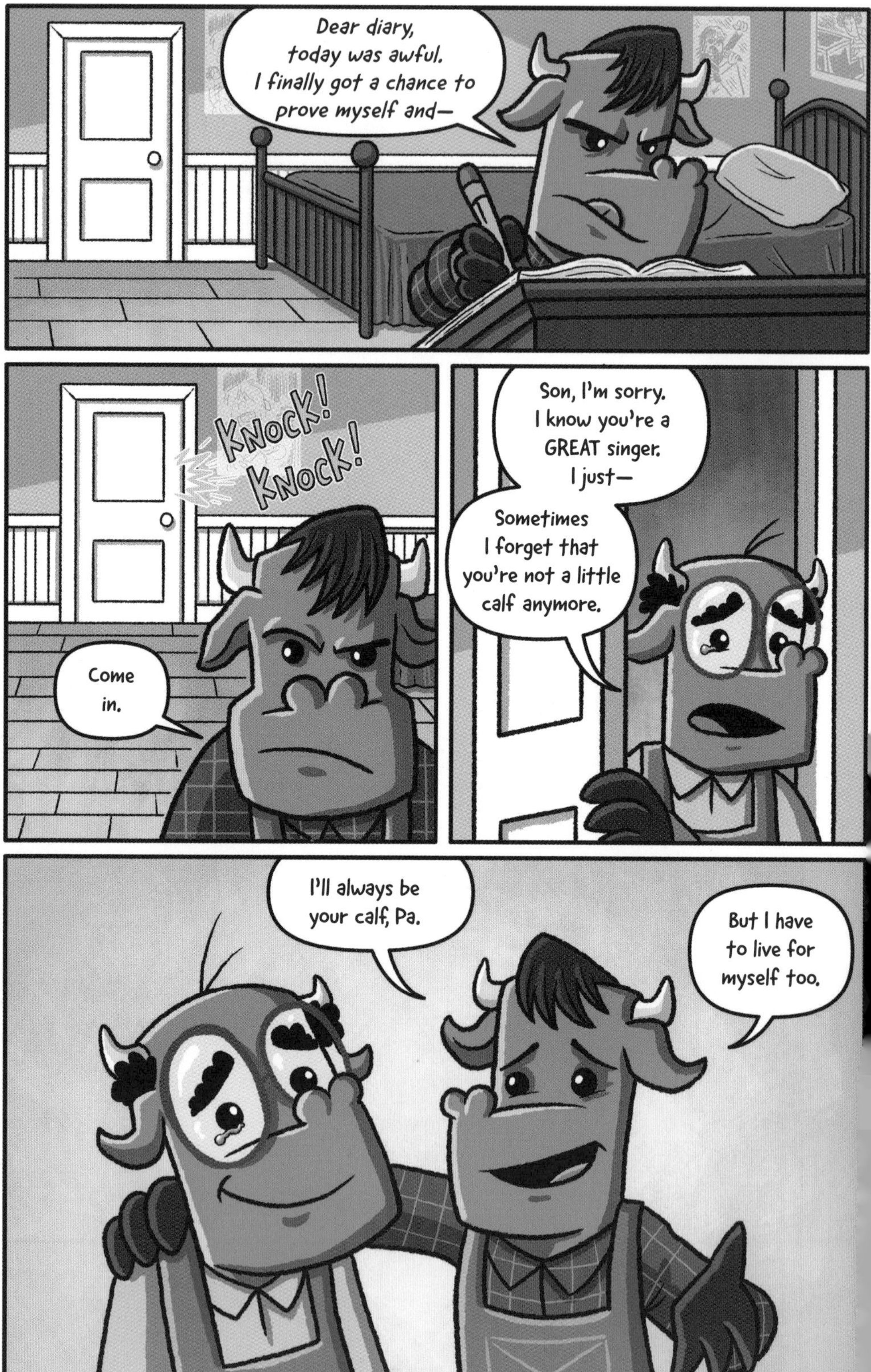
Dear diary, today was awful. I finally got a chance to prove myself and—
KNOCK! KNOCK!
Come in.
Son, I'm sorry. I know you're a GREAT singer. I just—
Sometimes I forget that you're not a little calf anymore.
I'll always be your calf, Pa.
But I have to live for myself too.

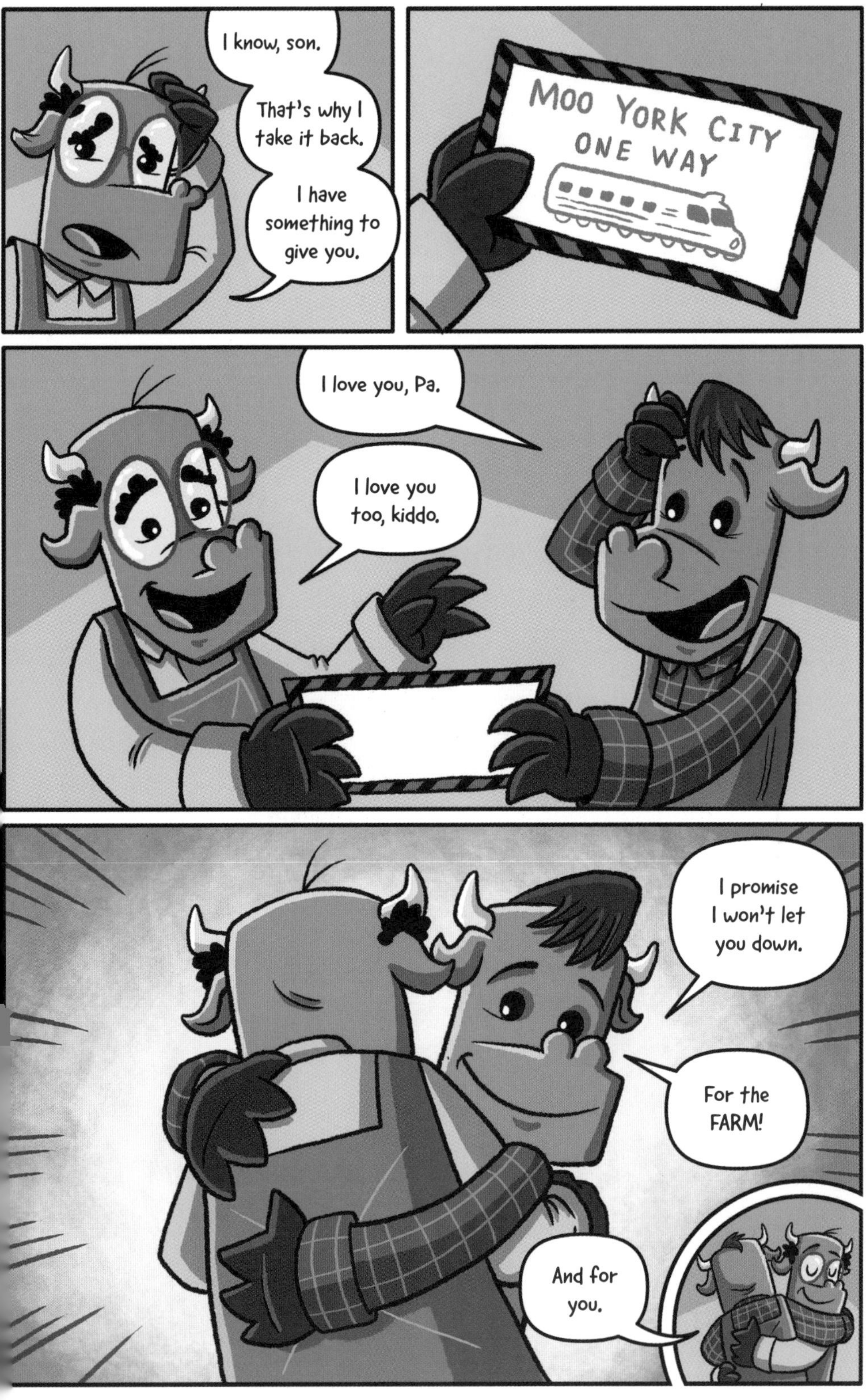
I know, son.
That's why I take it back.
I have something to give you.
MOO YORK CITY
ONE WAY
I love you, Pa.
I love you too, kiddo.
I promise I won't let you down.
For the FARM!
And for you.

CHAPTER 2

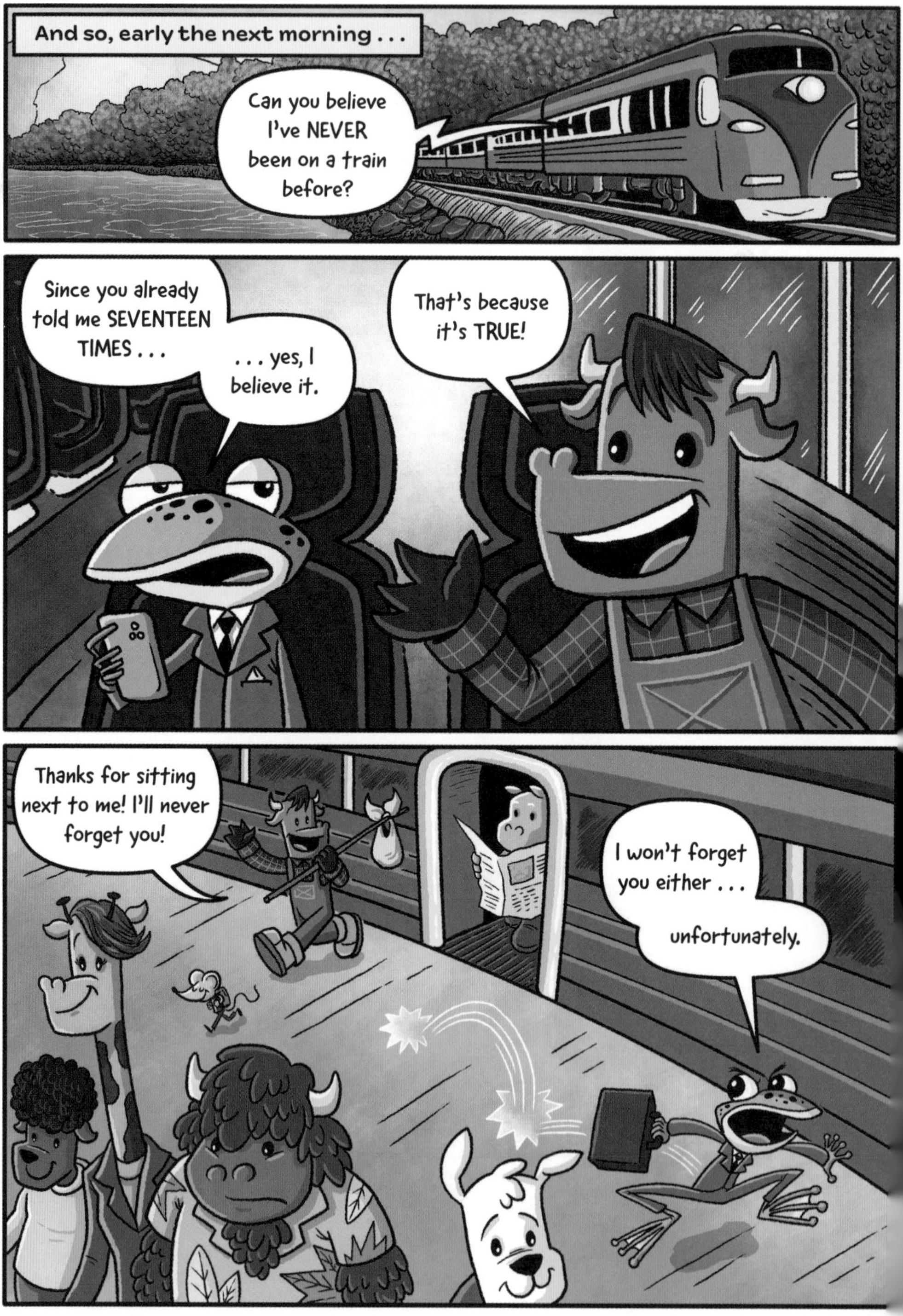
And so, early the next morning . . .
Can you believe I've NEVER been on a train before?
Since you already told me SEVENTEEN TIMES . . .
. . . yes, I believe it.
That's because it's TRUE!
Thanks for sitting next to me! I'll never forget you!
I won't forget you either . . .
unfortunately.

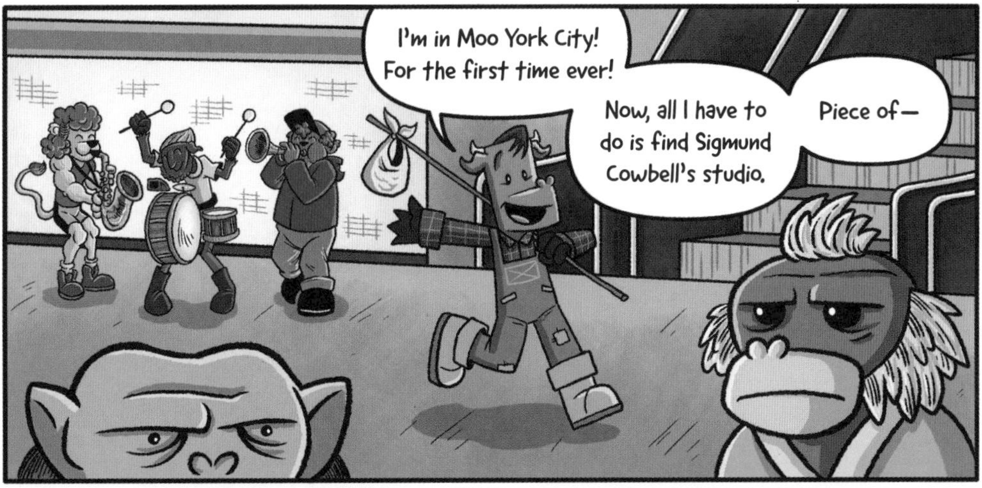
I'm in Moo York City! For the first time ever!
Now, all I have to do is find Sigmund Cowbell's studio.
Piece of—

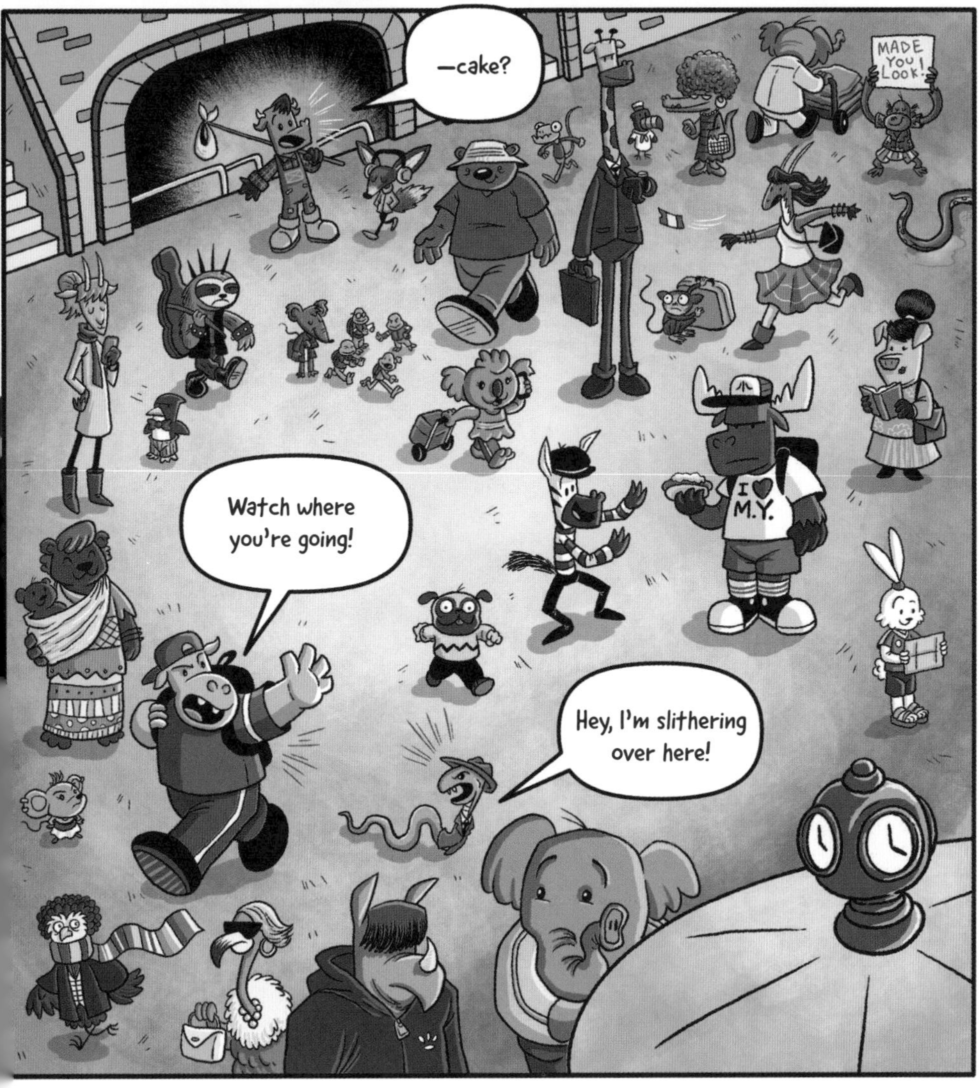
—cake?
MADE YOU LOOK!
Watch where you're going!
I ♥ M.Y.
Hey, I'm slithering over here!

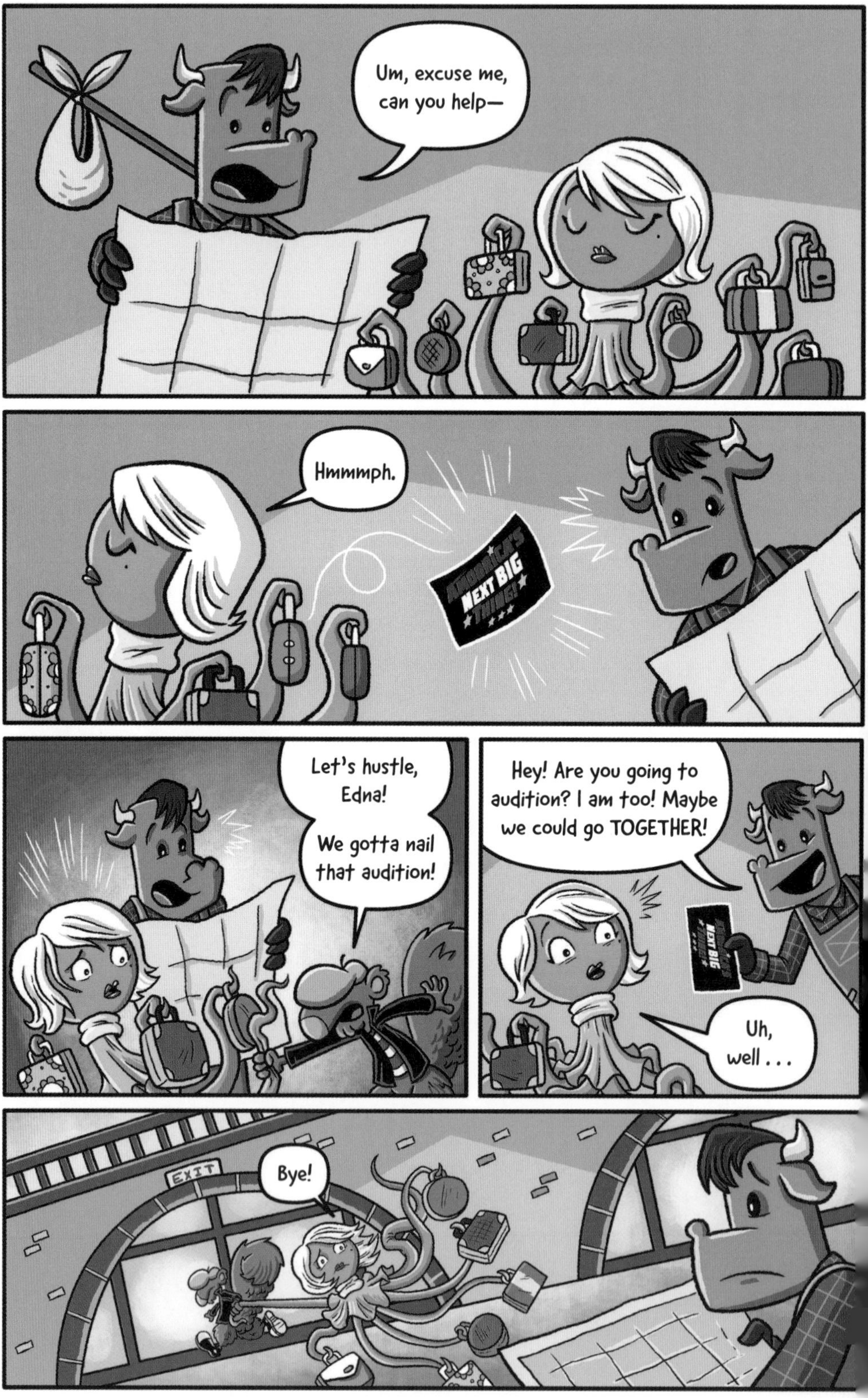
Um, excuse me, can you help—
Hmmmph.
AMERICA'S NEXT BIG THING!
Let's hustle, Edna!
We gotta nail that audition!
Hey! Are you going to audition? I am too! Maybe we could go TOGETHER!
Uh, well . . .
EXIT
Bye!

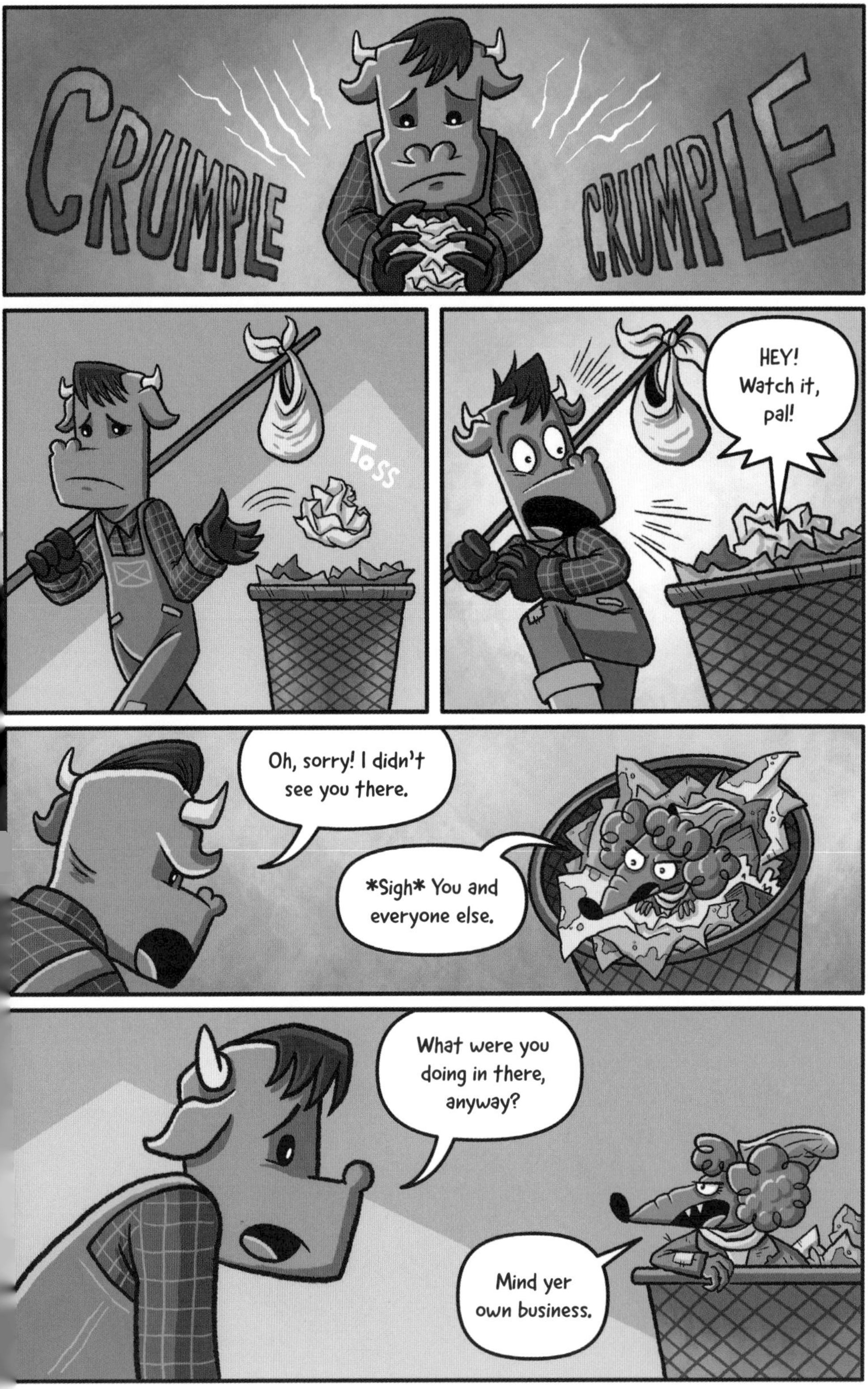
CRUMPLE
CRUMPLE
TOSS
HEY! Watch it, pal!
Oh, sorry! I didn't see you there.
Sigh You and everyone else.
What were you doing in there, anyway?
Mind yer own business.

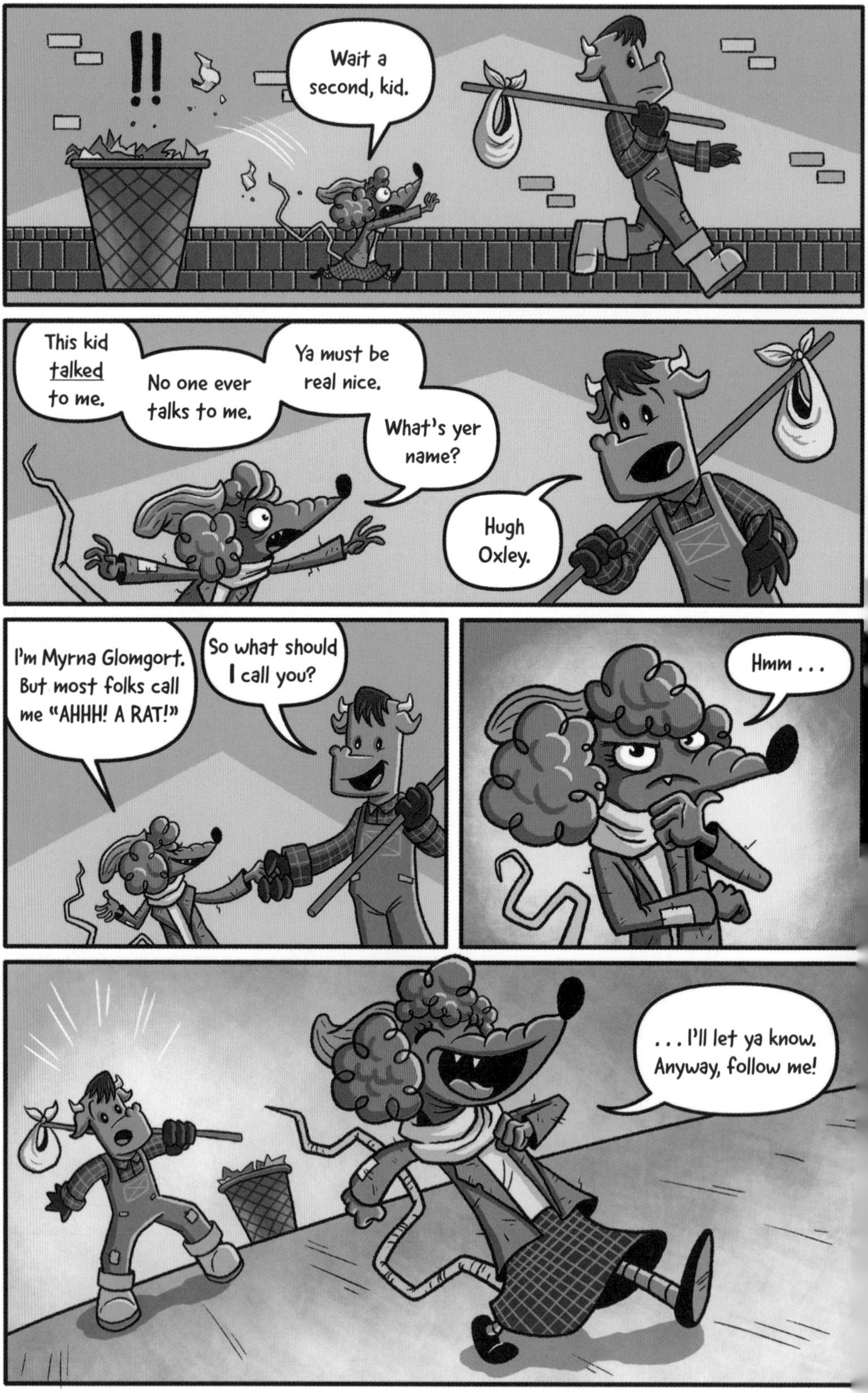
!!
Wait a second, kid.
This kid talked to me.
No one ever talks to me.
Ya must be real nice.
What's yer name?
Hugh Oxley.
I'm Myrna Glomgort. But most folks call me "AHHH! A RAT!"
So what should I call you?
Hmm . . .
. . . I'll let ya know. Anyway, follow me!

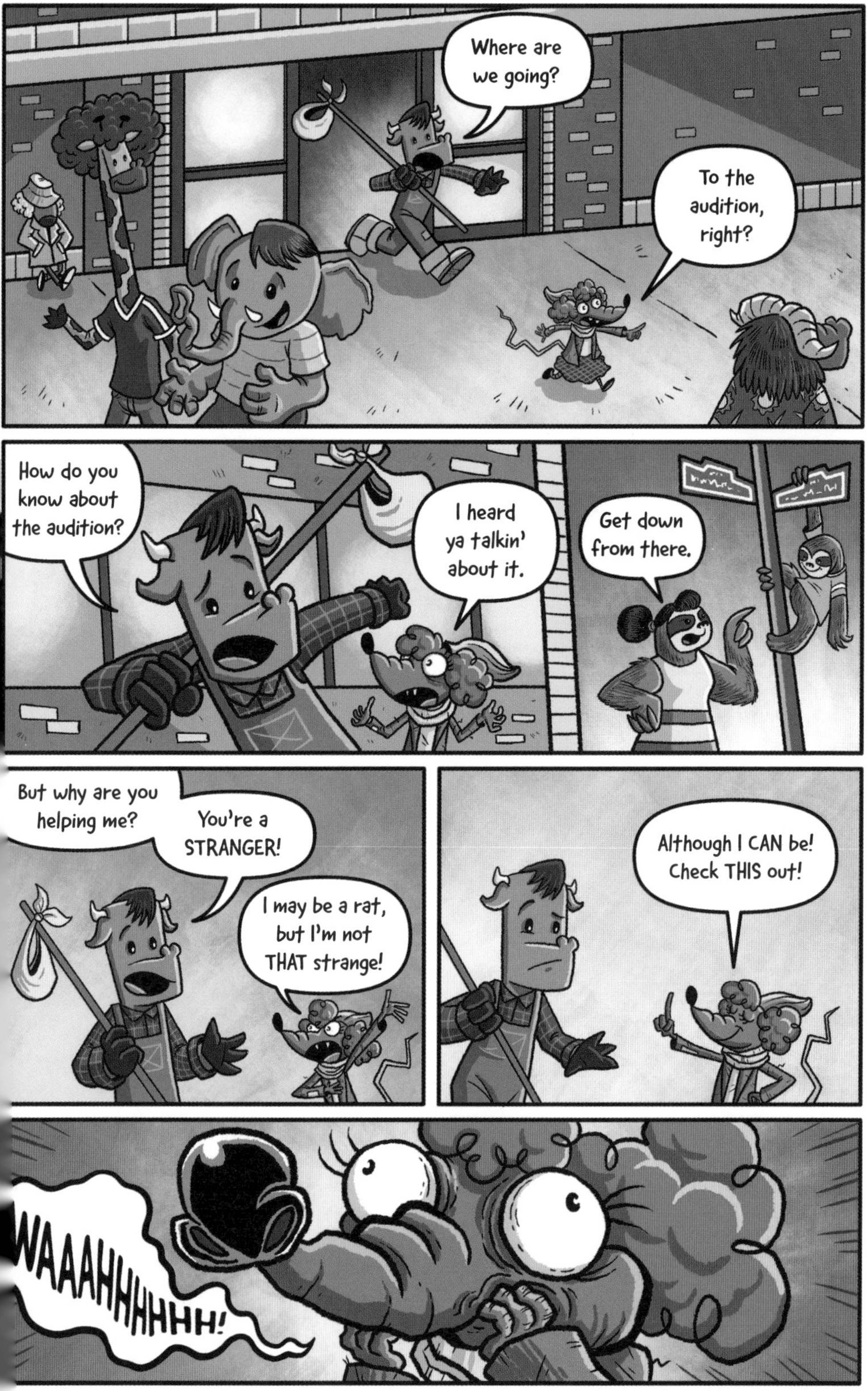
Where are we going?
To the audition, right?
How do you know about the audition?
I heard ya talkin' about it.
Get down from there.
But why are you helping me?
You're a STRANGER!
I may be a rat, but I'm not THAT strange!
Although I CAN be! Check THIS out!
WAAAHHHHHH!

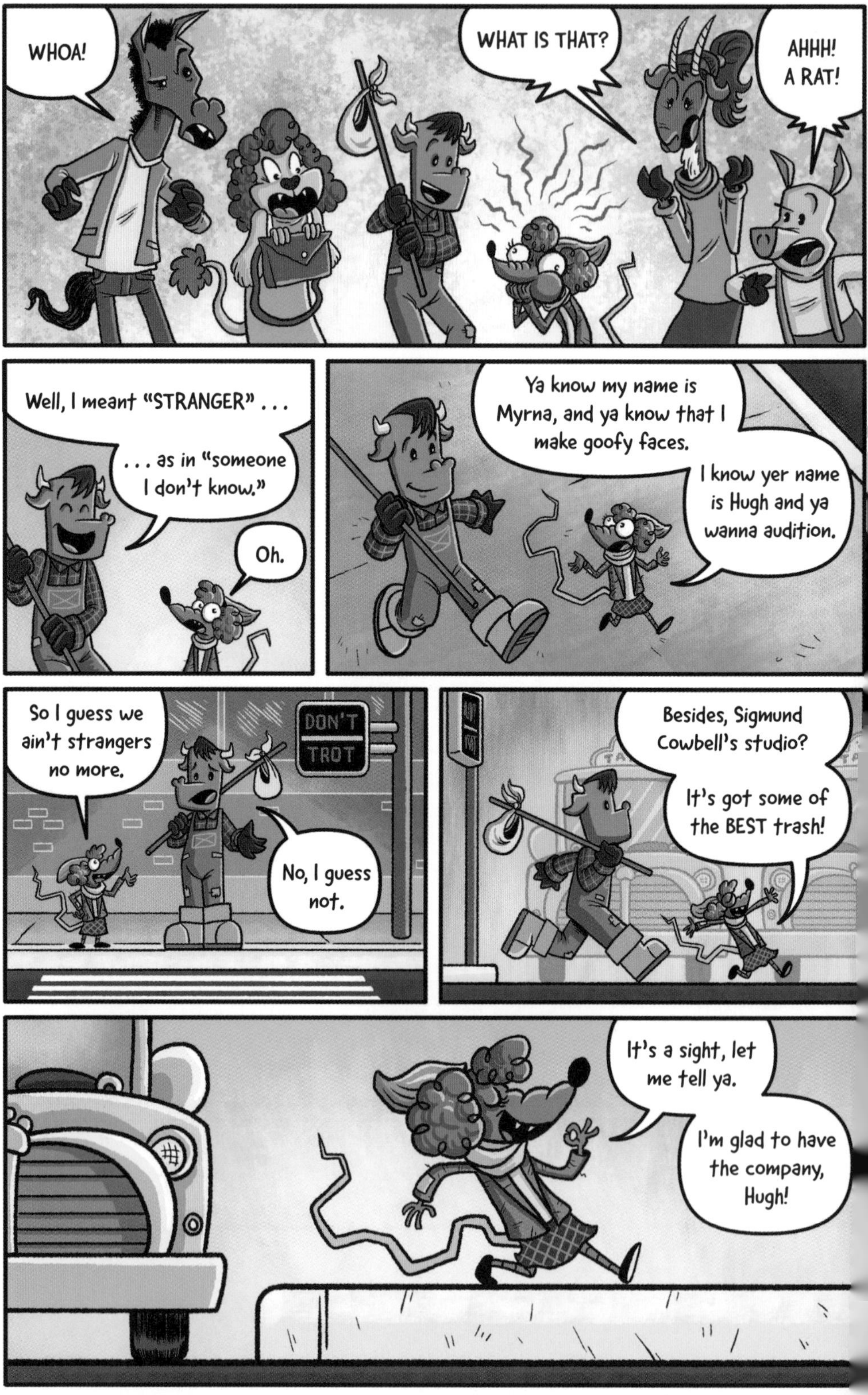

WHOA!
WHAT IS THAT?
AHHH! A RAT!
Well, I meant "STRANGER" . . .
. . . as in "someone I don't know."
Oh.
Ya know my name is Myrna, and ya know that I make goofy faces.
I know yer name is Hugh and ya wanna audition.
So I guess we ain't strangers no more.
DON'T TROT
No, I guess not.
Besides, Sigmund Cowbell's studio?
It's got some of the BEST trash!
It's a sight, let me tell ya.
I'm glad to have the company, Hugh!

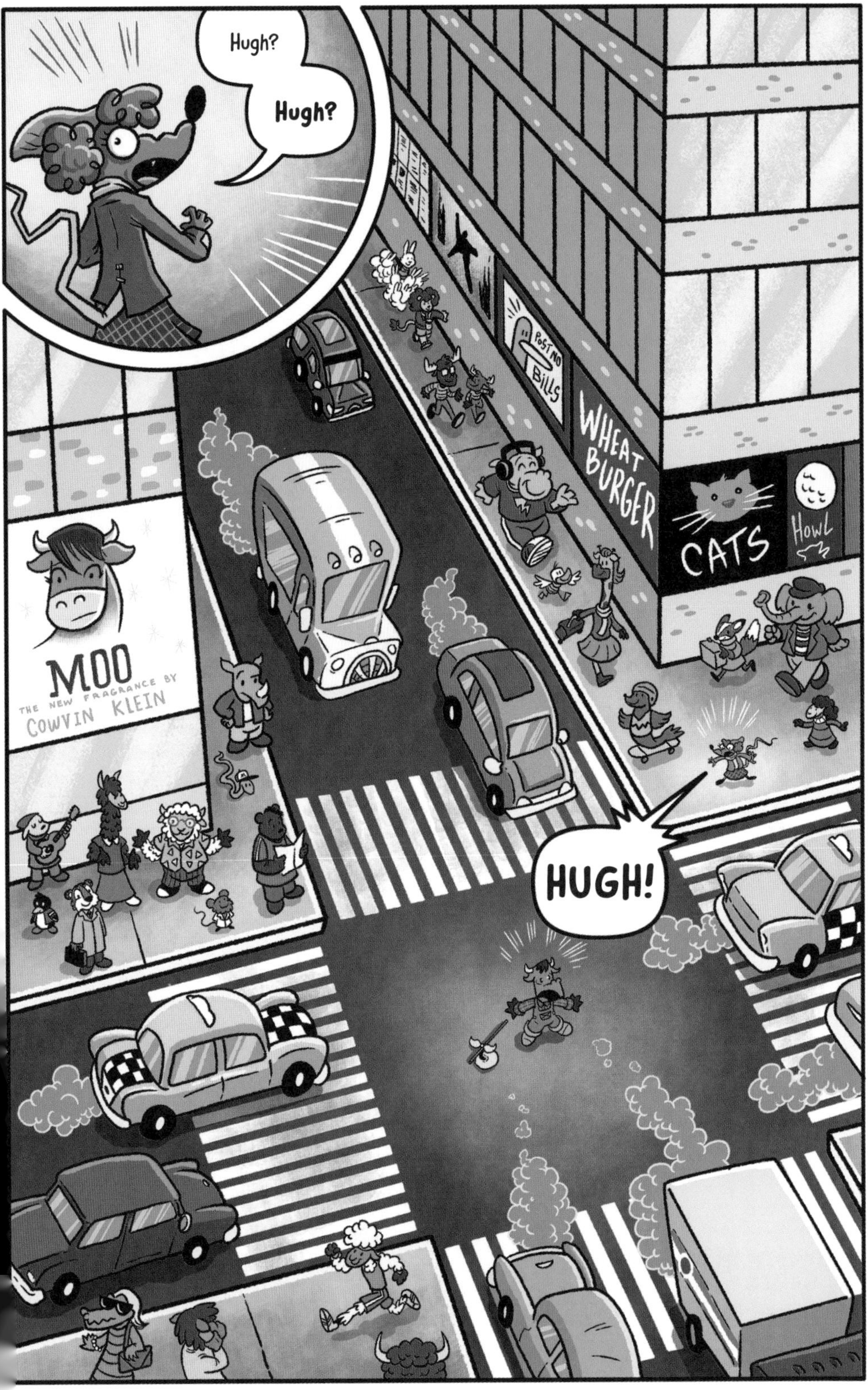
Hugh?
Hugh?
POST NO BILLS
WHEAT BURGER
CATS
HOWL
MOO
THE NEW FRAGRANCE BY
COWVIN KLEIN
HUGH!

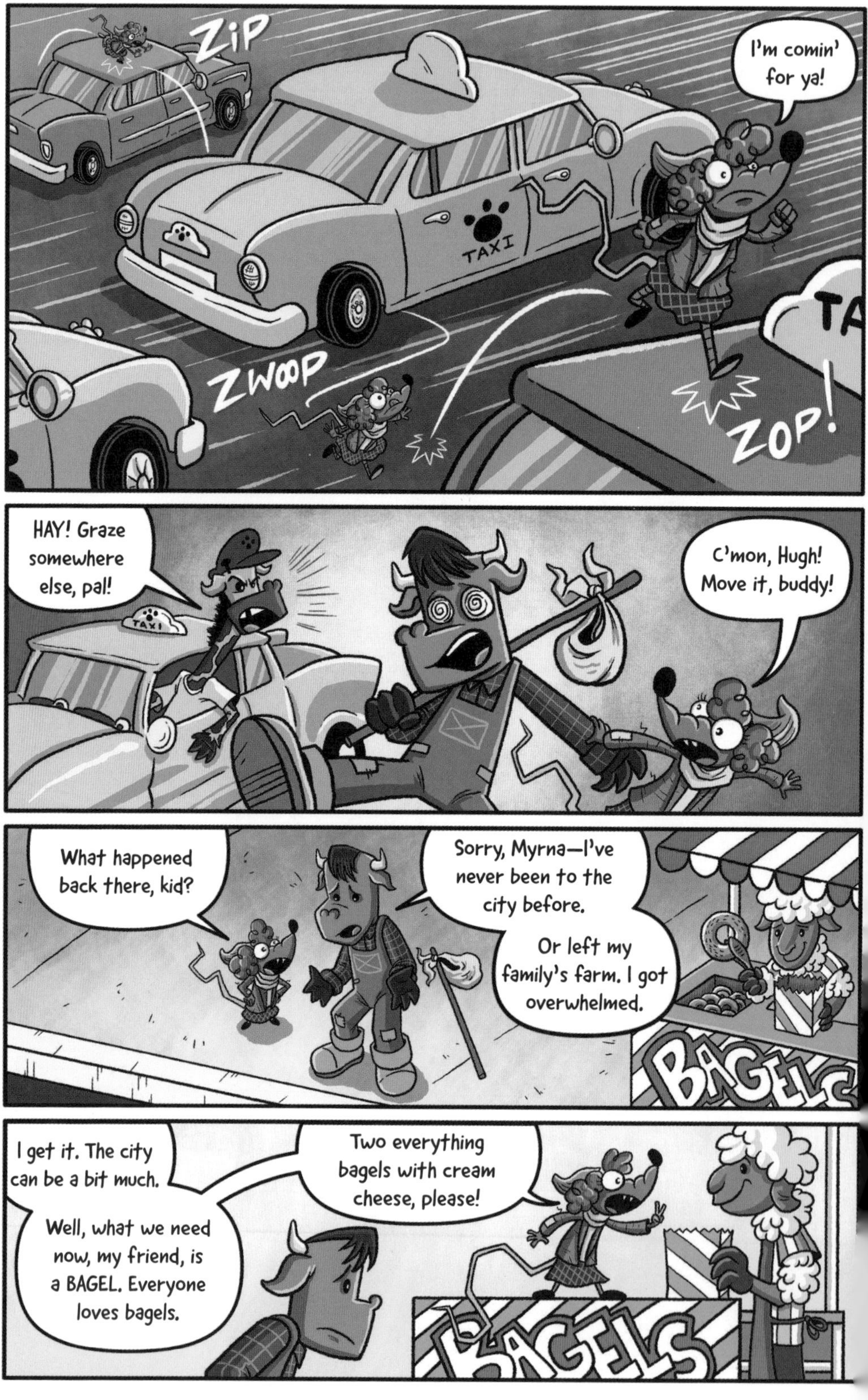
ZIP
I'm comin' for ya!
TAXI
ZWOOP
ZOP!
HAY! Graze somewhere else, pal!
TAXI
C'mon, Hugh! Move it, buddy!
What happened back there, kid?
Sorry, Myrna—I've never been to the city before.
Or left my family's farm. I got overwhelmed.
BAGELS
I get it. The city can be a bit much.
Well, what we need now, my friend, is a BAGEL. Everyone loves bagels.
Two everything bagels with cream cheese, please!
BAGELS

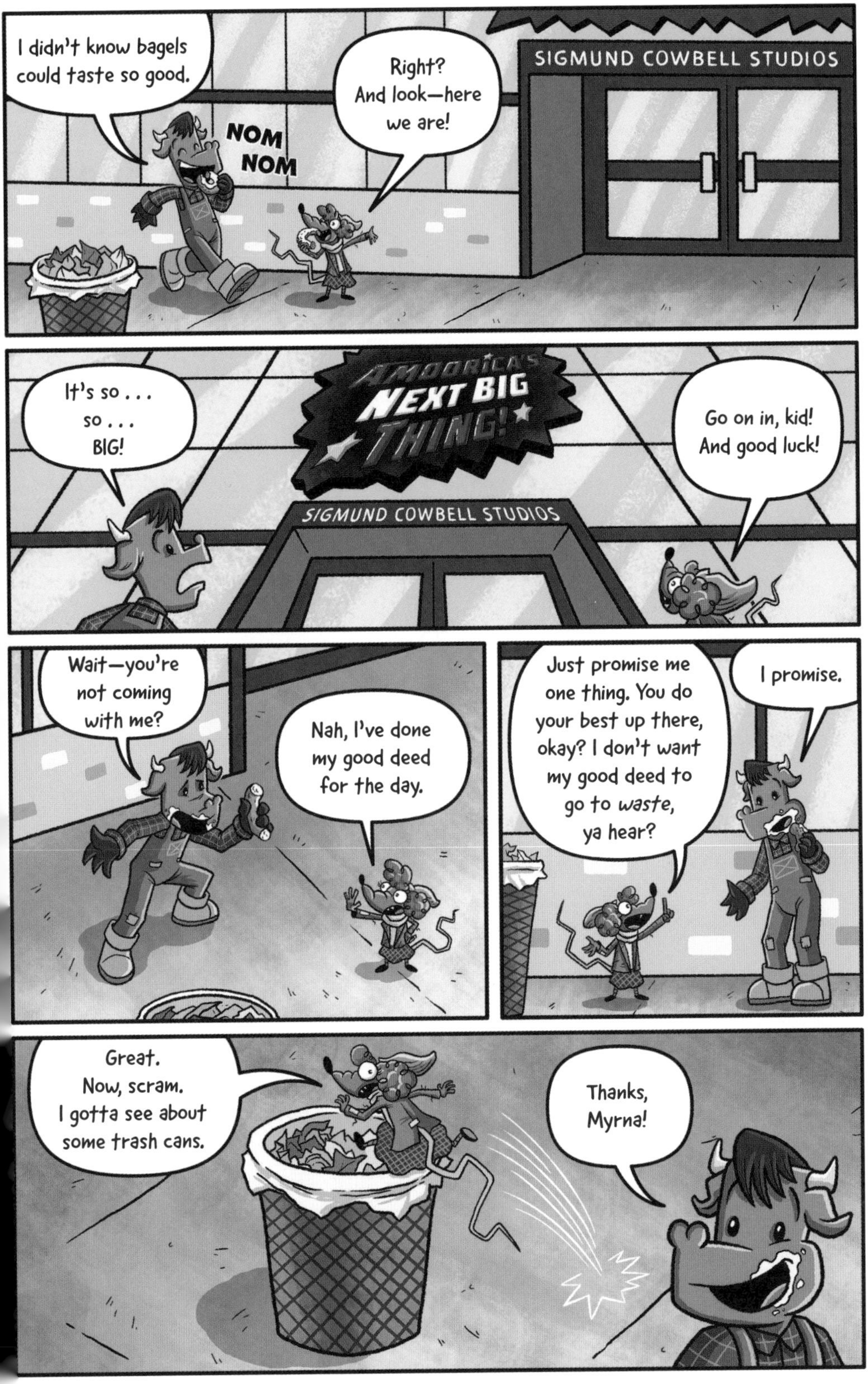
SIGMUND COWBELL STUDIOS
I didn't know bagels could taste so good.
NOM NOM
Right? And look—here we are!
It's so . . . so . . . BIG!
AMOORICA'S NEXT BIG THING!
SIGMUND COWBELL STUDIOS
Go on in, kid! And good luck!
Wait—you're not coming with me?
Nah, I've done my good deed for the day.
Just promise me one thing. You do your best up there, okay? I don't want my good deed to go to *waste*, ya hear?
I promise.
Great. Now, scram. I gotta see about some trash cans.
Thanks, Myrna!

CHAPTER 3

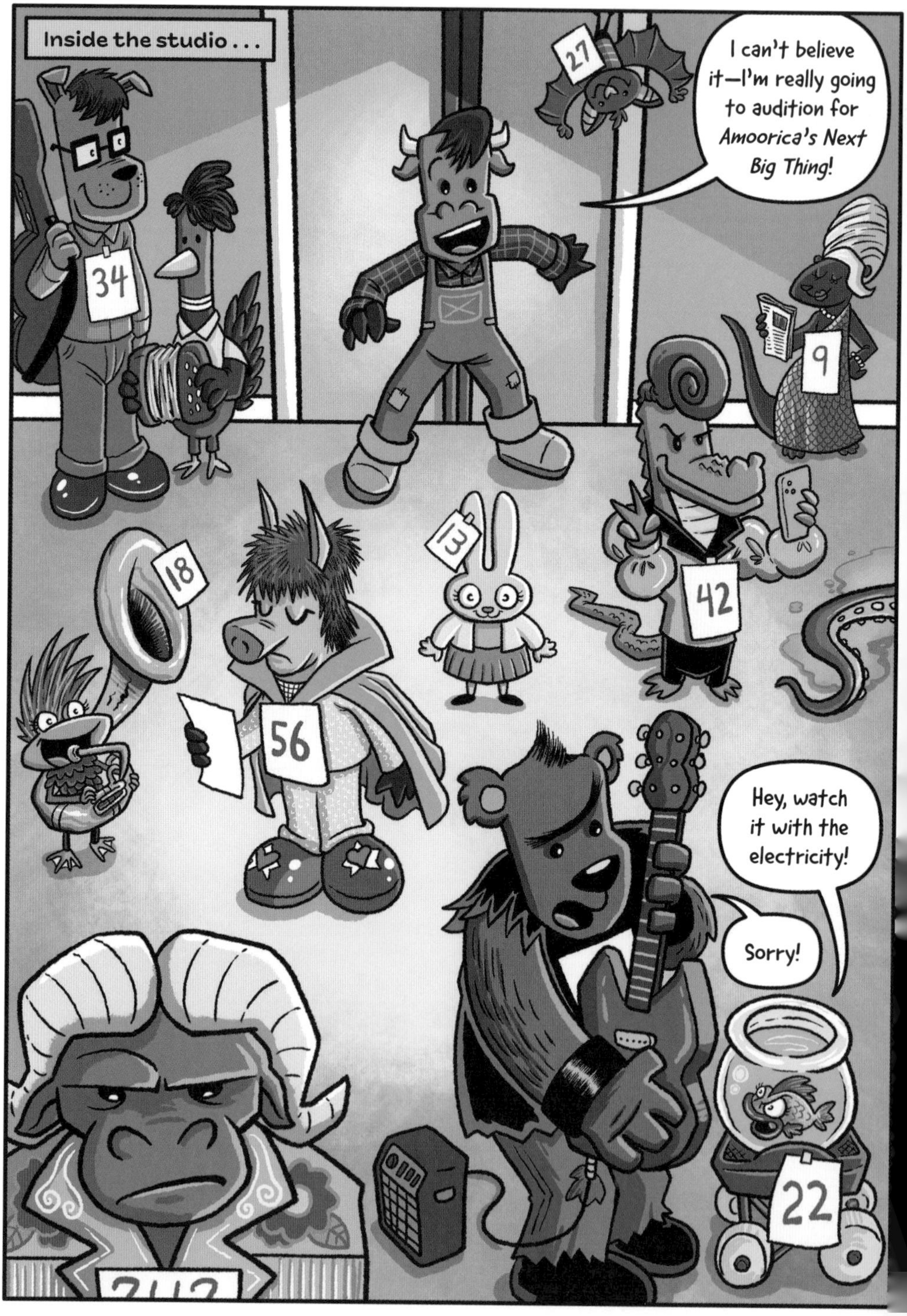
Inside the studio . . .
I can't believe it—I'm really going to audition for *Amoorica's Next Big Thing!*
Hey, watch it with the electricity!
Sorry!

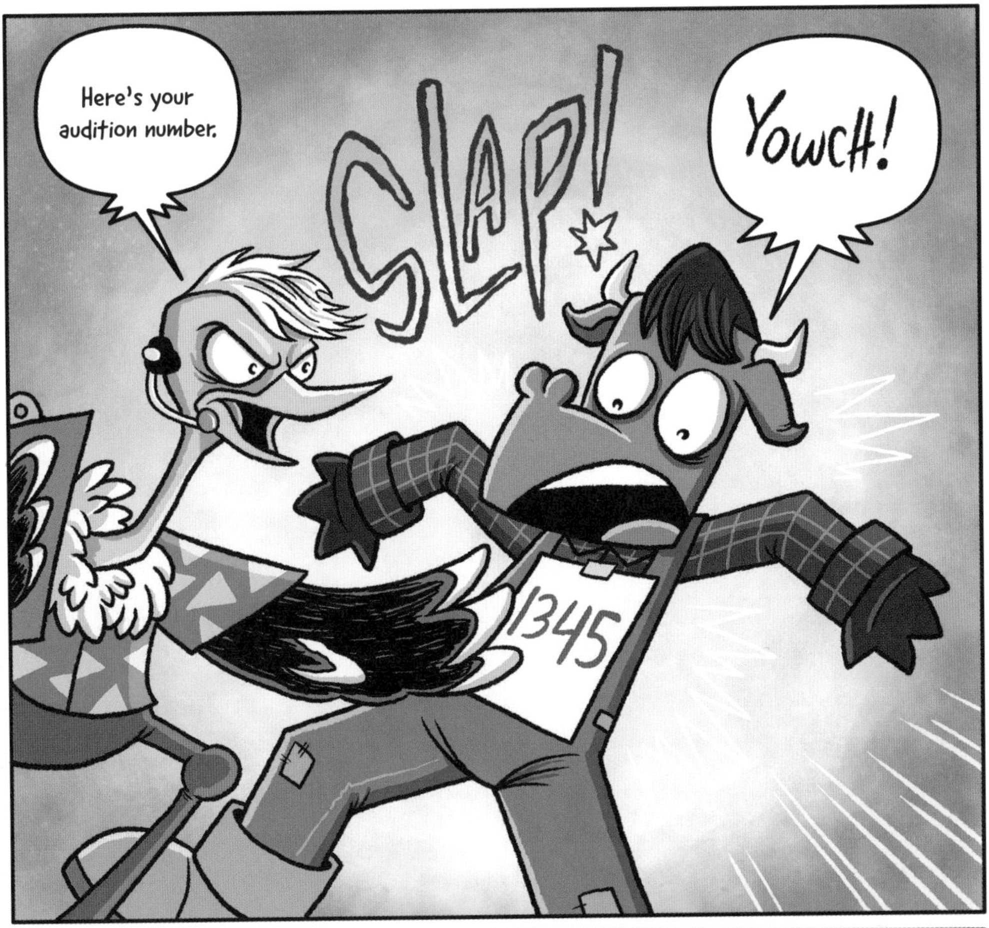
Here's your audition number.
SLAP!
YOWCH!
1345

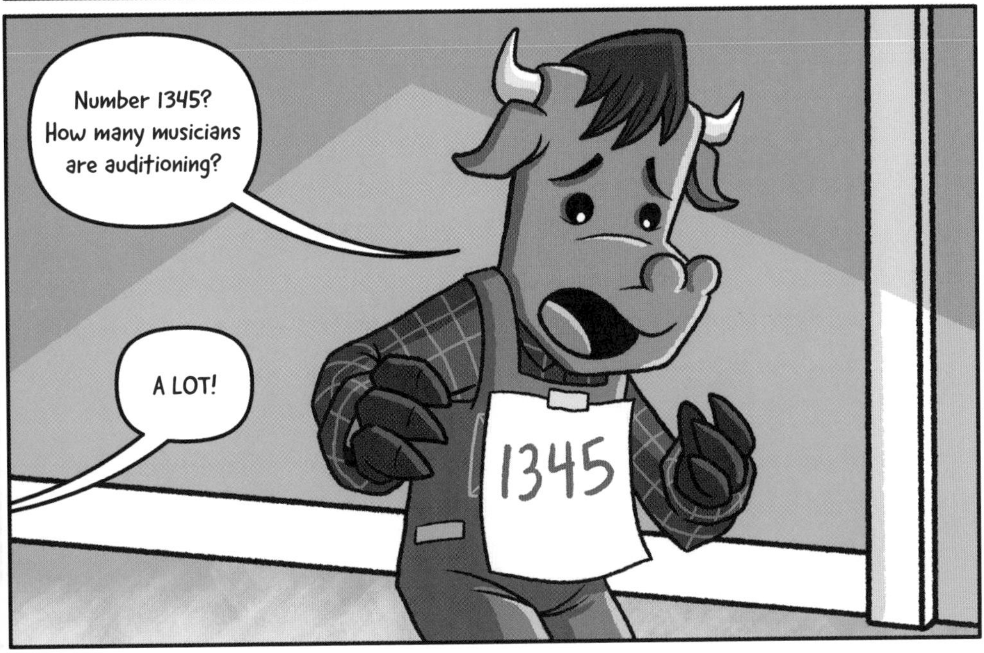
Number 1345? How many musicians are auditioning?
A LOT!
1345

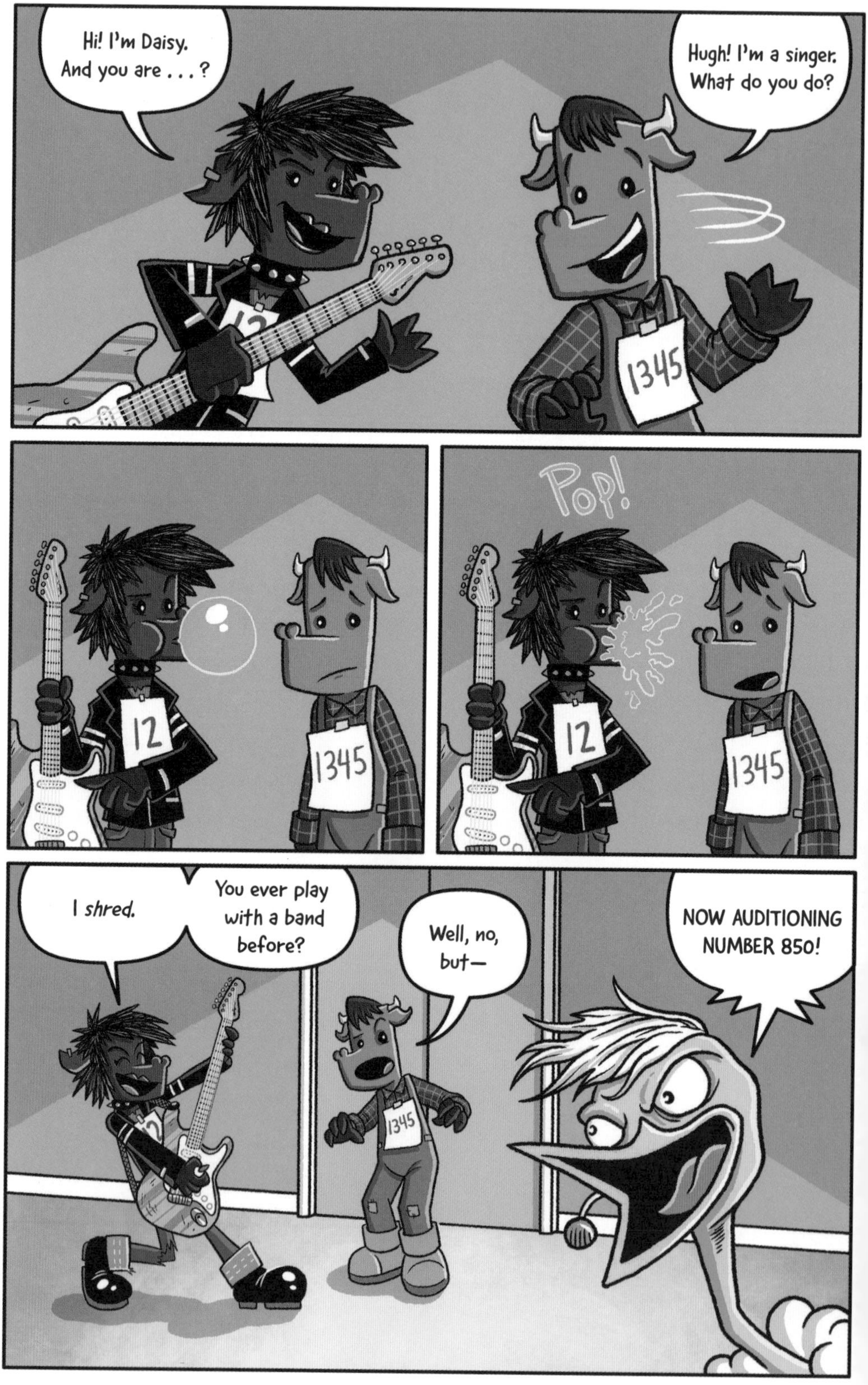
Hi! I'm Daisy. And you are . . . ?
Hugh! I'm a singer. What do you do?
12
1345
Pop!
I *shred.*
You ever play with a band before?
Well, no, but—
NOW AUDITIONING NUMBER 850!

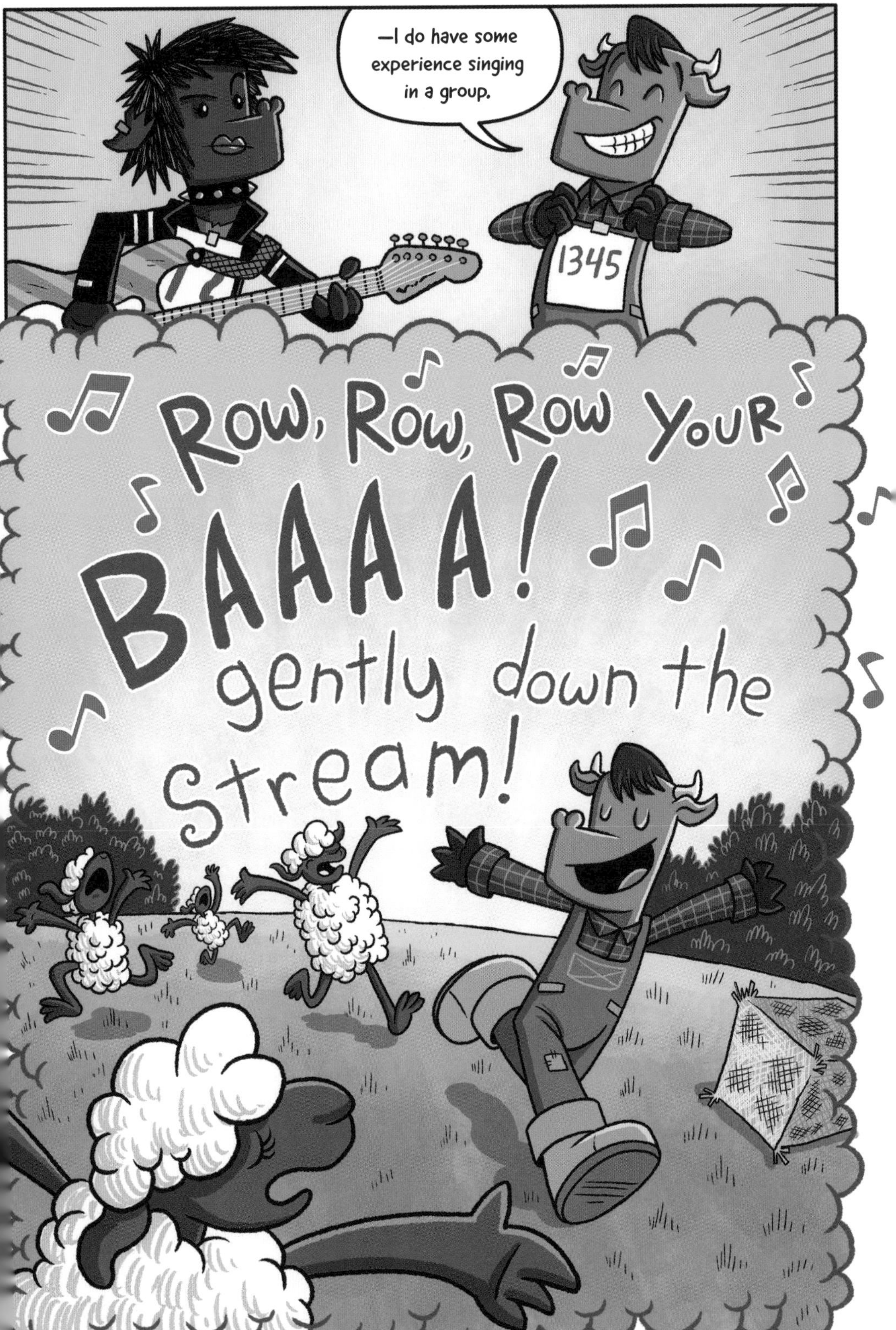
—I do have some experience singing in a group.
1345
Row, Row, Row your
BAAAA!
gently down the
stream!

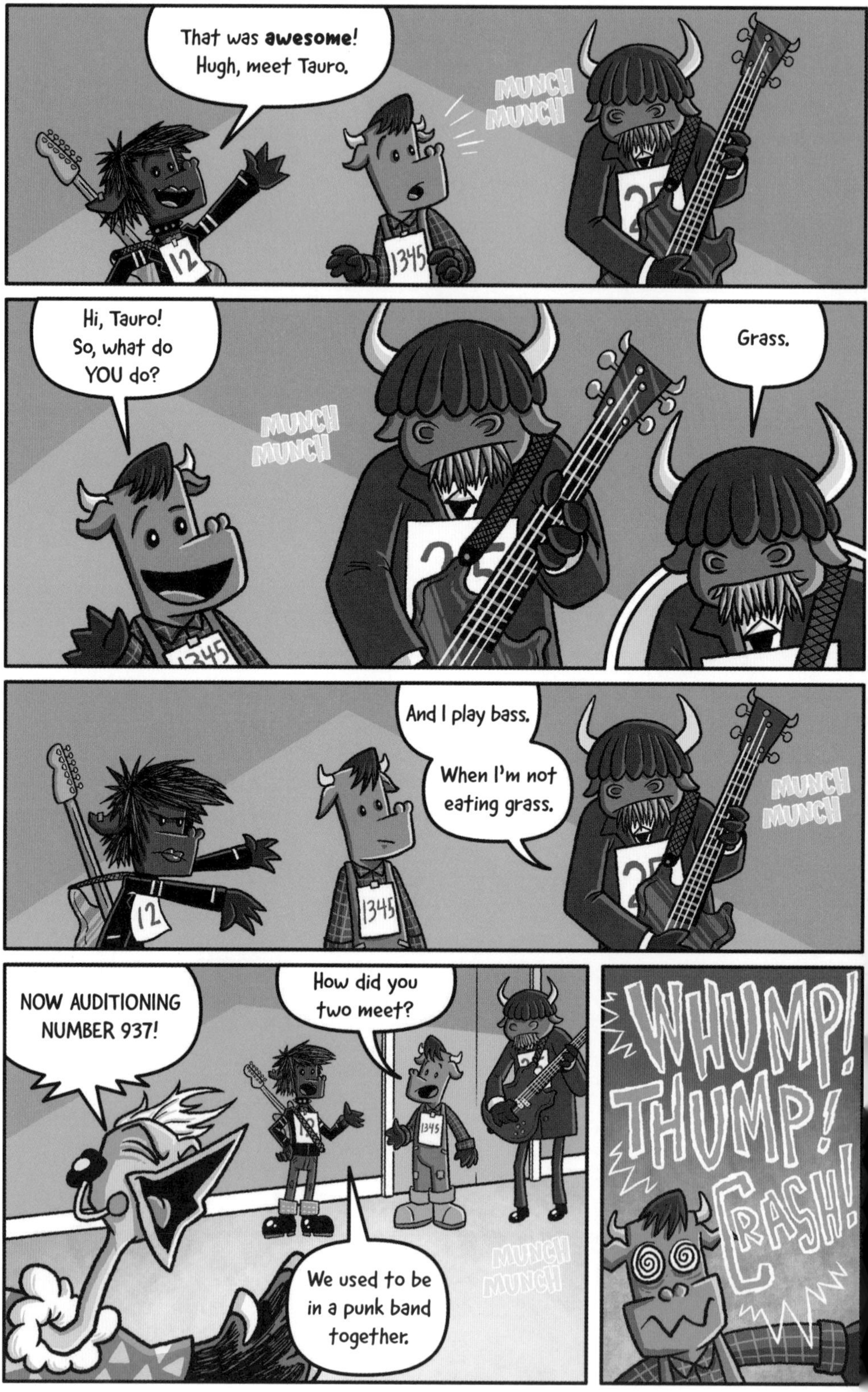
That was **awesome**! Hugh, meet Tauro.
MUNCH MUNCH
12
1345
Hi, Tauro! So, what do YOU do?
MUNCH MUNCH
Grass.
And I play bass.
When I'm not eating grass.
MUNCH MUNCH
NOW AUDITIONING NUMBER 937!
How did you two meet?
We used to be in a punk band together.
MUNCH MUNCH
WHUMP! THUMP! CRASH!

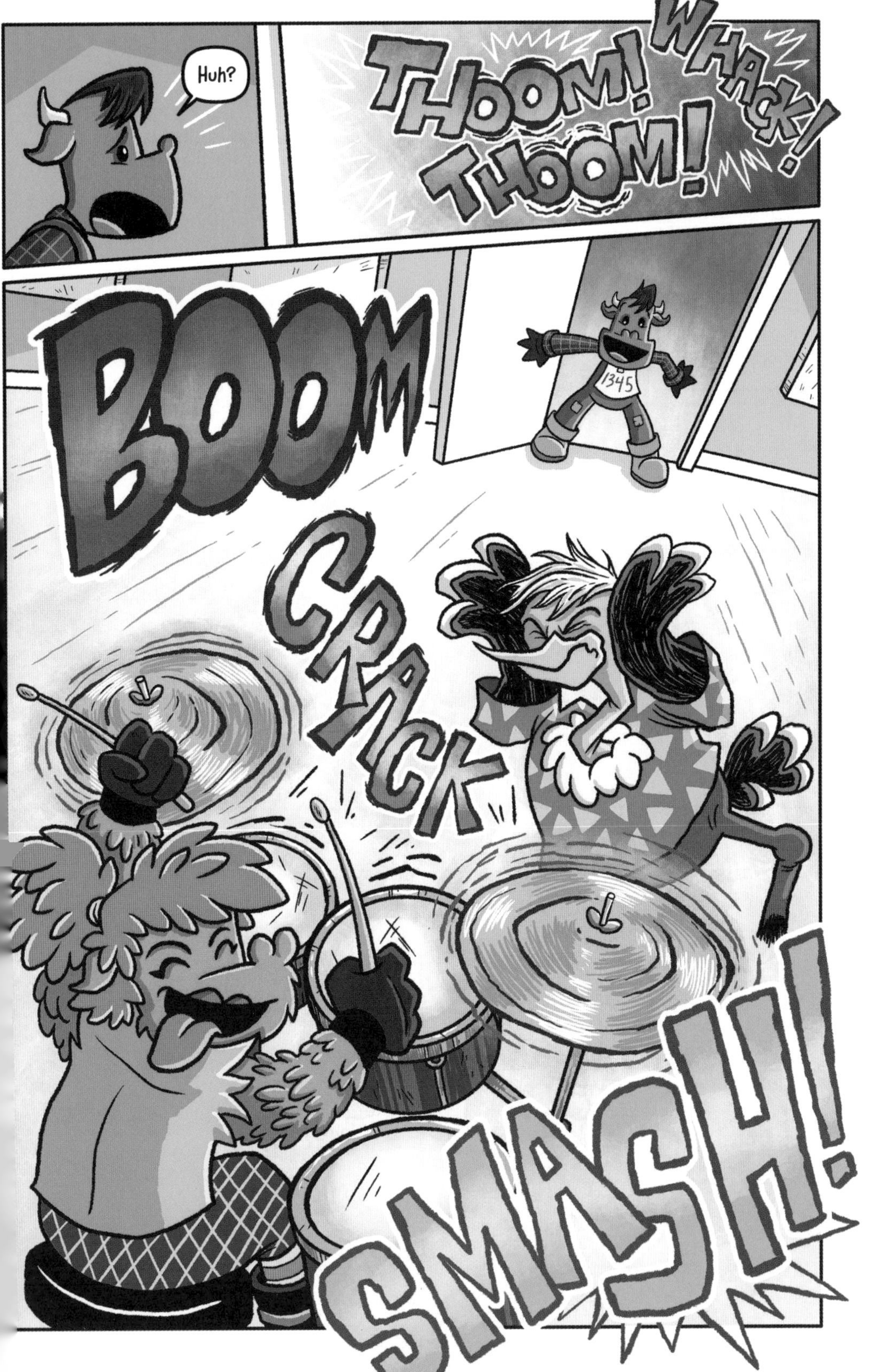

Huh?
THOOM! WHACK! THOOM!
BOOM
1345
CRACK
SMASH!!

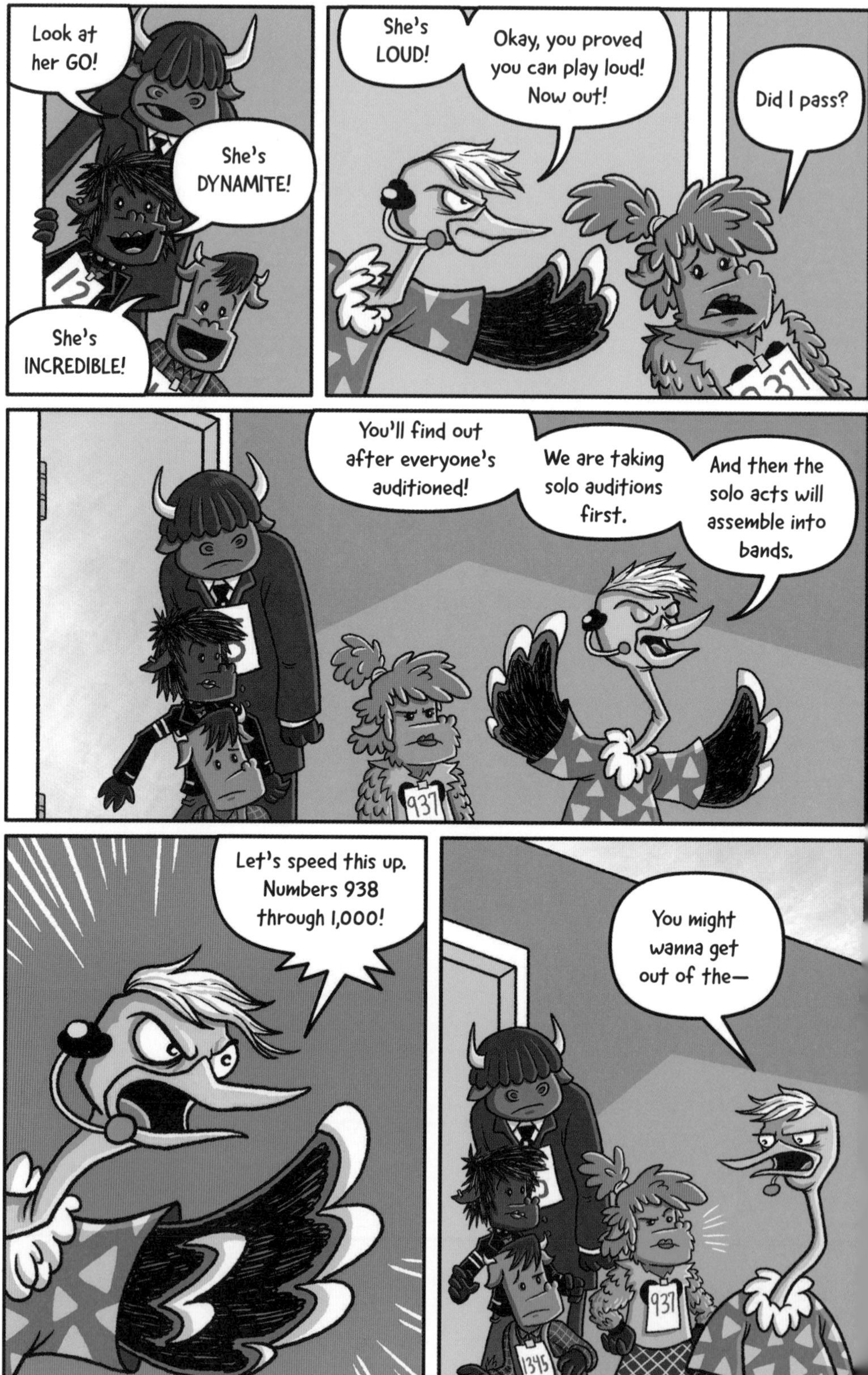
Look at her GO!
She's DYNAMITE!
She's INCREDIBLE!
She's LOUD!
Okay, you proved you can play loud! Now out!
Did I pass?
You'll find out after everyone's auditioned!
We are taking solo auditions first.
And then the solo acts will assemble into bands.
Let's speed this up. Numbers 938 through 1,000!
You might wanna get out of the—

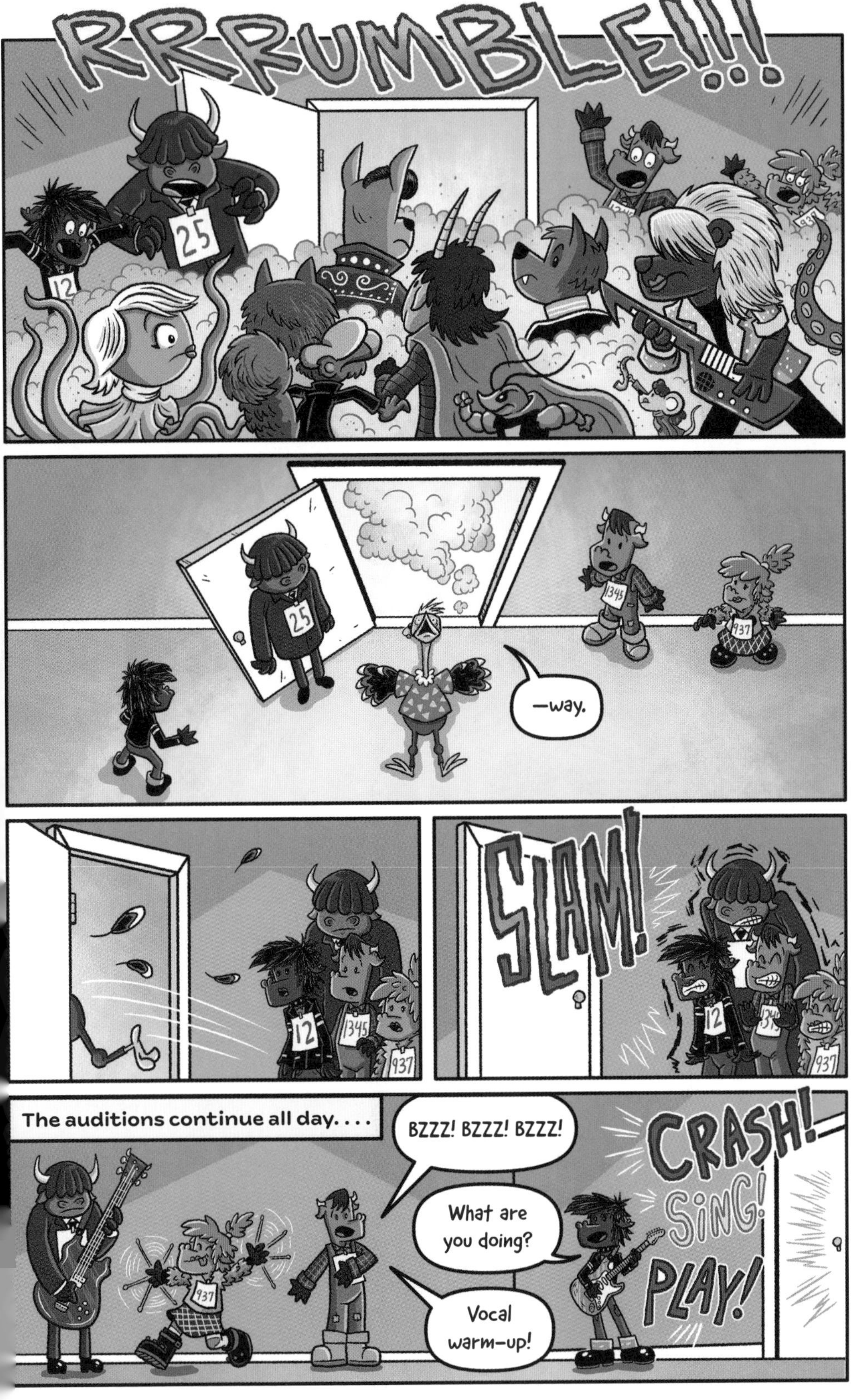
RRRUMBLE!!!
—way.
SLAM!
The auditions continue all day. . . .
BZZZ! BZZZ! BZZZ!
What are you doing?
Vocal warm-up!
CRASH!
SING!
PLAY!

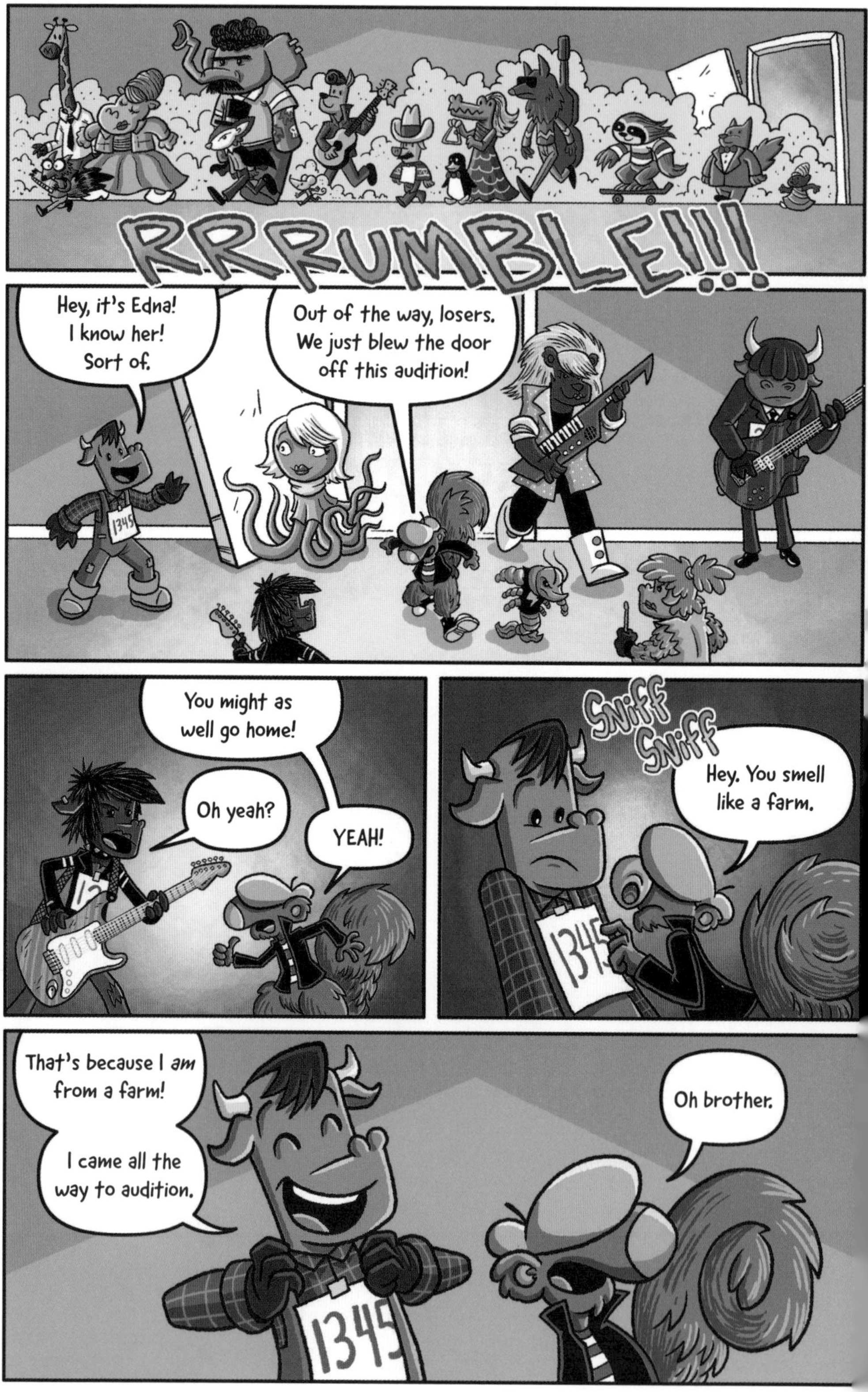
RRRUMBLE!!!
Hey, it's Edna! I know her! Sort of.
Out of the way, losers. We just blew the door off this audition!
You might as well go home!
Oh yeah?
YEAH!
Sniff Sniff
Hey. You smell like a farm.
That's because I *am* from a farm!
I came all the way to audition.
Oh brother.

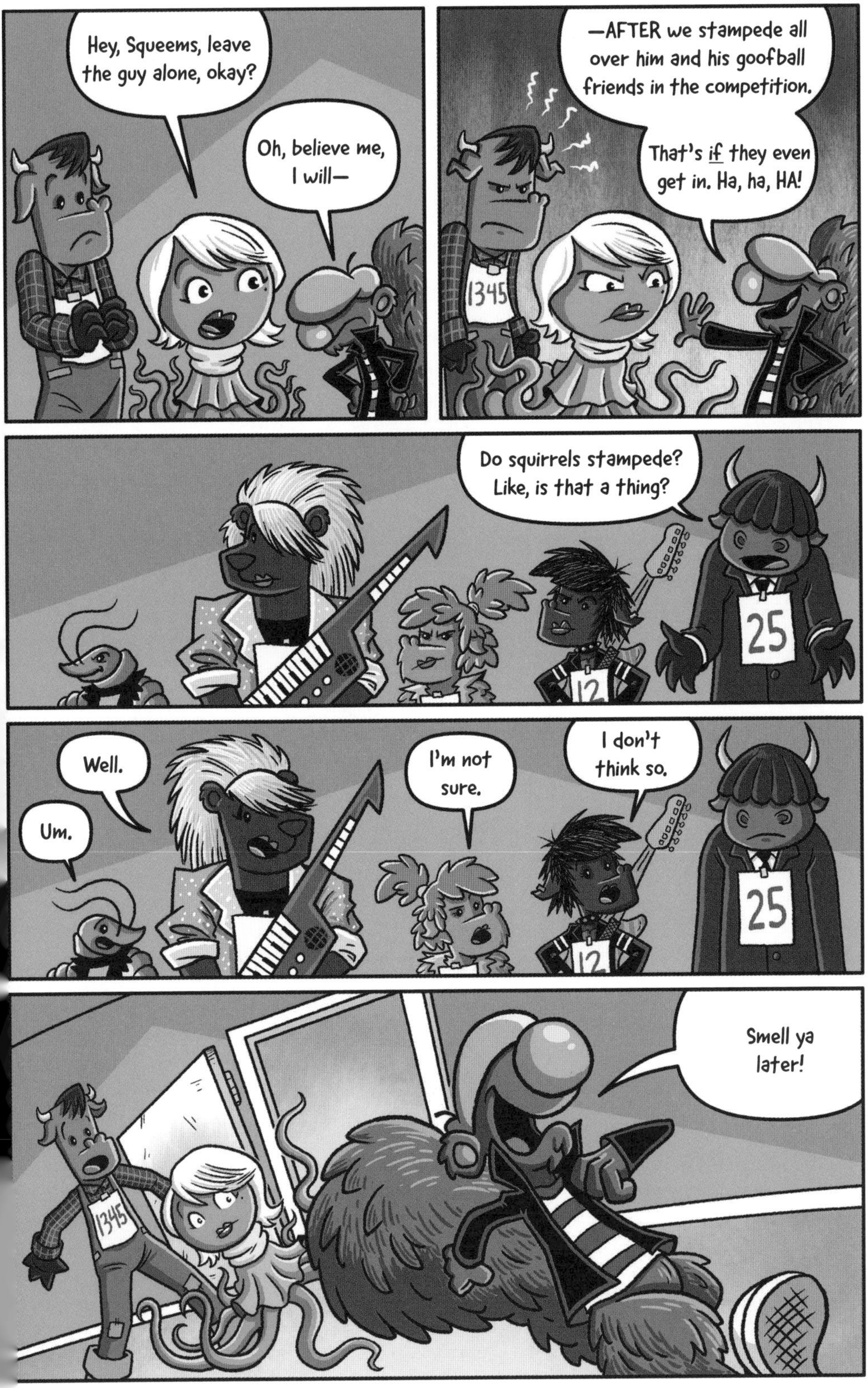
Hey, Squeems, leave the guy alone, okay?
Oh, believe me, I will—
—AFTER we stampede all over him and his goofball friends in the competition.
That's if they even get in. Ha, ha, HA!
1345
Do squirrels stampede? Like, is that a thing?
25
12
Well.
Um.
I'm not sure.
I don't think so.
25
12
Smell ya later!
1345

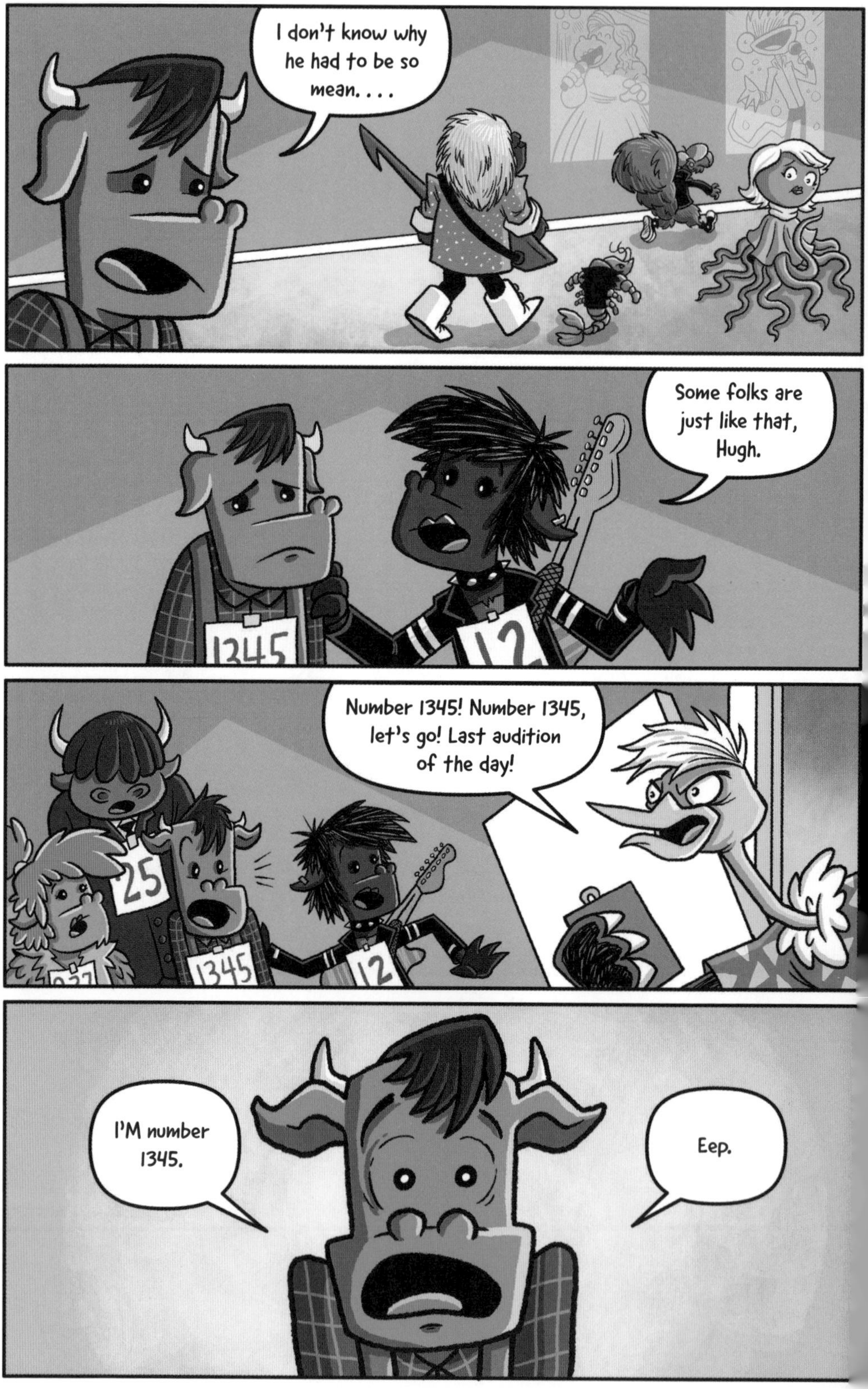
I don't know why he had to be so mean. . . .
Some folks are just like that, Hugh.
1345
12
Number 1345! Number 1345, let's go! Last audition of the day!
25
1345
12
I'M number 1345.
Eep.

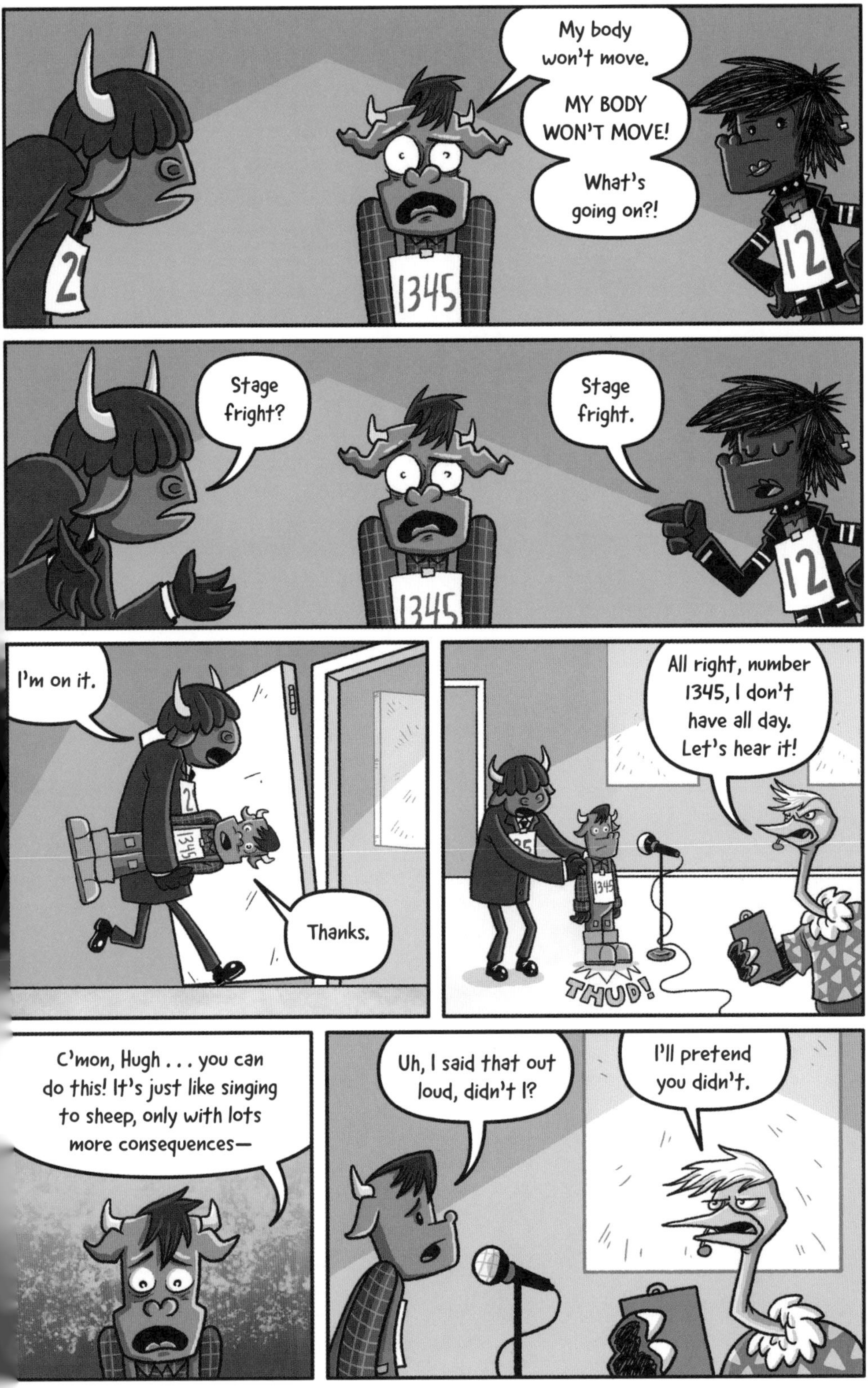
My body won't move.
MY BODY WON'T MOVE!
What's going on?!
Stage fright?
Stage fright.
I'm on it.
Thanks.
All right, number 1345, I don't have all day. Let's hear it!
THUD!
C'mon, Hugh . . . you can do this! It's just like singing to sheep, only with lots more consequences—
Uh, I said that out loud, didn't I?
I'll pretend you didn't.

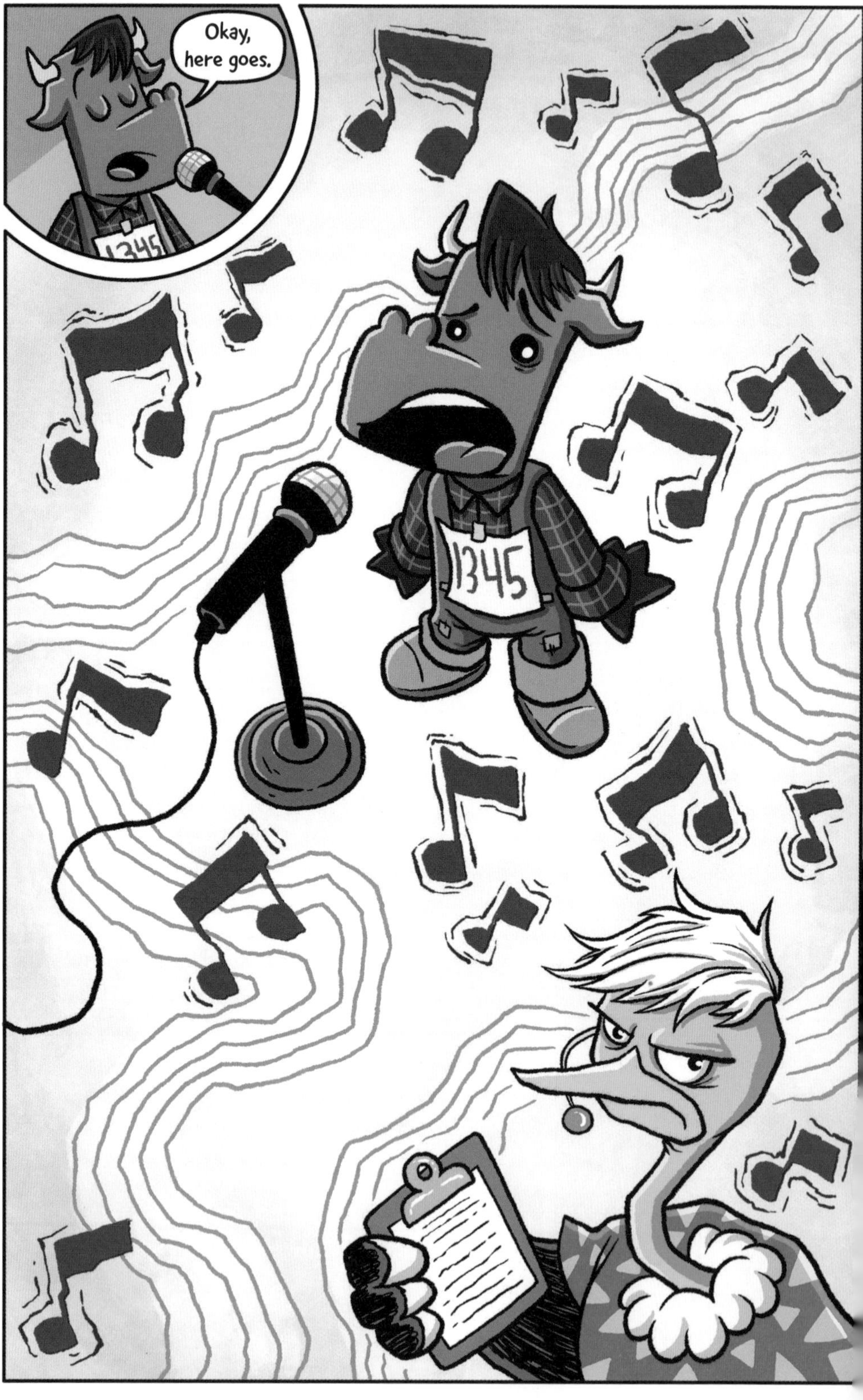
Okay,
here goes.
1345
1345

CHAPTER 4

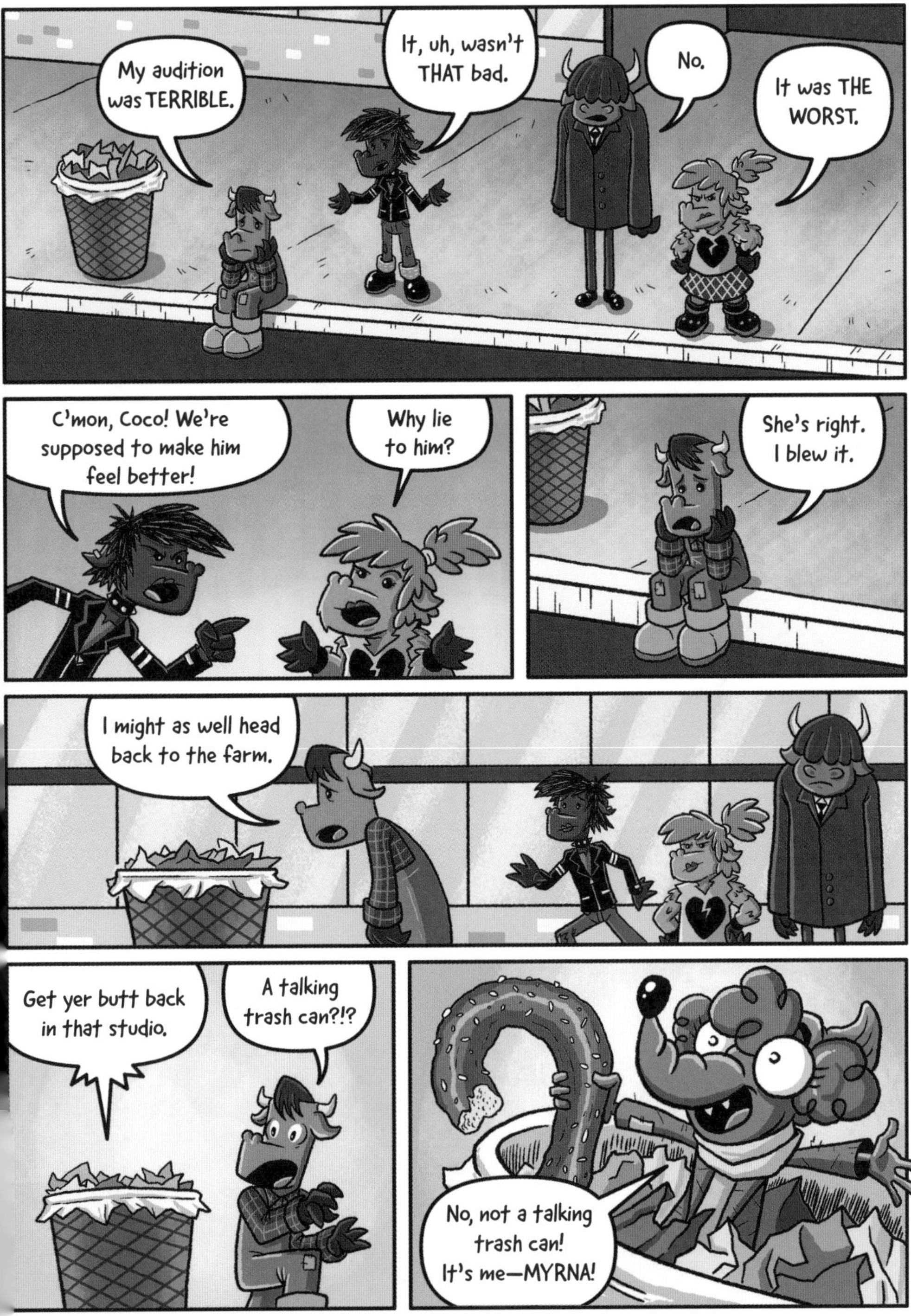
My audition was TERRIBLE.
It, uh, wasn't THAT bad.
No.
It was THE WORST.
C'mon, Coco! We're supposed to make him feel better!
Why lie to him?
She's right. I blew it.
I might as well head back to the farm.
Get yer butt back in that studio.
A talking trash can?!?
No, not a talking trash can! It's me—MYRNA!

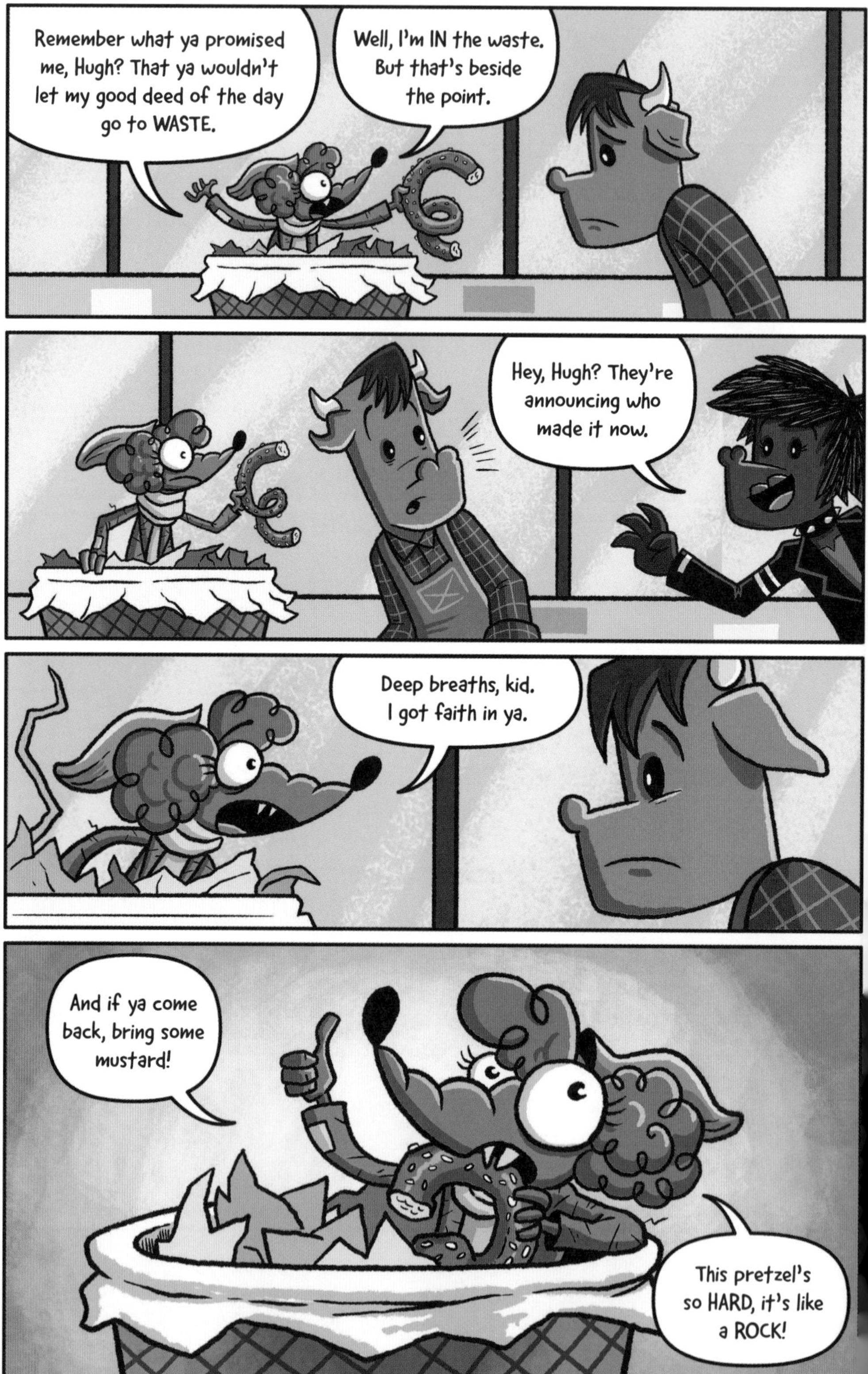
Remember what ya promised me, Hugh? That ya wouldn't let my good deed of the day go to WASTE.
Well, I'm IN the waste. But that's beside the point.
Hey, Hugh? They're announcing who made it now.
Deep breaths, kid. I got faith in ya.
And if ya come back, bring some mustard!
This pretzel's so HARD, it's like a ROCK!

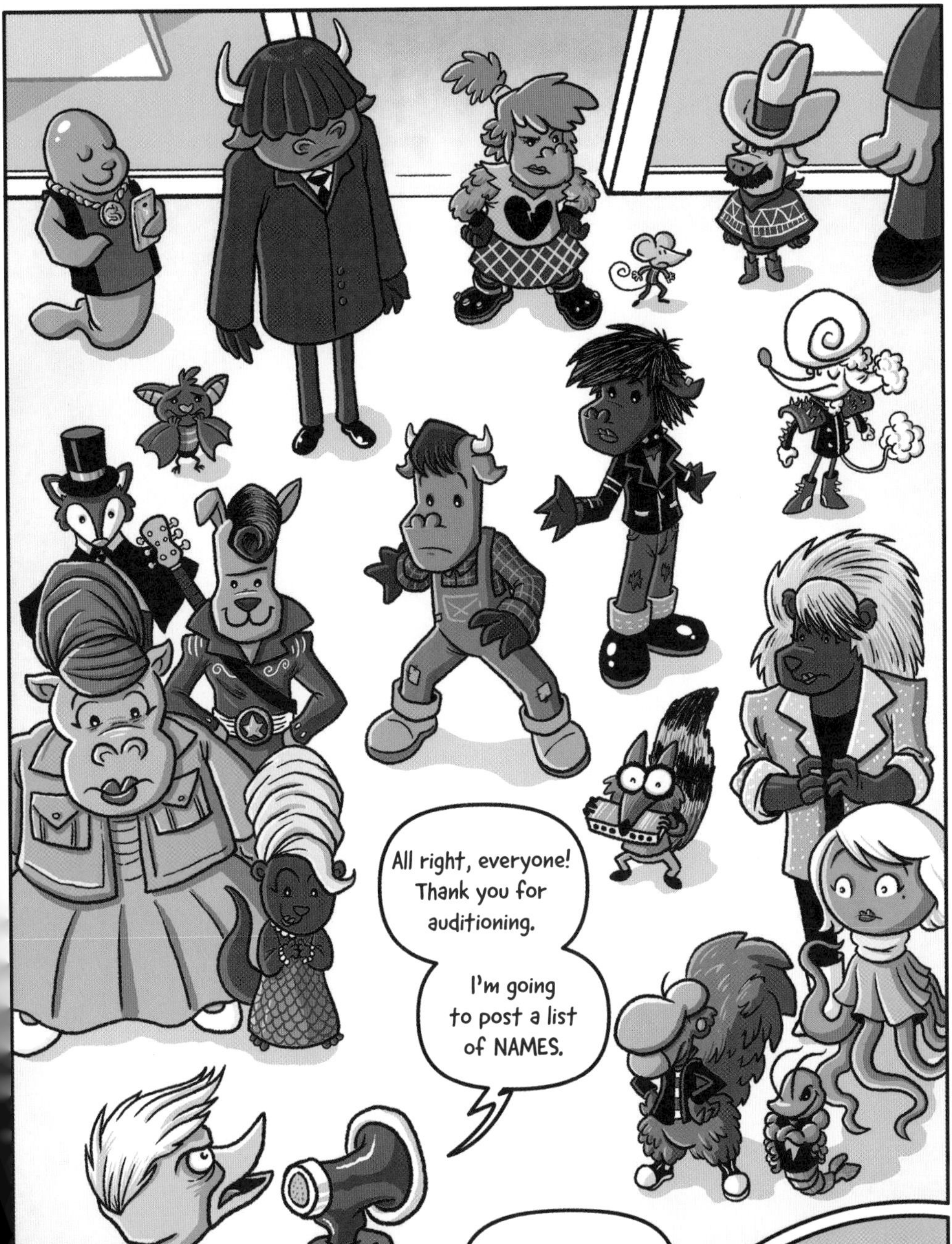
All right, everyone! Thank you for auditioning.
I'm going to post a list of NAMES.

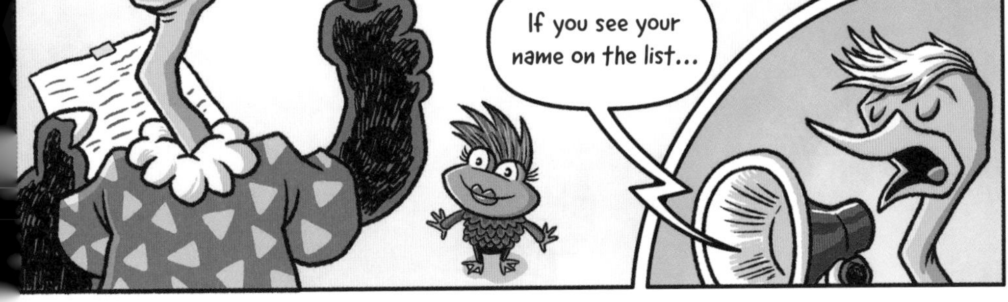
If you see your name on the list...

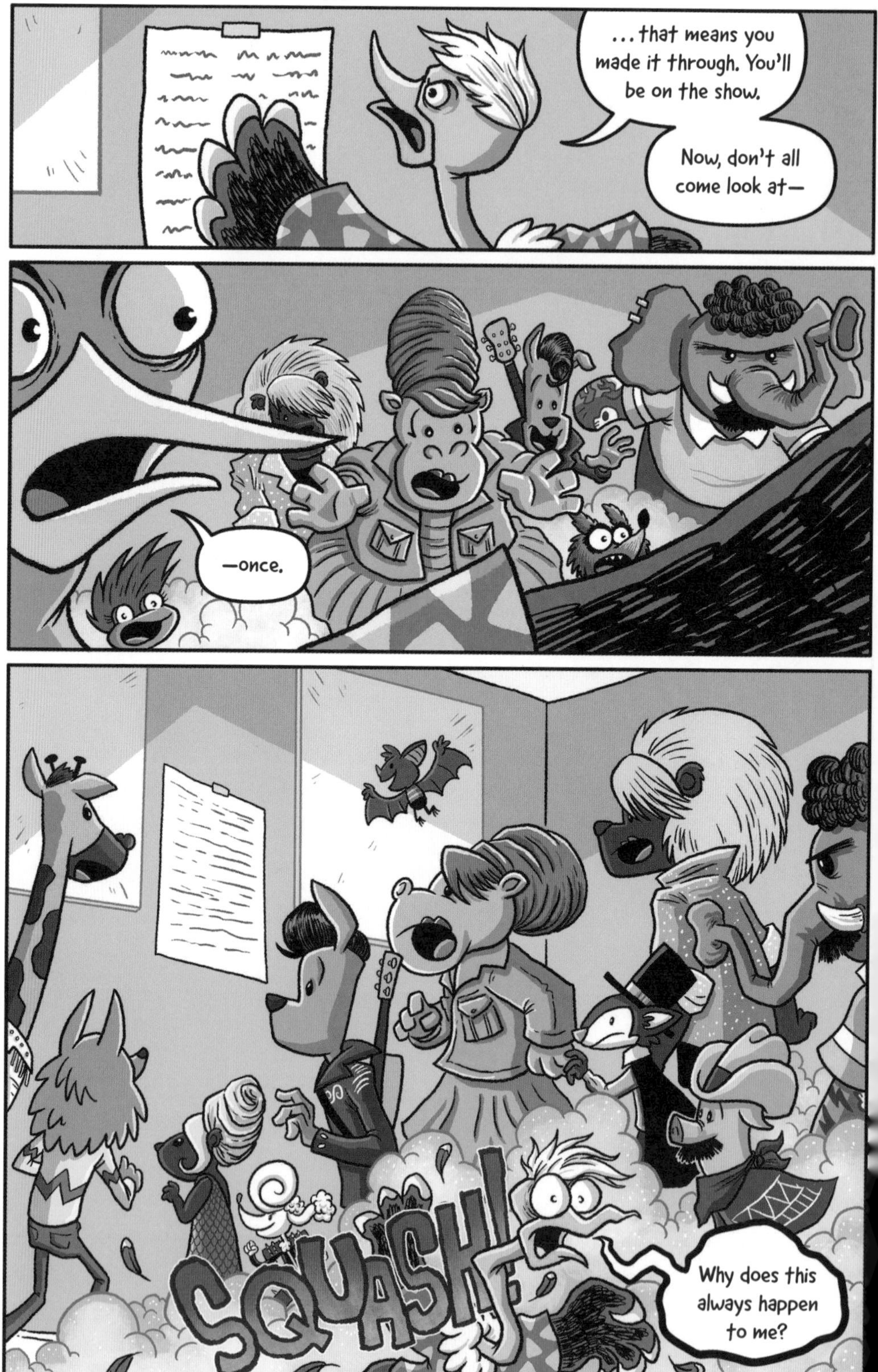
...that means you made it through. You'll be on the show.
Now, don't all come look at—
—once.
SQUASH!
Why does this always happen to me?

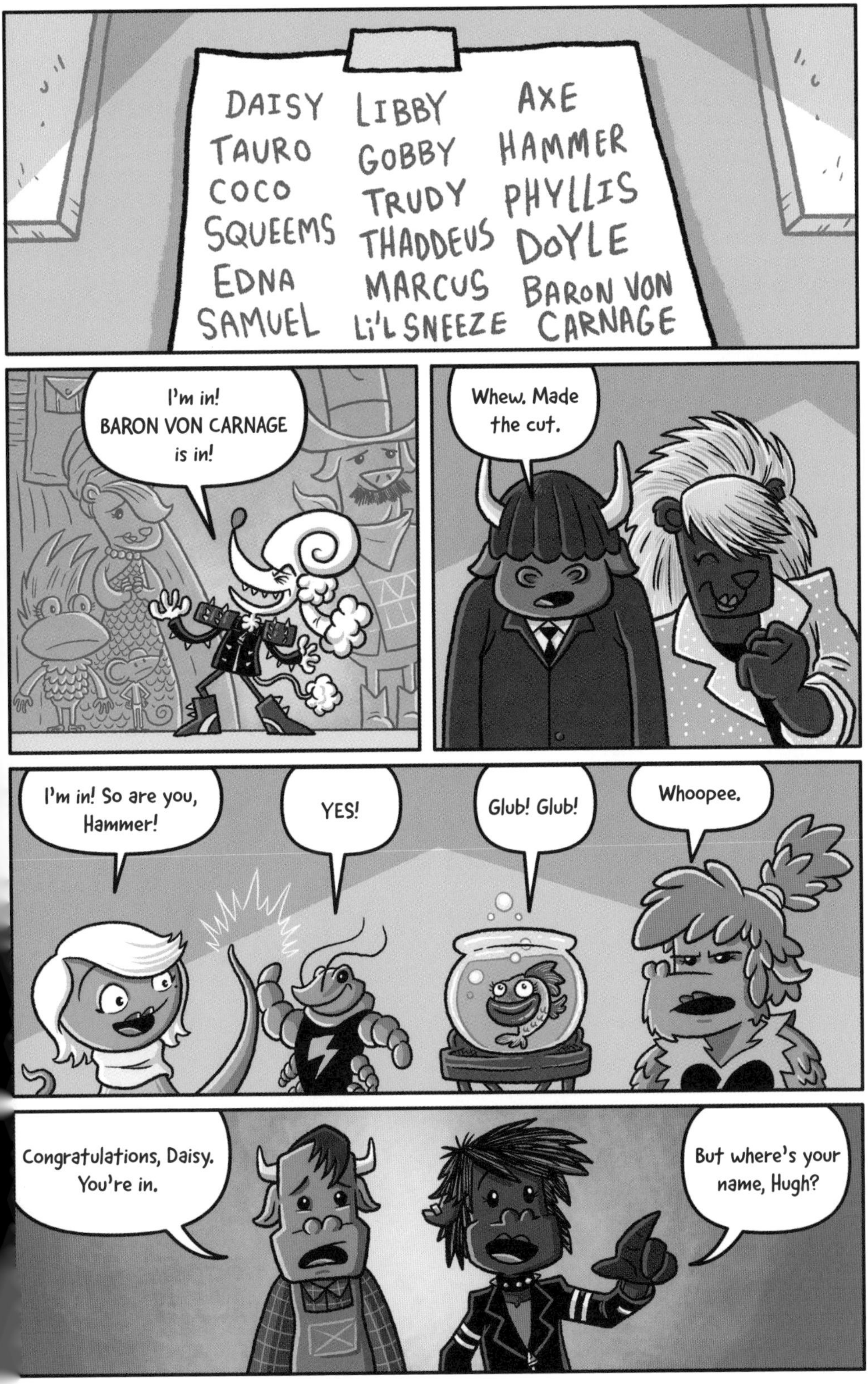
DAISY LIBBY AXE
TAURO GOBBY HAMMER
COCO TRUDY PHYLLIS
SQUEEMS THADDEUS DOYLE
EDNA MARCUS BARON VON
SAMUEL LI'L SNEEZE CARNAGE
I'm in! BARON VON CARNAGE is in!
Whew. Made the cut.
I'm in! So are you, Hammer!
YES!
Glub! Glub!
Whoopee.
Congratulations, Daisy. You're in.
But where's your name, Hugh?

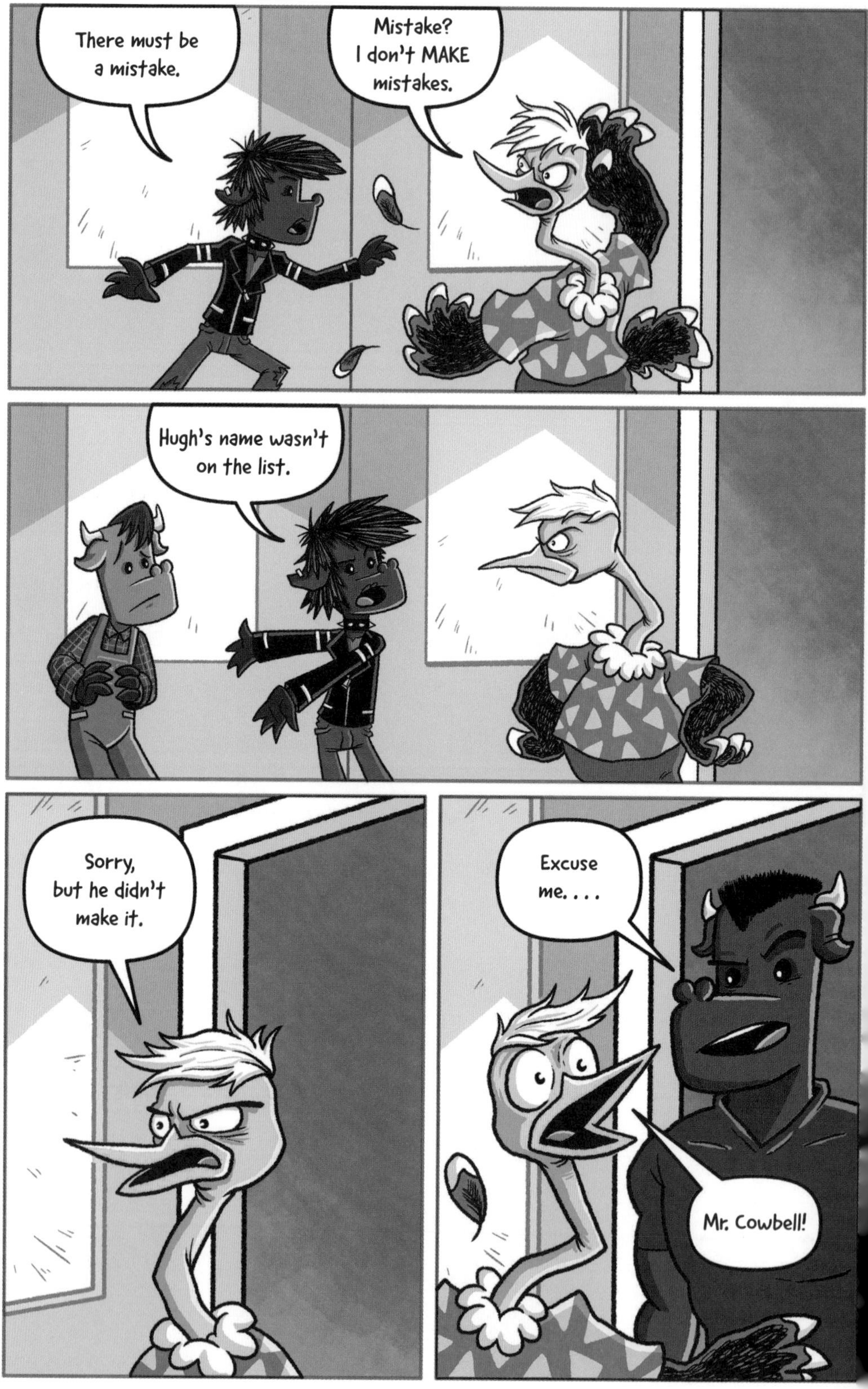

There must be a mistake.
Mistake? I don't MAKE mistakes.
Hugh's name wasn't on the list.
Sorry, but he didn't make it.
Excuse me. . . .
Mr. Cowbell!

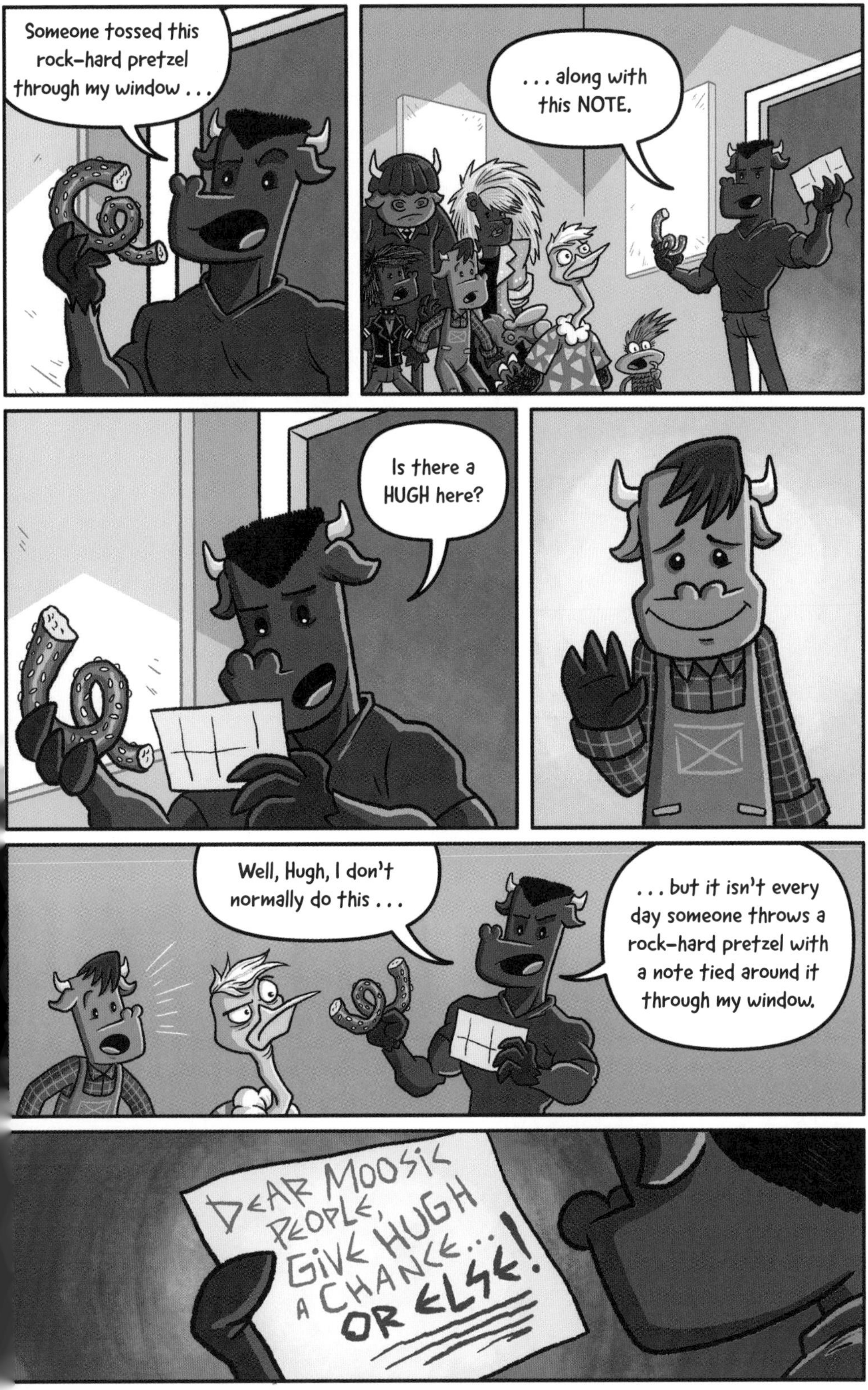
Someone tossed this rock-hard pretzel through my window . . .
. . . along with this NOTE.
Is there a HUGH here?
Well, Hugh, I don't normally do this . . .
. . . but it isn't every day someone throws a rock-hard pretzel with a note tied around it through my window.
DEAR MOOSIC PEOPLE, GIVE HUGH A CHANCE... OR ELSE!

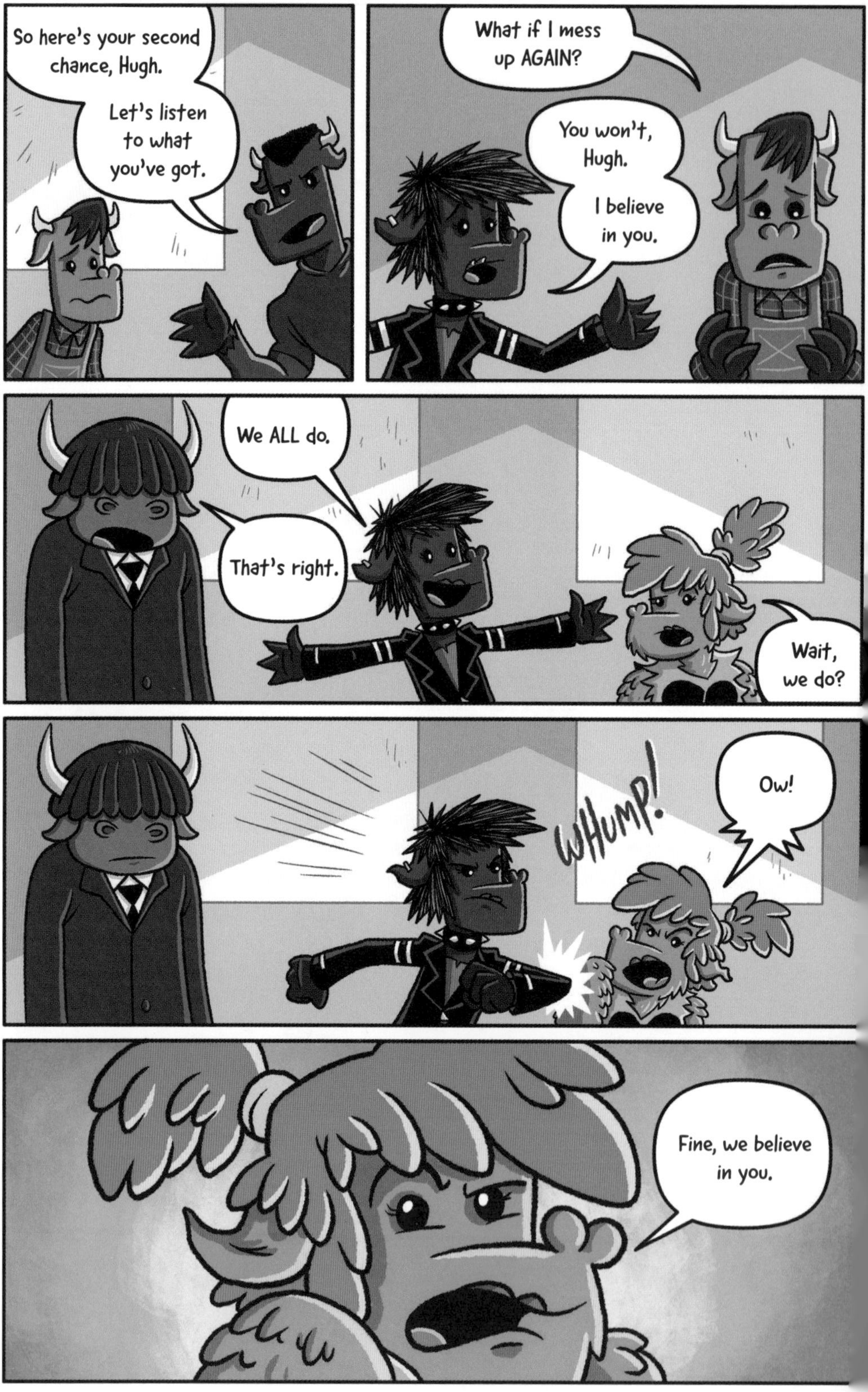
So here's your second chance, Hugh.
Let's listen to what you've got.
What if I mess up AGAIN?
You won't, Hugh.
I believe in you.
We ALL do.
That's right.
Wait, we do?
WHUMP!
Ow!
Fine, we believe in you.

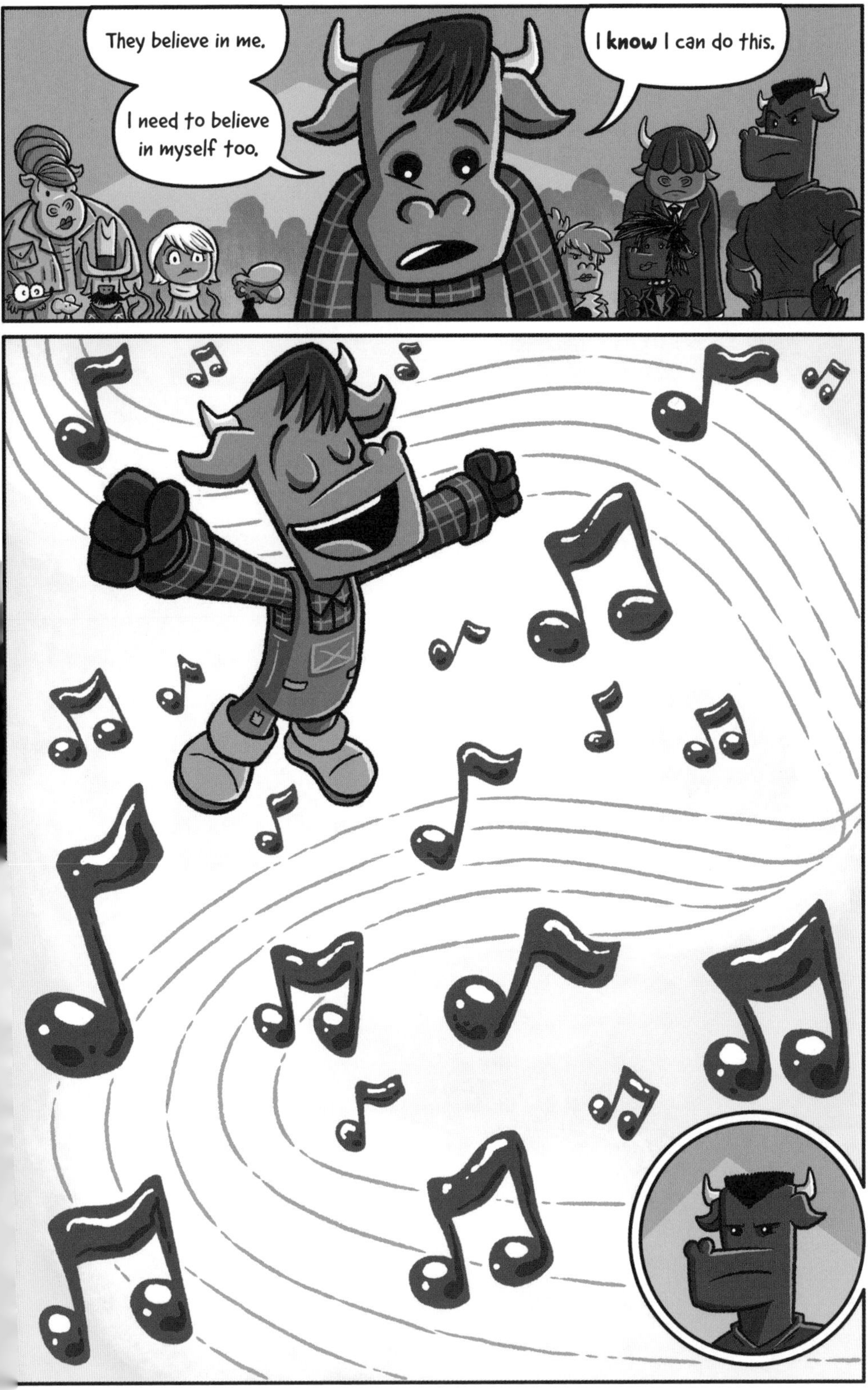
They believe in me.
I need to believe in myself too.
I **know** I can do this.

CHAPTER 5

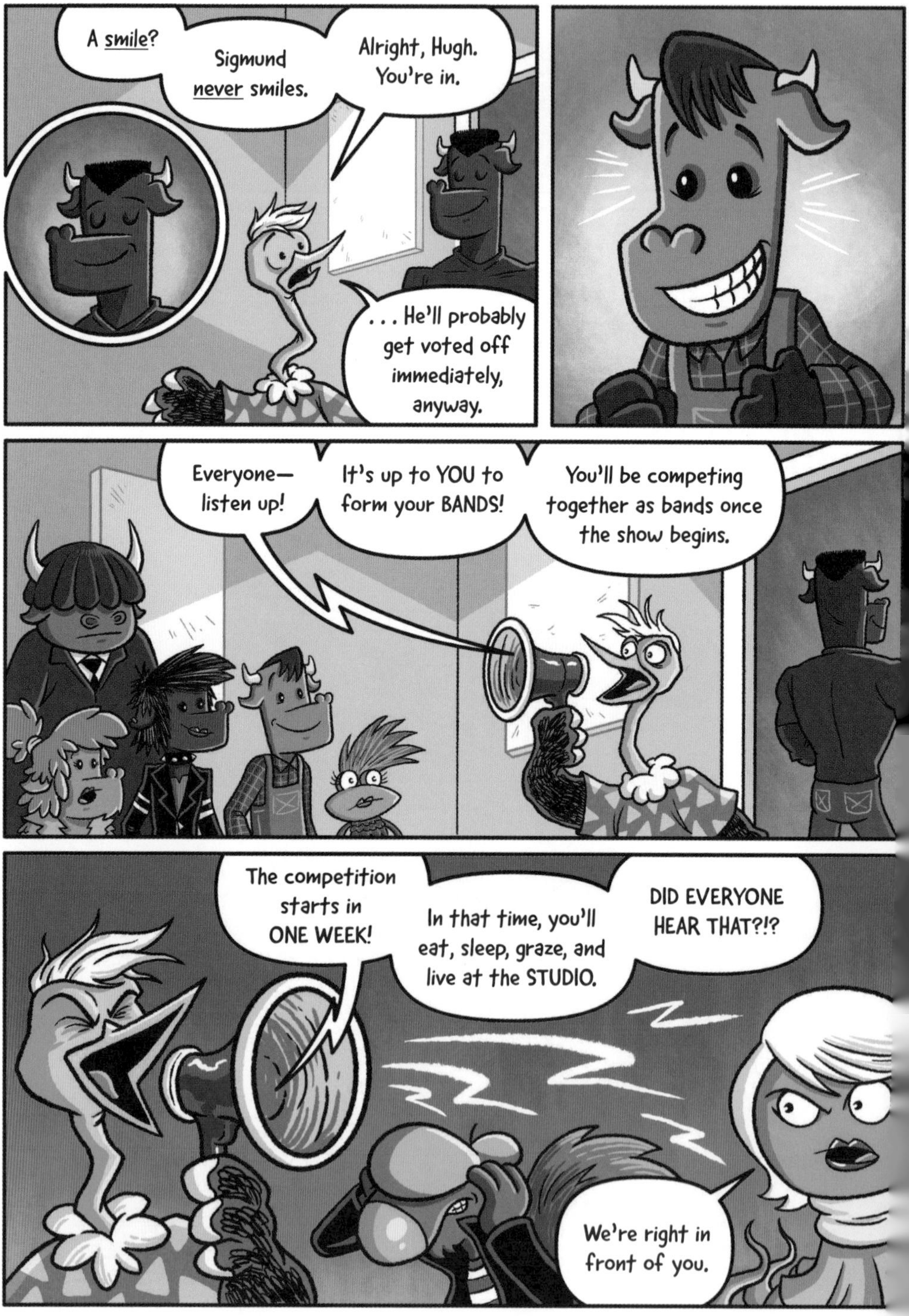
A smile?
Sigmund never smiles.
Alright, Hugh. You're in.
. . . He'll probably get voted off immediately, anyway.
Everyone—listen up!
It's up to YOU to form your BANDS!
You'll be competing together as bands once the show begins.
The competition starts in ONE WEEK!
In that time, you'll eat, sleep, graze, and live at the STUDIO.
DID EVERYONE HEAR THAT?!?
We're right in front of you.

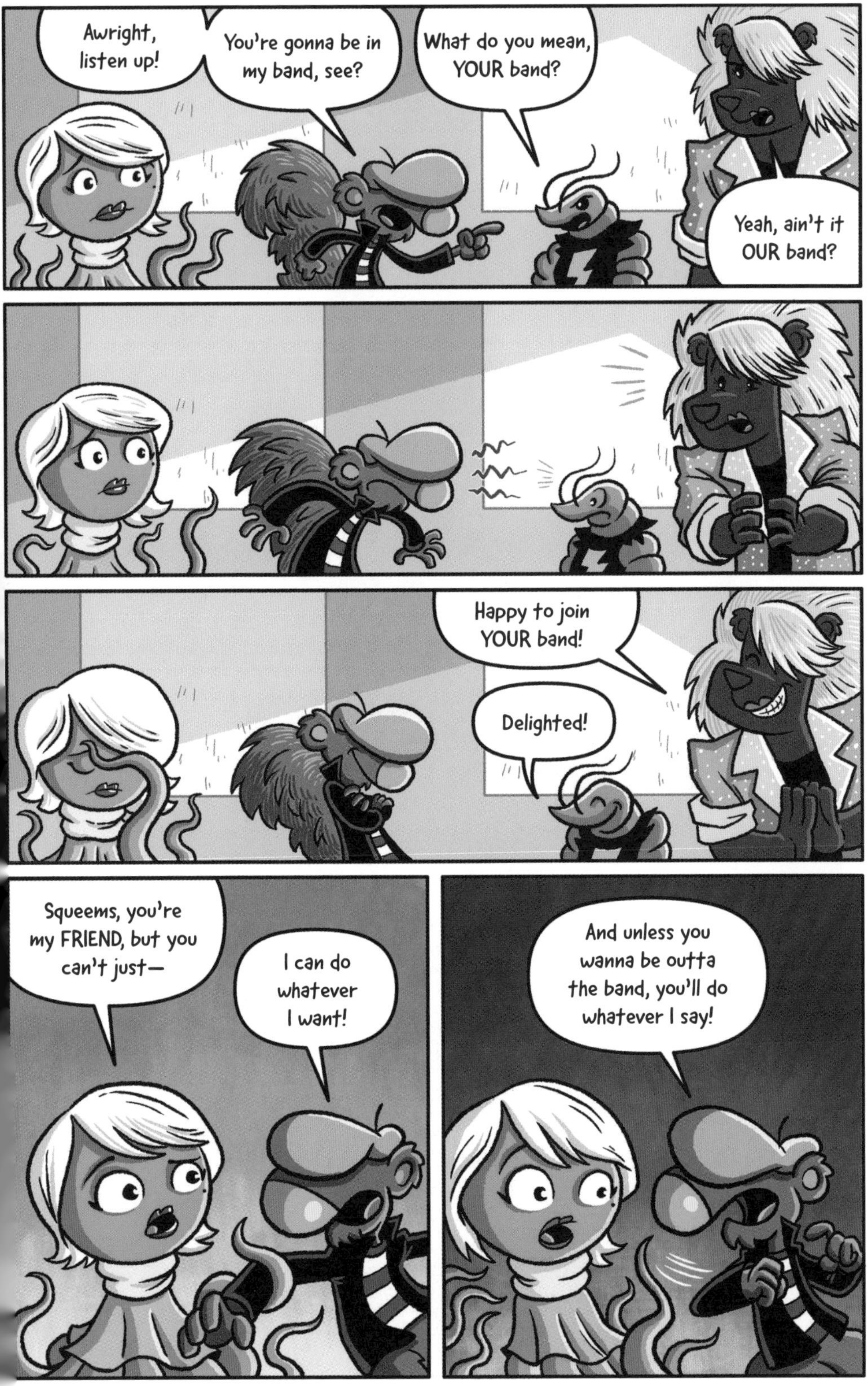
Awright, listen up!
You're gonna be in my band, see?
What do you mean, YOUR band?
Yeah, ain't it OUR band?
Happy to join YOUR band!
Delighted!
Squeems, you're my FRIEND, but you can't just—
I can do whatever I want!
And unless you wanna be outta the band, you'll do whatever I say!

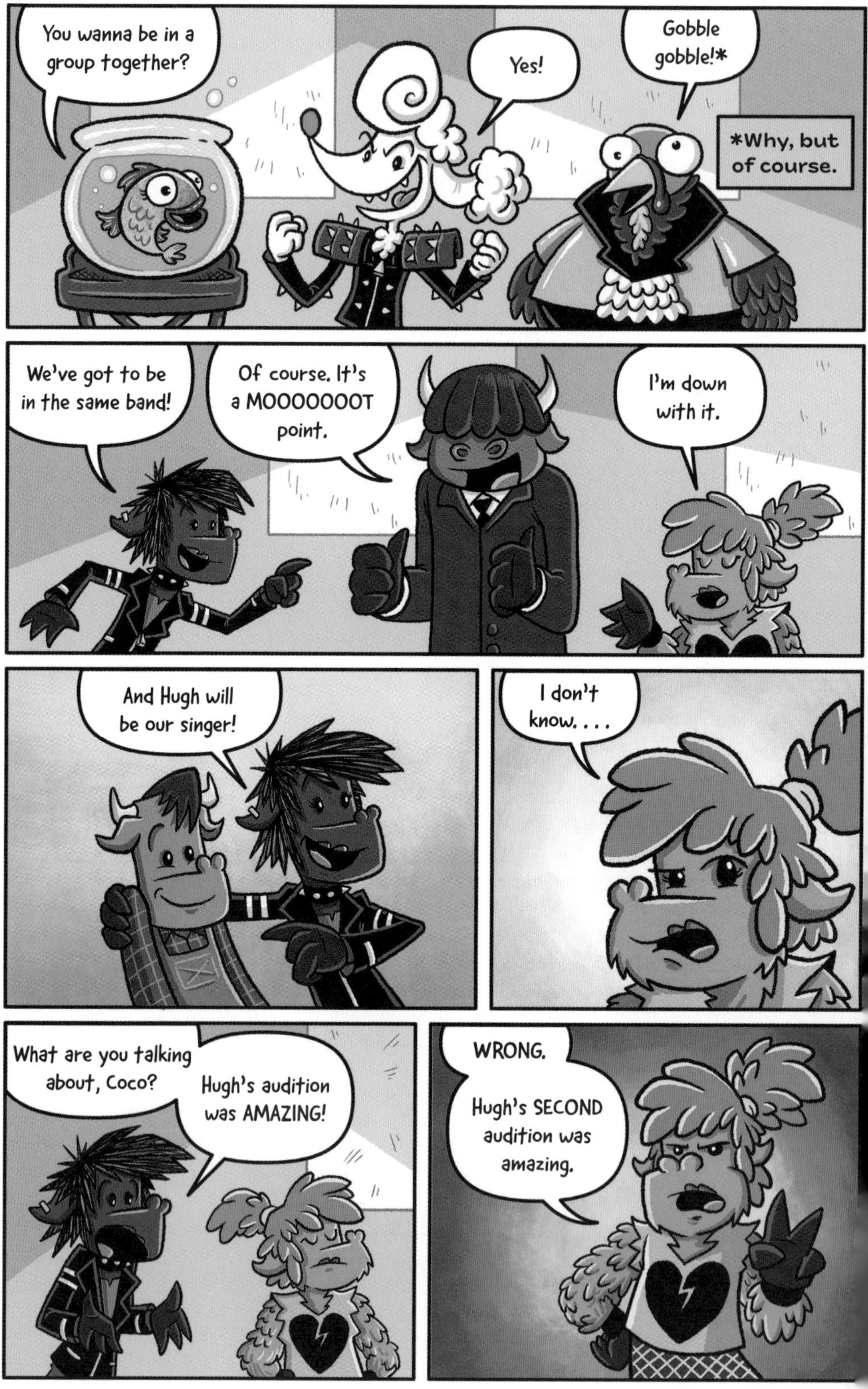
You wanna be in a group together?
Yes!
Gobble gobble!*
*Why, but of course.
We've got to be in the same band!
Of course. It's a MOOOOOOOT point.
I'm down with it.
And Hugh will be our singer!
I don't know. . . .
What are you talking about, Coco?
Hugh's audition was AMAZING!
WRONG.
Hugh's SECOND audition was amazing.

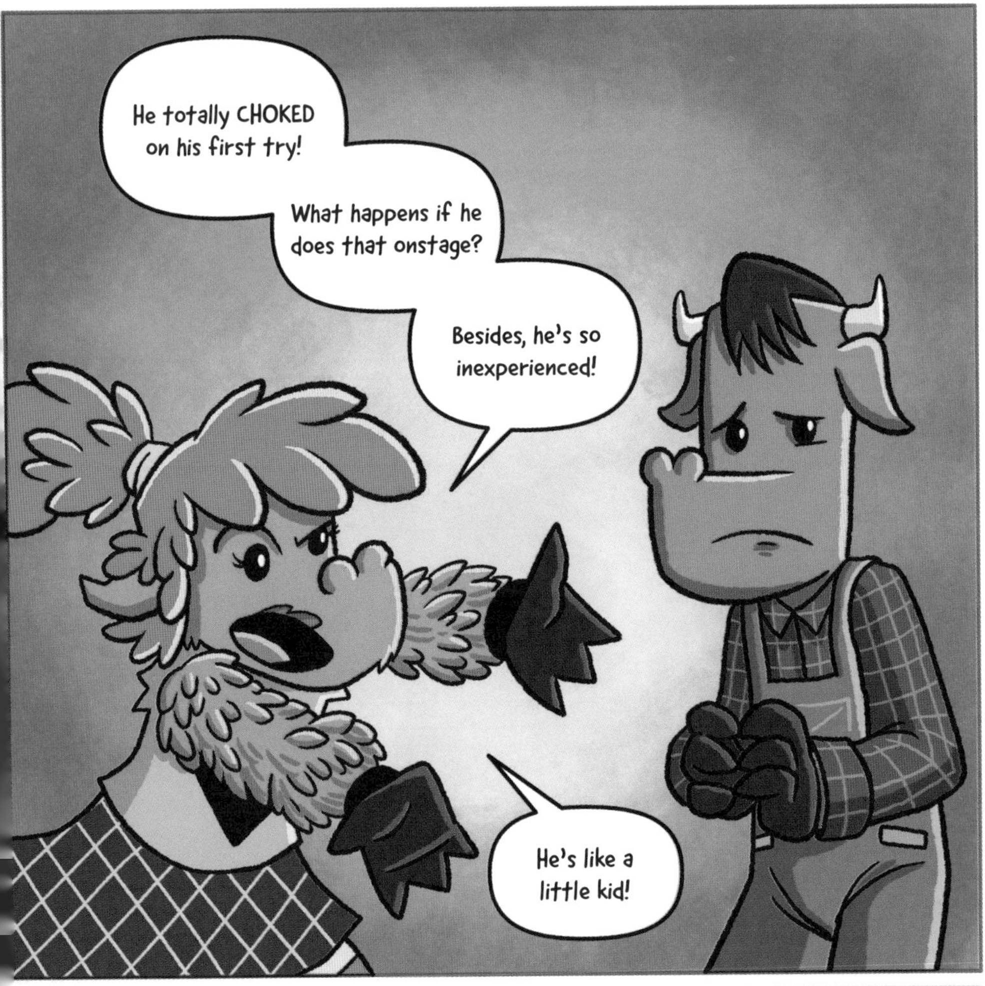
He totally CHOKED on his first try!
What happens if he does that onstage?
Besides, he's so inexperienced!
He's like a little kid!

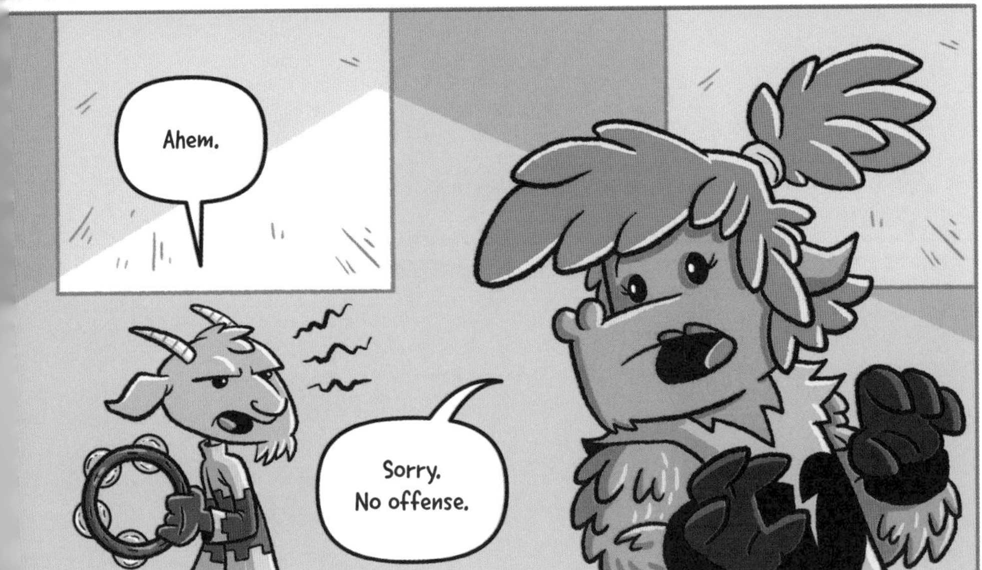
Ahem.
Sorry. No offense.

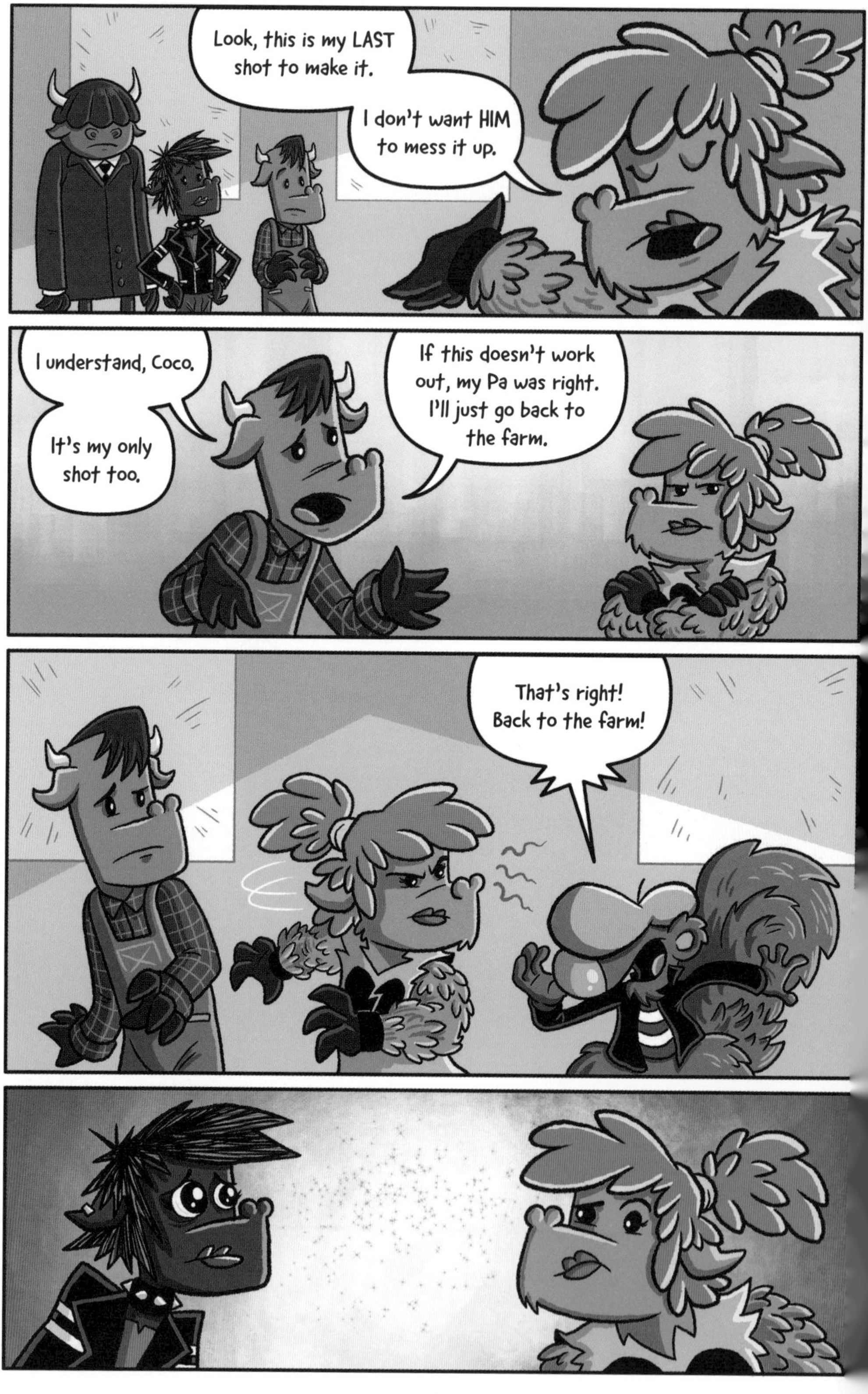
Look, this is my LAST shot to make it.
I don't want HIM to mess it up.
I understand, Coco.
It's my only shot too.
If this doesn't work out, my Pa was right. I'll just go back to the farm.
That's right! Back to the farm!

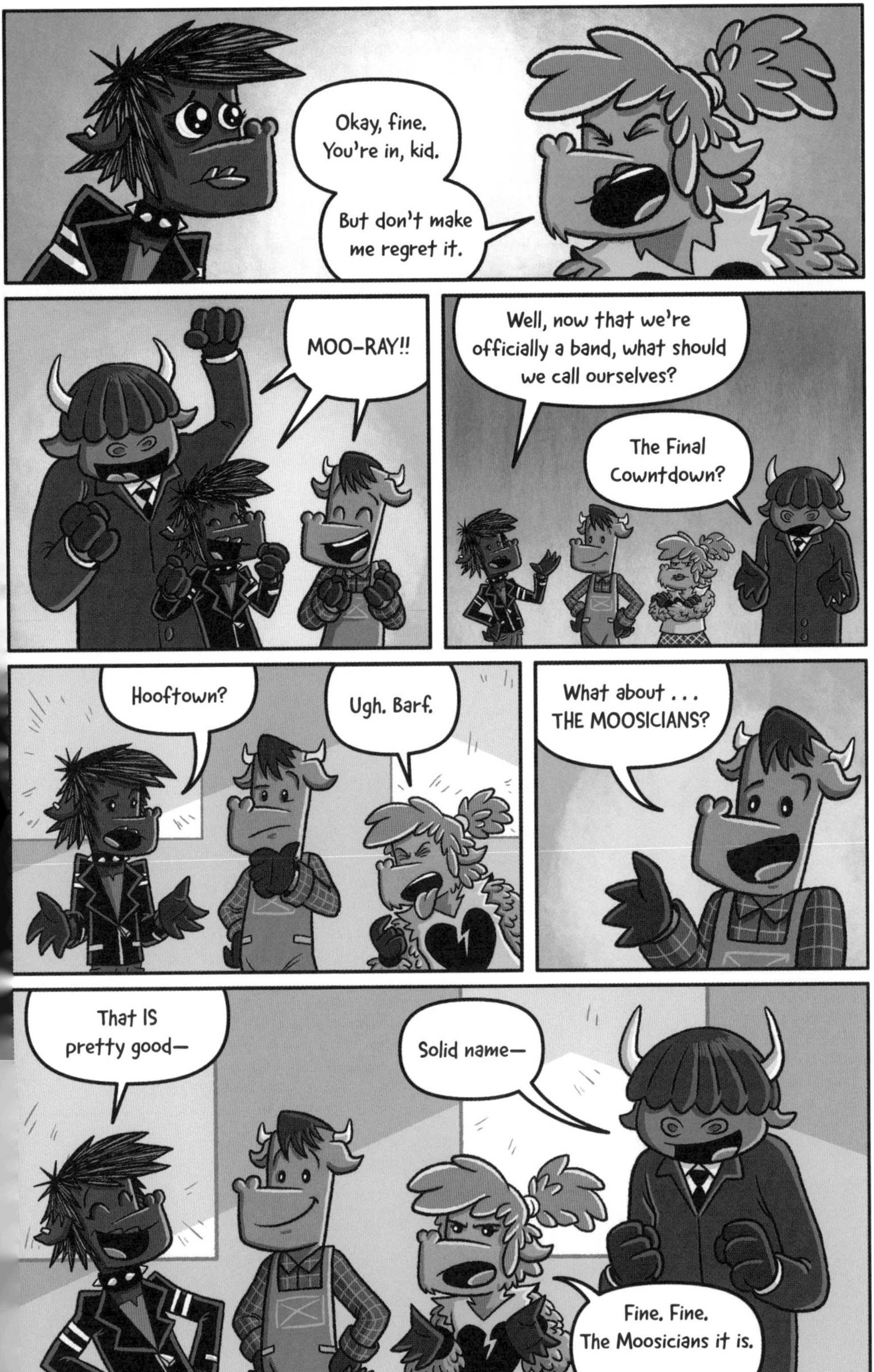
Okay, fine. You're in, kid.
But don't make me regret it.
MOO-RAY!!
Well, now that we're officially a band, what should we call ourselves?
The Final Cowntdown?
Hooftown?
Ugh. Barf.
What about . . . THE MOOSICIANS?
That IS pretty good—
Solid name—
Fine. Fine. The Moosicians it is.

CHAPTER 6

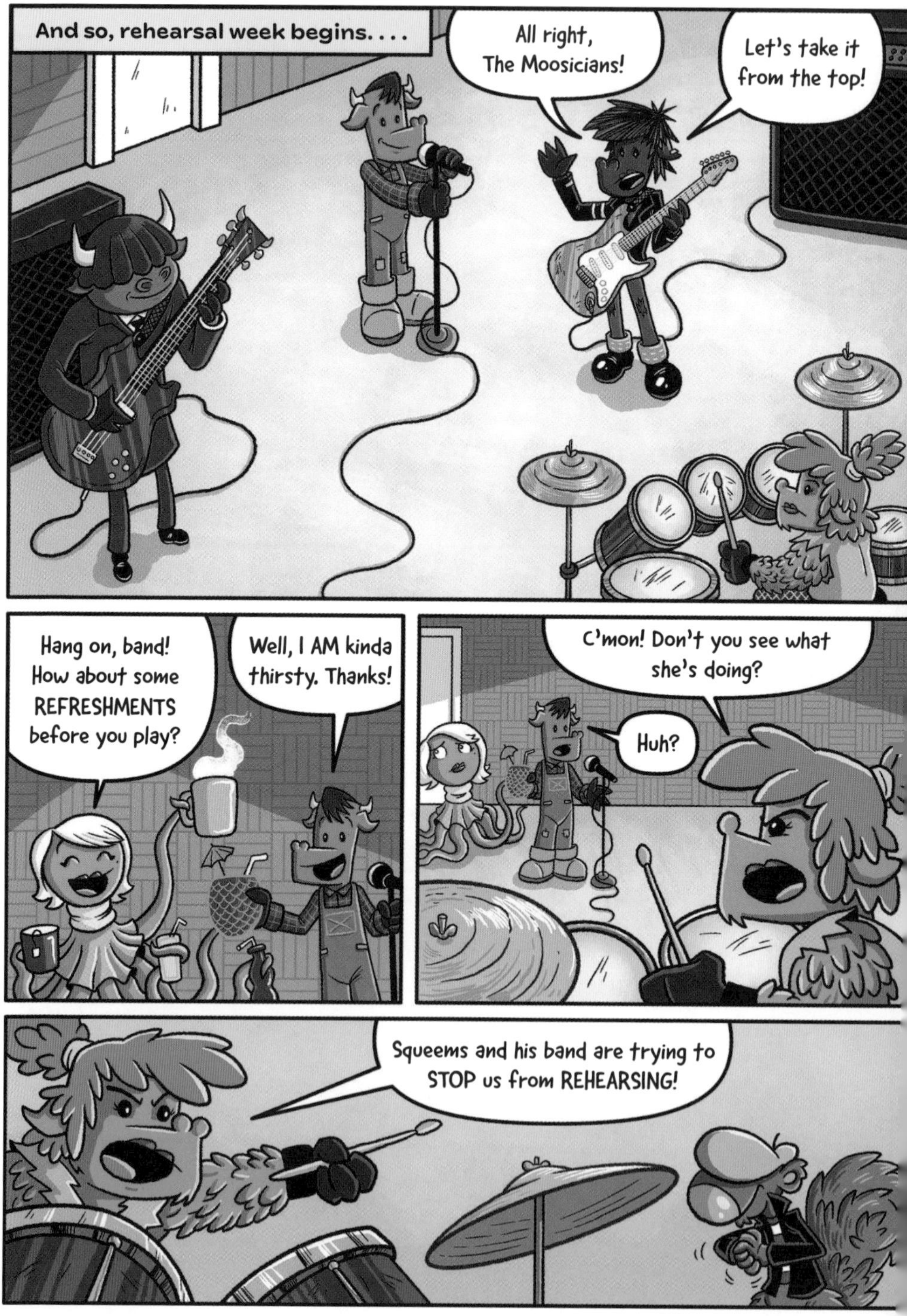

And so, rehearsal week begins. . . .
All right, The Moosicians!
Let's take it from the top!
Hang on, band! How about some REFRESHMENTS before you play?
Well, I AM kinda thirsty. Thanks!
C'mon! Don't you see what she's doing?
Huh?
Squeems and his band are trying to STOP us from REHEARSING!

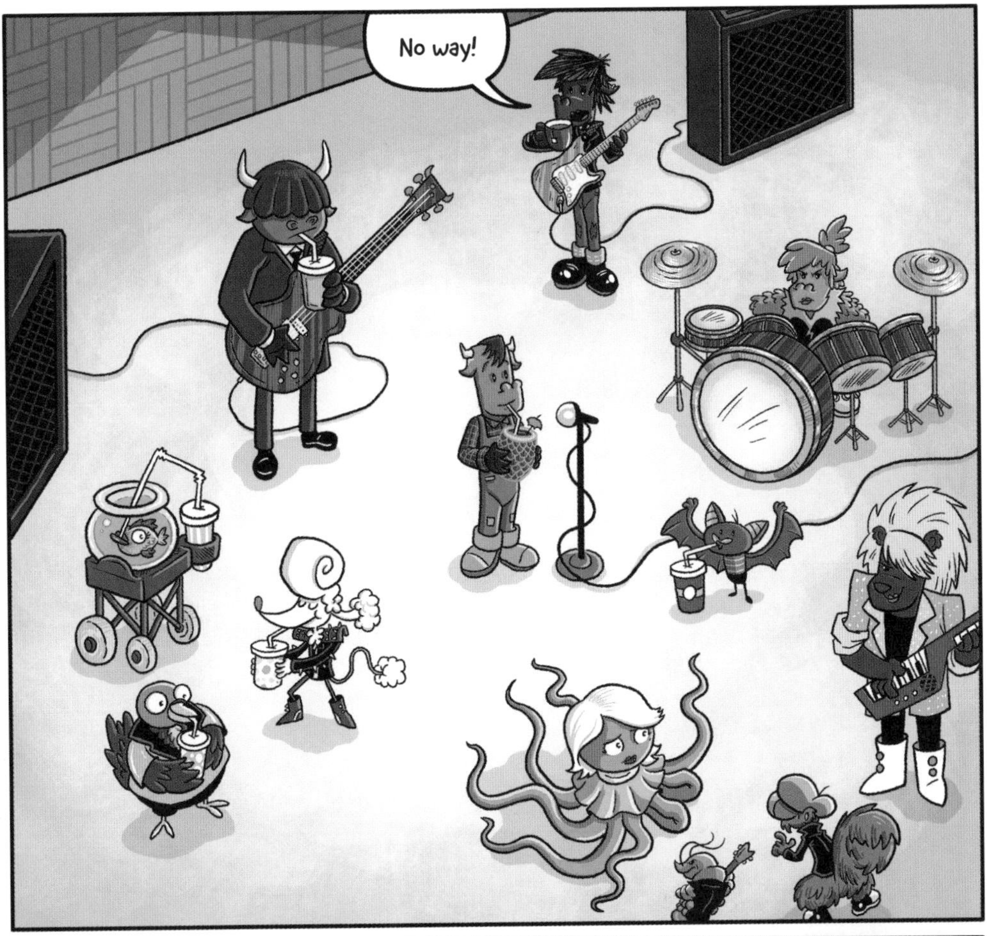
No way!

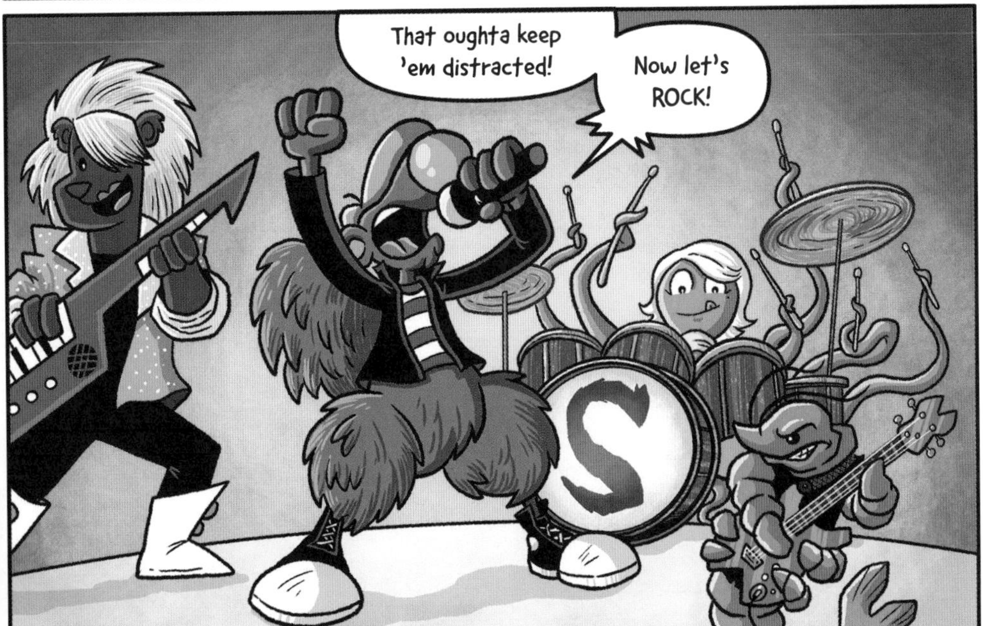
That oughta keep
'em distracted!
Now let's
ROCK!

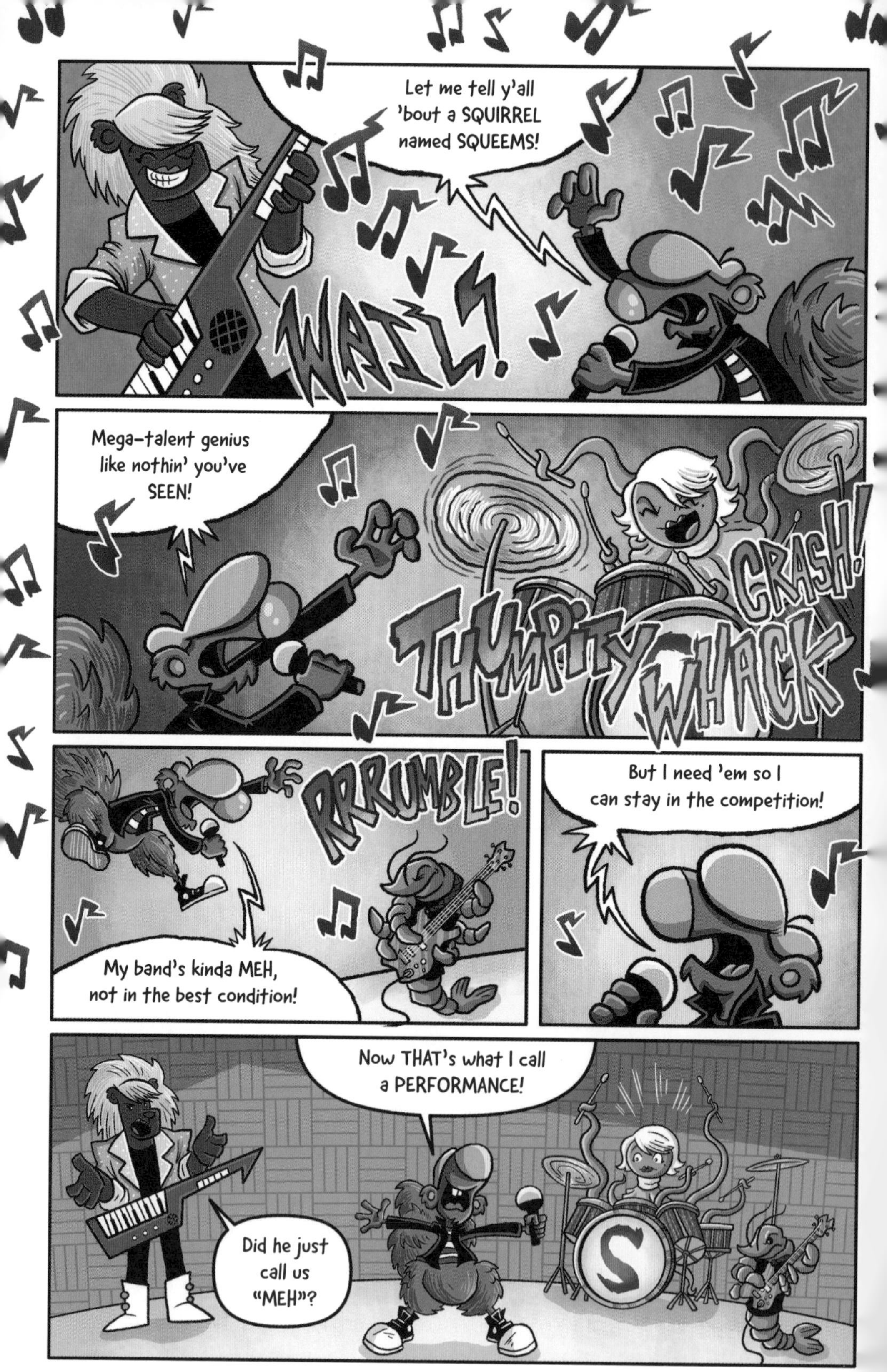
Let me tell y'all 'bout a SQUIRREL named SQUEEMS!
WAIL!
Mega-talent genius like nothin' you've SEEN!
THUMPITY WHACK
CRASH!
RRRUMBLE!
My band's kinda MEH, not in the best condition!
But I need 'em so I can stay in the competition!
Now THAT's what I call a PERFORMANCE!
Did he just call us "MEH"?

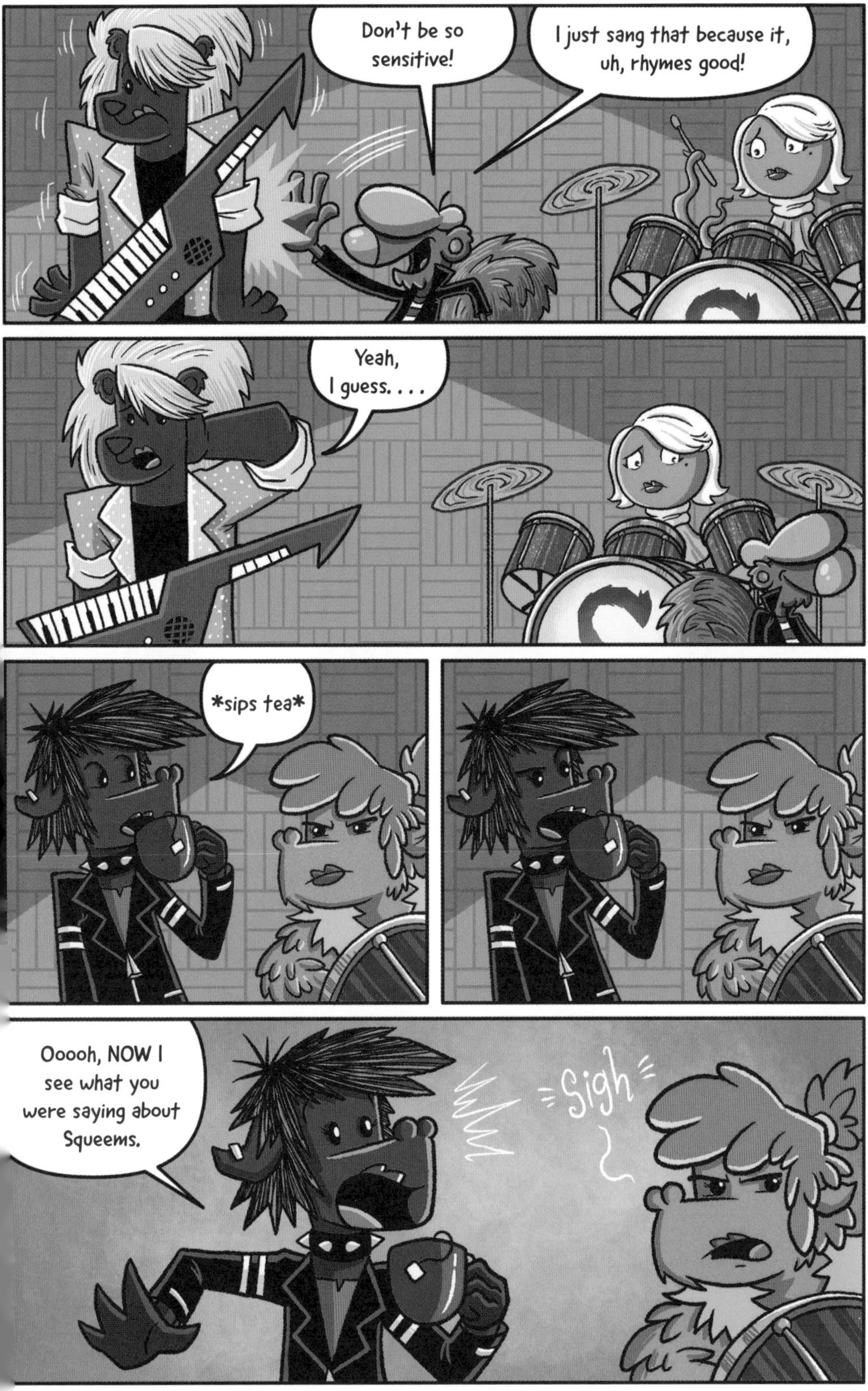
Don't be so sensitive!
I just sang that because it, uh, rhymes good!
Yeah, I guess. . . .
sips tea
Ooooh, NOW I see what you were saying about Squeems.
Sigh

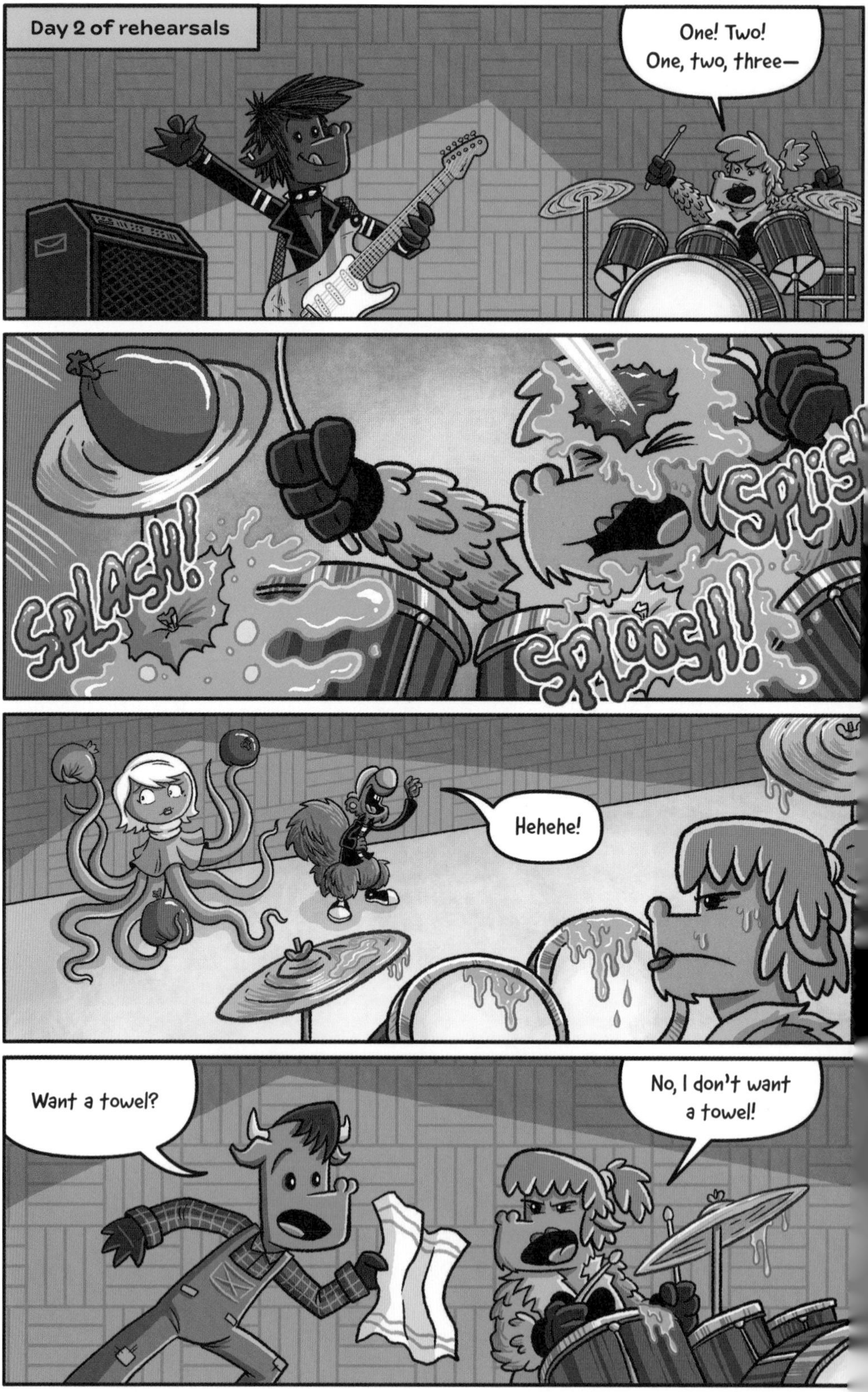
Day 2 of rehearsals
One! Two! One, two, three—
SPLASH!
SPLOOSH!
Hehehe!
Want a towel?
No, I don't want a towel!

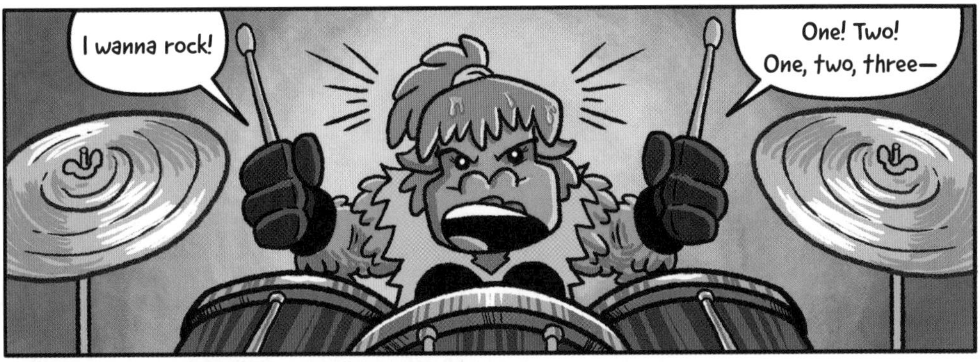
I wanna rock!
One! Two!
One, two, three—

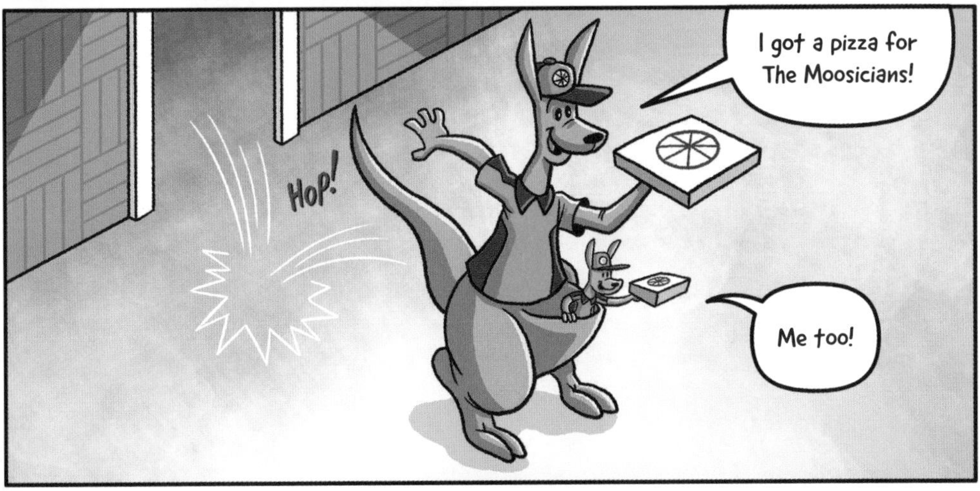
HOP!
I got a pizza for
The Moosicians!
Me too!

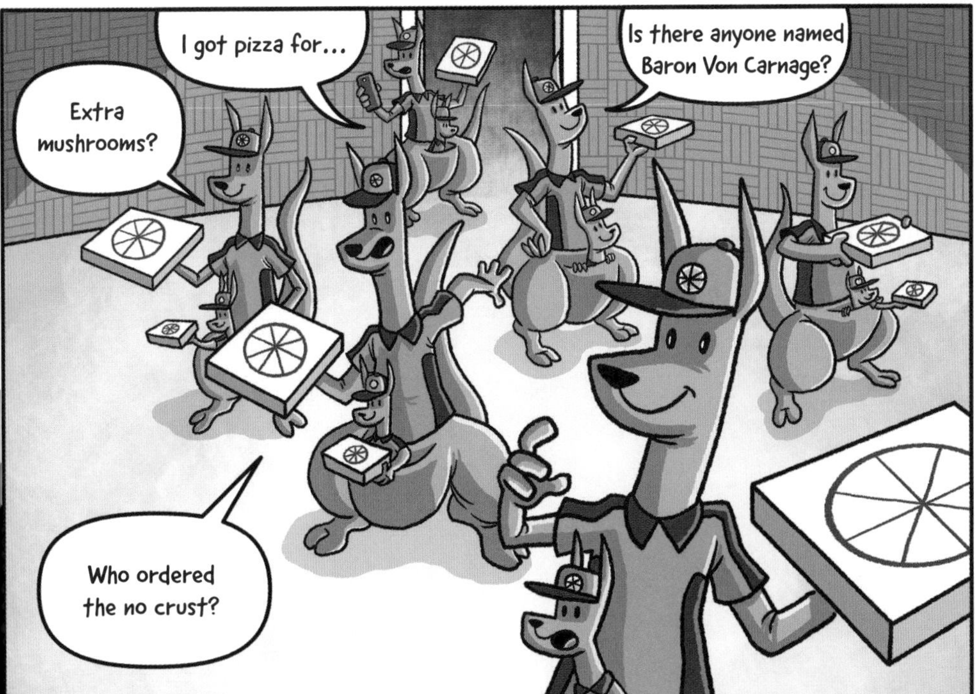
I got pizza for...
Is there anyone named
Baron Von Carnage?
Extra
mushrooms?
Who ordered
the no crust?

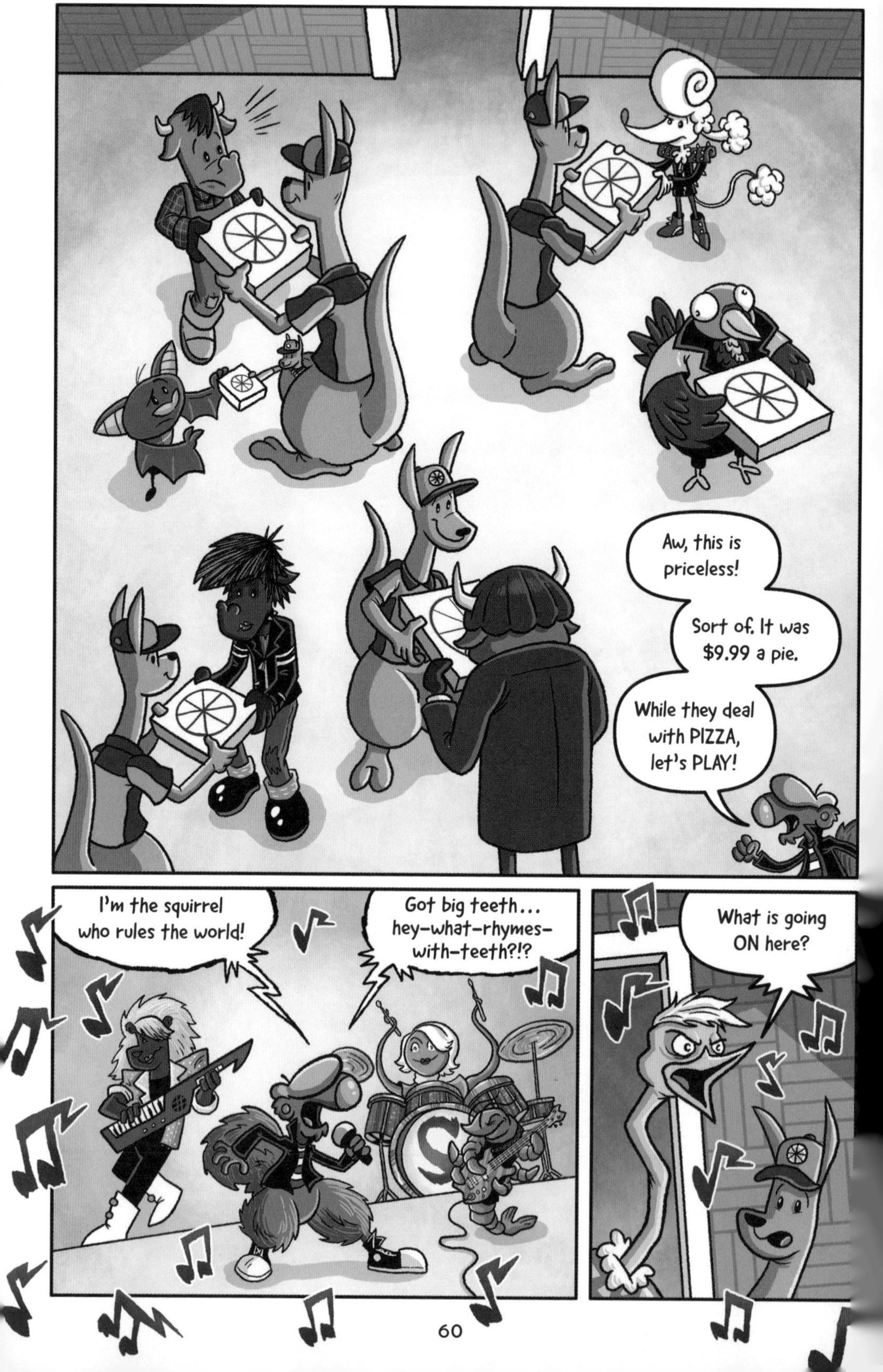
Aw, this is priceless!
Sort of. It was $9.99 a pie.
While they deal with PIZZA, let's PLAY!
I'm the squirrel who rules the world!
Got big teeth... hey-what-rhymes-with-teeth?!?
What is going ON here?

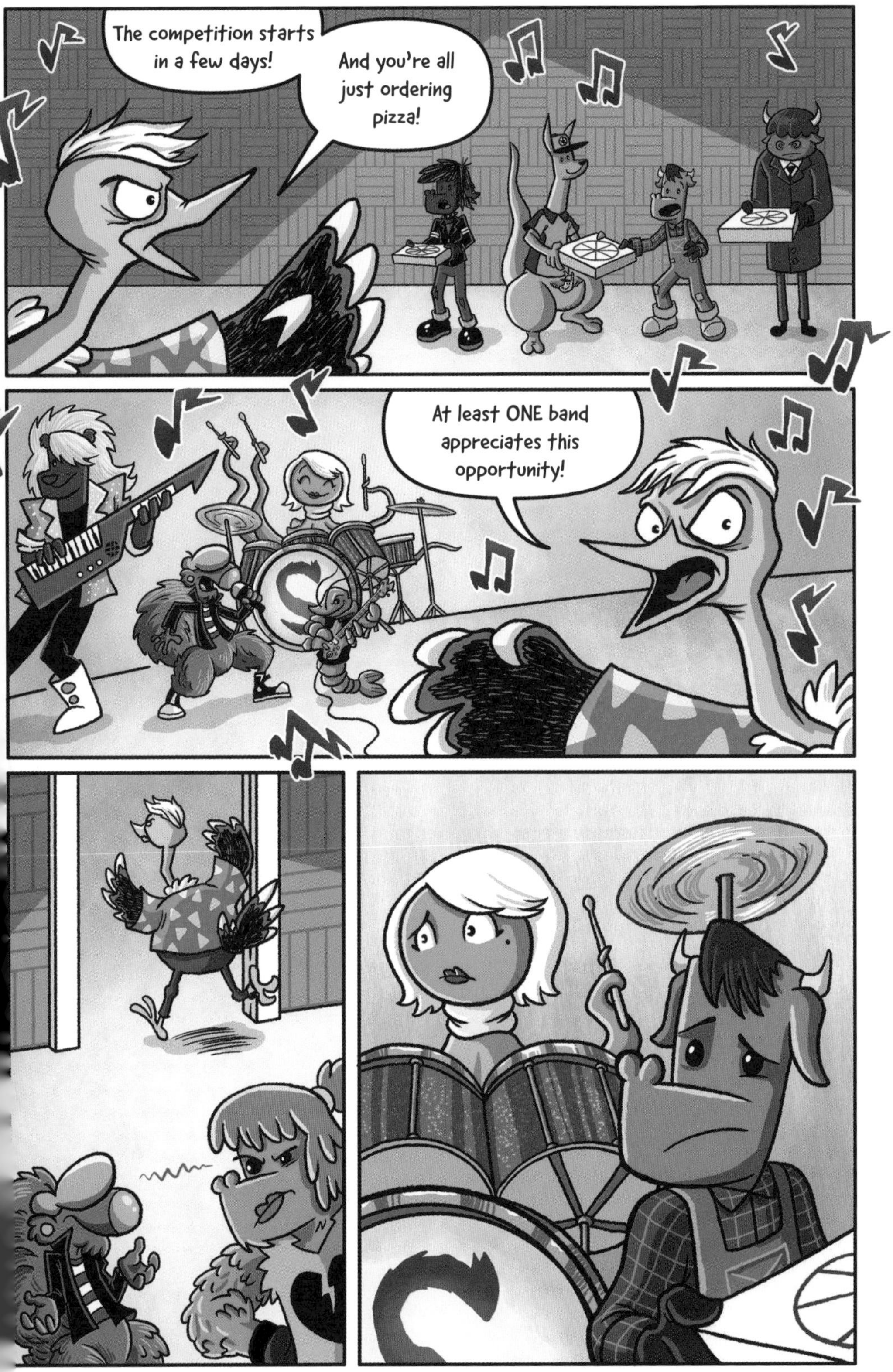

The competition starts in a few days!
And you're all just ordering pizza!
At least ONE band appreciates this opportunity!

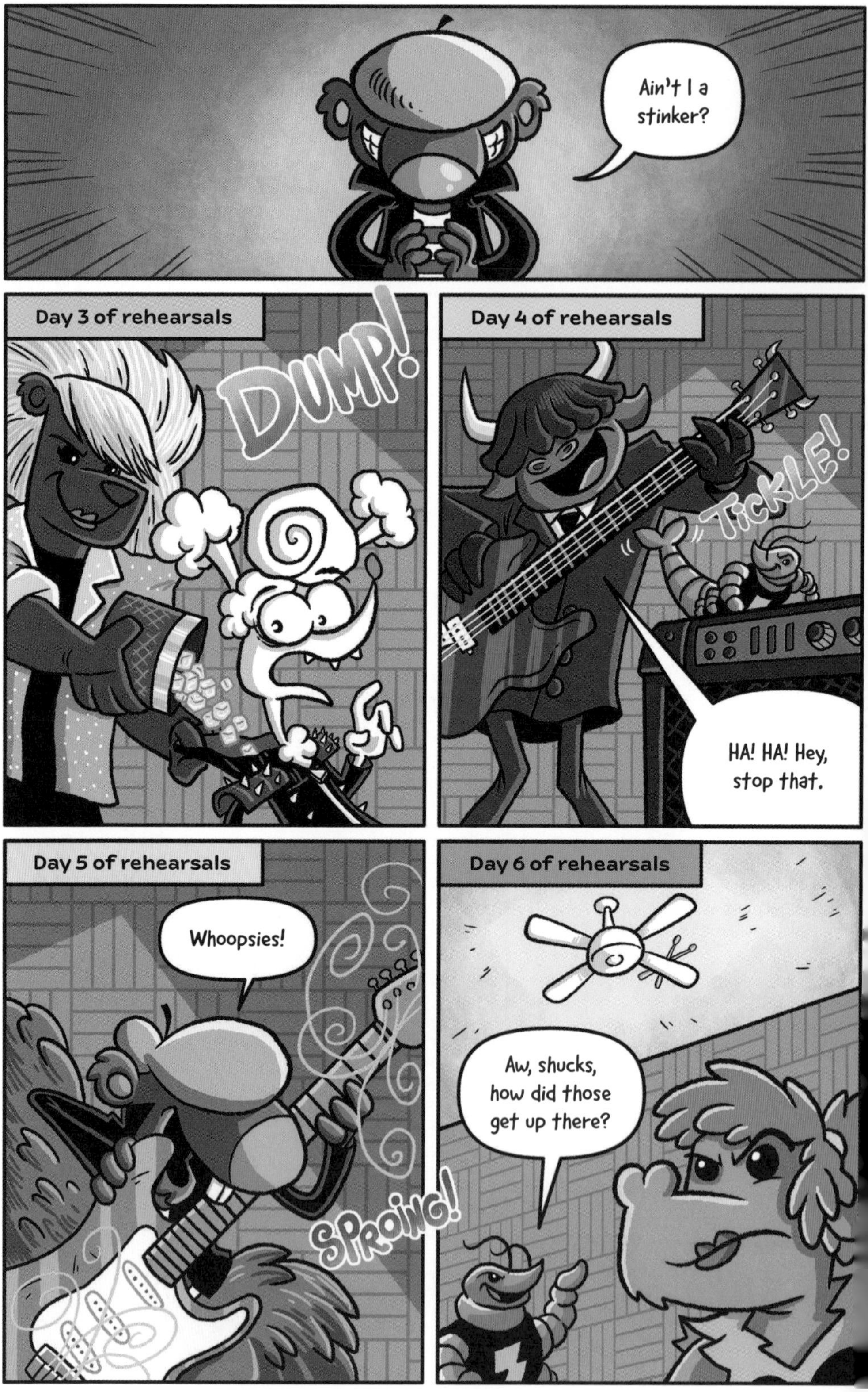
Ain't I a stinker?
Day 3 of rehearsals
DUMP!
Day 4 of rehearsals
TICKLE!
HA! HA! Hey, stop that.
Day 5 of rehearsals
Whoopsies!
SPROING!
Day 6 of rehearsals
Aw, shucks, how did those get up there?

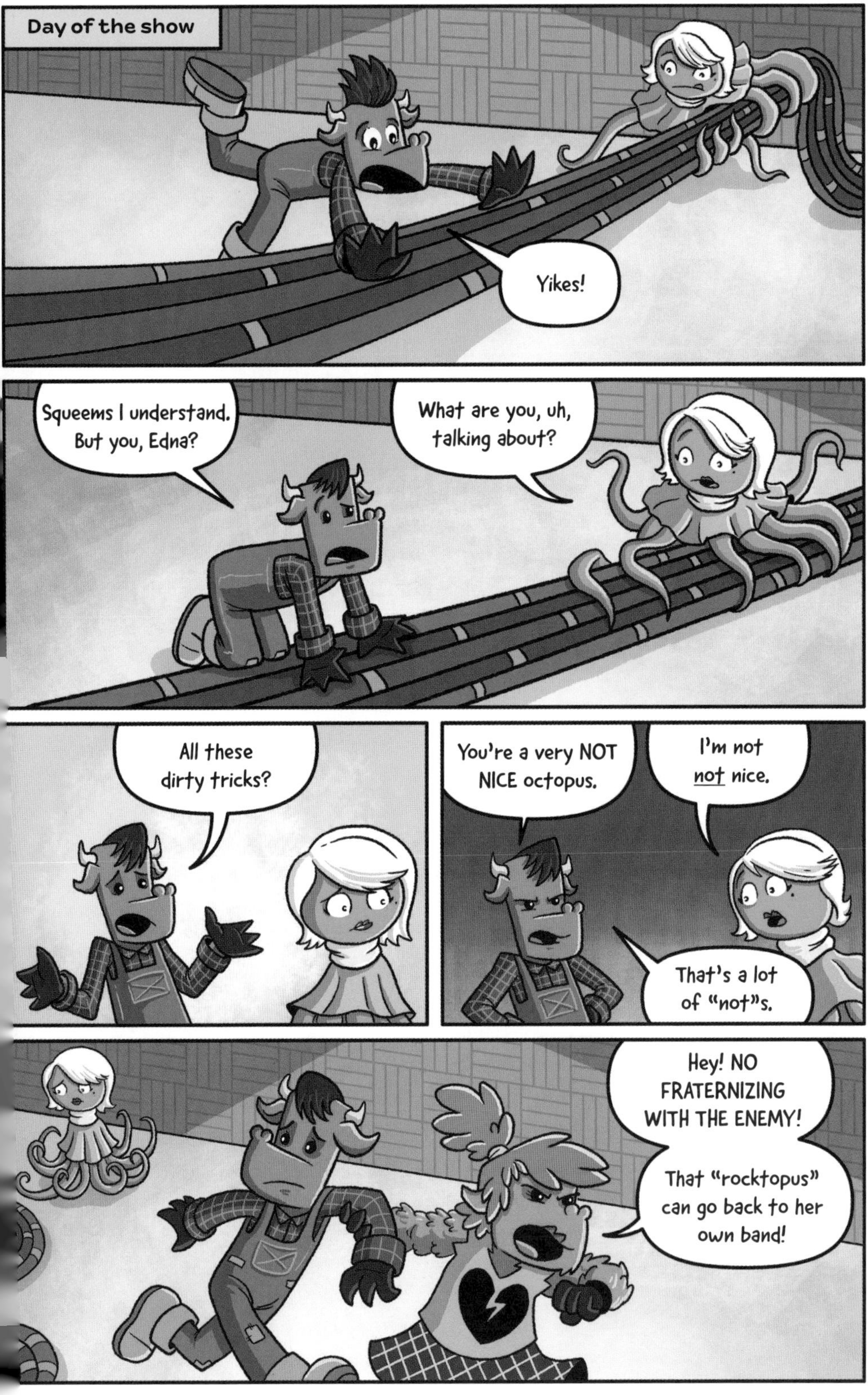
Day of the show
Yikes!
Squeems I understand. But you, Edna?
What are you, uh, talking about?
All these dirty tricks?
You're a very NOT NICE octopus.
I'm not not nice.
That's a lot of "not"s.
Hey! NO FRATERNIZING WITH THE ENEMY!
That "rocktopus" can go back to her own band!

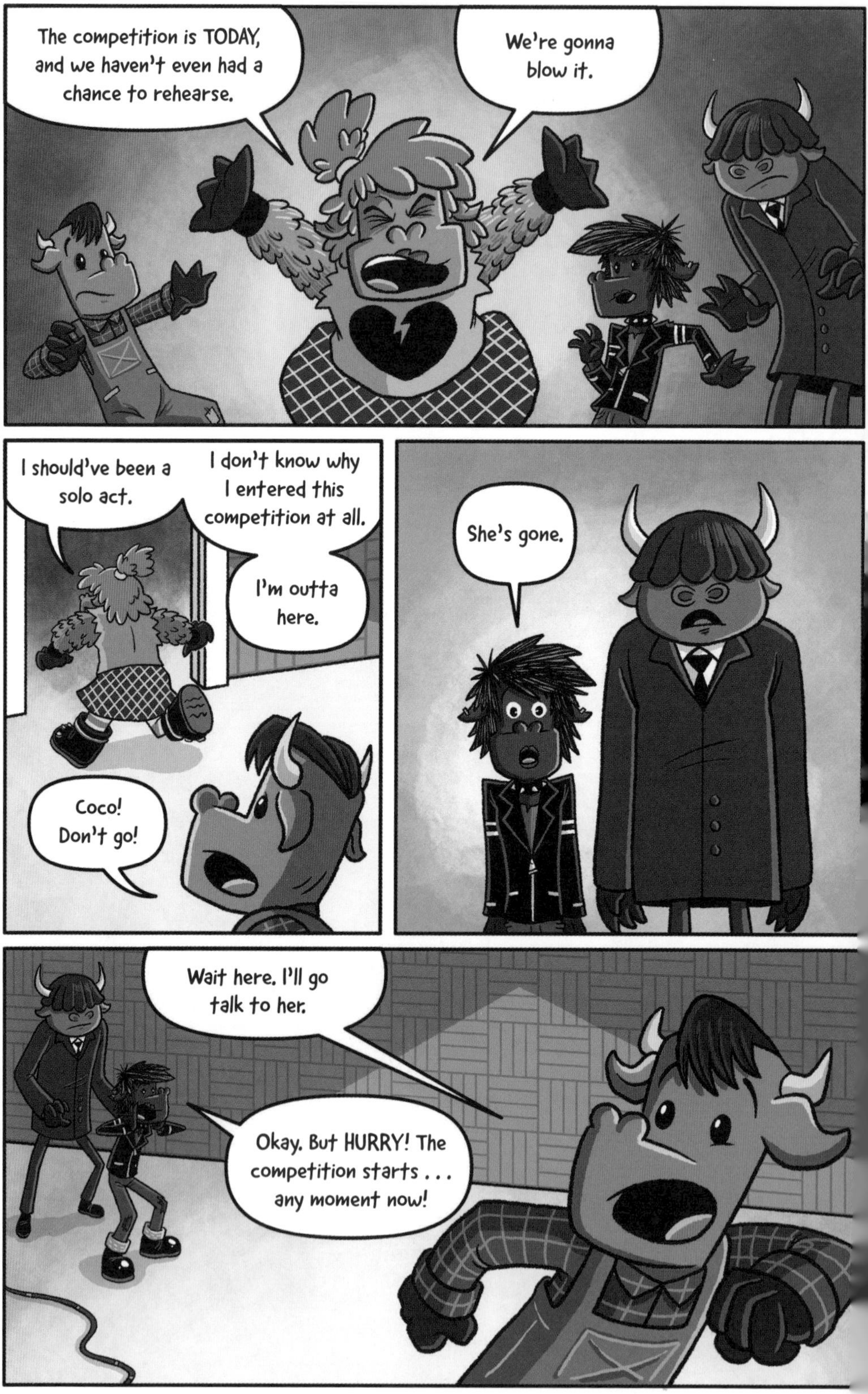
The competition is TODAY, and we haven't even had a chance to rehearse.
We're gonna blow it.
I should've been a solo act.
I don't know why I entered this competition at all.
I'm outta here.
Coco! Don't go!
She's gone.
Wait here. I'll go talk to her.
Okay. But HURRY! The competition starts . . . any moment now!

CHAPTER 7

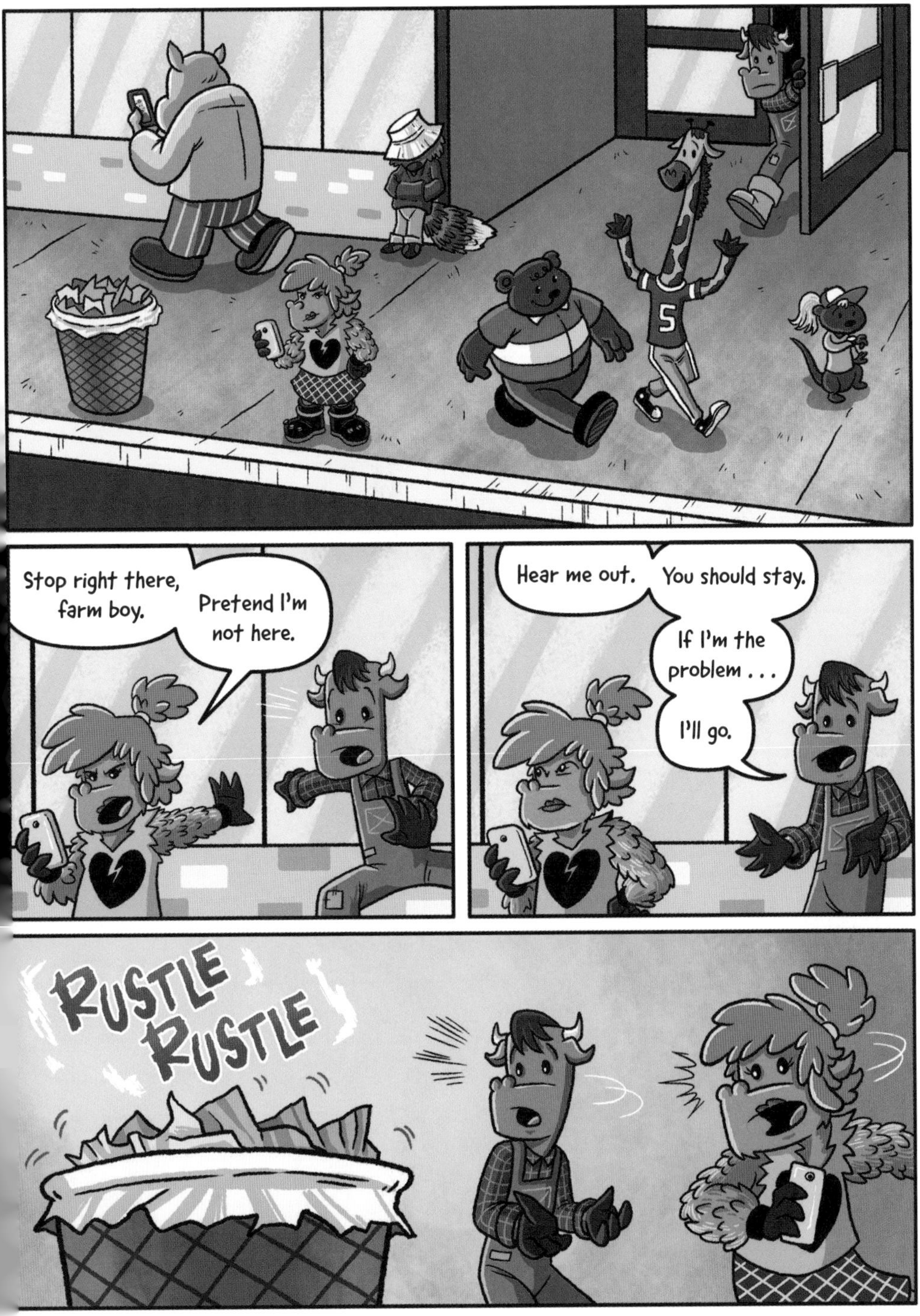
Stop right there, farm boy.
Pretend I'm not here.
Hear me out.
You should stay.
If I'm the problem . . .
I'll go.
RUSTLE RUSTLE

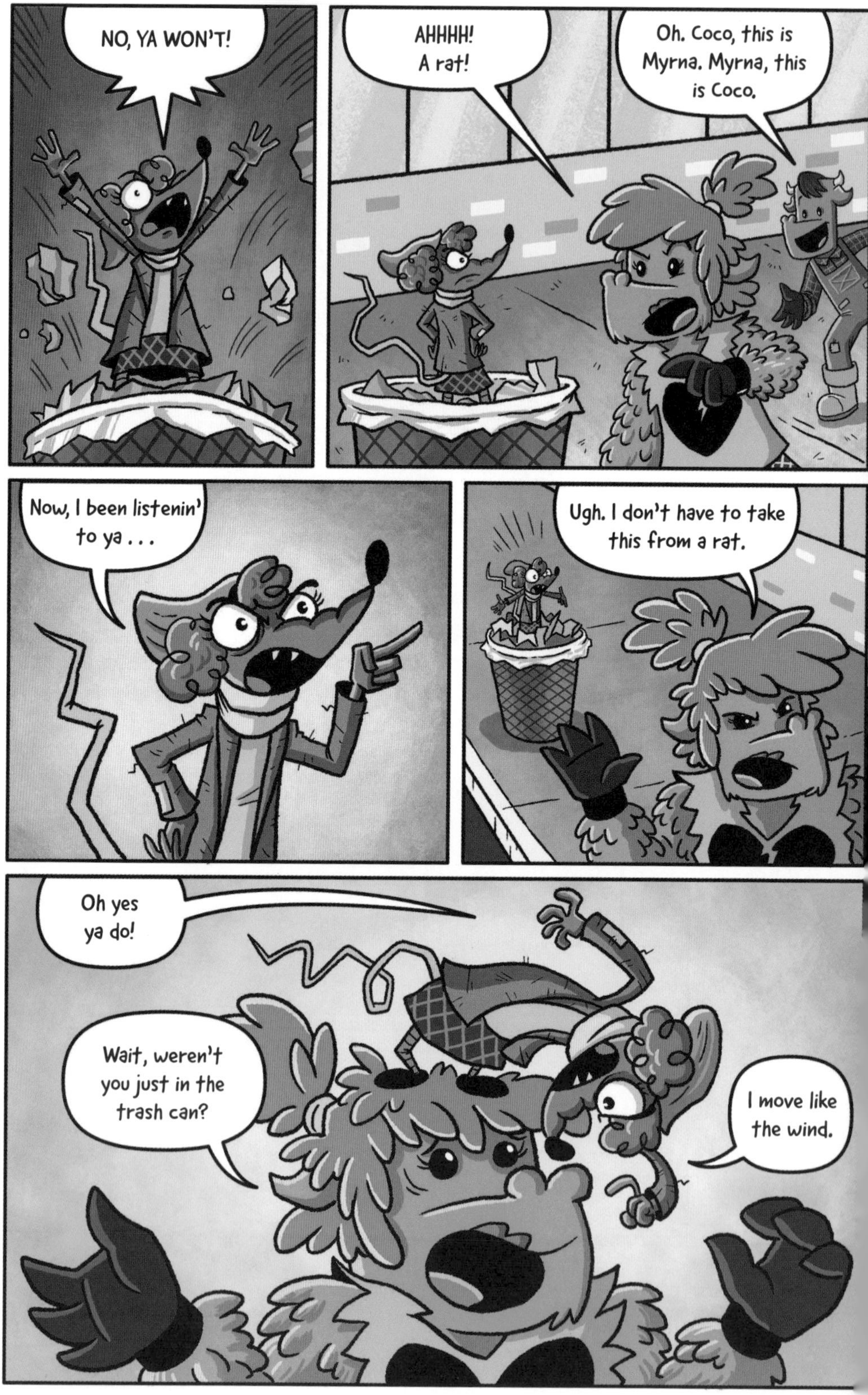
NO, YA WON'T!
AHHHH!
A rat!
Oh. Coco, this is
Myrna. Myrna, this
is Coco.
Now, I been listenin'
to ya . . .
Ugh. I don't have to take
this from a rat.
Oh yes
ya do!
Wait, weren't
you just in the
trash can?
I move like
the wind.

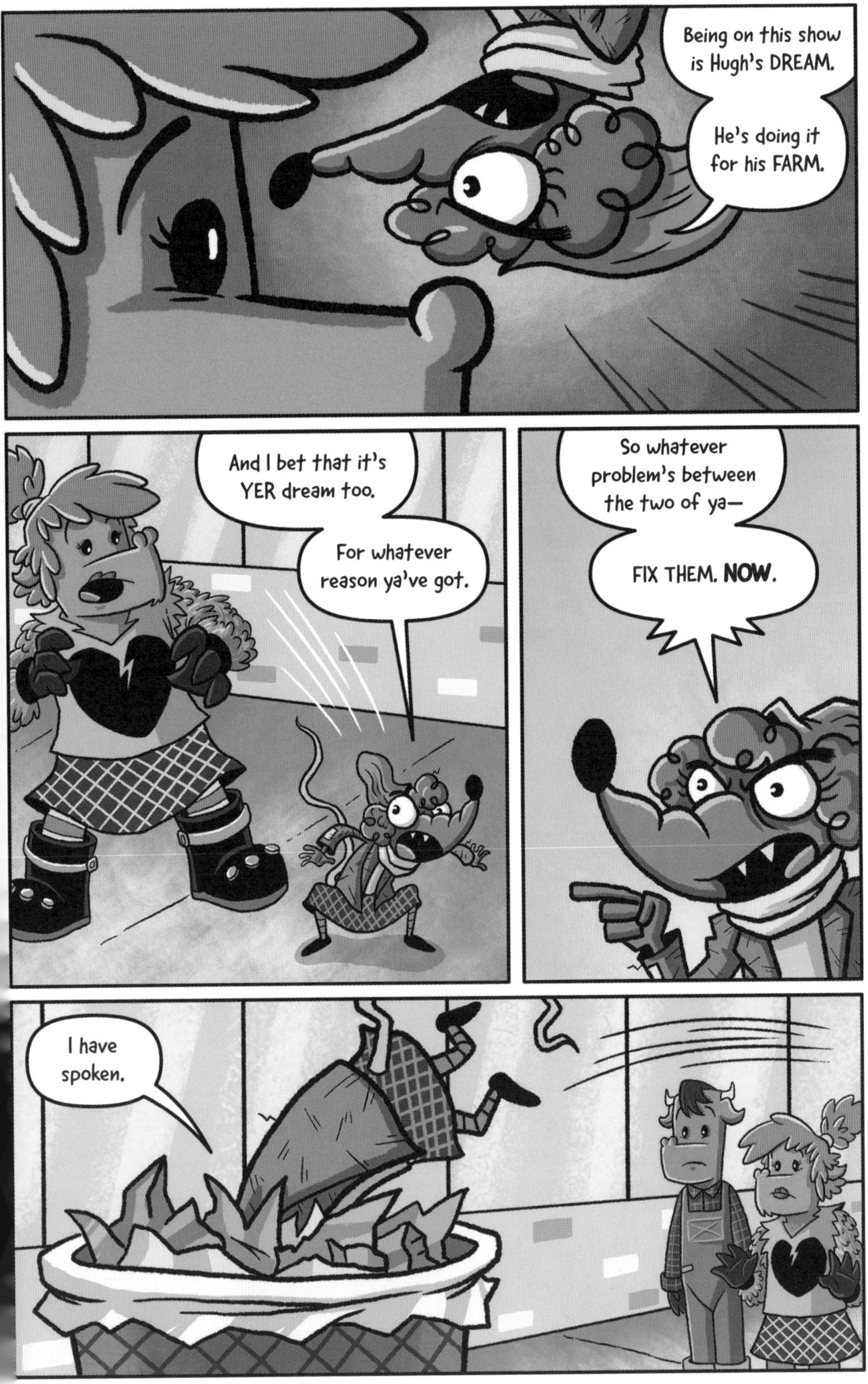
Being on this show is Hugh's DREAM.
He's doing it for his FARM.
And I bet that it's YER dream too.
For whatever reason ya've got.
So whatever problem's between the two of ya—
FIX THEM. **NOW**.
I have spoken.

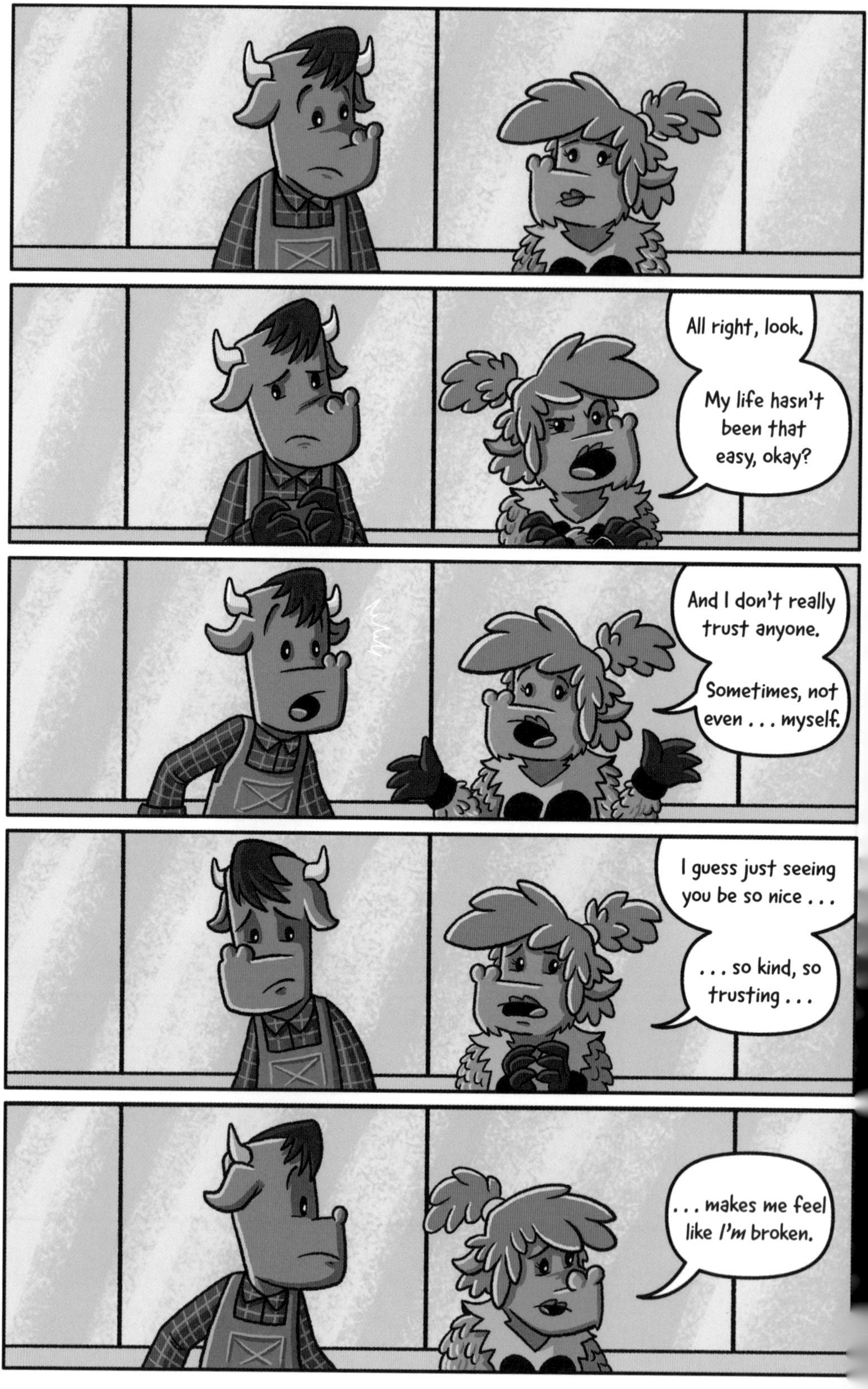
All right, look.
My life hasn't been that easy, okay?
And I don't really trust anyone.
Sometimes, not even . . . myself.
I guess just seeing you be so nice . . .
. . . so kind, so trusting . . .
. . . makes me feel like *I'm* broken.

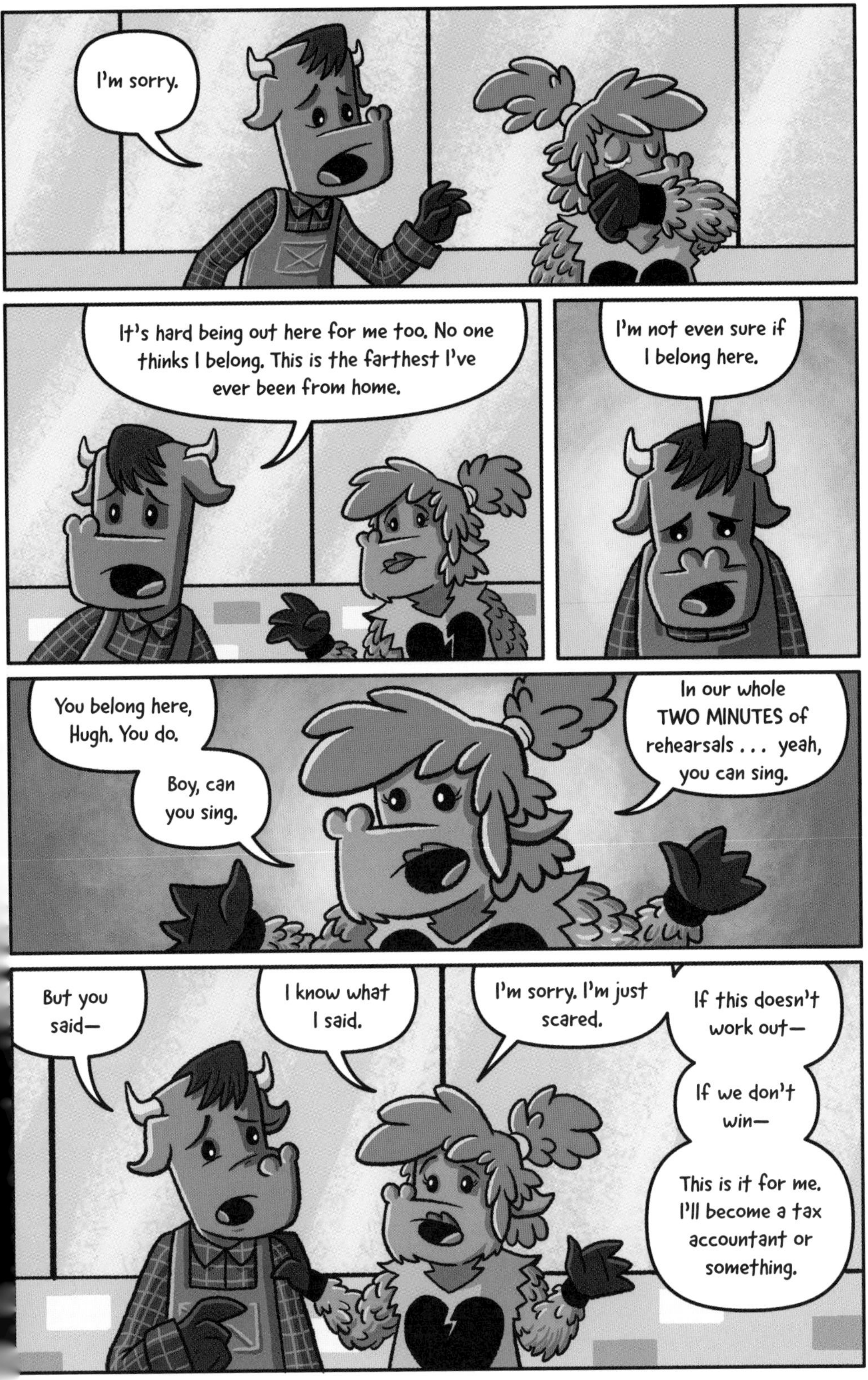
I'm sorry.
It's hard being out here for me too. No one thinks I belong. This is the farthest I've ever been from home.
I'm not even sure if I belong here.
You belong here, Hugh. You do.
Boy, can you sing.
In our whole TWO MINUTES of rehearsals . . . yeah, you can sing.
But you said—
I know what I said.
I'm sorry. I'm just scared.
If this doesn't work out—
If we don't win—
This is it for me. I'll become a tax accountant or something.

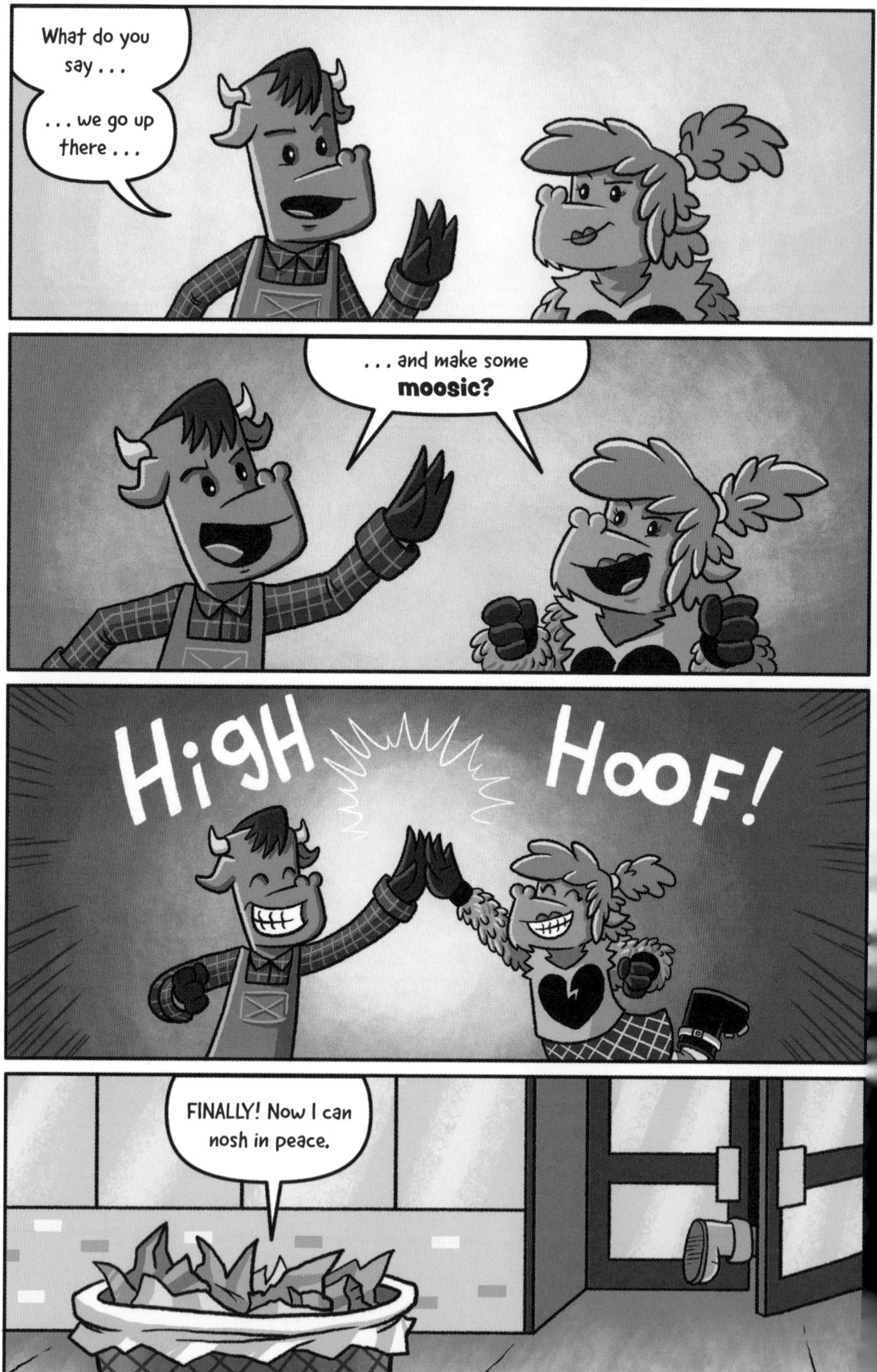
What do you say . . .
. . . we go up there . . .
. . . and make some moosic?
HigH HOOF!
FINALLY! Now I can nosh in peace.

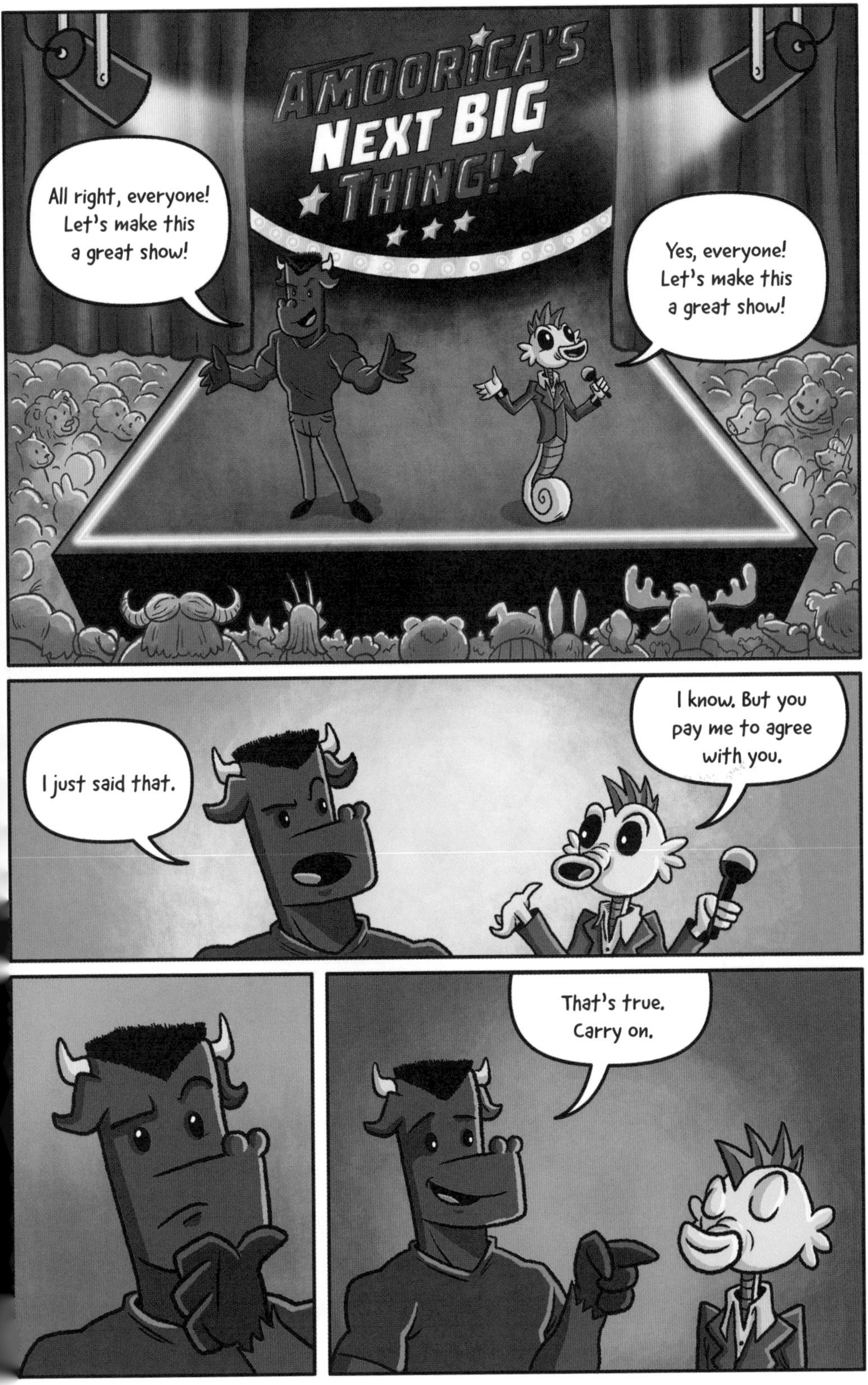
AMOORICA'S NEXT BIG THING!
All right, everyone! Let's make this a great show!
Yes, everyone! Let's make this a great show!
I just said that.
I know. But you pay me to agree with you.
That's true. Carry on.

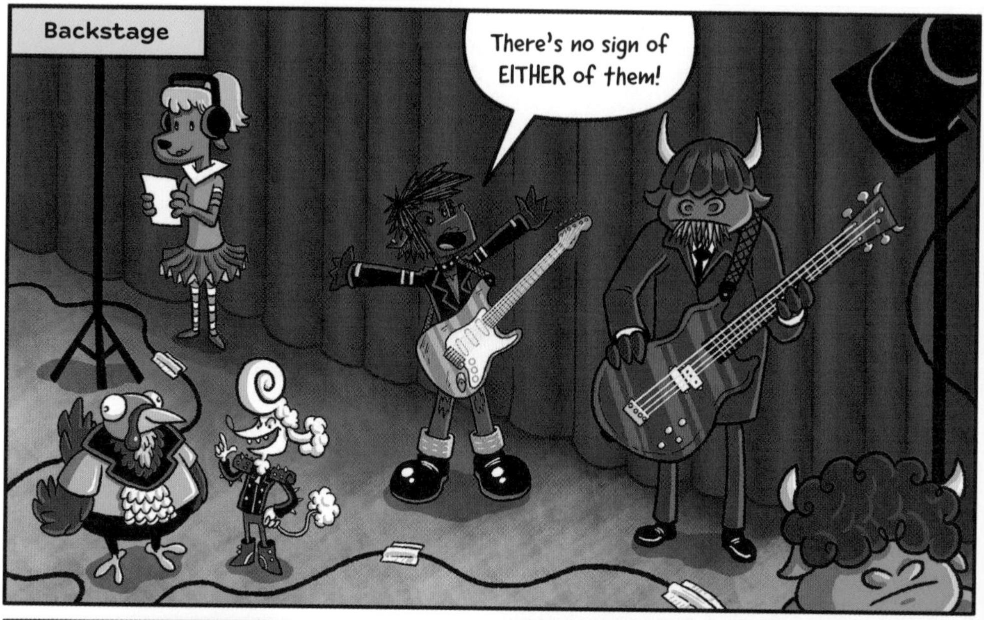
Backstage
There's no sign of EITHER of them!

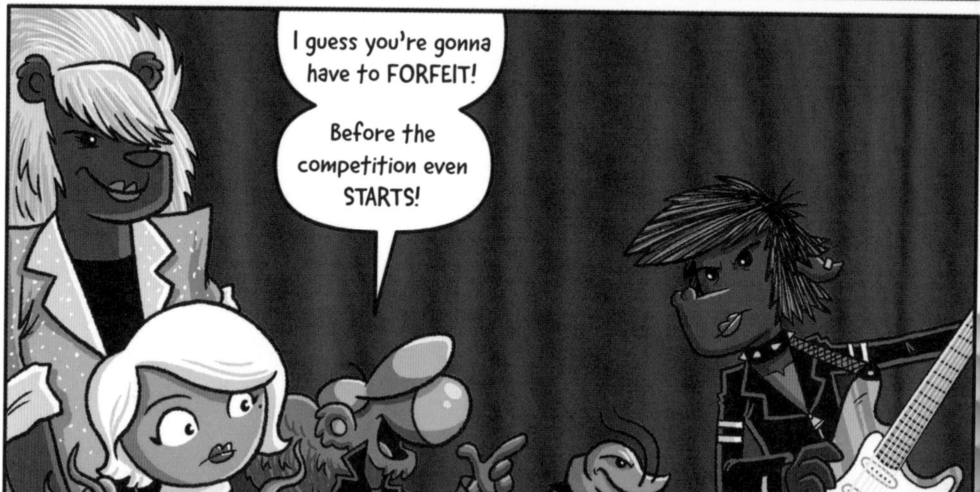
I guess you're gonna have to FORFEIT!
Before the competition even STARTS!

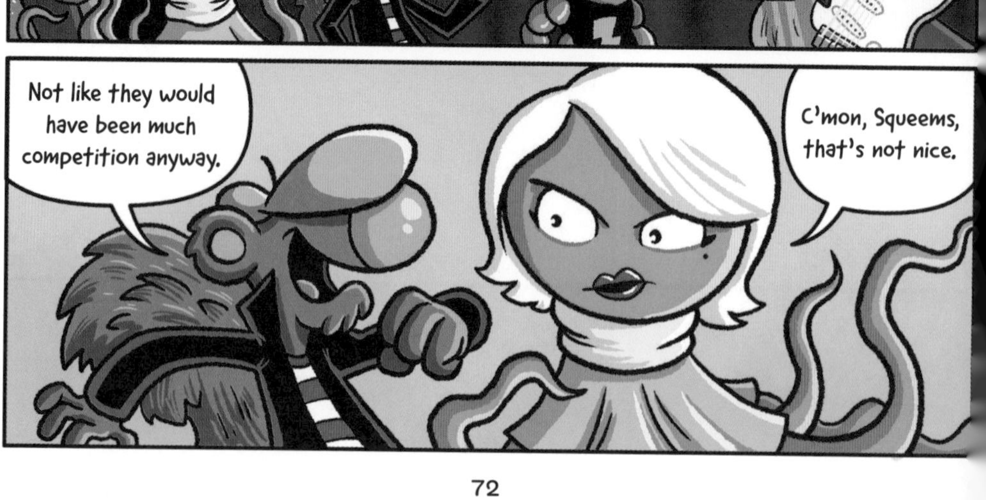
Not like they would have been much competition anyway.
C'mon, Squeems, that's not nice.

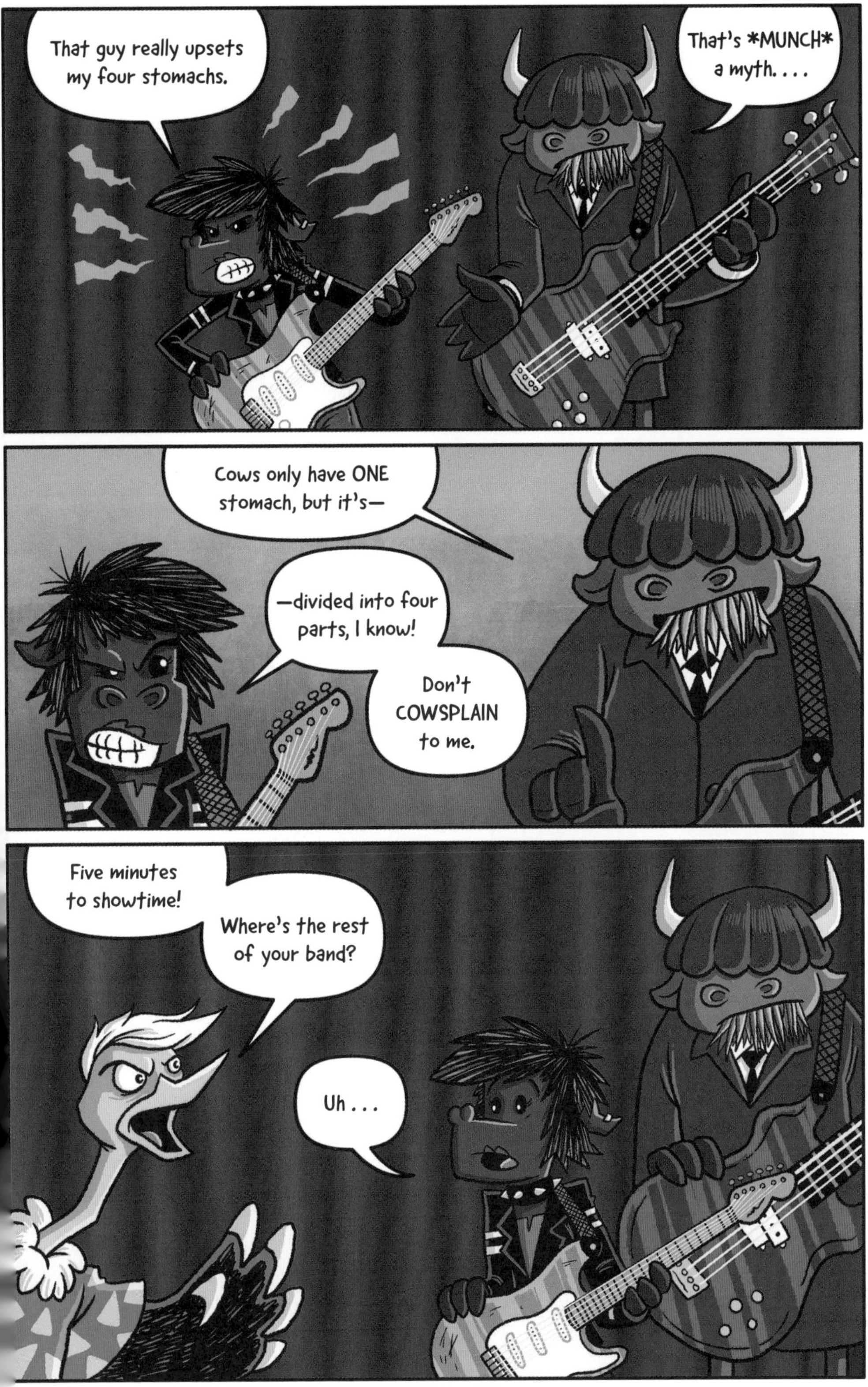
That guy really upsets my four stomachs.
That's *MUNCH* a myth. . . .
Cows only have ONE stomach, but it's—
—divided into four parts, I know!
Don't COWSPLAIN to me.
Five minutes to showtime!
Where's the rest of your band?
Uh . . .

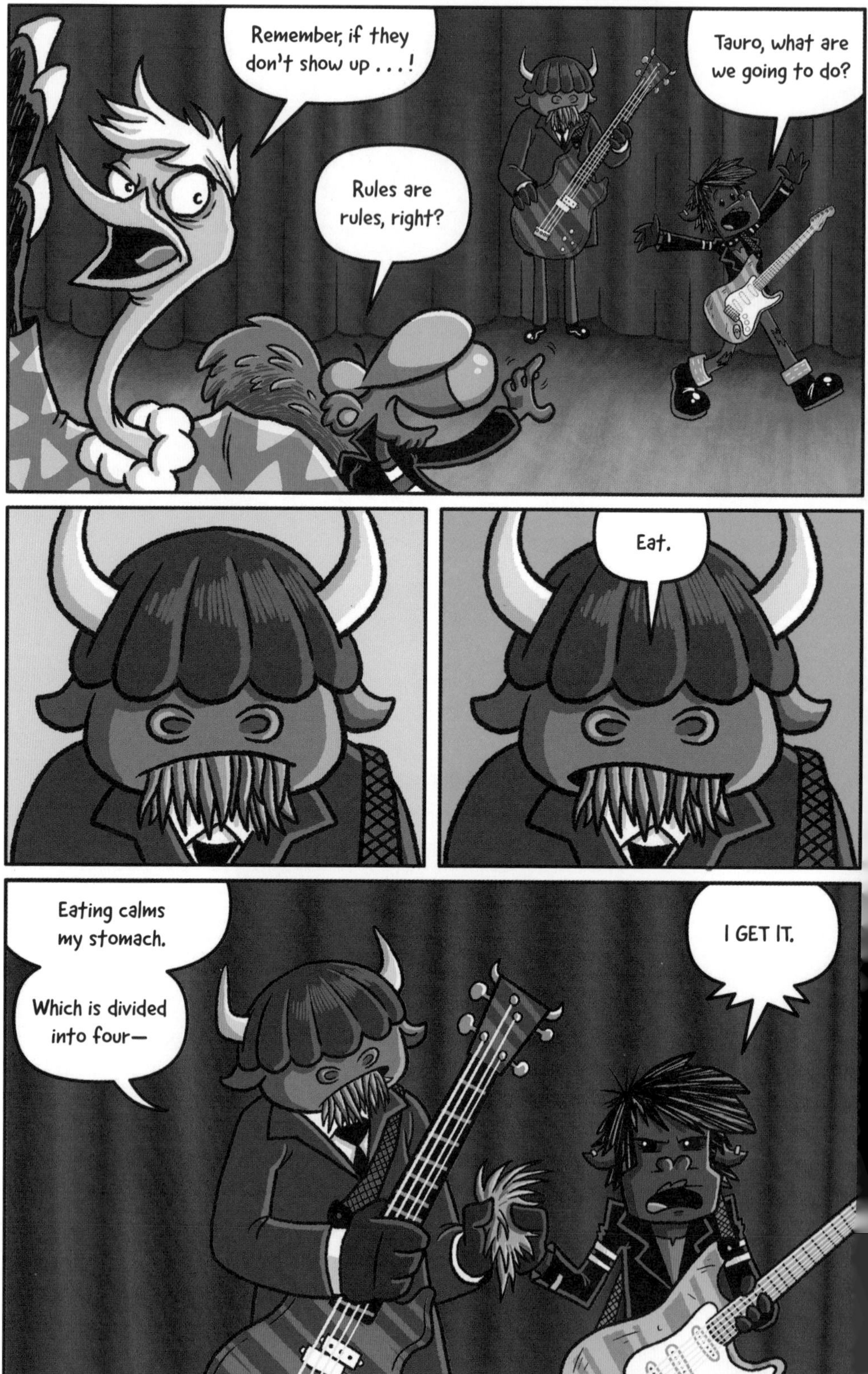
Remember, if they don't show up . . . !
Rules are rules, right?
Tauro, what are we going to do?
Eat.
Eating calms my stomach.
Which is divided into four—
I GET IT.

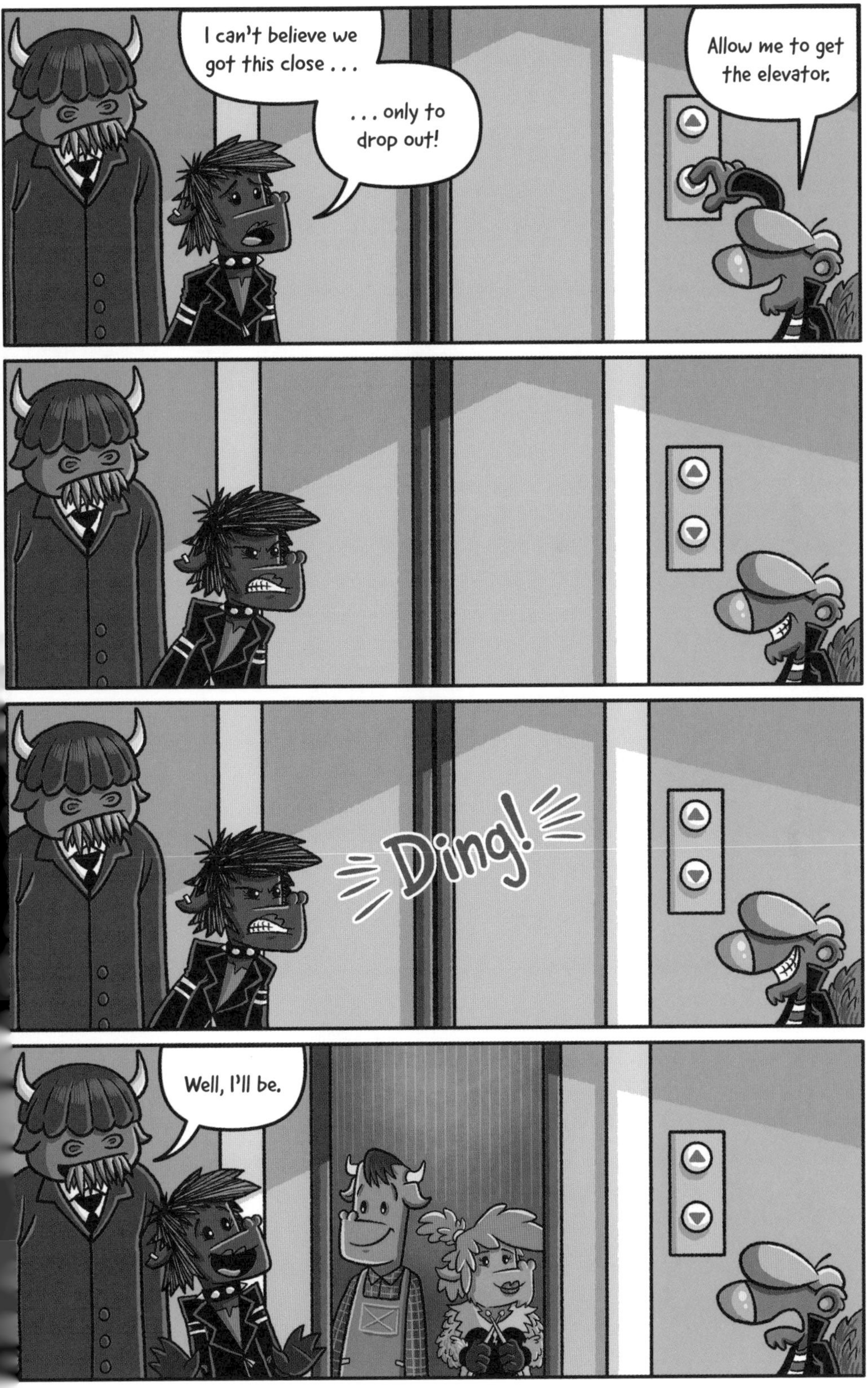
I can't believe we got this close . . .
. . . only to drop out!
Allow me to get the elevator.
Ding!
Well, I'll be.

CHAPTER 8

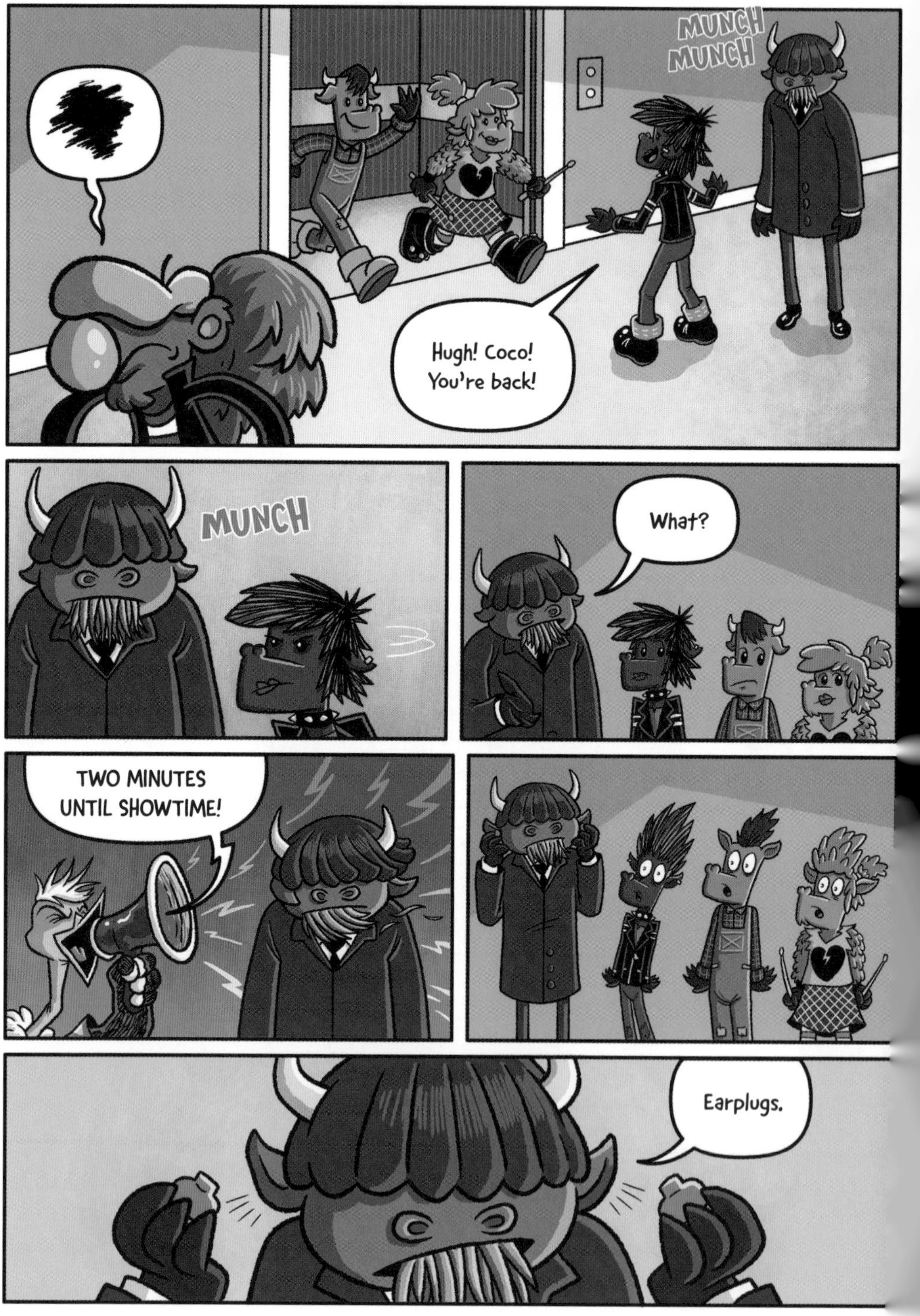
MUNCH
MUNCH
Hugh! Coco!
You're back!
MUNCH
What?
TWO MINUTES
UNTIL SHOWTIME!
Earplugs.

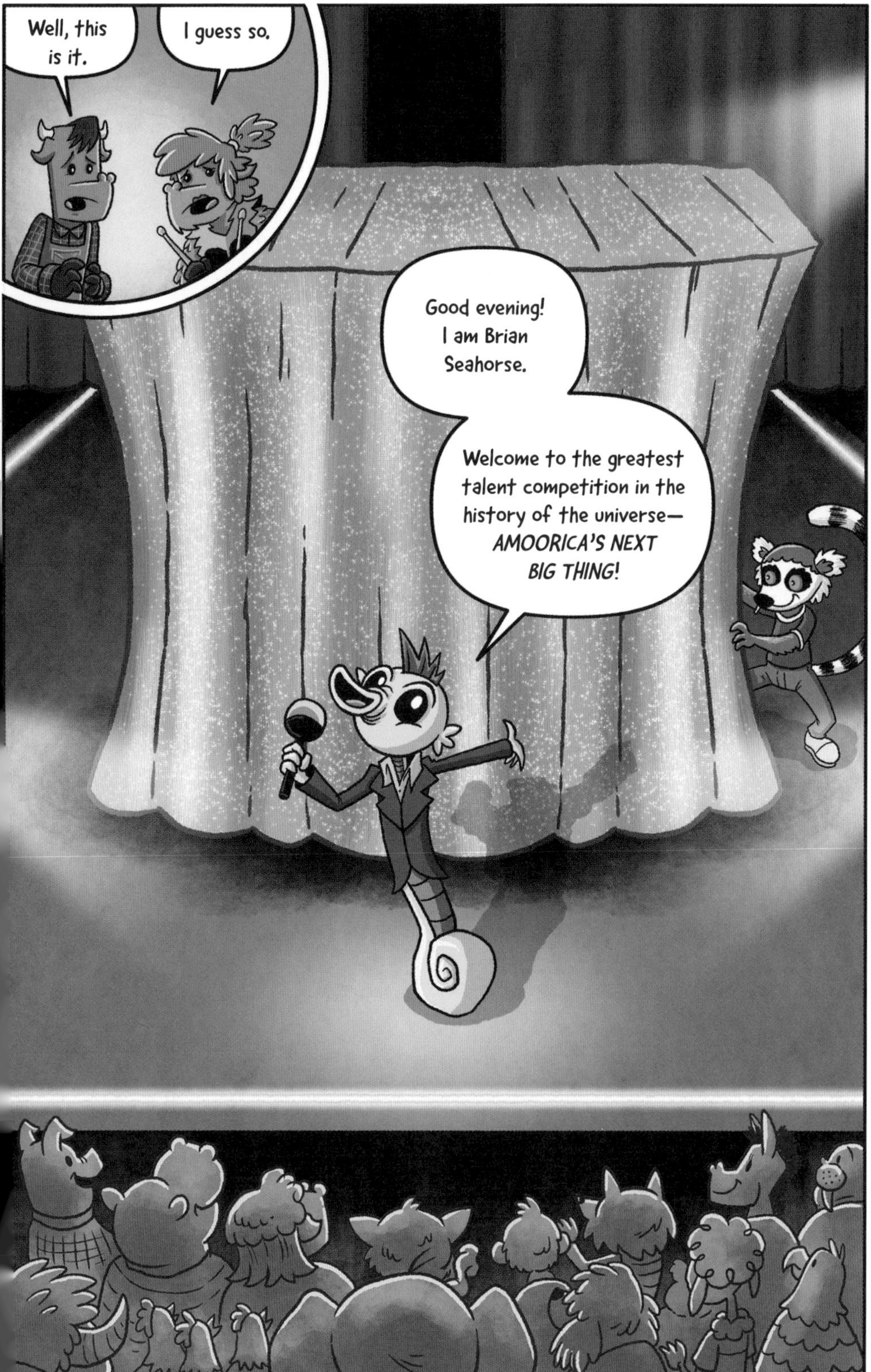
Well, this is it.
I guess so.
Good evening! I am Brian Seahorse.
Welcome to the greatest talent competition in the history of the universe— *AMOORICA'S NEXT BIG THING!*

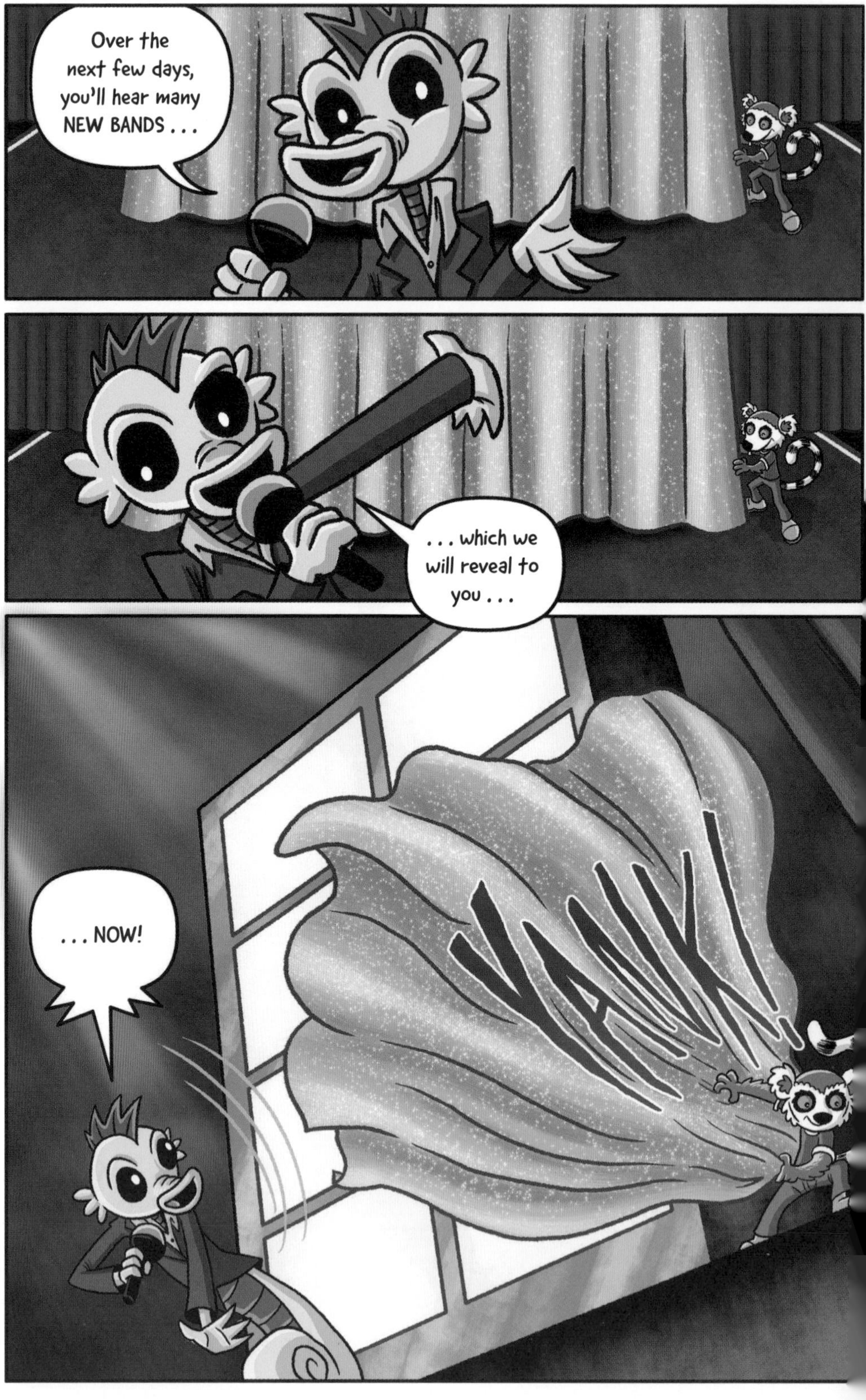
Over the next few days, you'll hear many NEW BANDS . . .
. . . which we will reveal to you . . .
. . . NOW!
YANK!

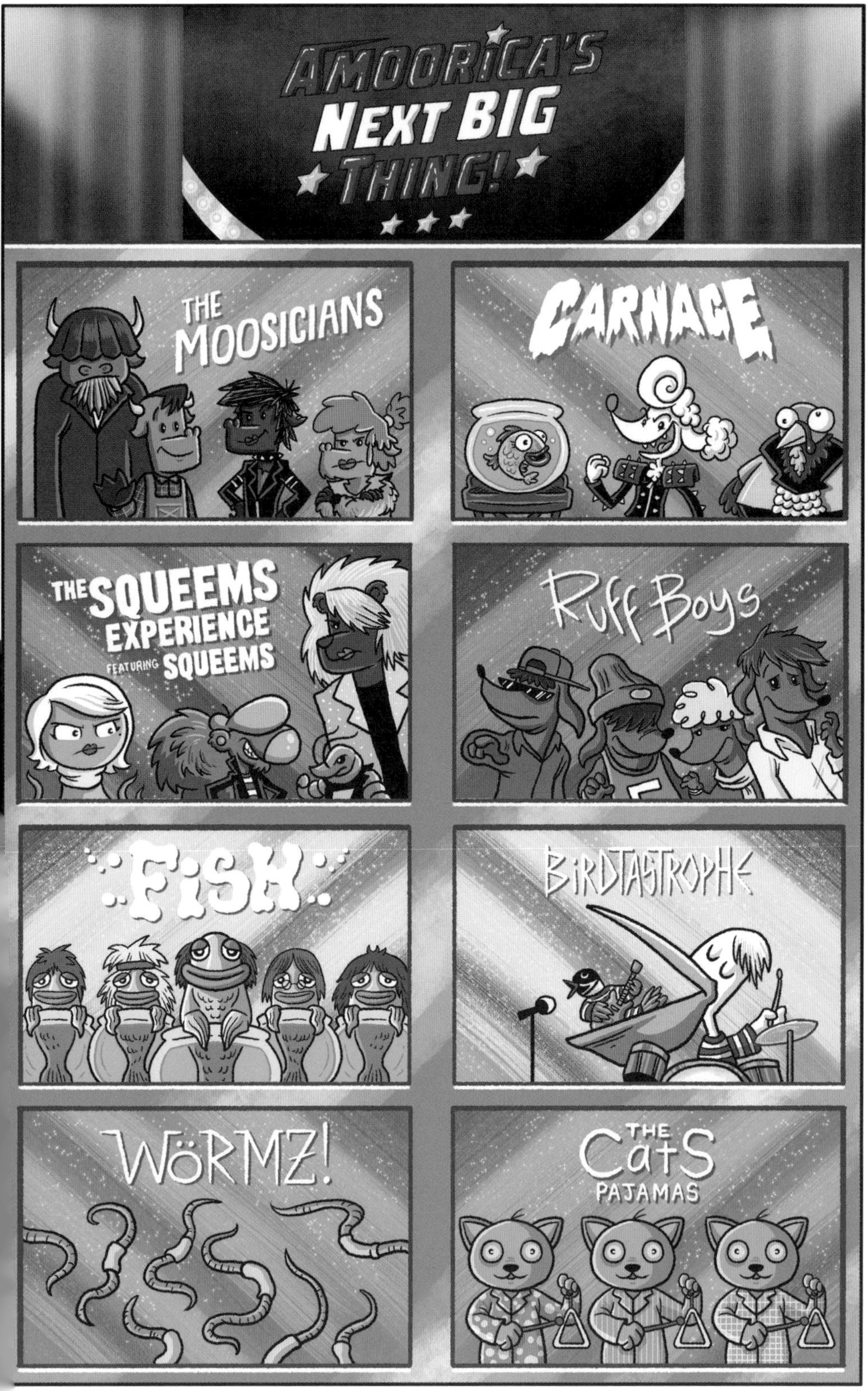
AMOORICA'S NEXT BIG THING!
THE MOOSICIANS
CARNAGE
THE SQUEEMS EXPERIENCE FEATURING SQUEEMS
Ruff Boys
FISH
BIRDTASTROPHE
WÖRMZ!
THE CATS PAJAMAS

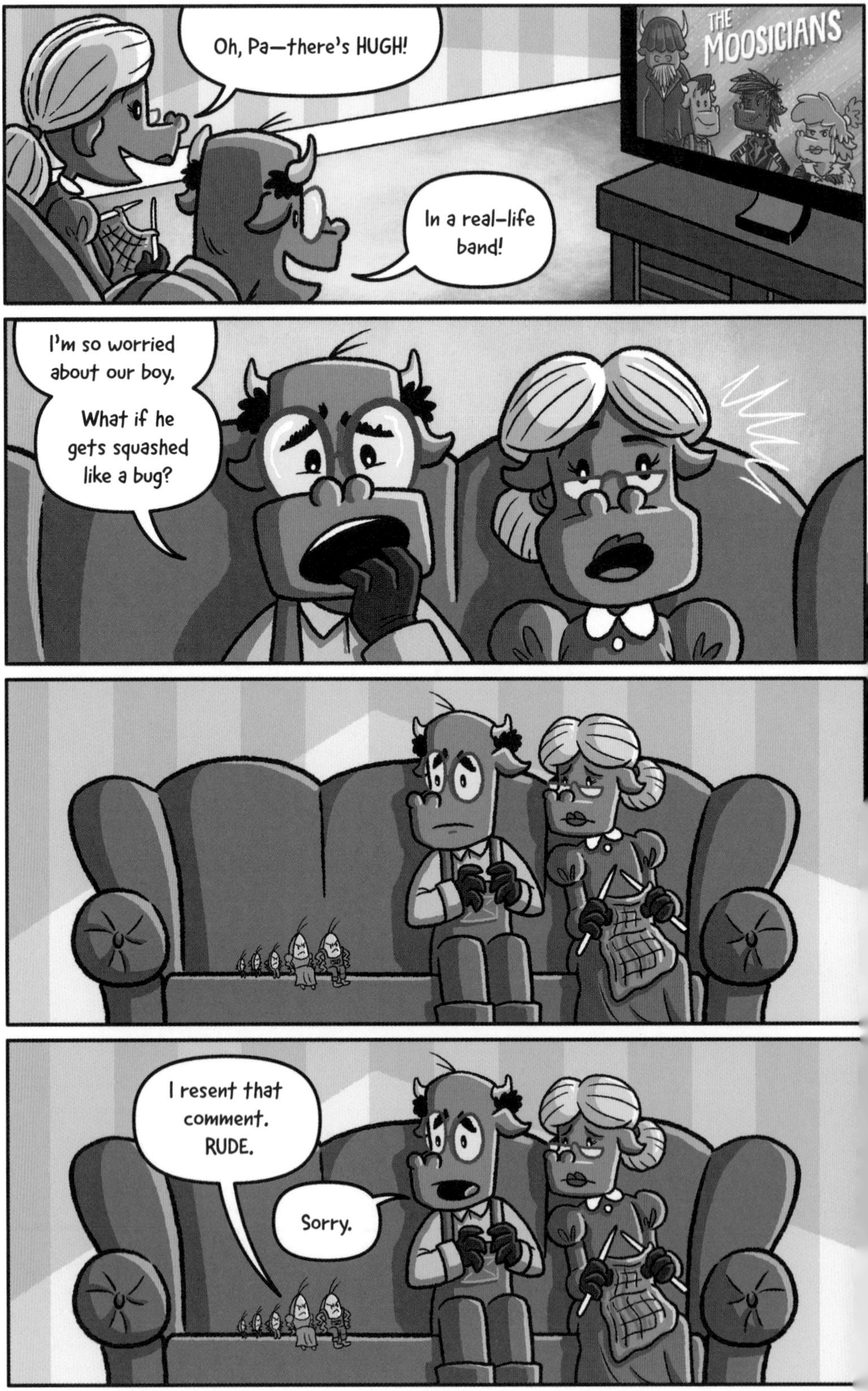
THE MOOSICIANS
Oh, Pa—there's HUGH!
In a real-life band!
I'm so worried about our boy.
What if he gets squashed like a bug?
I resent that comment. RUDE.
Sorry.

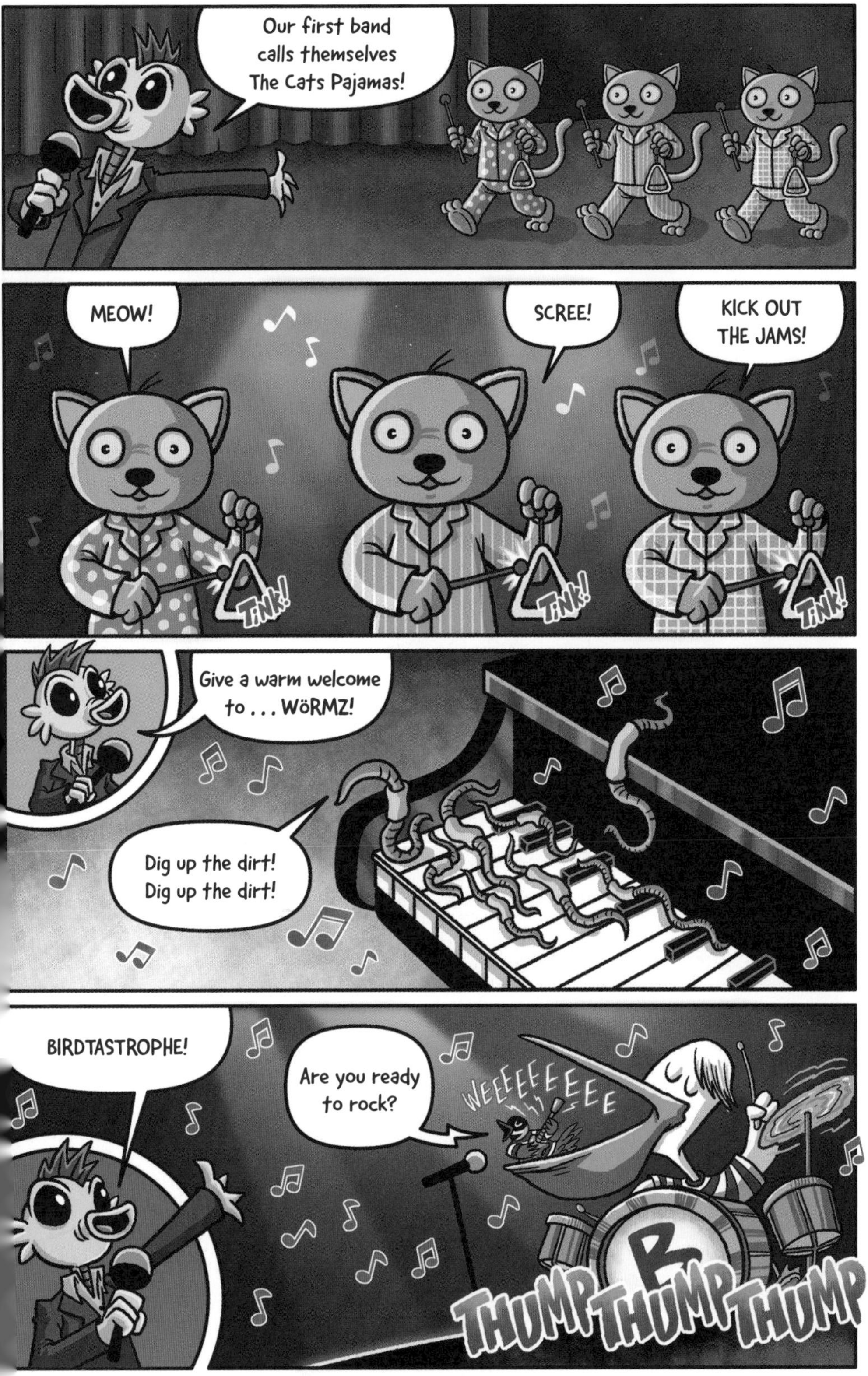
Our first band calls themselves The Cats Pajamas!
MEOW!
SCREE!
KICK OUT THE JAMS!
TINK!
TINK!
TINK!
Give a warm welcome to . . . WÖRMZ!
Dig up the dirt! Dig up the dirt!
BIRDTASTROPHE!
Are you ready to rock?
WEEEEEEEEE
THUMP THUMP THUMP

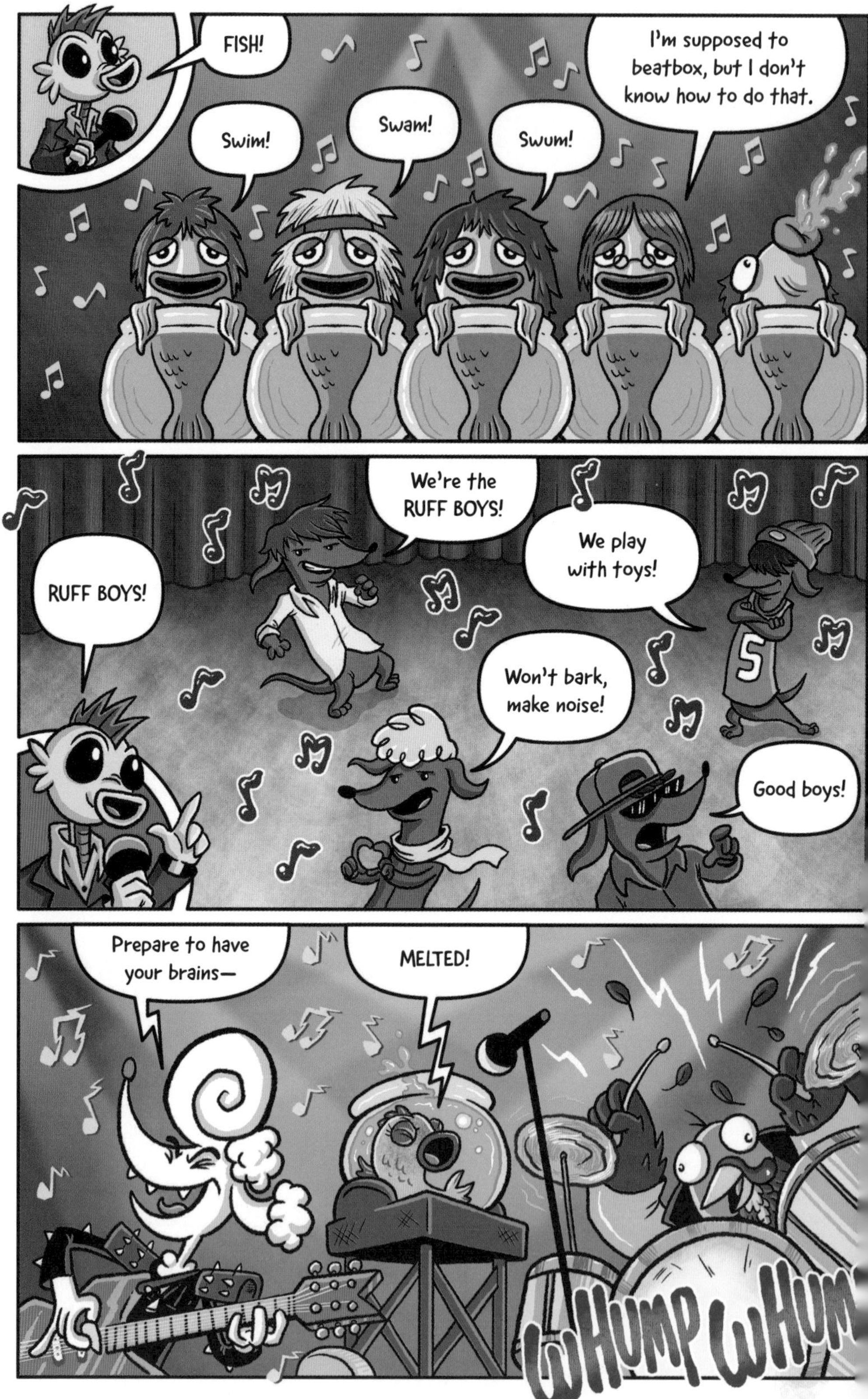
FISH!
Swim!
Swam!
Swum!
I'm supposed to beatbox, but I don't know how to do that.
We're the RUFF BOYS!
RUFF BOYS!
We play with toys!
Won't bark, make noise!
Good boys!
Prepare to have your brains—
MELTED!
WHUMP WHUM

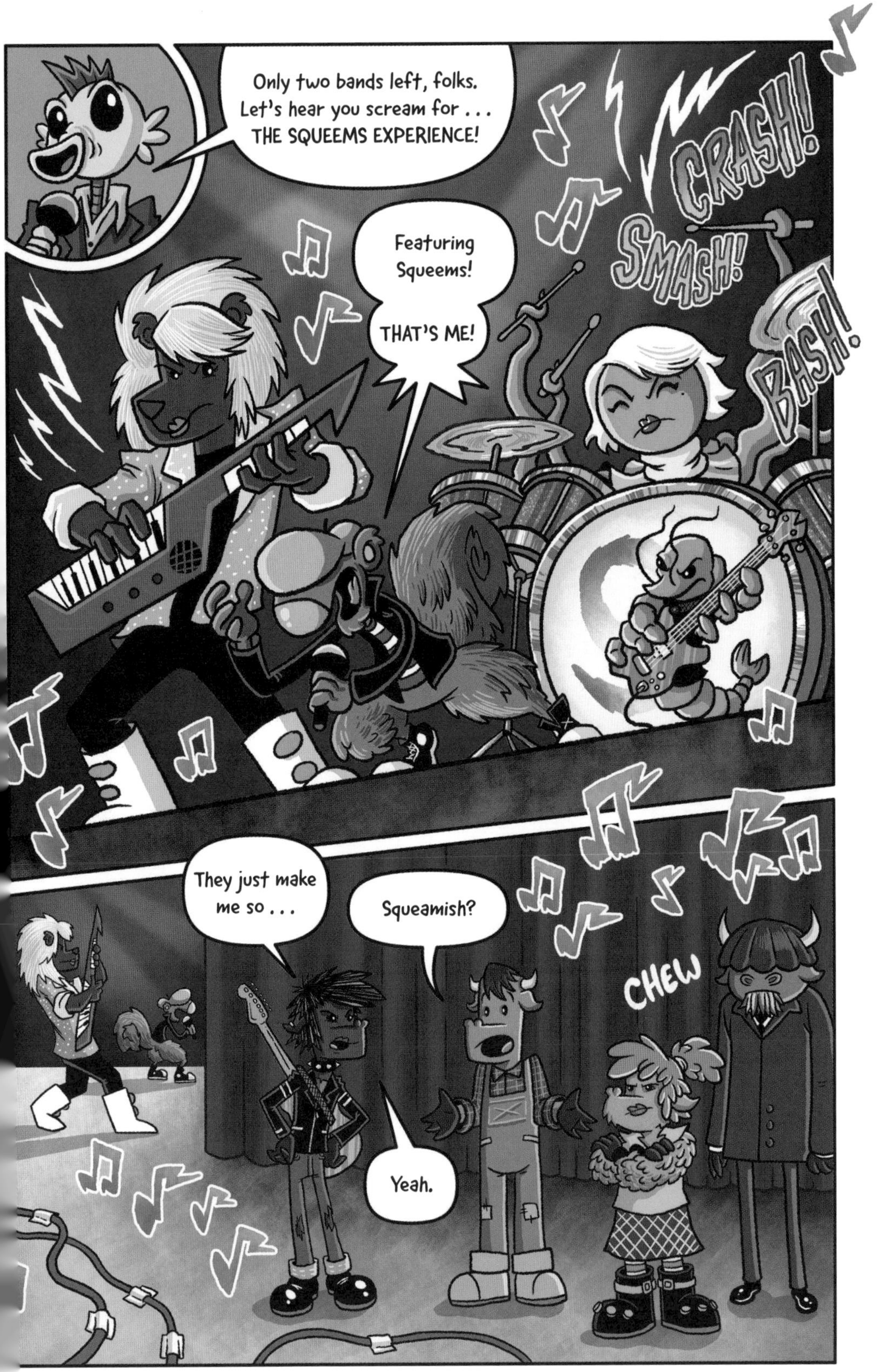
Only two bands left, folks. Let's hear you scream for . . . THE SQUEEMS EXPERIENCE!
CRASH!
SMASH!
Featuring Squeems!
THAT'S ME!
BASH!
They just make me so . . .
Squeamish?
CHEW
Yeah.

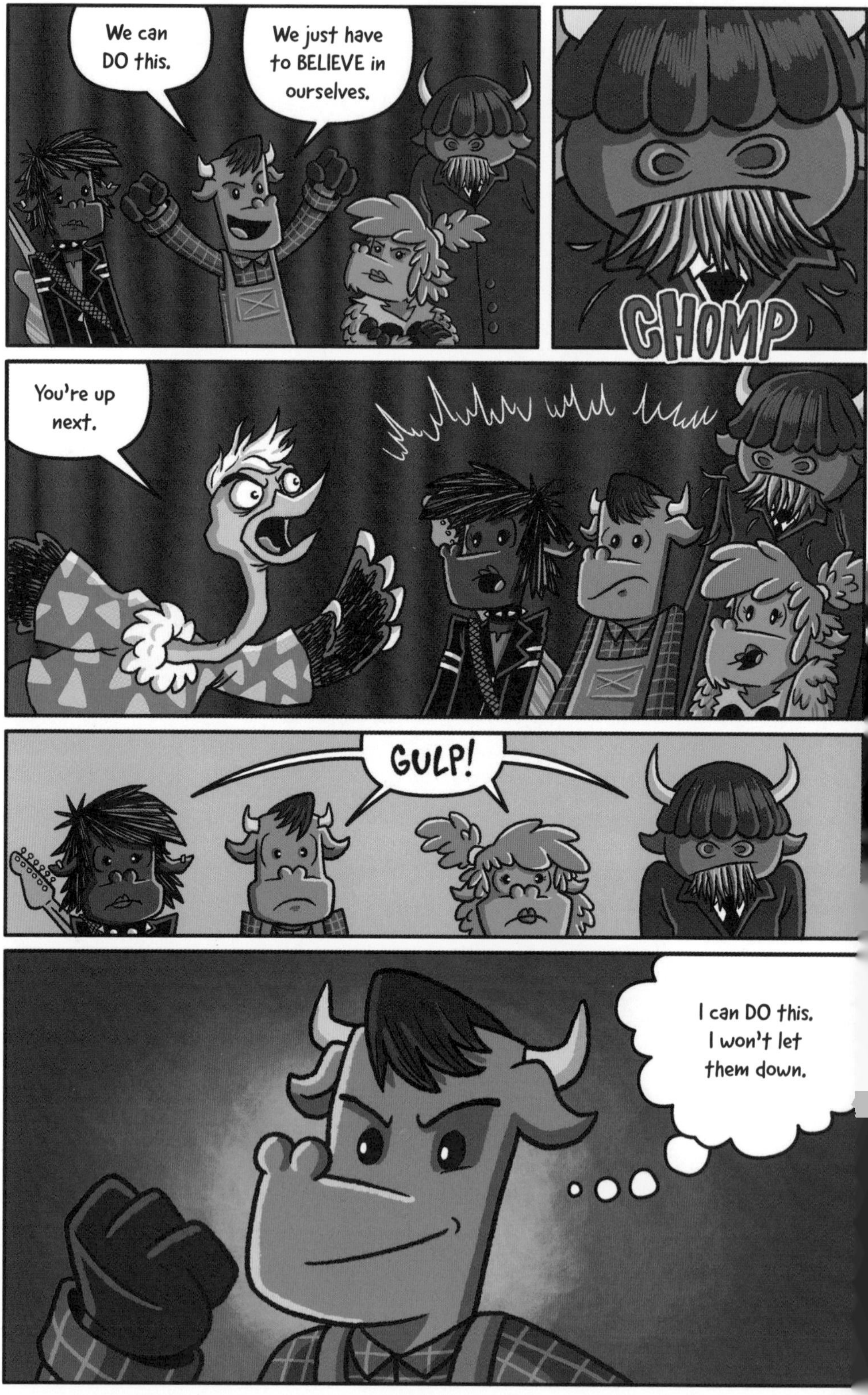
We can DO this.
We just have to BELIEVE in ourselves.
CHOMP
You're up next.
GULP!
I can DO this. I won't let them down.

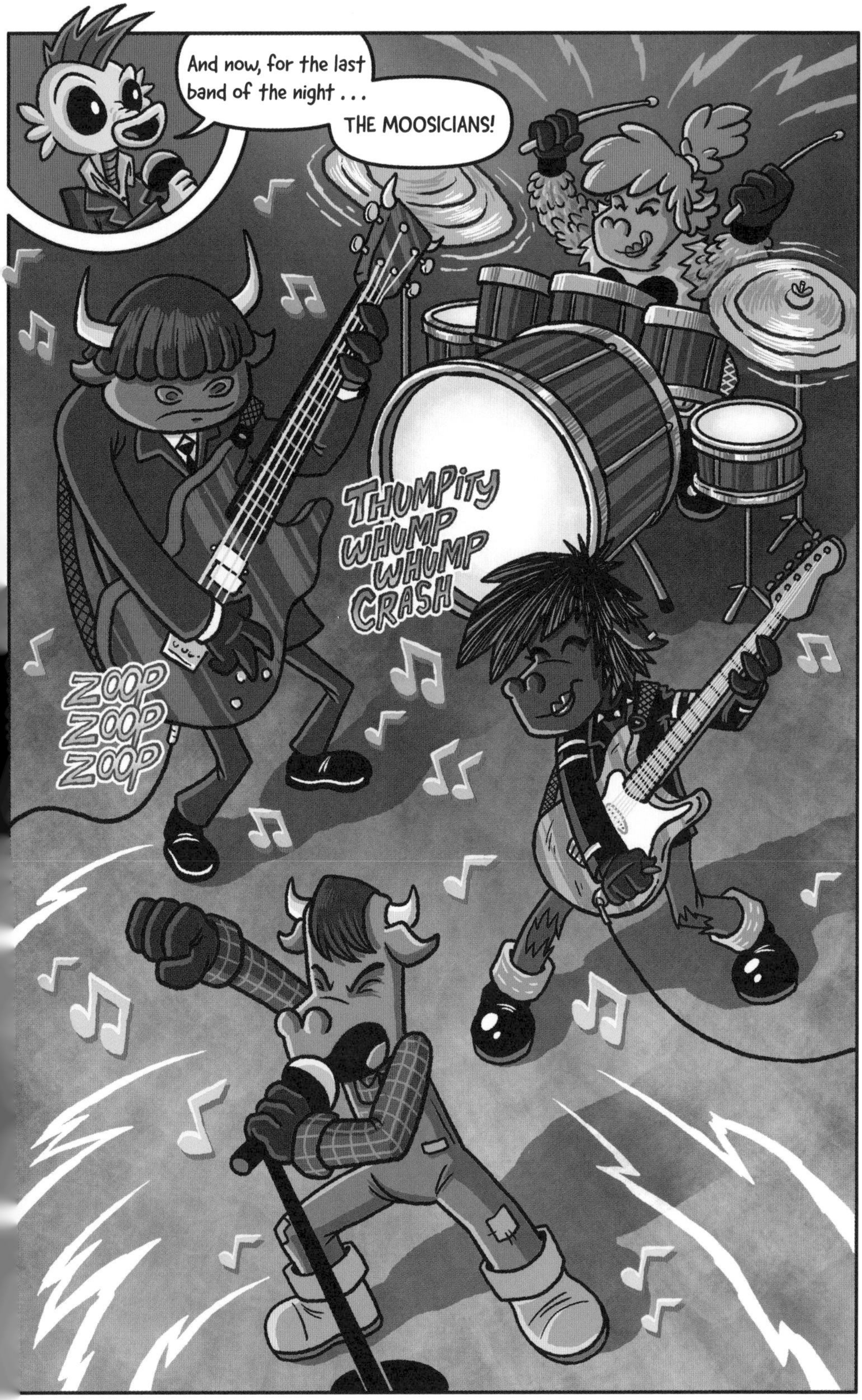
And now, for the last band of the night . . .
THE MOOSICIANS!
THUMPITY WHUMP WHUMP CRASH
ZOOP ZOOP ZOOP

CHAPTER 9

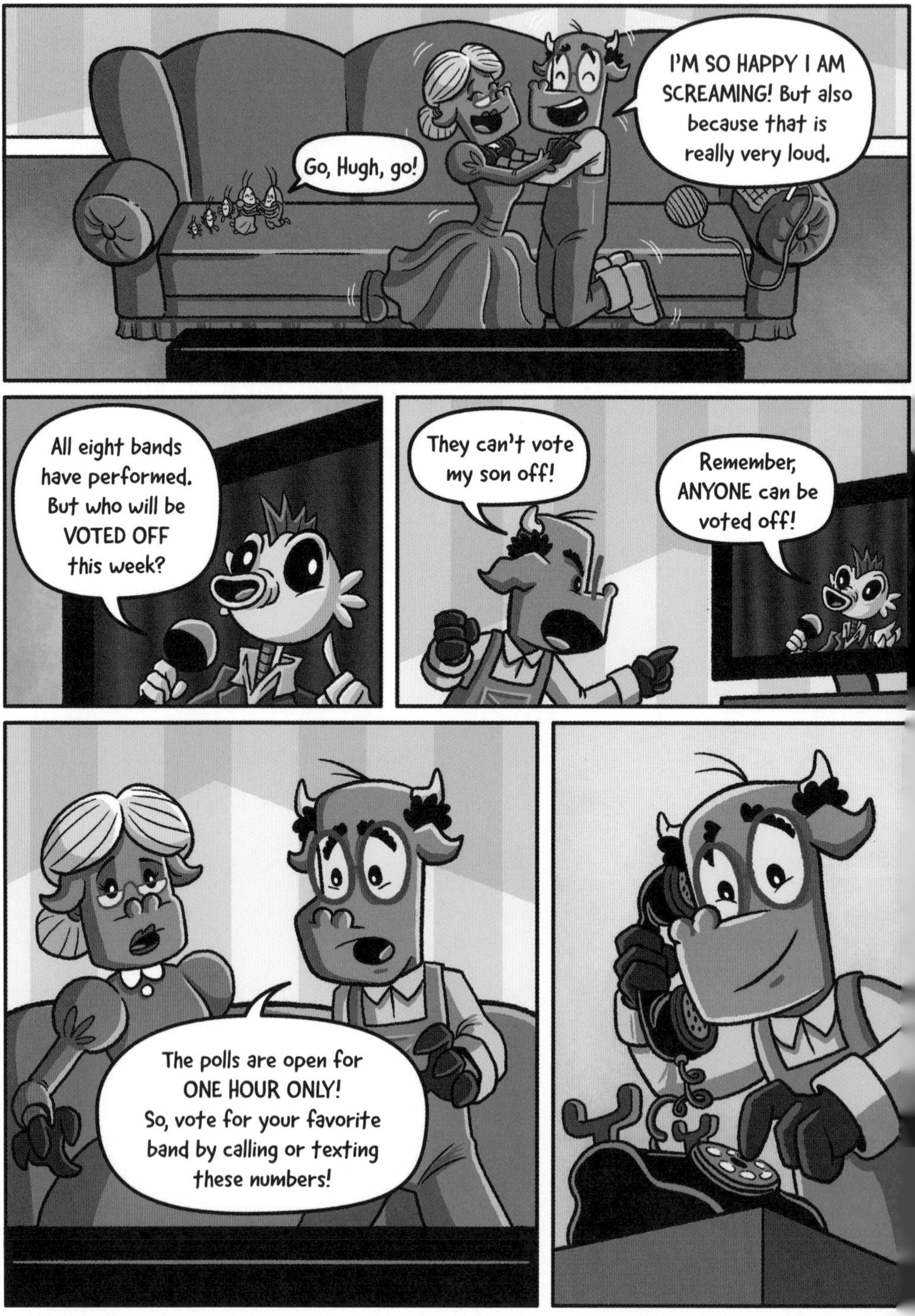

I'M SO HAPPY I AM SCREAMING! But also because that is really very loud.
Go, Hugh, go!
All eight bands have performed. But who will be VOTED OFF this week?
They can't vote my son off!
Remember, ANYONE can be voted off!
The polls are open for ONE HOUR ONLY! So, vote for your favorite band by calling or texting these numbers!

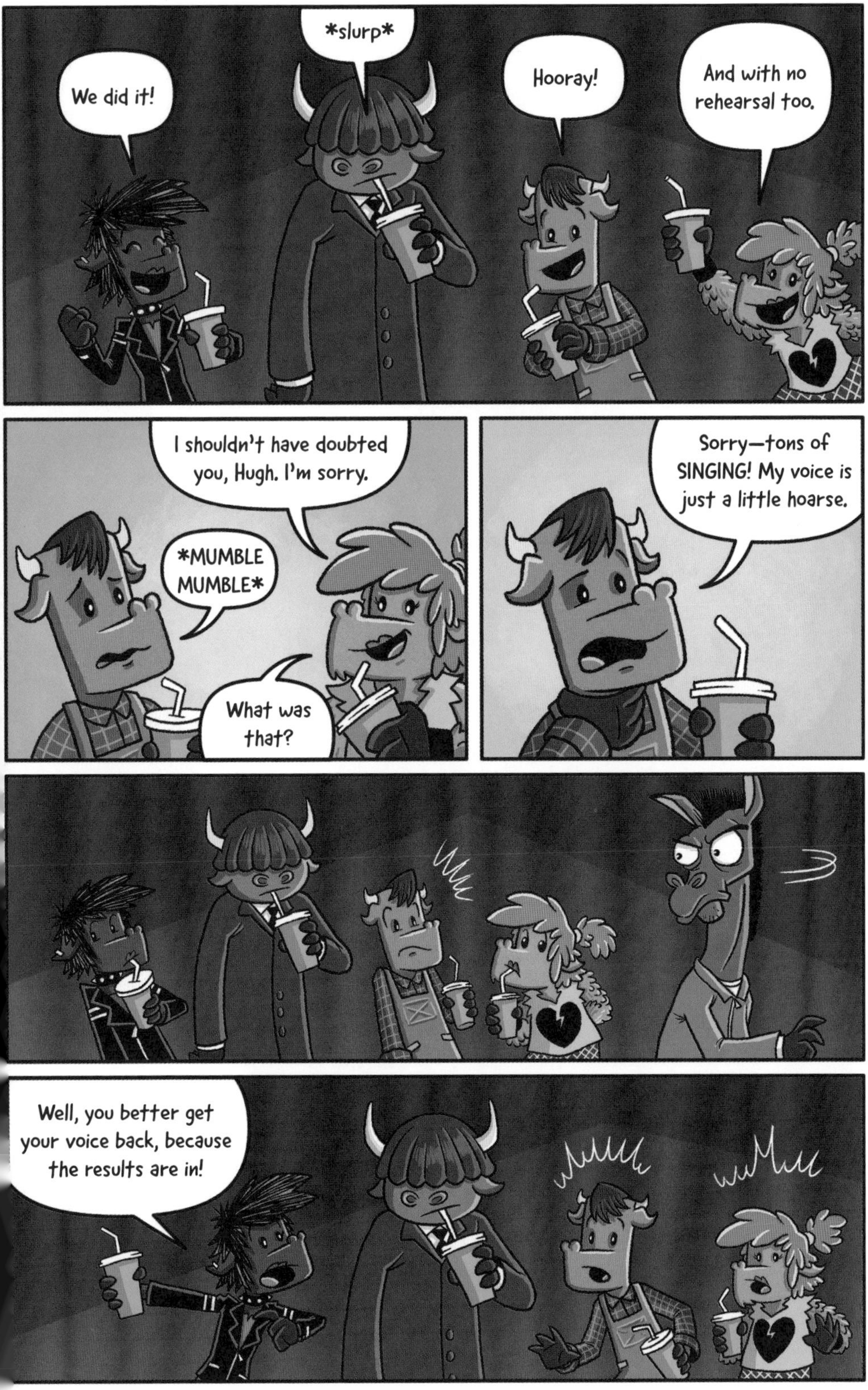
We did it!
slurp
Hooray!
And with no rehearsal too.
I shouldn't have doubted you, Hugh. I'm sorry.
MUMBLE MUMBLE
What was that?
Sorry—tons of SINGING! My voice is just a little hoarse.
Well, you better get your voice back, because the results are in!

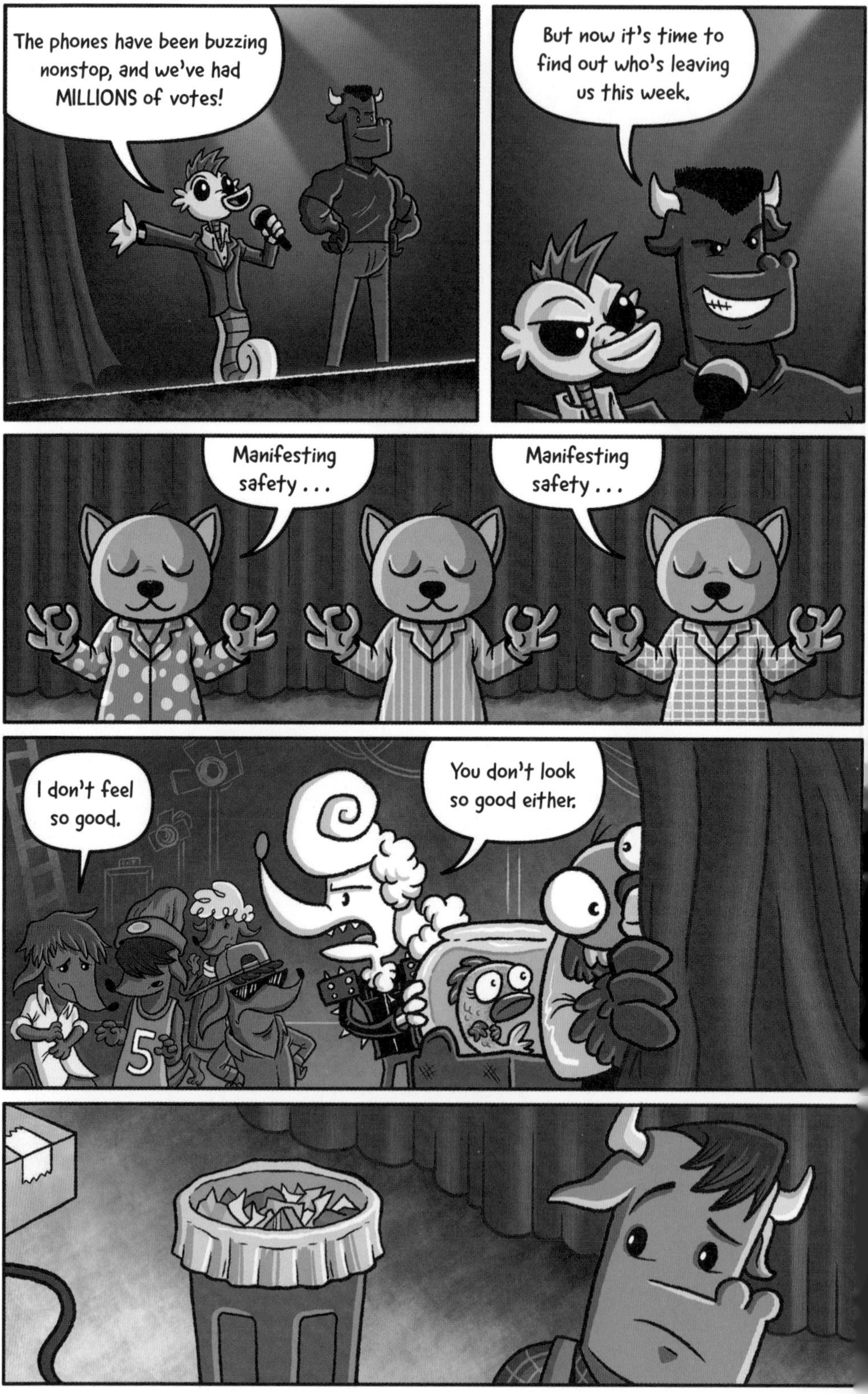
The phones have been buzzing nonstop, and we've had MILLIONS of votes!
But now it's time to find out who's leaving us this week.
Manifesting safety . . .
Manifesting safety . . .
I don't feel so good.
You don't look so good either.

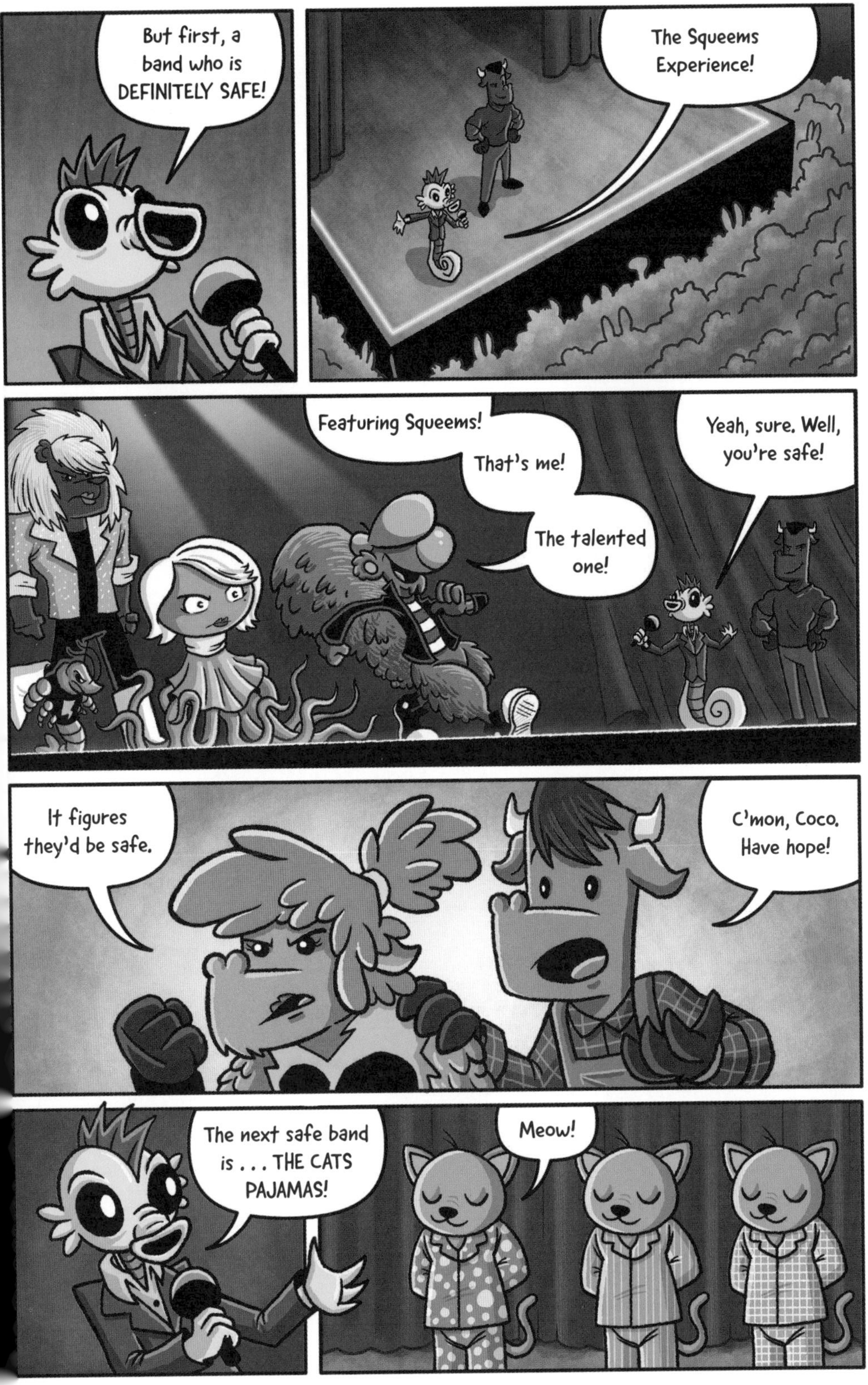
But first, a band who is DEFINITELY SAFE!
The Squeems Experience!
Featuring Squeems!
That's me!
The talented one!
Yeah, sure. Well, you're safe!
It figures they'd be safe.
C'mon, Coco. Have hope!
The next safe band is . . . THE CATS PAJAMAS!
Meow!

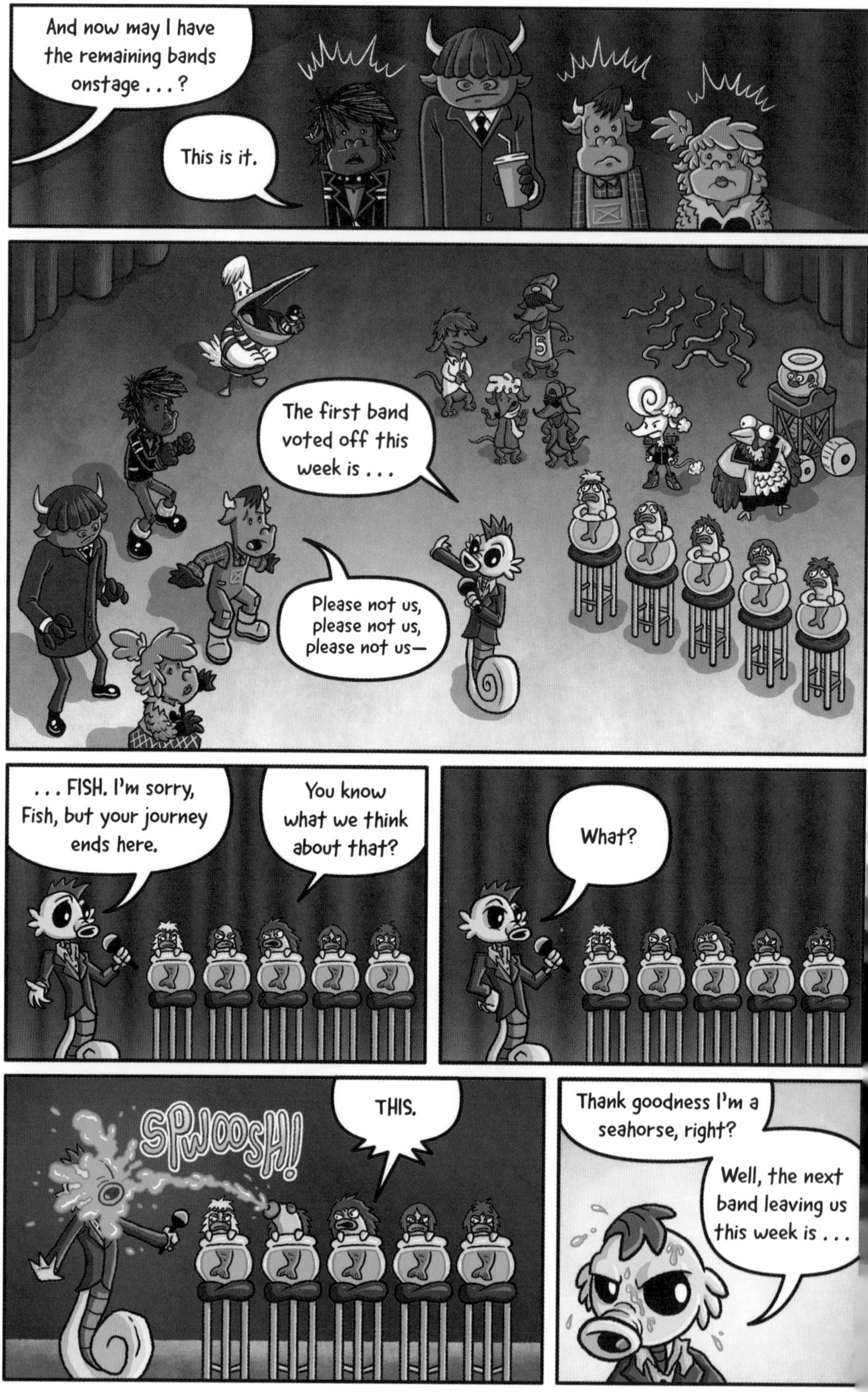
And now may I have the remaining bands onstage . . . ?
This is it.
The first band voted off this week is . . .
Please not us, please not us, please not us—
. . . FISH. I'm sorry, Fish, but your journey ends here.
You know what we think about that?
What?
SPWOOSH!
THIS.
Thank goodness I'm a seahorse, right?
Well, the next band leaving us this week is . . .

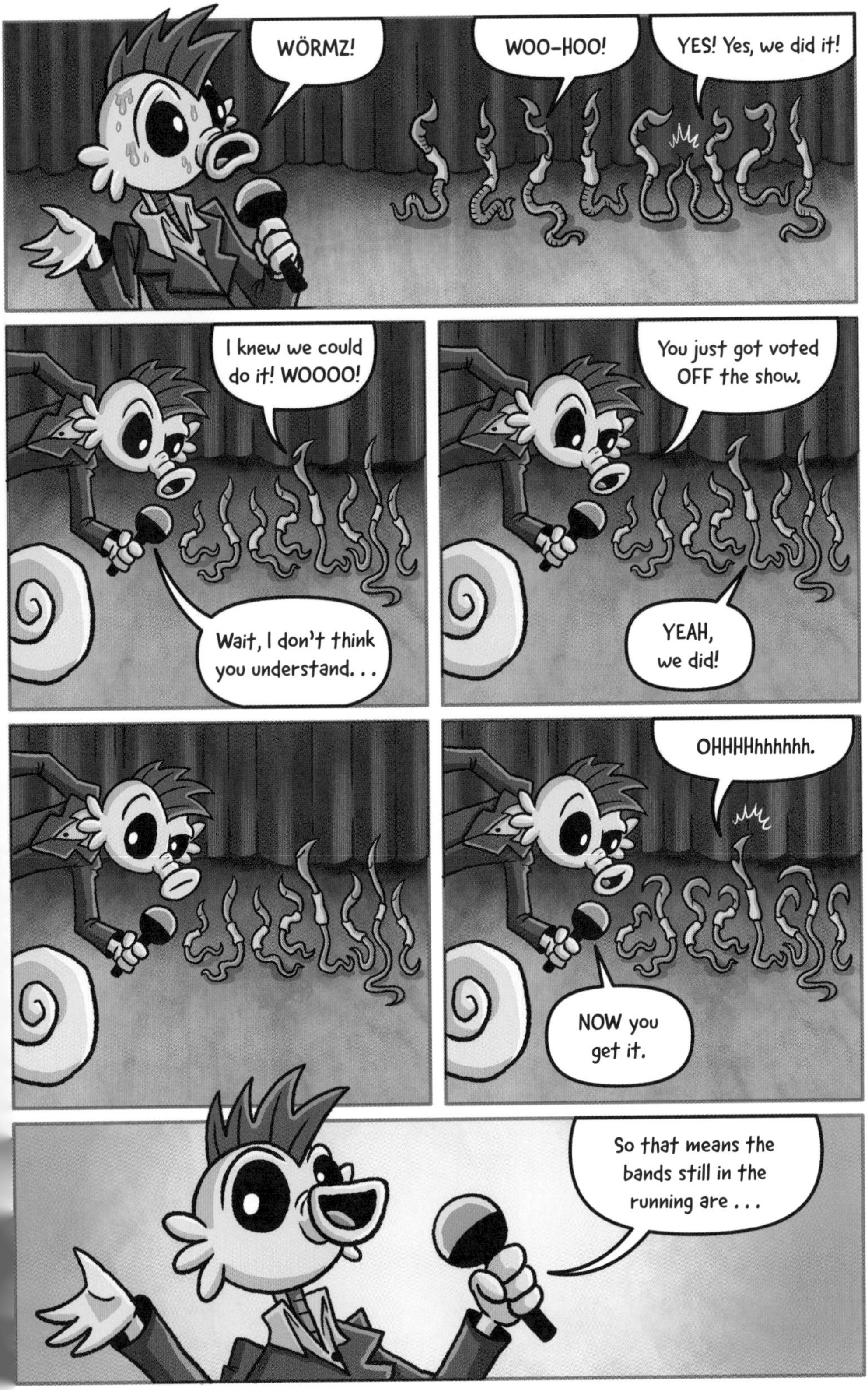
WÖRMZ!
WOO-HOO!
YES! Yes, we did it!
I knew we could do it! WOOOO!
Wait, I don't think you understand. . .
You just got voted OFF the show.
YEAH, we did!
OHHHHhhhhh.
NOW you get it.
So that means the bands still in the running are . . .

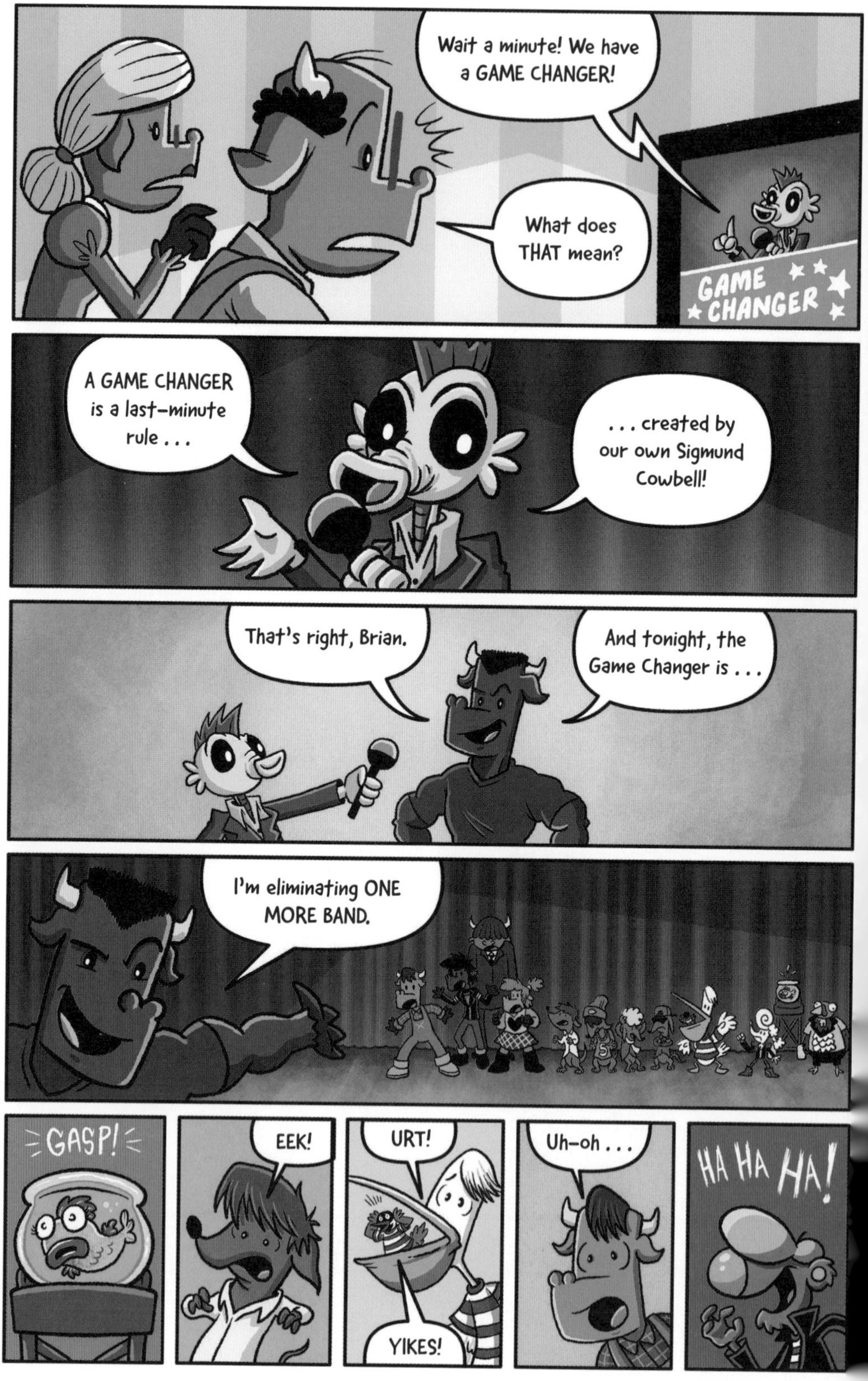
Wait a minute! We have a GAME CHANGER!
What does THAT mean?
GAME CHANGER
A GAME CHANGER is a last-minute rule . . .
. . . created by our own Sigmund Cowbell!
That's right, Brian.
And tonight, the Game Changer is . . .
I'm eliminating ONE MORE BAND.
GASP!
EEK!
URT!
YIKES!
Uh-oh . . .
HA HA HA!

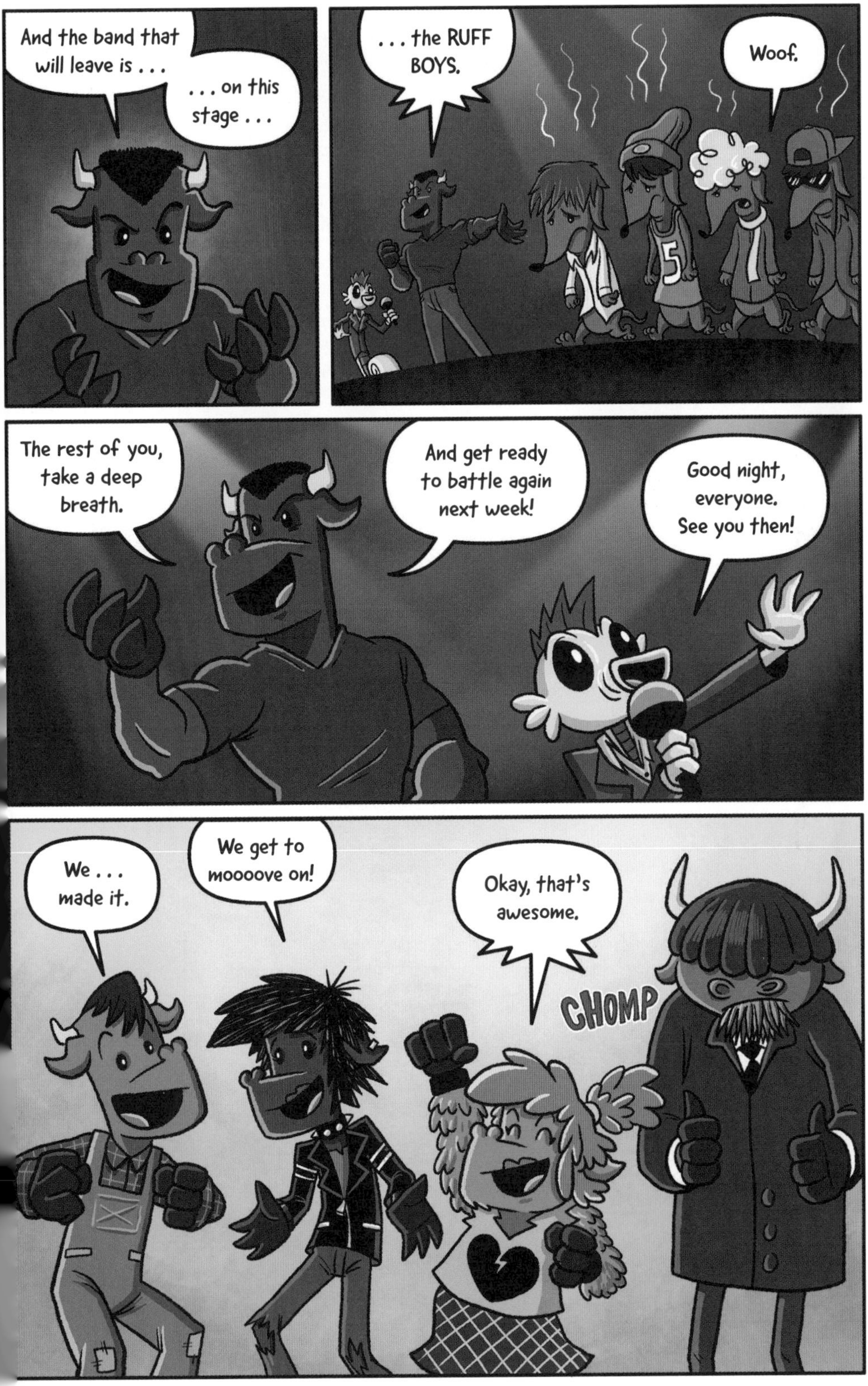
And the band that will leave is . . .
. . . on this stage . . .
. . . the RUFF BOYS.
Woof.
The rest of you, take a deep breath.
And get ready to battle again next week!
Good night, everyone. See you then!
We . . . made it.
We get to moooove on!
Okay, that's awesome.
CHOMP

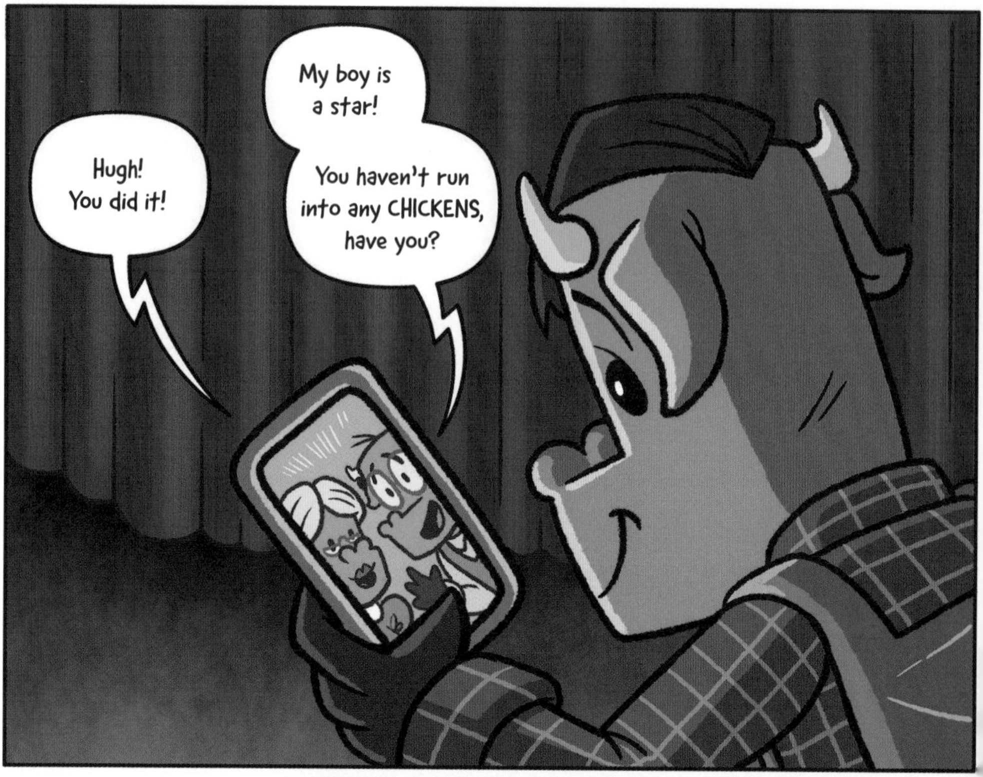
Hugh!
You did it!
My boy is
a star!
You haven't run
into any CHICKENS,
have you?

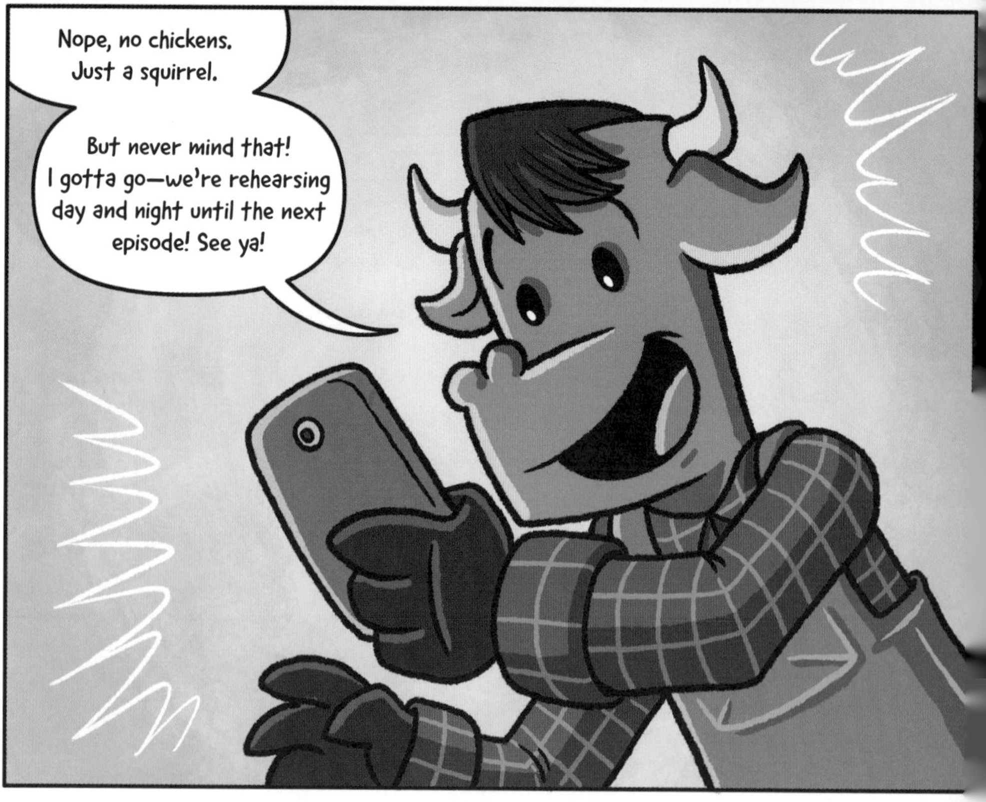
Nope, no chickens.
Just a squirrel.
But never mind that!
I gotta go—we're rehearsing
day and night until the next
episode! See ya!

CHAPTER 10

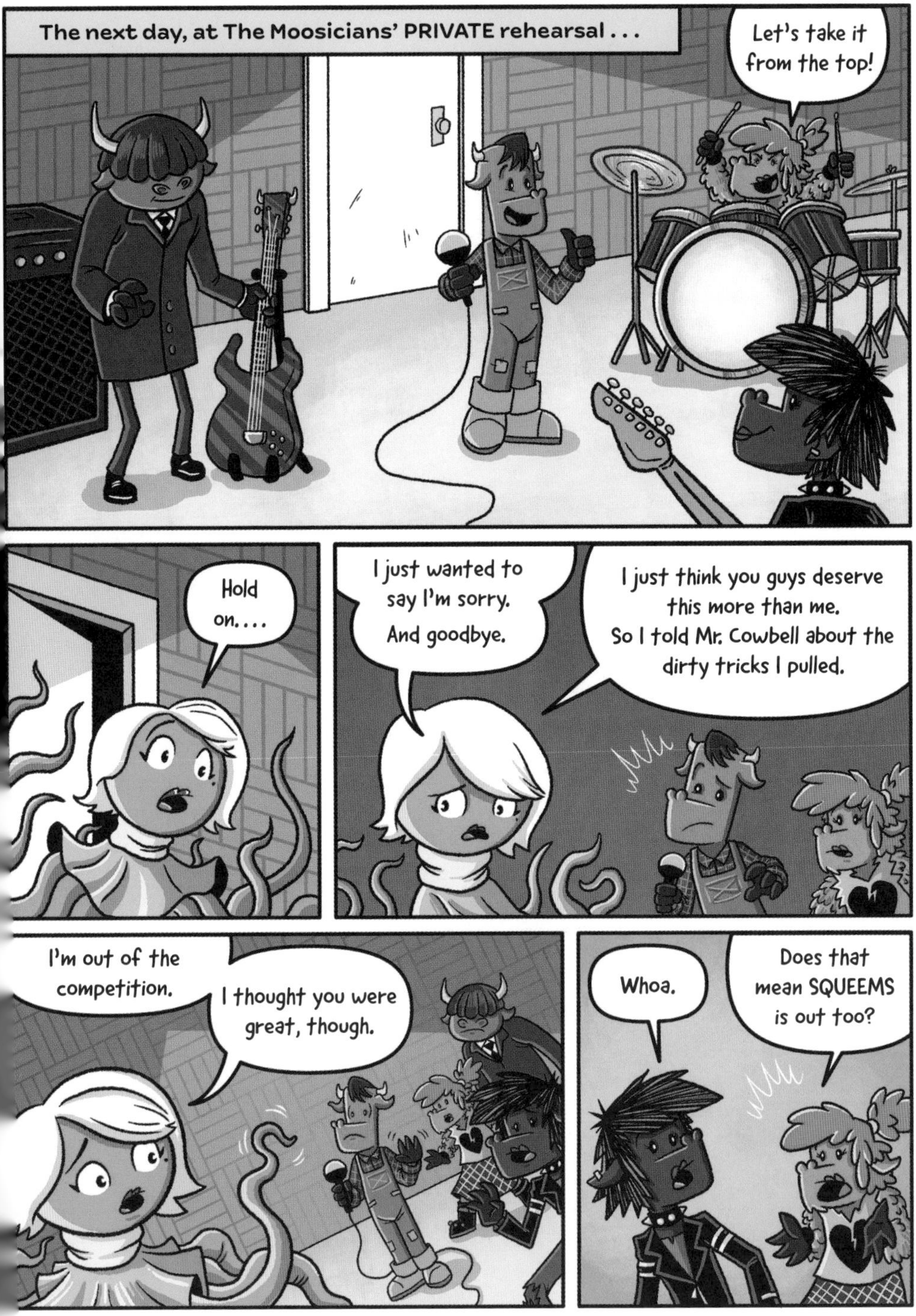
The next day, at The Moosicians' PRIVATE rehearsal . . .
Let's take it from the top!
Hold on. . . .
I just wanted to say I'm sorry. And goodbye.
I just think you guys deserve this more than me. So I told Mr. Cowbell about the dirty tricks I pulled.
I'm out of the competition.
I thought you were great, though.
Whoa.
Does that mean SQUEEMS is out too?

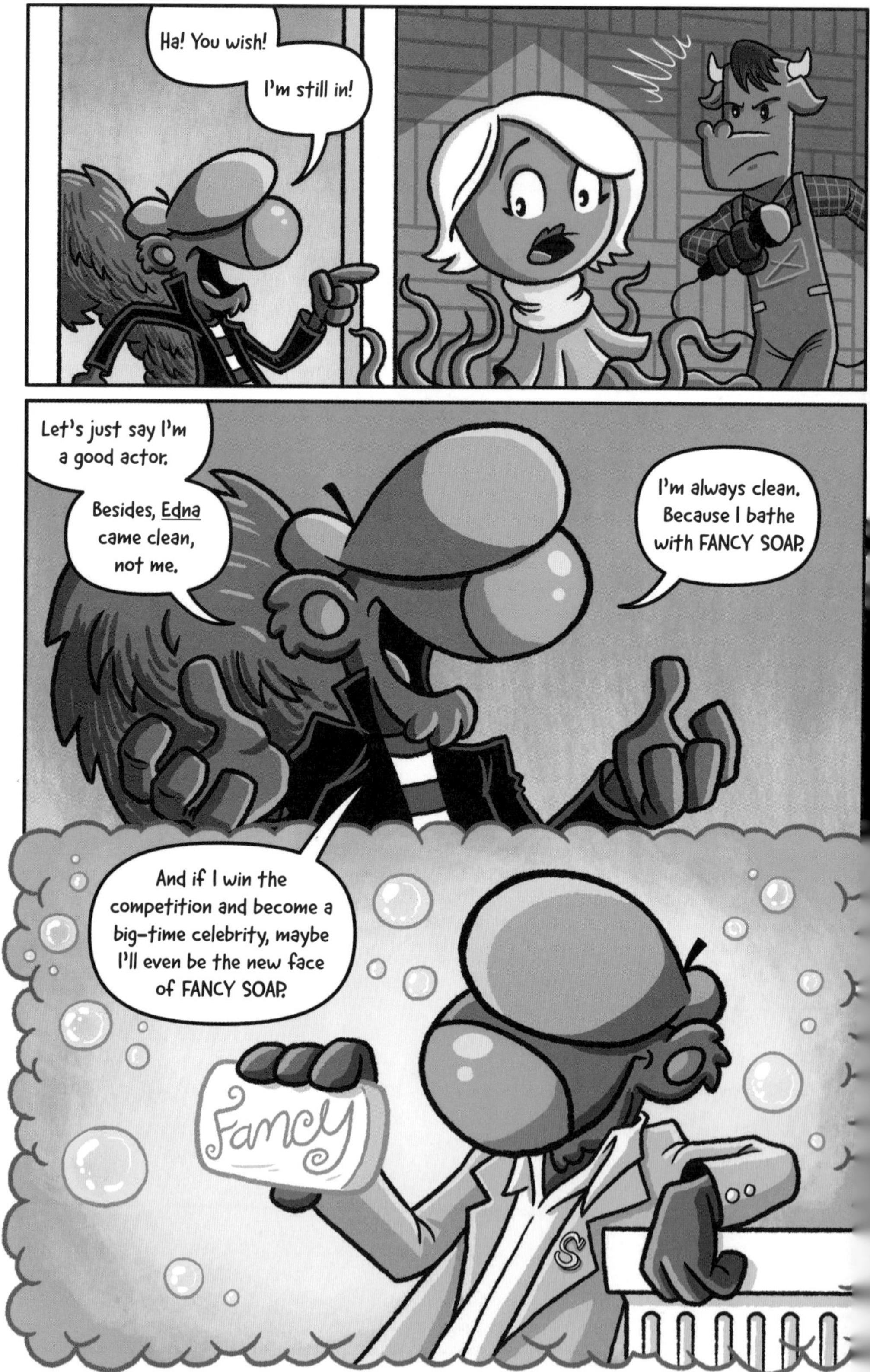

Ha! You wish!
I'm still in!
Let's just say I'm a good actor.
Besides, Edna came clean, not me.
I'm always clean. Because I bathe with FANCY SOAP.
And if I win the competition and become a big-time celebrity, maybe I'll even be the new face of FANCY SOAP.
Fancy

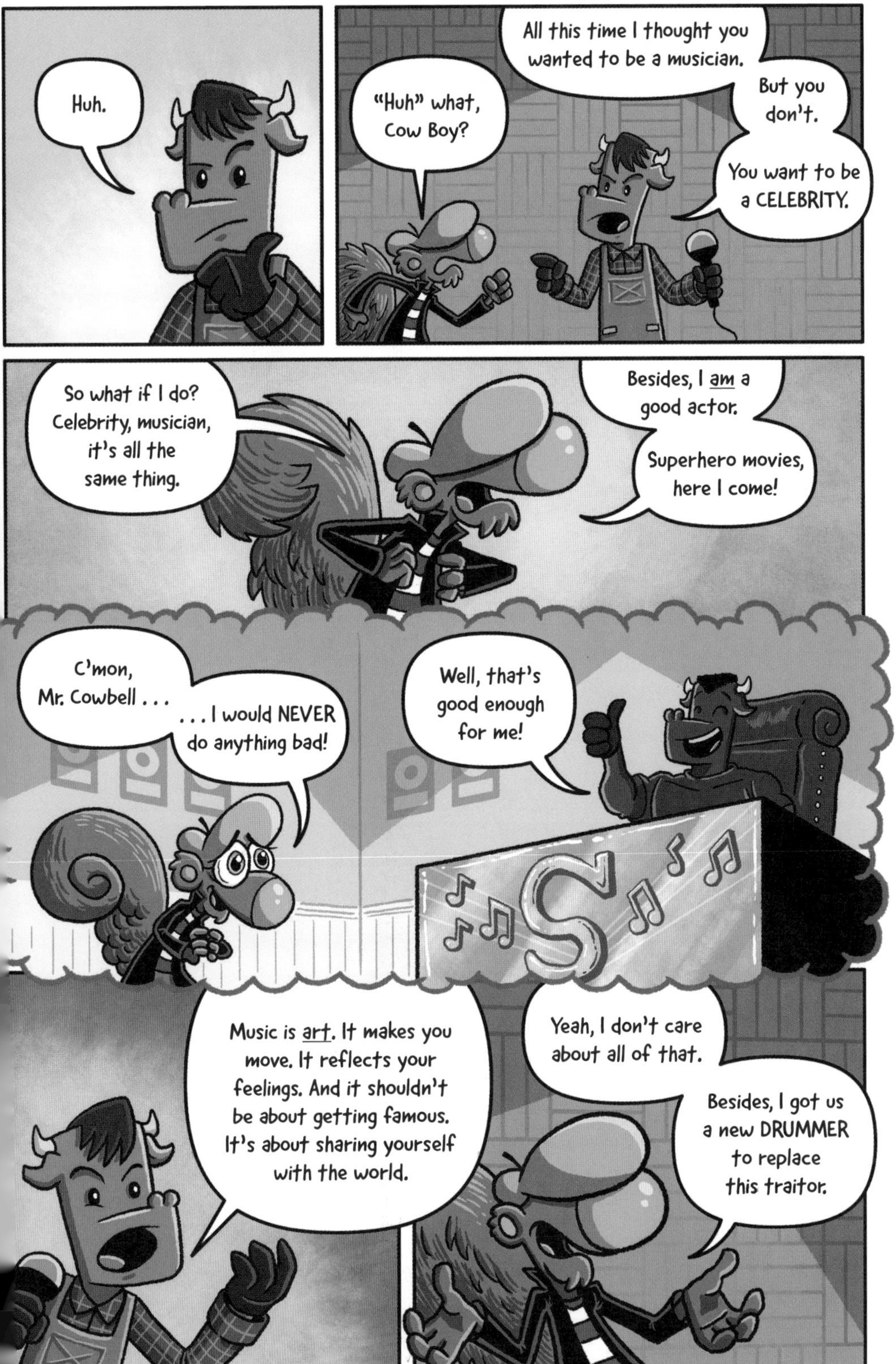
Huh.
"Huh" what, Cow Boy?
All this time I thought you wanted to be a musician.
But you don't.
You want to be a CELEBRITY.
So what if I do? Celebrity, musician, it's all the same thing.
Besides, I am a good actor.
Superhero movies, here I come!
C'mon, Mr. Cowbell . . .
. . . I would NEVER do anything bad!
Well, that's good enough for me!
Music is art. It makes you move. It reflects your feelings. And it shouldn't be about getting famous. It's about sharing yourself with the world.
Yeah, I don't care about all of that.
Besides, I got us a new DRUMMER to replace this traitor.

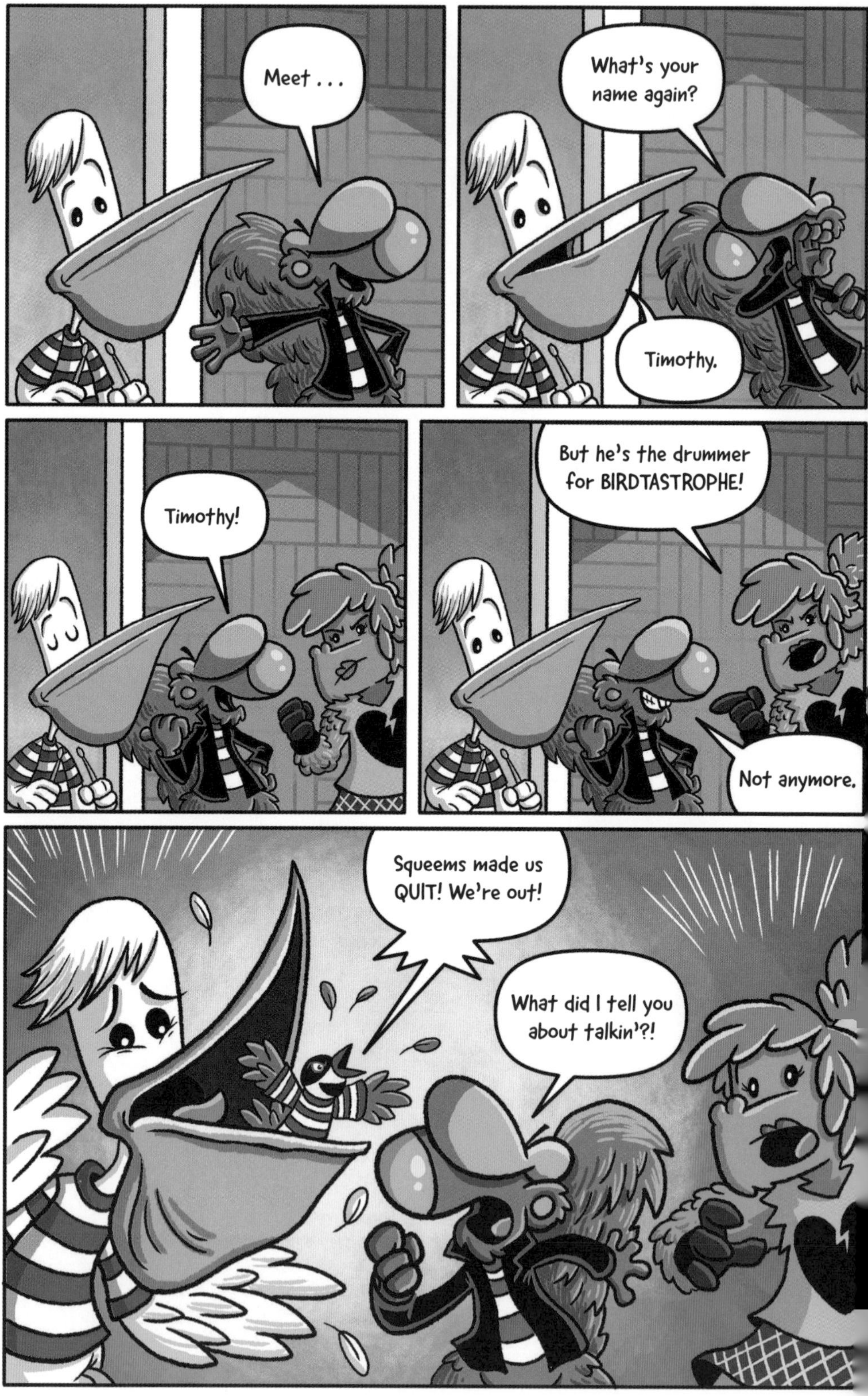
Meet . . .
What's your name again?
Timothy.
Timothy!
But he's the drummer for BIRDTASTROPHE!
Not anymore.
Squeems made us QUIT! We're out!
What did I tell you about talkin'?!

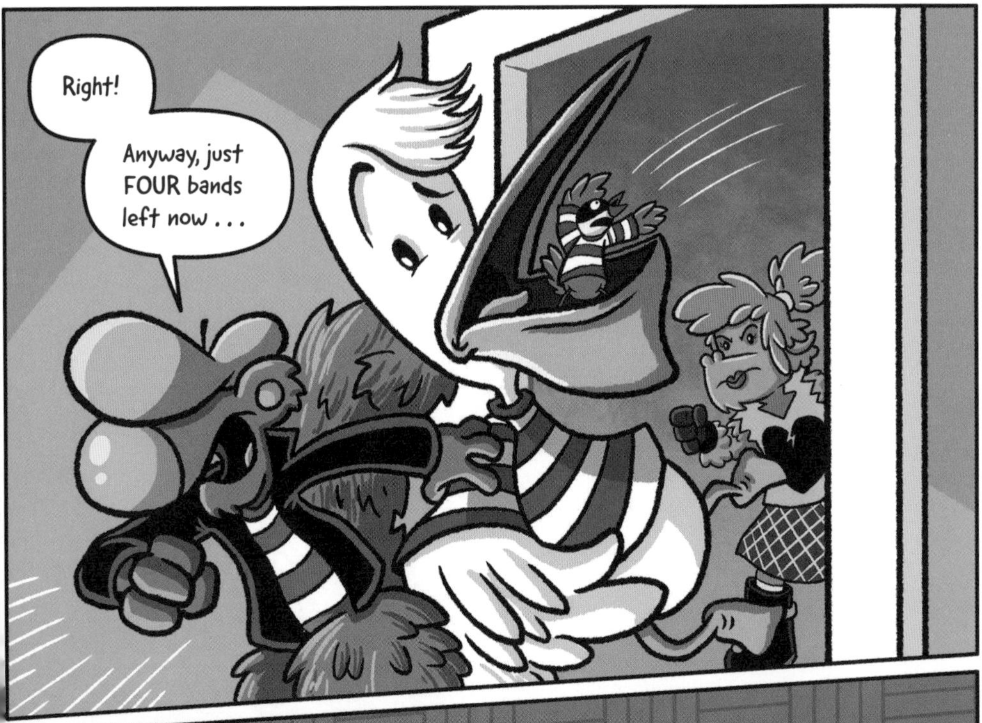
Right!
Anyway, just FOUR bands left now . . .

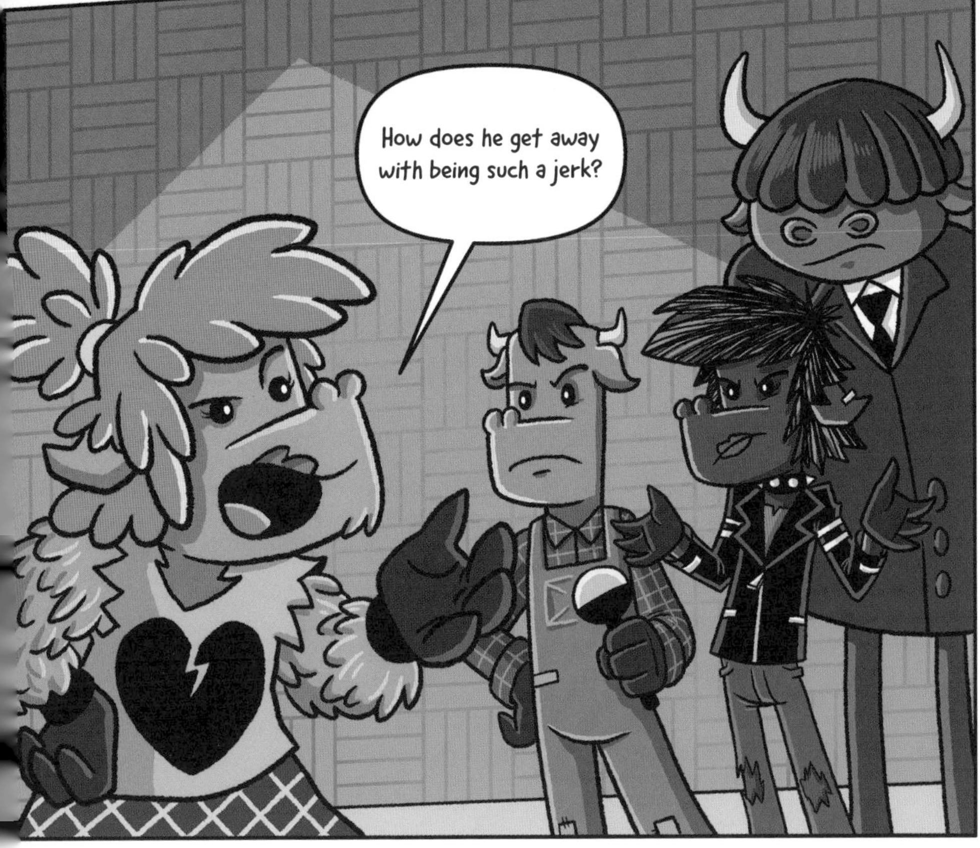
How does he get away with being such a jerk?

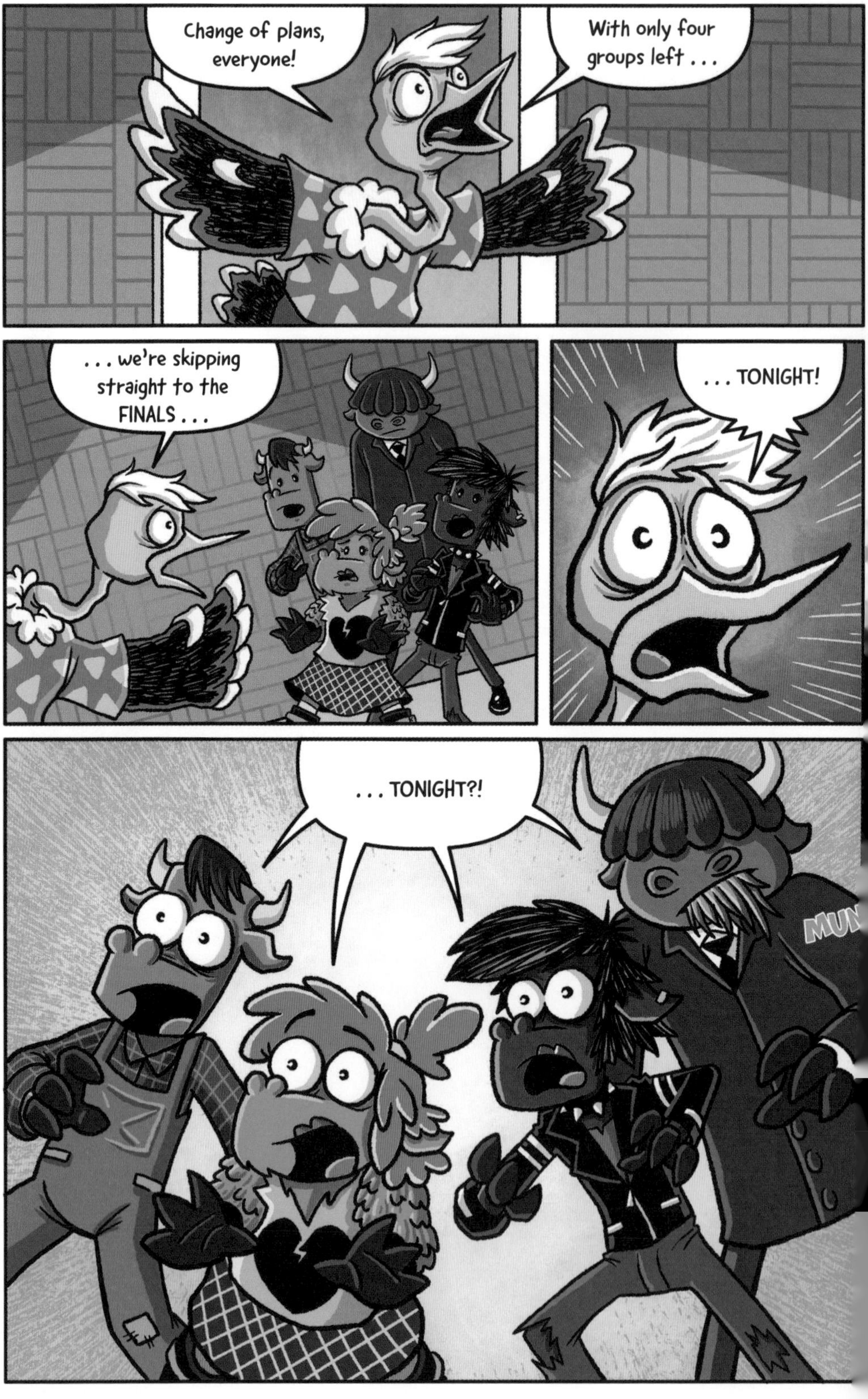
Change of plans, everyone!
With only four groups left . . .
. . . we're skipping straight to the FINALS . . .
. . . TONIGHT!
. . . TONIGHT?!

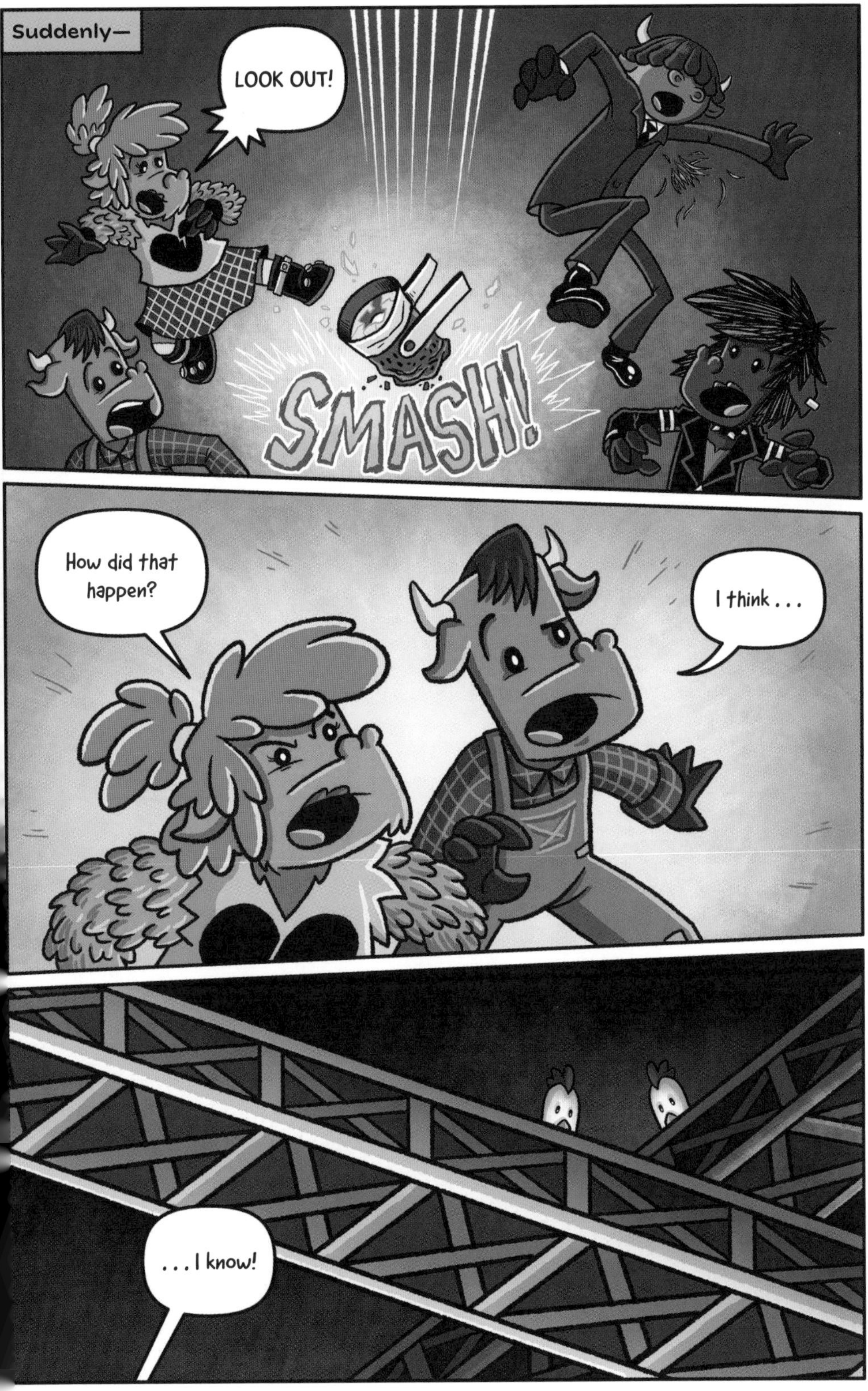
Suddenly—
LOOK OUT!
SMASH!
How did that happen?
I think . . .
. . . I know!

CHAPTER 11

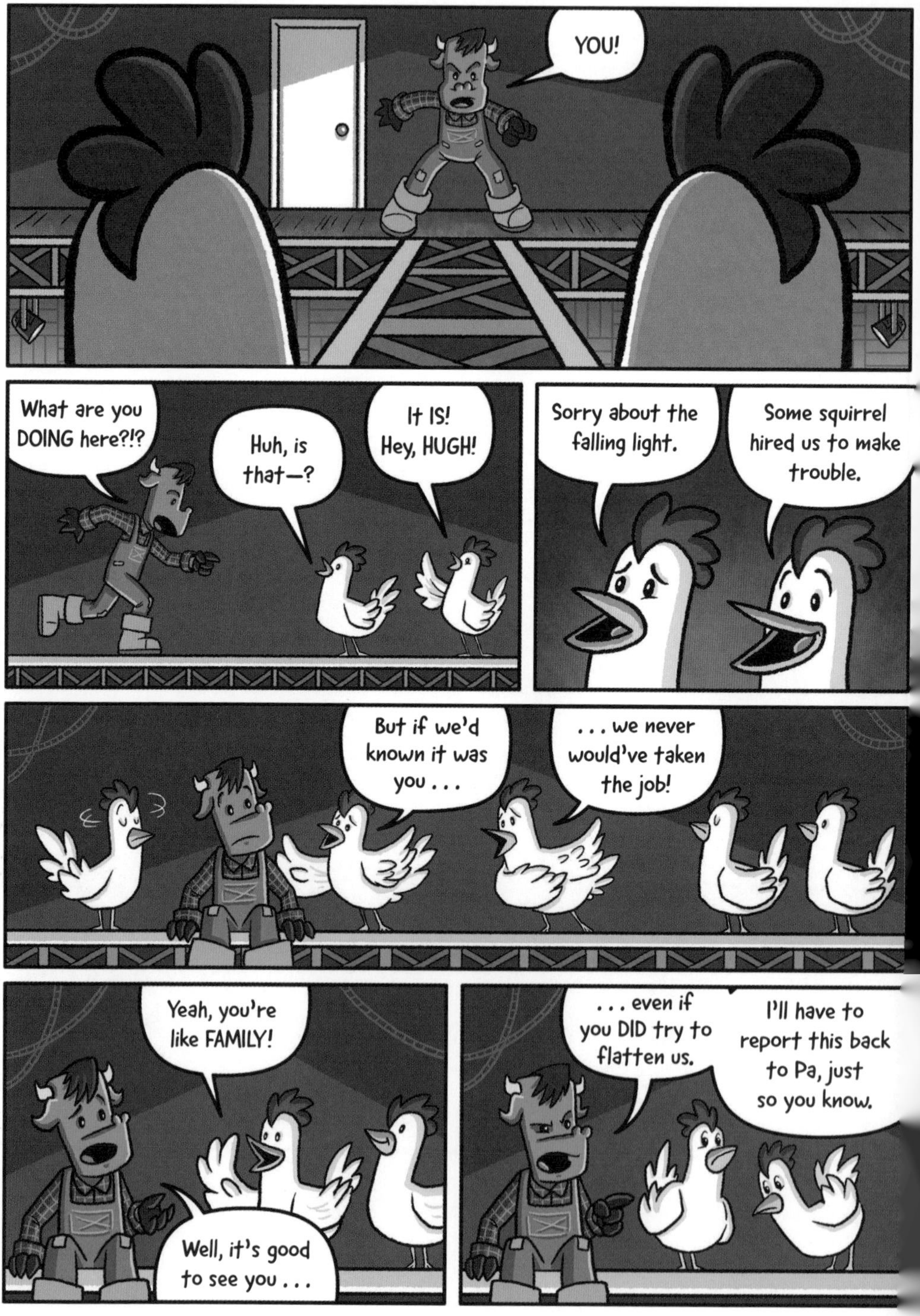
YOU!
What are you DOING here?!?
Huh, is that—?
It IS! Hey, HUGH!
Sorry about the falling light.
Some squirrel hired us to make trouble.
But if we'd known it was you . . .
. . . we never would've taken the job!
Yeah, you're like FAMILY!
Well, it's good to see you . . .
. . . even if you DID try to flatten us.
I'll have to report this back to Pa, just so you know.

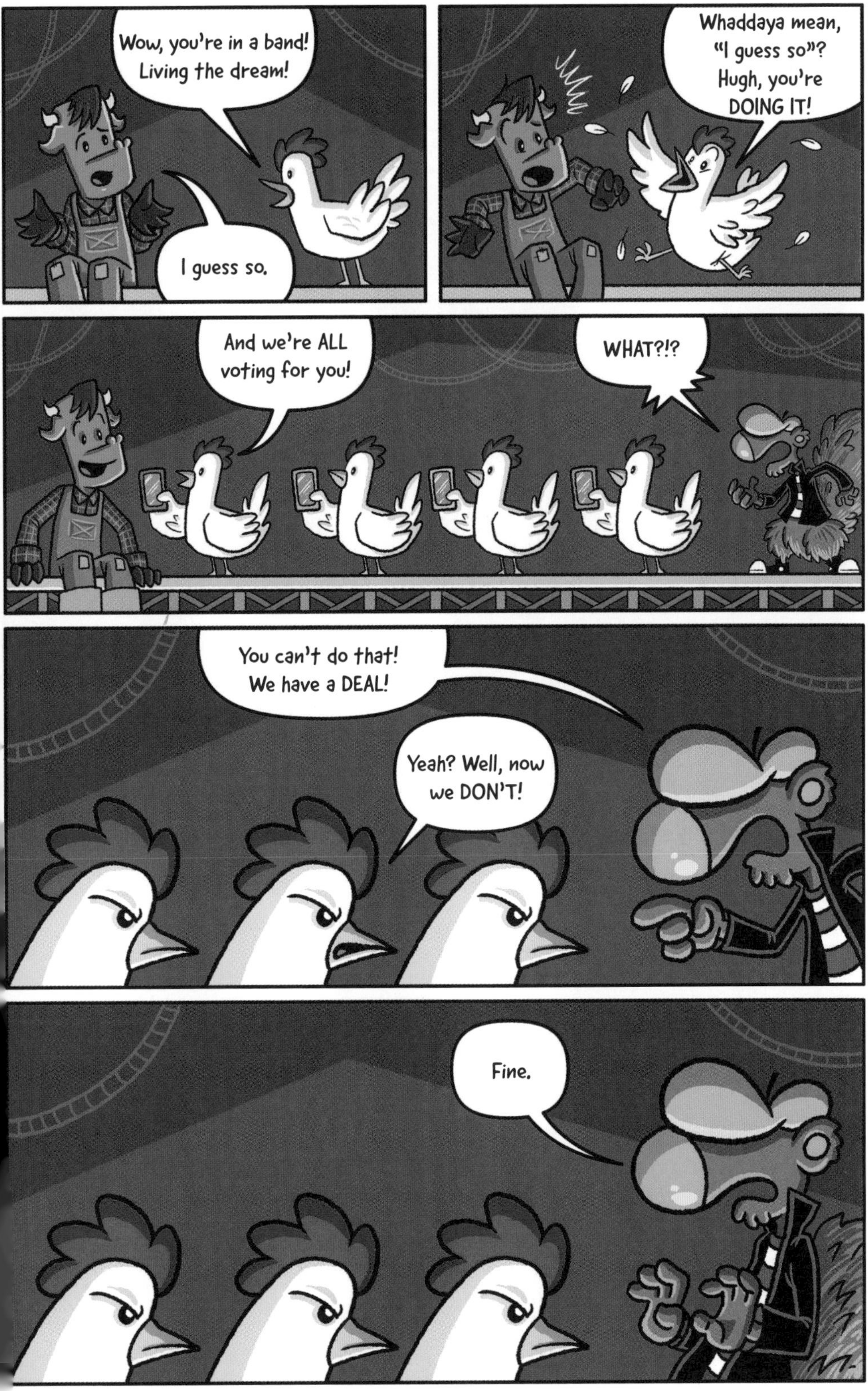
Wow, you're in a band! Living the dream!
I guess so.
Whaddaya mean, "I guess so"? Hugh, you're DOING IT!
And we're ALL voting for you!
WHAT?!?
You can't do that! We have a DEAL!
Yeah? Well, now we DON'T!
Fine.

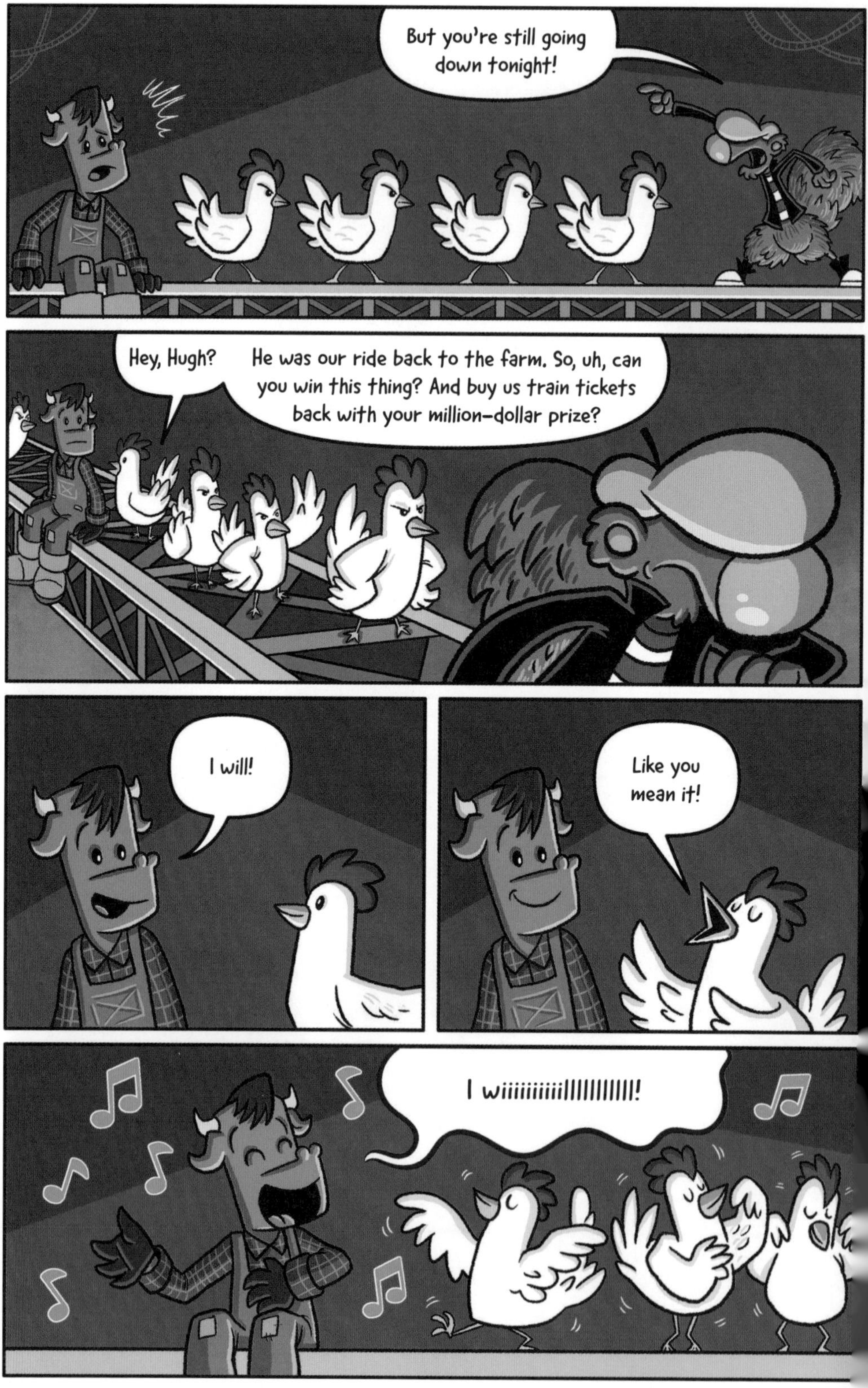

But you're still going down tonight!
Hey, Hugh?
He was our ride back to the farm. So, uh, can you win this thing? And buy us train tickets back with your million-dollar prize?
I will!
Like you mean it!
I wiiiiiiiiilllllllllll!

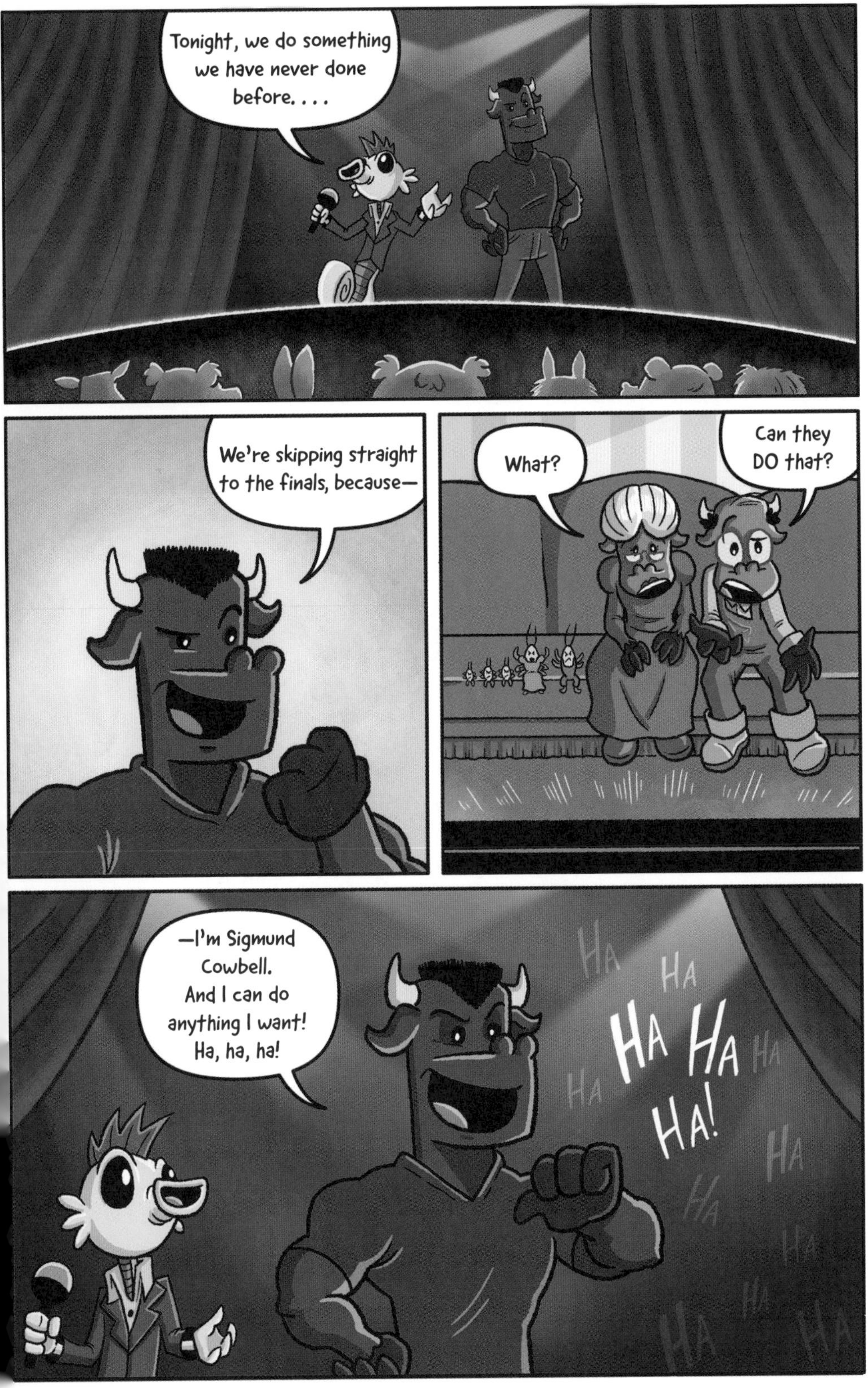
Tonight, we do something we have never done before. . . .
We're skipping straight to the finals, because—
What?
Can they DO that?
—I'm Sigmund Cowbell. And I can do anything I want! Ha, ha, ha!
HA HA HA HA HA! HA HA HA HA HA HA HA HA HA

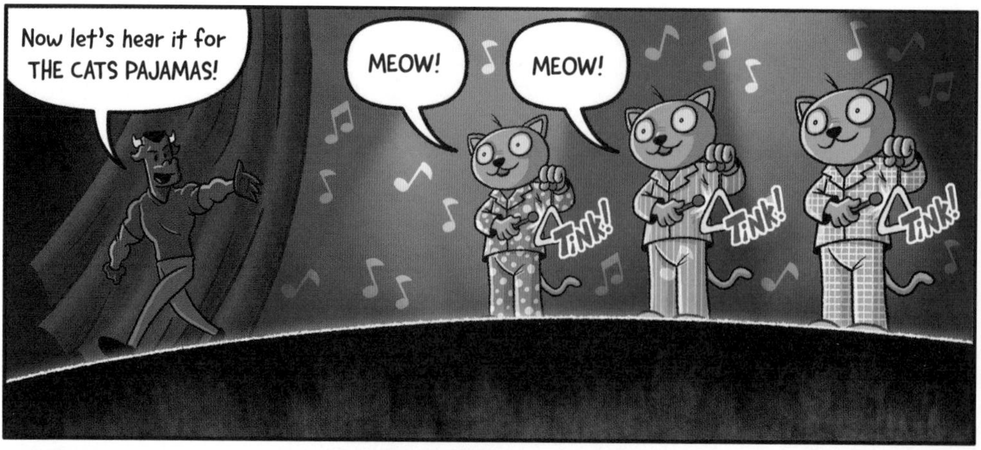
Now let's hear it for THE CATS PAJAMAS!
MEOW!
MEOW!
TINK!
TINK!
TINK!

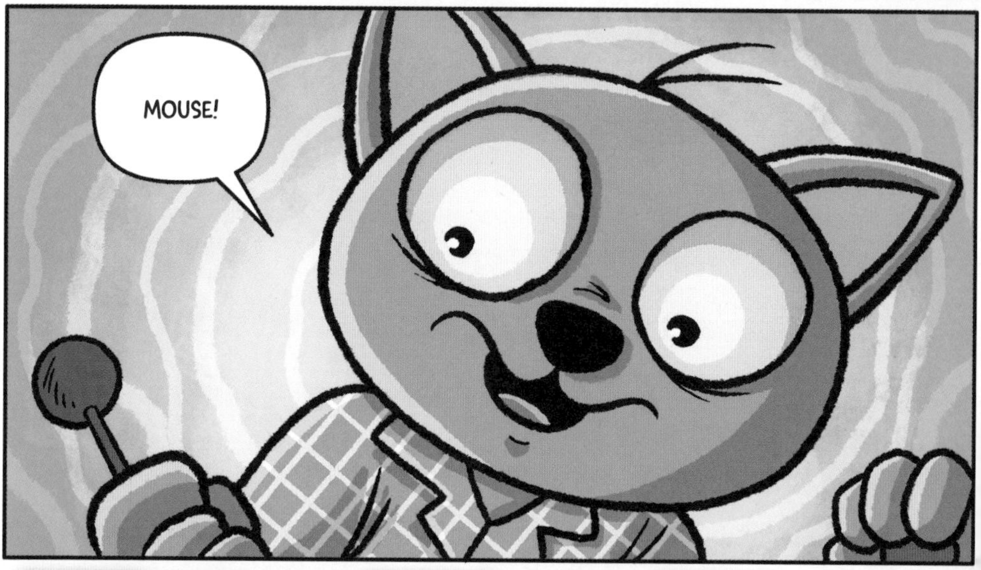
MOUSE!

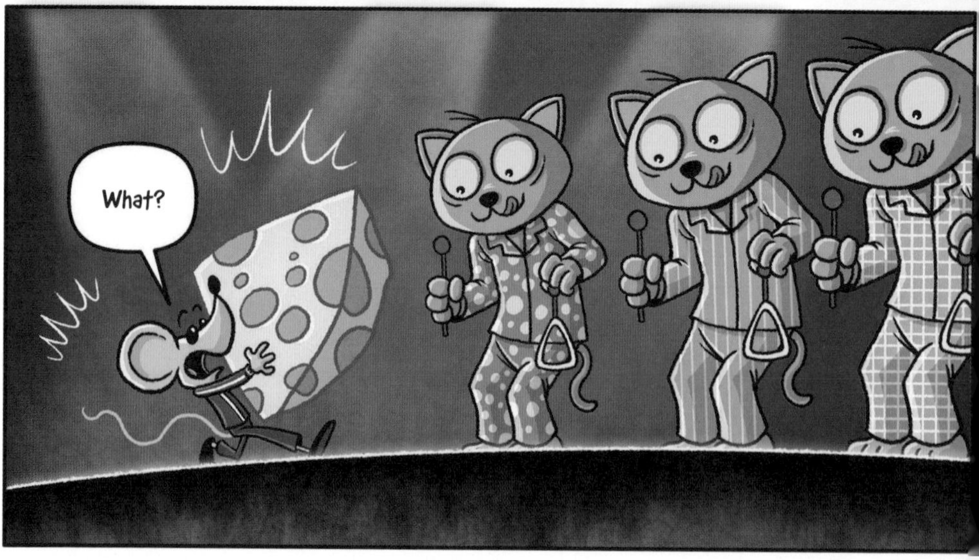
What?

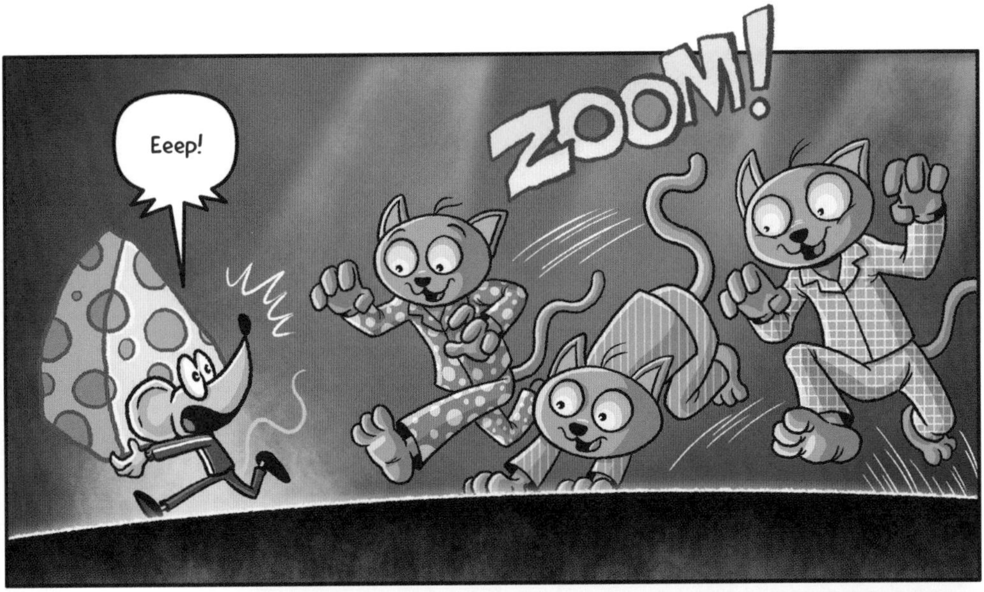
Eeep!
ZOOM!

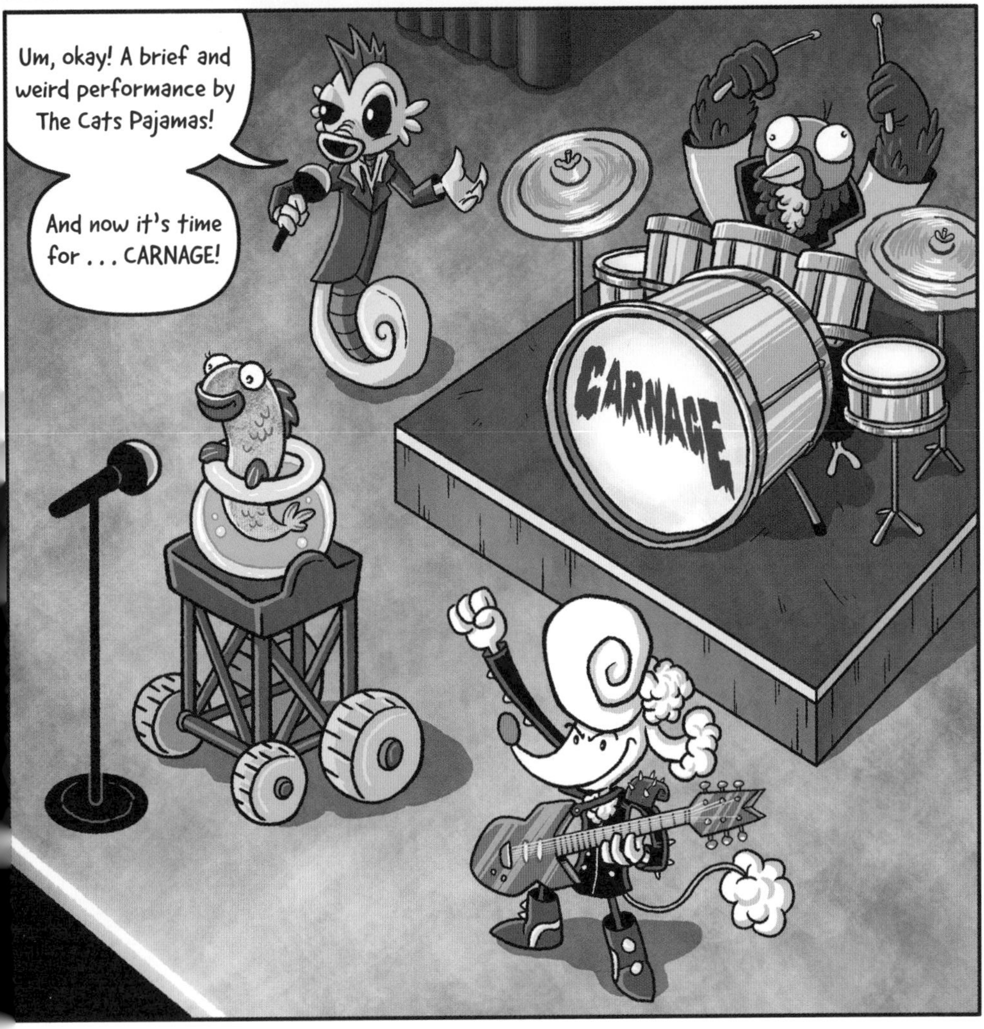
Um, okay! A brief and weird performance by The Cats Pajamas!
And now it's time for . . . CARNAGE!
CARNAGE

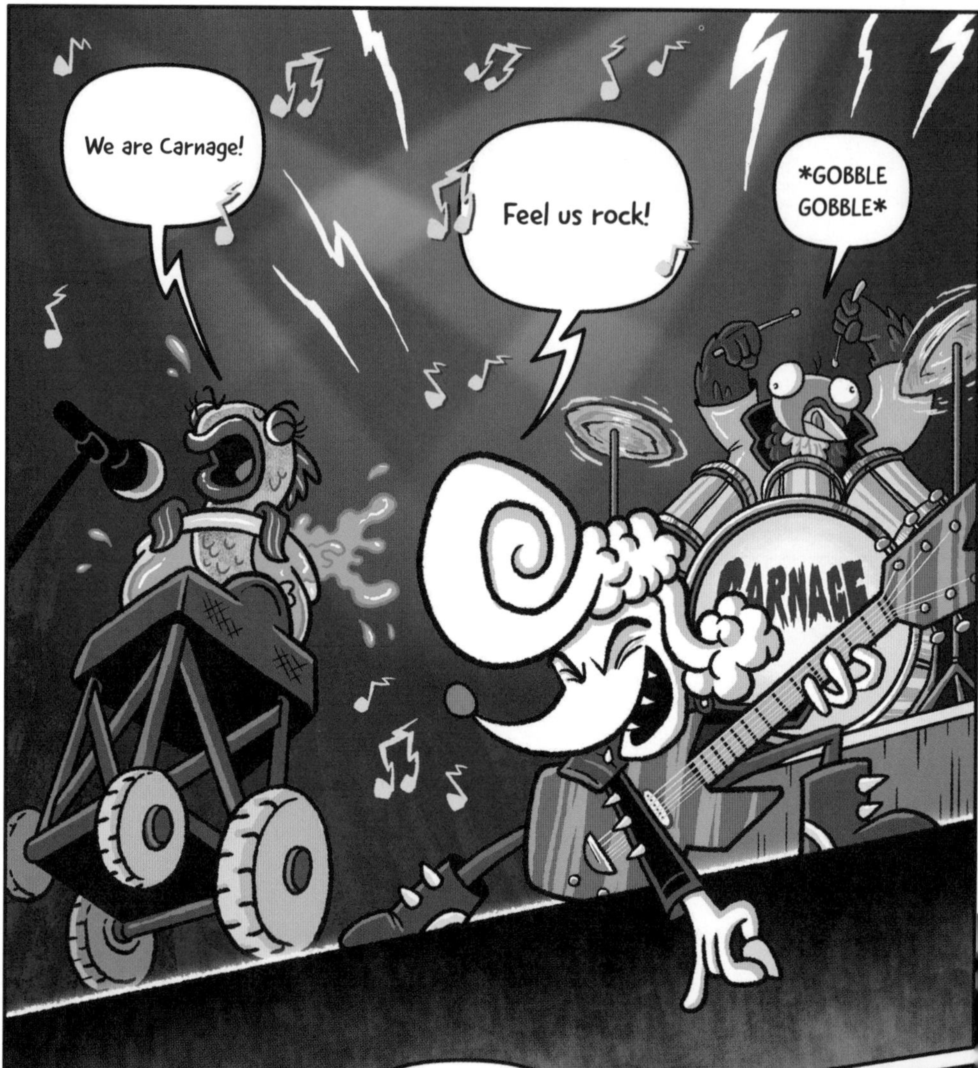
We are Carnage!
Feel us rock!
GOBBLE GOBBLE
CARNAGE

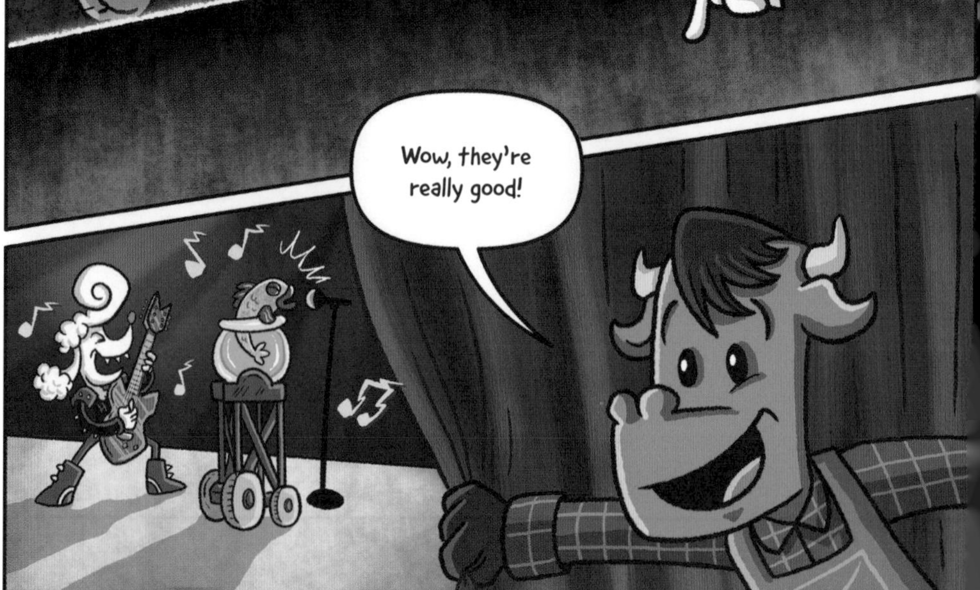
Wow, they're really good!

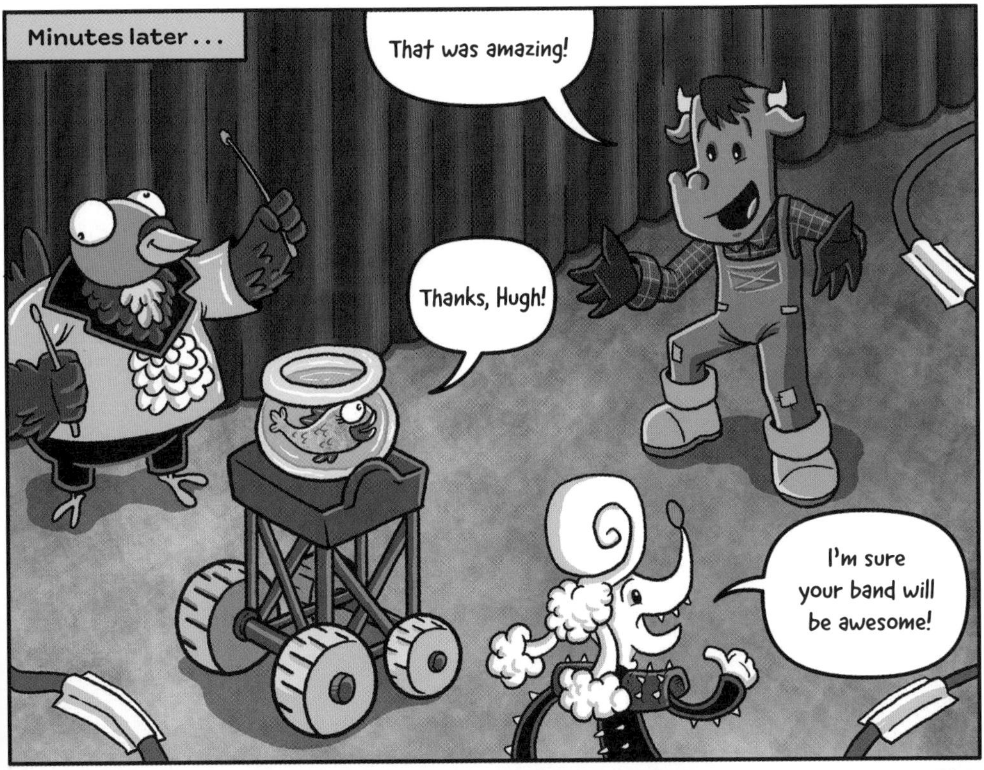
Minutes later . . .
That was amazing!
Thanks, Hugh!
I'm sure your band will be awesome!

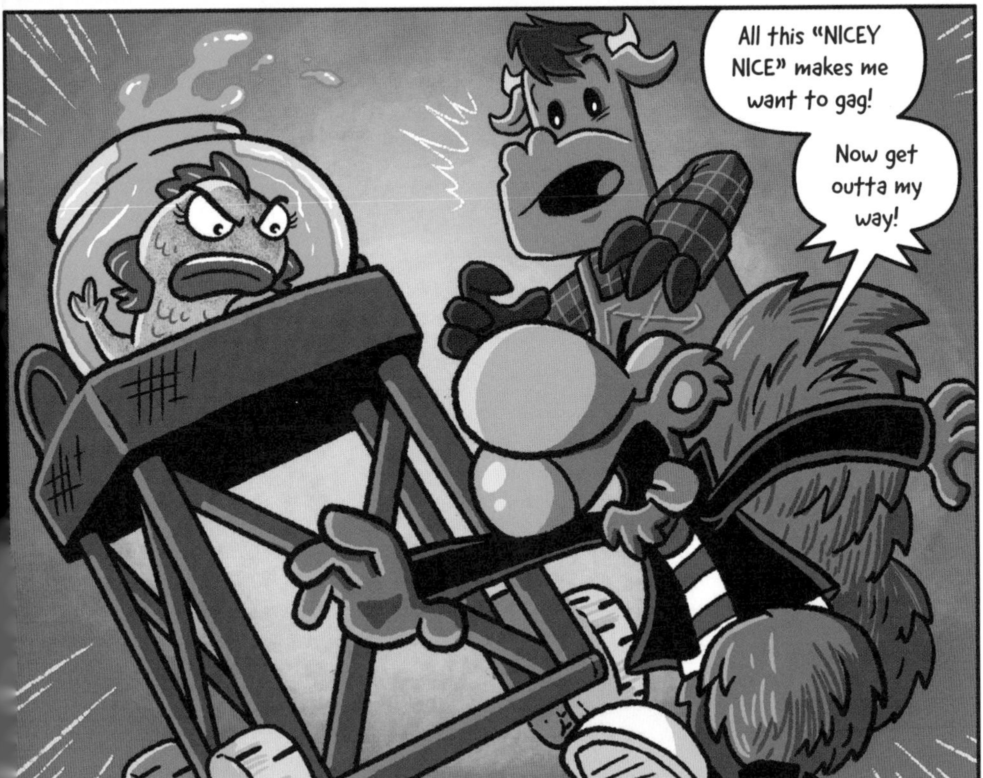
All this "NICEY NICE" makes me want to gag!
Now get outta my way!

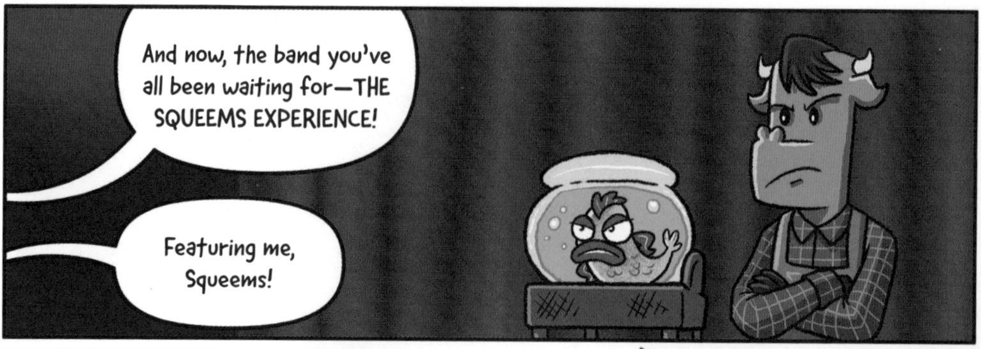
And now, the band you've all been waiting for—THE SQUEEMS EXPERIENCE!
Featuring me, Squeems!

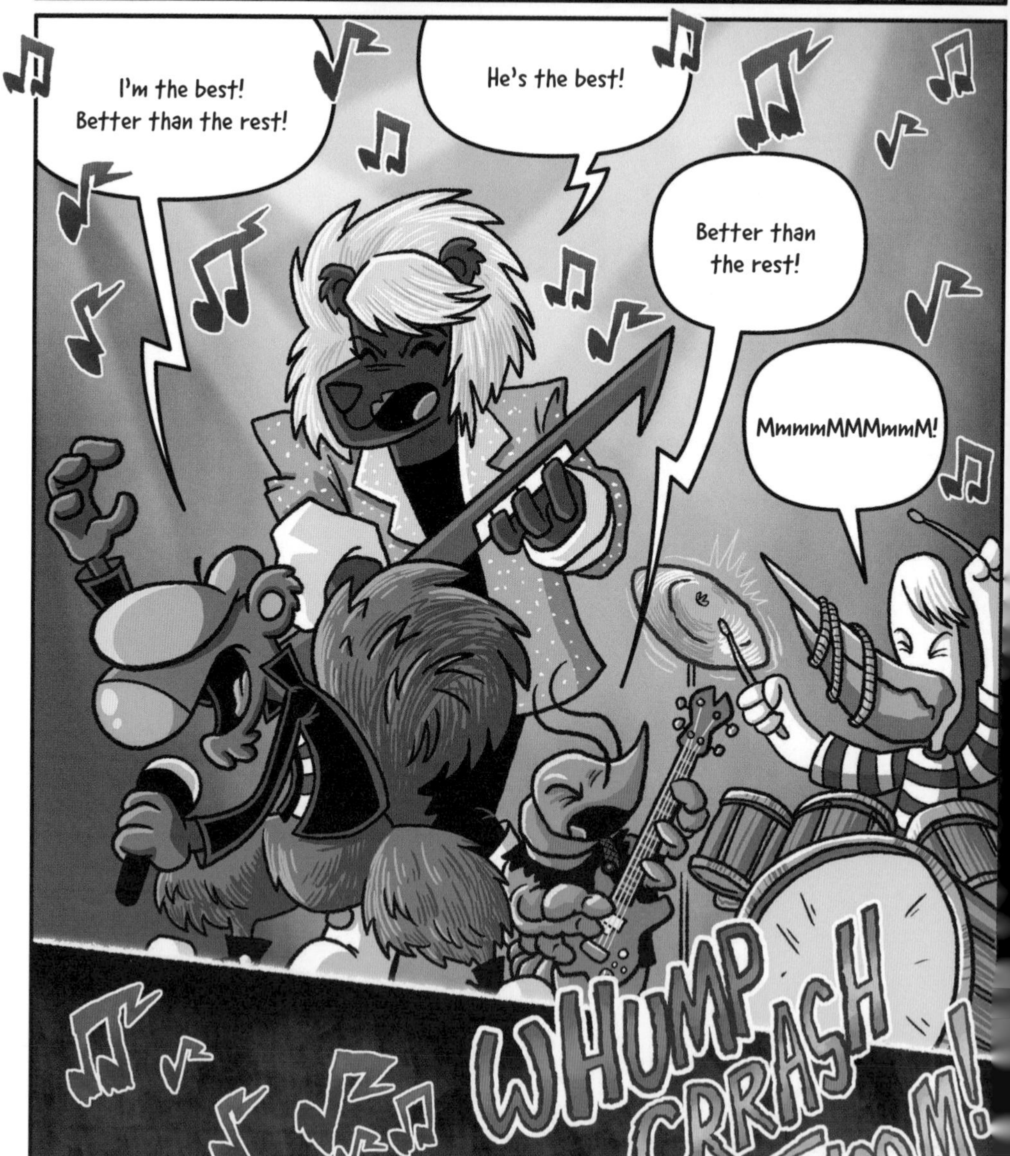
I'm the best! Better than the rest!
He's the best!
Better than the rest!
MmmmMMMmmM!
WHUMP CRRASH THOOM!

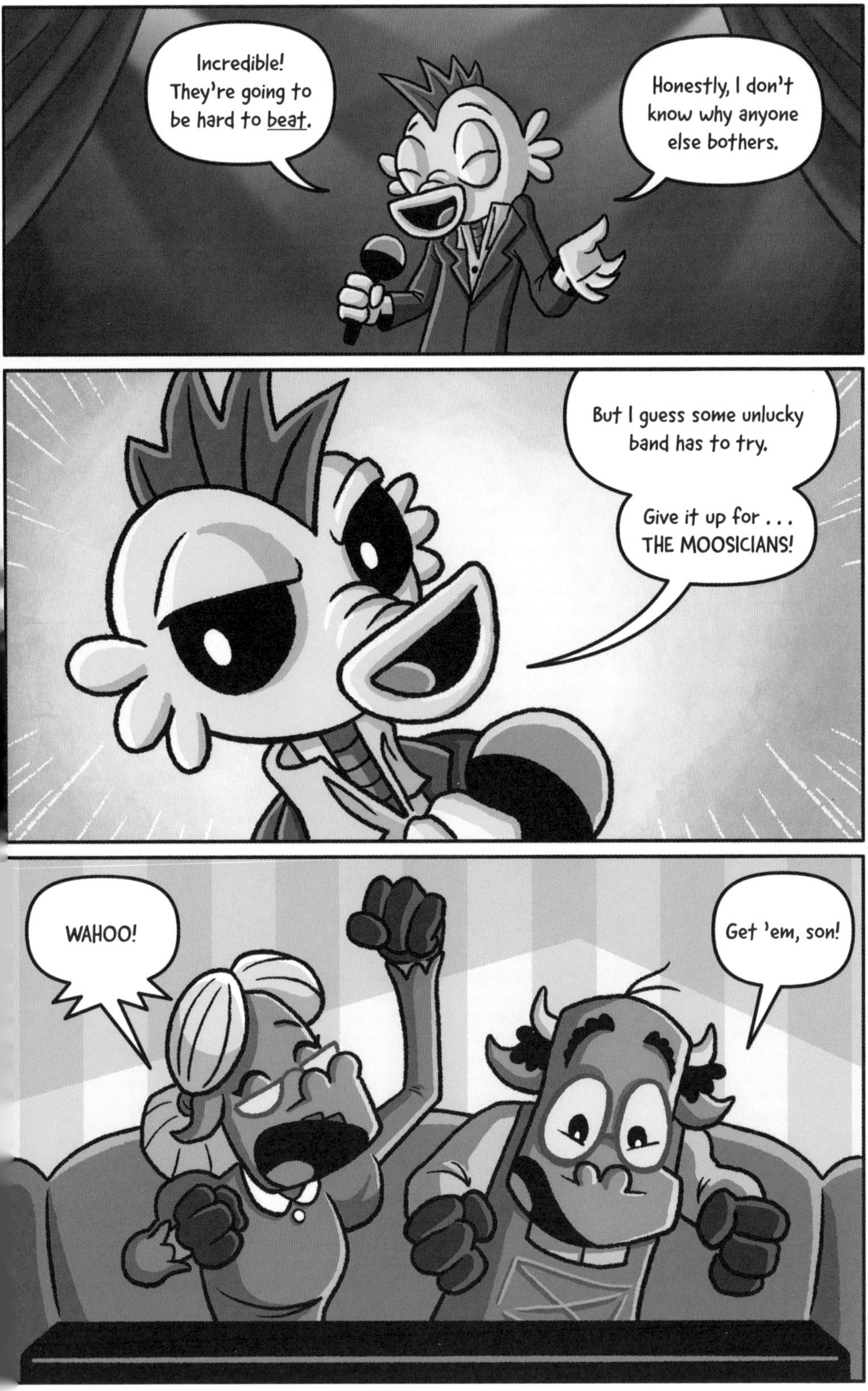
Incredible! They're going to be hard to beat.
Honestly, I don't know why anyone else bothers.
But I guess some unlucky band has to try.
Give it up for . . . THE MOOSICIANS!
WAHOO!
Get 'em, son!

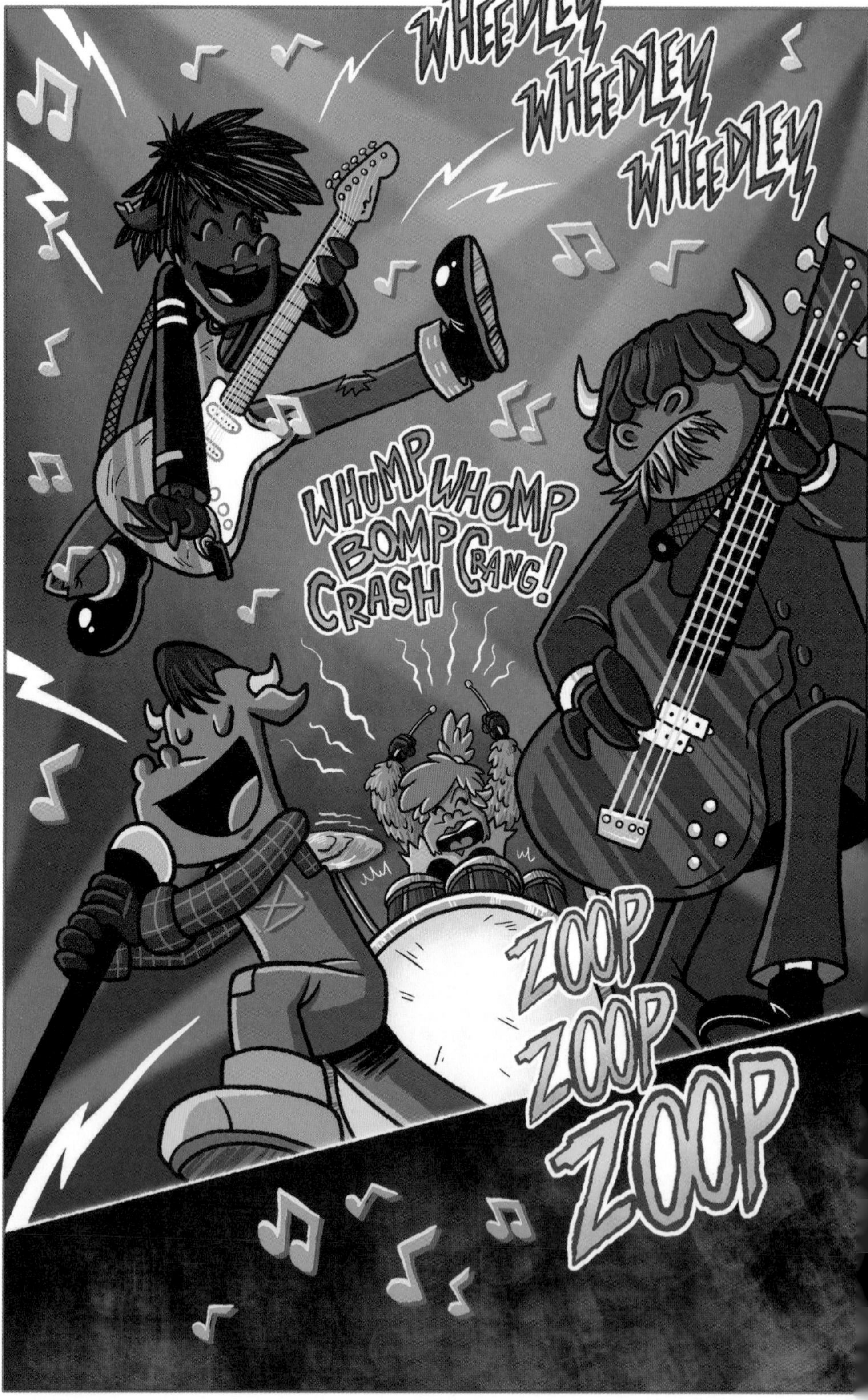
WHEEDLEY WHEEDLEY WHEEDLEY
WHUMP WHOMP BOMP CRASH CRANG!
ZOOP ZOOP ZOOP

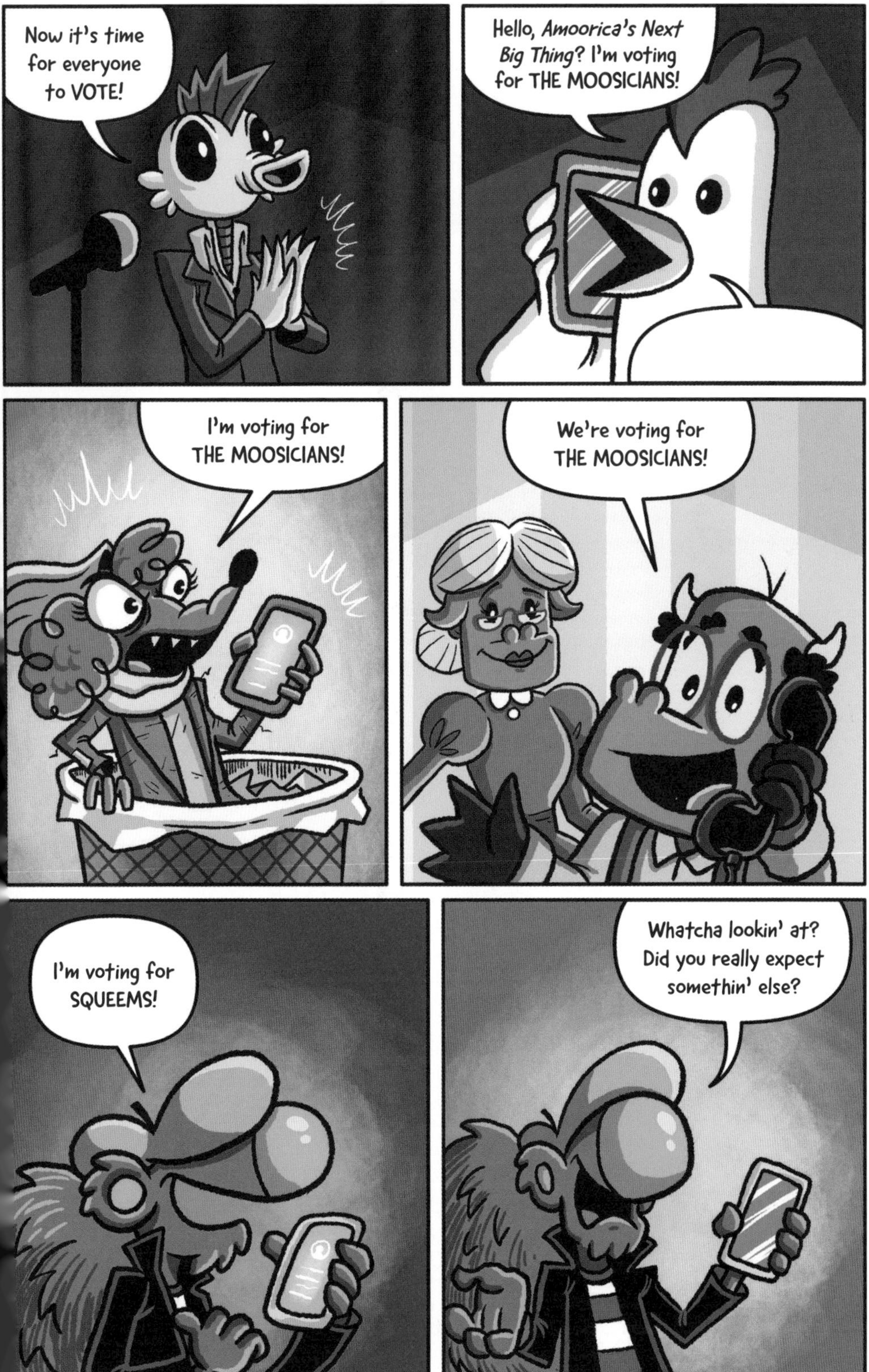
Now it's time for everyone to VOTE!
Hello, *Amoorica's Next Big Thing*? I'm voting for THE MOOSICIANS!
I'm voting for THE MOOSICIANS!
We're voting for THE MOOSICIANS!
I'm voting for SQUEEMS!
Whatcha lookin' at? Did you really expect somethin' else?

CHAPTER 12

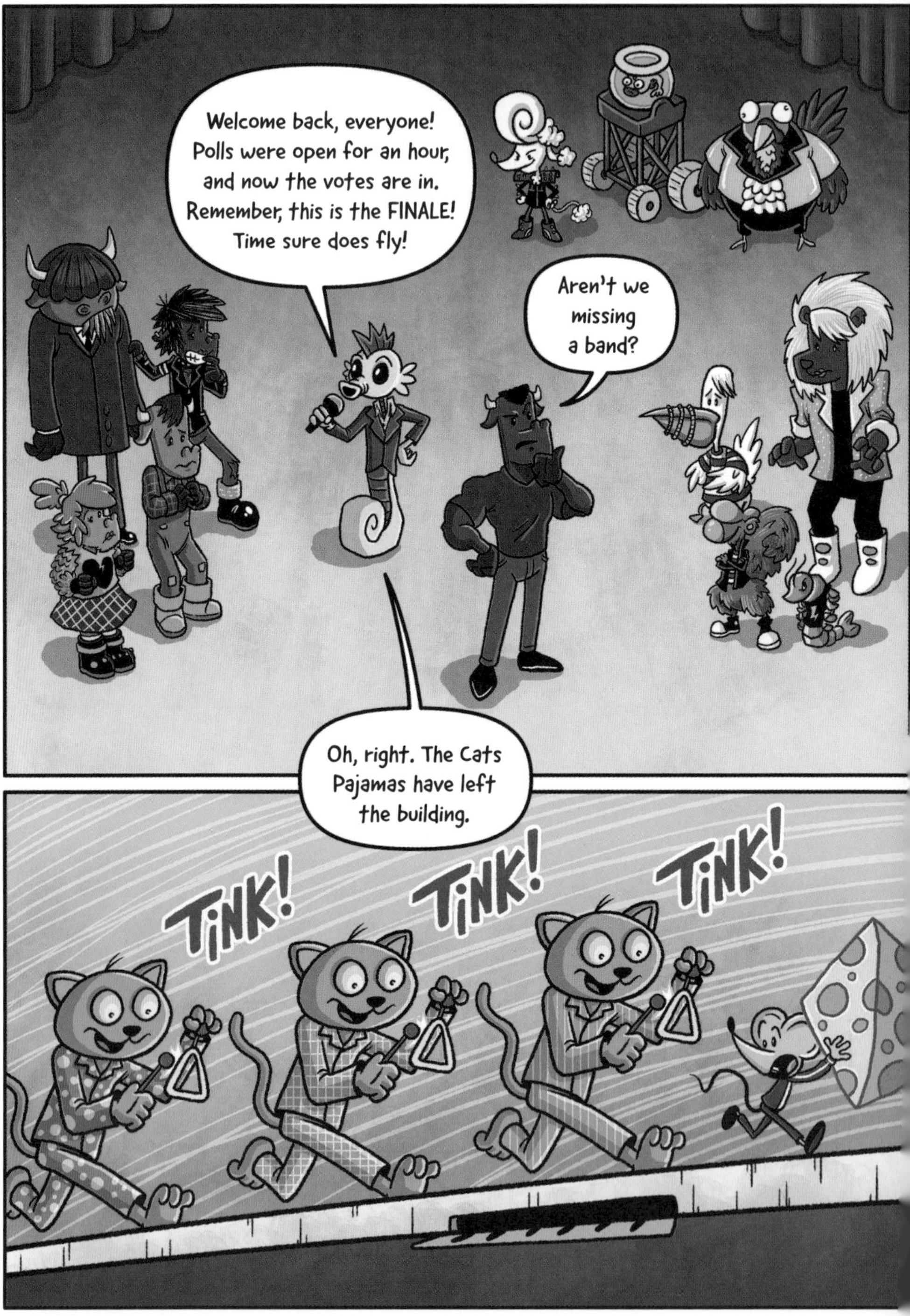

Welcome back, everyone! Polls were open for an hour, and now the votes are in. Remember, this is the FINALE! Time sure does fly!
Aren't we missing a band?
Oh, right. The Cats Pajamas have left the building.
TiNK!
TiNK!
TiNK!

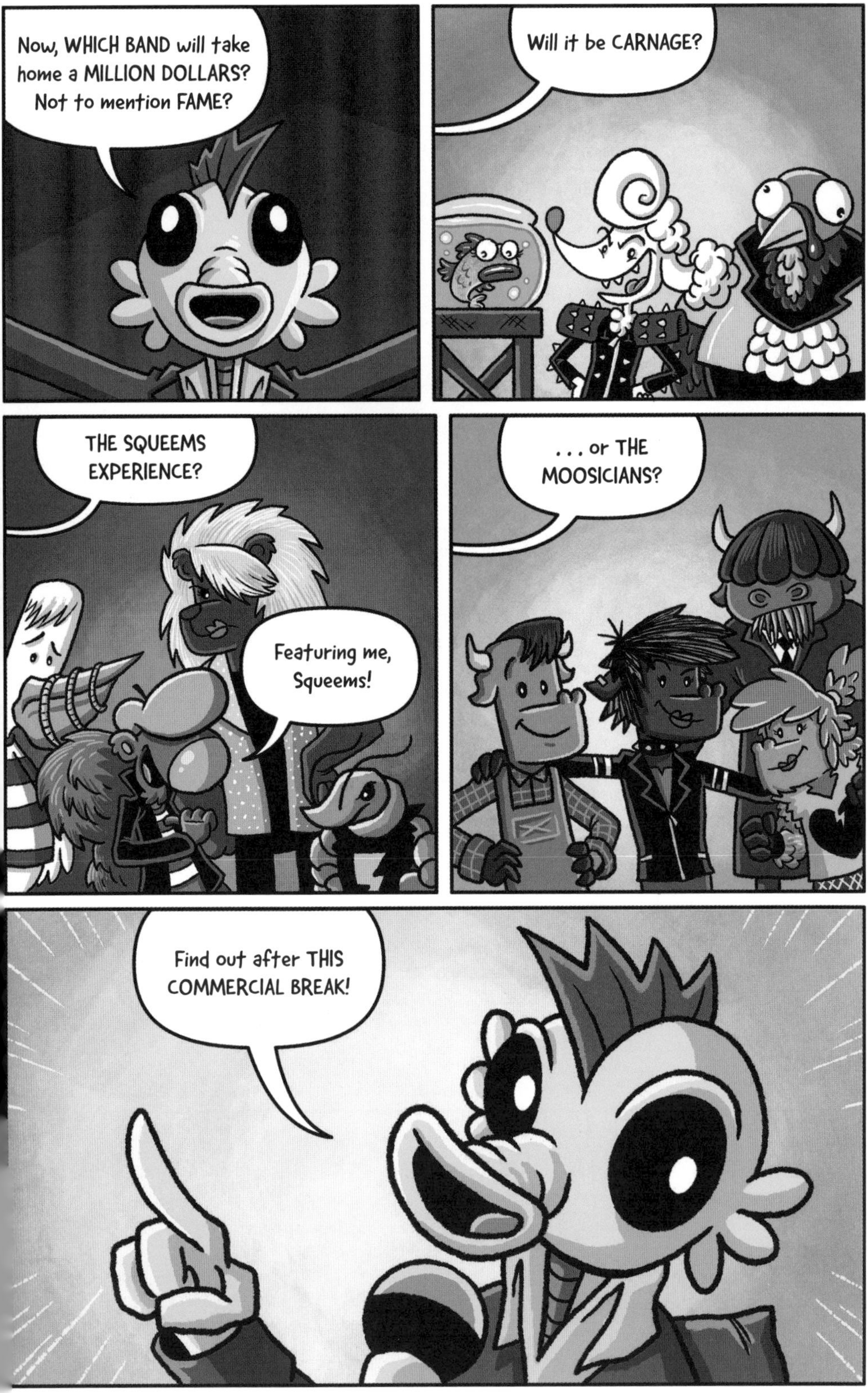
Now, WHICH BAND will take home a MILLION DOLLARS? Not to mention FAME?
Will it be CARNAGE?
THE SQUEEMS EXPERIENCE?
Featuring me, Squeems!
. . . or THE MOOSICIANS?
Find out after THIS COMMERCIAL BREAK!

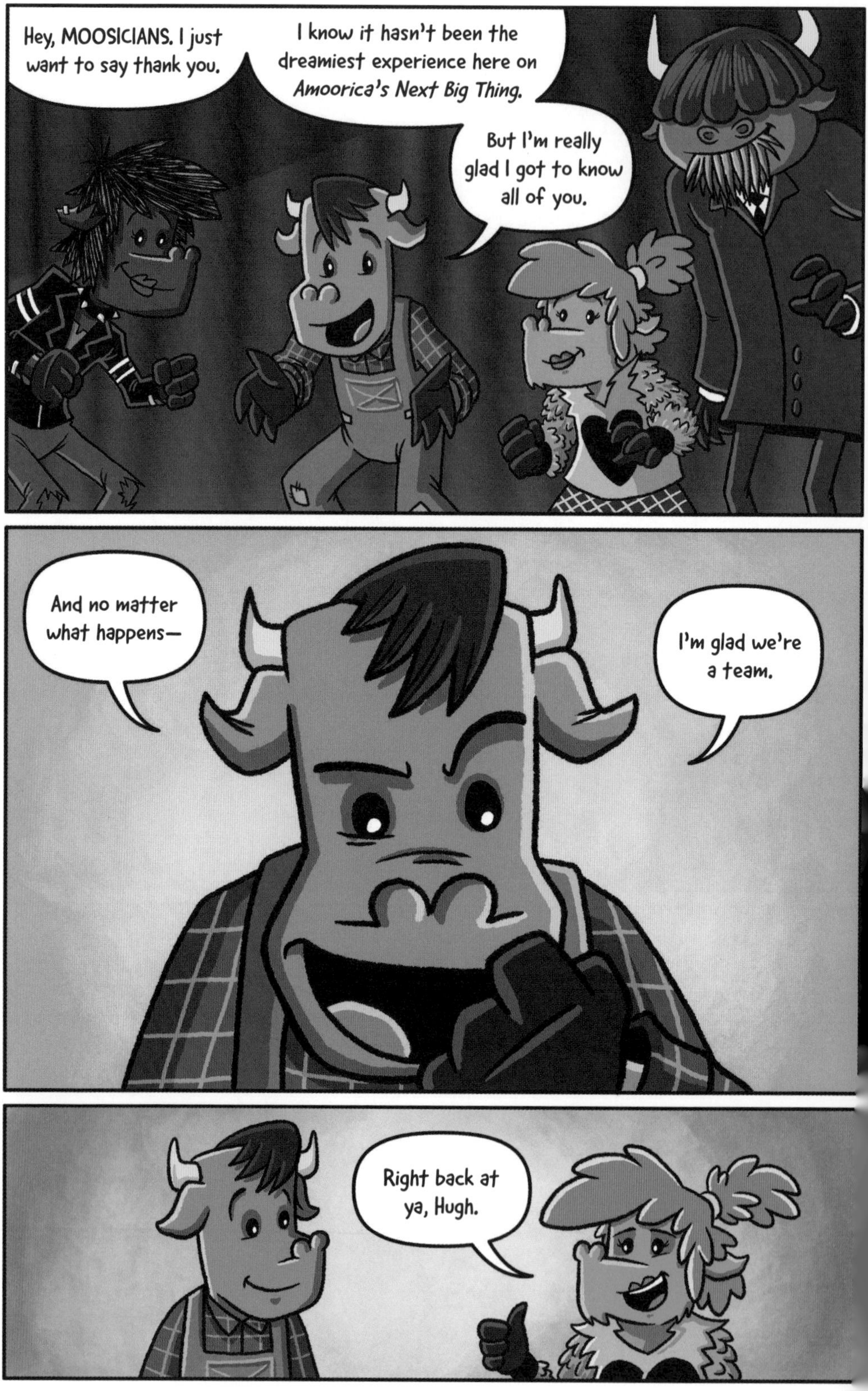
Hey, MOOSICIANS. I just want to say thank you.
I know it hasn't been the dreamiest experience here on *Amoorica's Next Big Thing.*
But I'm really glad I got to know all of you.
And no matter what happens—
I'm glad we're a team.
Right back at ya, Hugh.

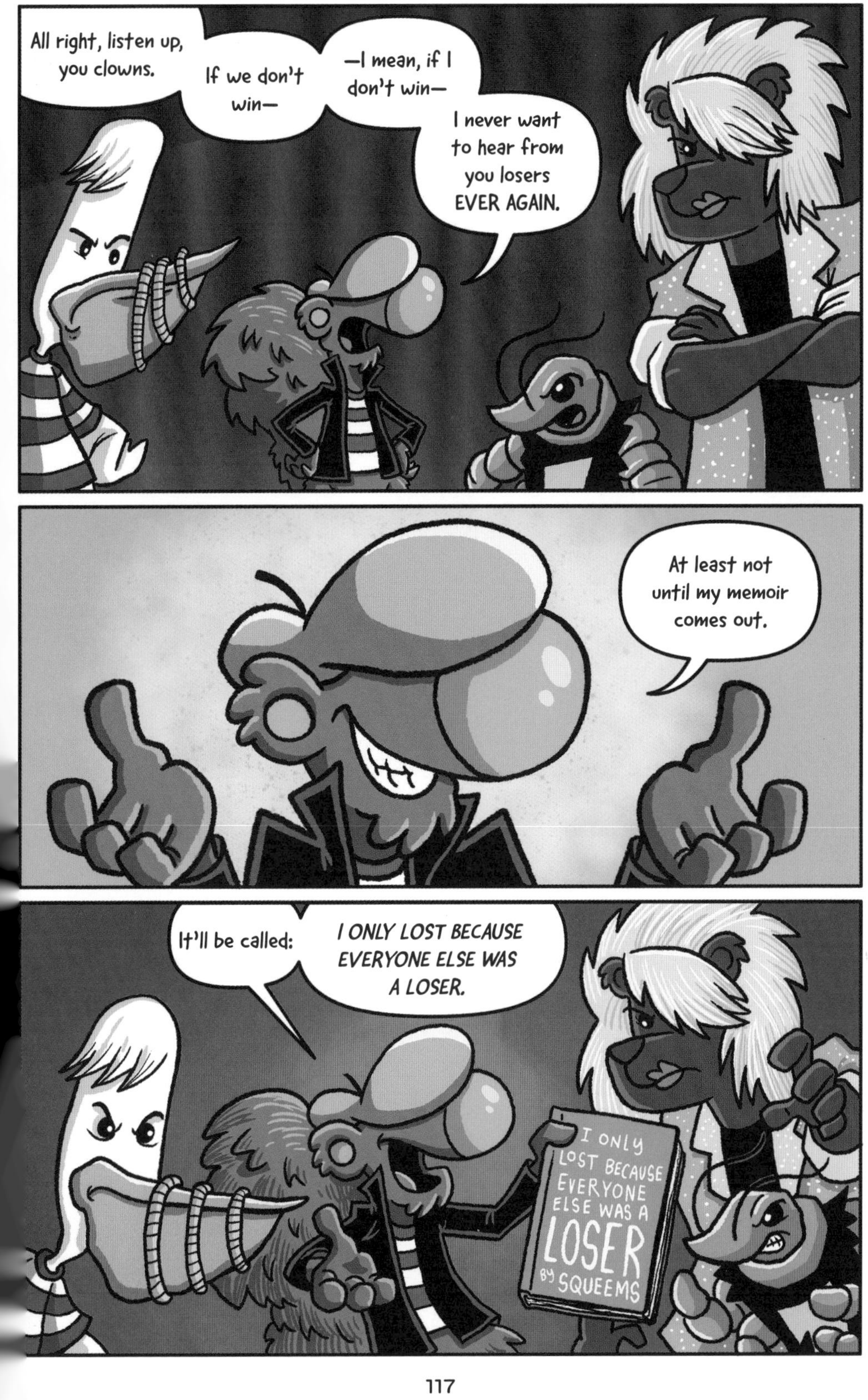
All right, listen up, you clowns.
If we don't win—
—I mean, if I don't win—
I never want to hear from you losers EVER AGAIN.
At least not until my memoir comes out.
It'll be called:
I ONLY LOST BECAUSE EVERYONE ELSE WAS A LOSER.
I ONLY LOST BECAUSE EVERYONE ELSE WAS A LOSER BY SQUEEMS

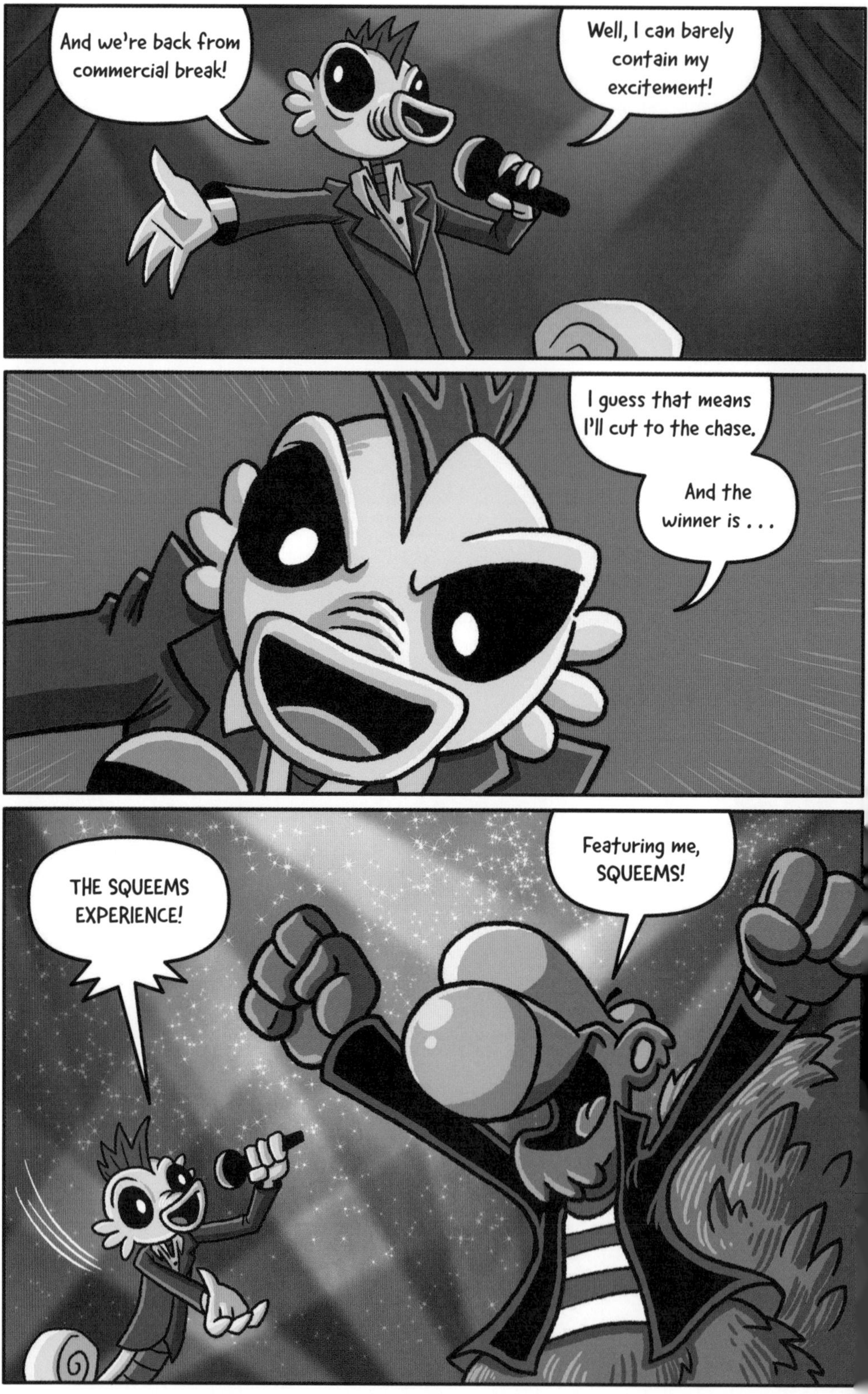
And we're back from commercial break!
Well, I can barely contain my excitement!
I guess that means I'll cut to the chase.
And the winner is . . .
THE SQUEEMS EXPERIENCE!
Featuring me, SQUEEMS!

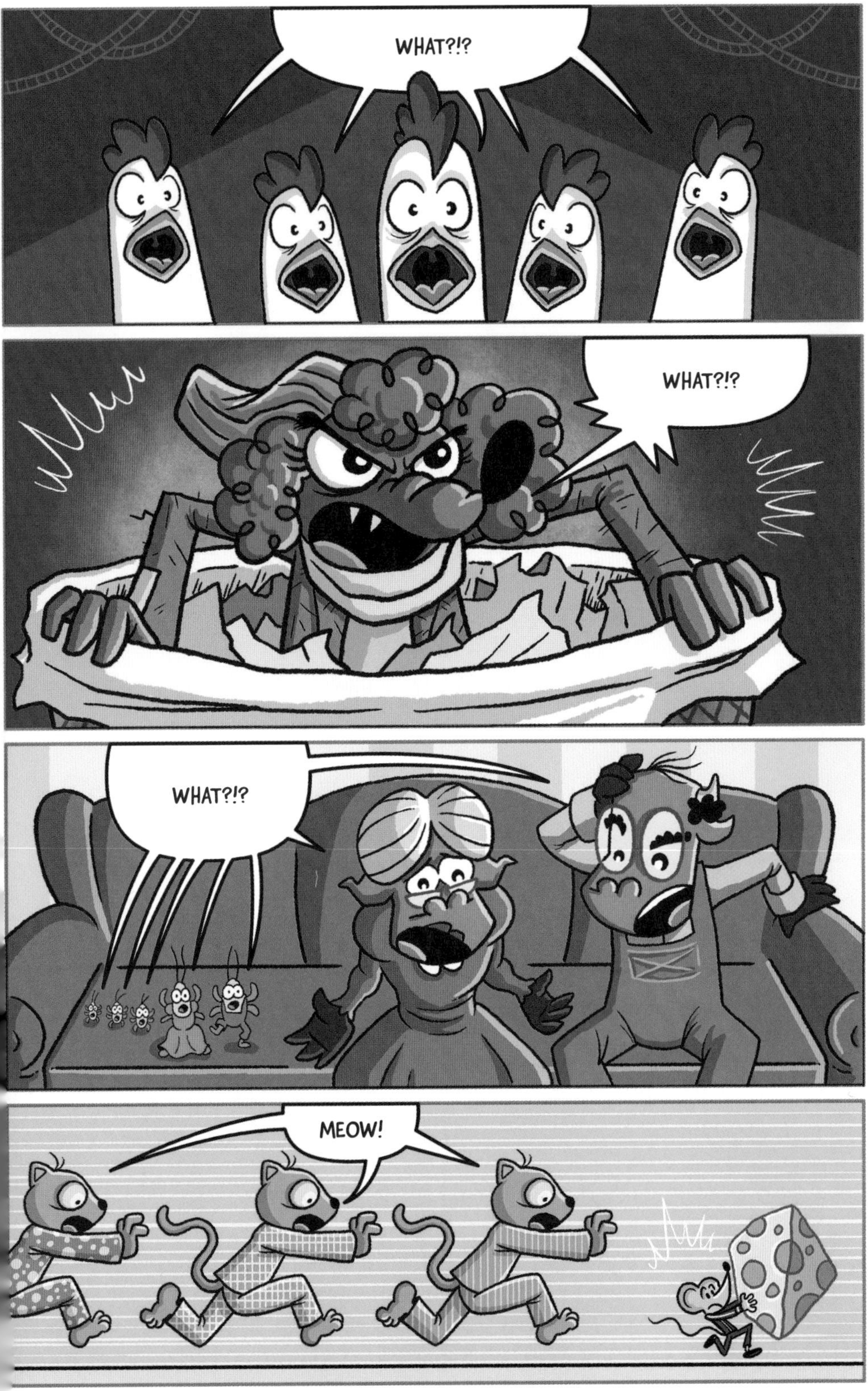
WHAT?!?
WHAT?!?
WHAT?!?
MEOW!

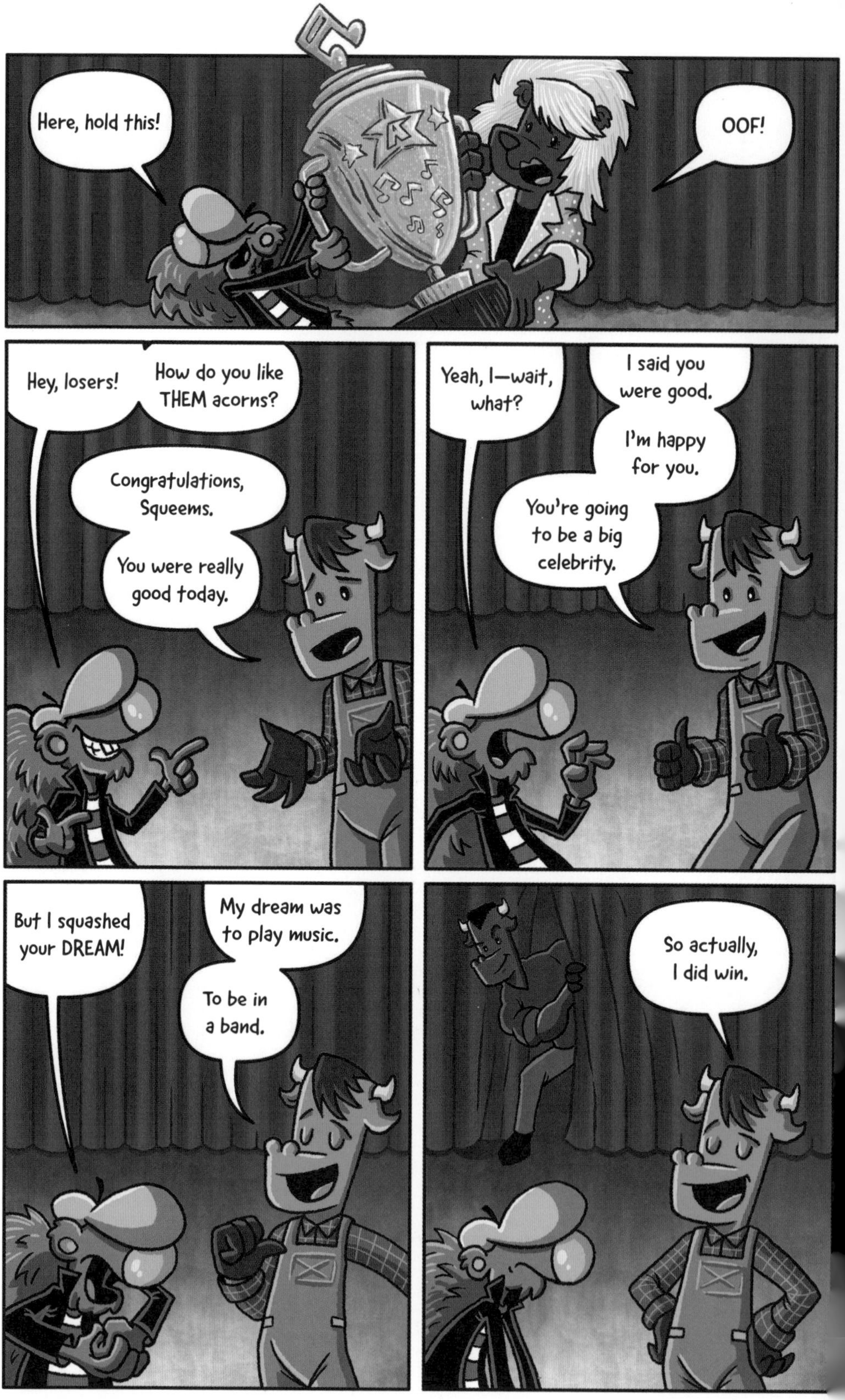
Here, hold this!
OOF!
Hey, losers!
How do you like THEM acorns?
Congratulations, Squeems.
You were really good today.
Yeah, I—wait, what?
I said you were good.
I'm happy for you.
You're going to be a big celebrity.
But I squashed your DREAM!
My dream was to play music.
To be in a band.
So actually, I did win.

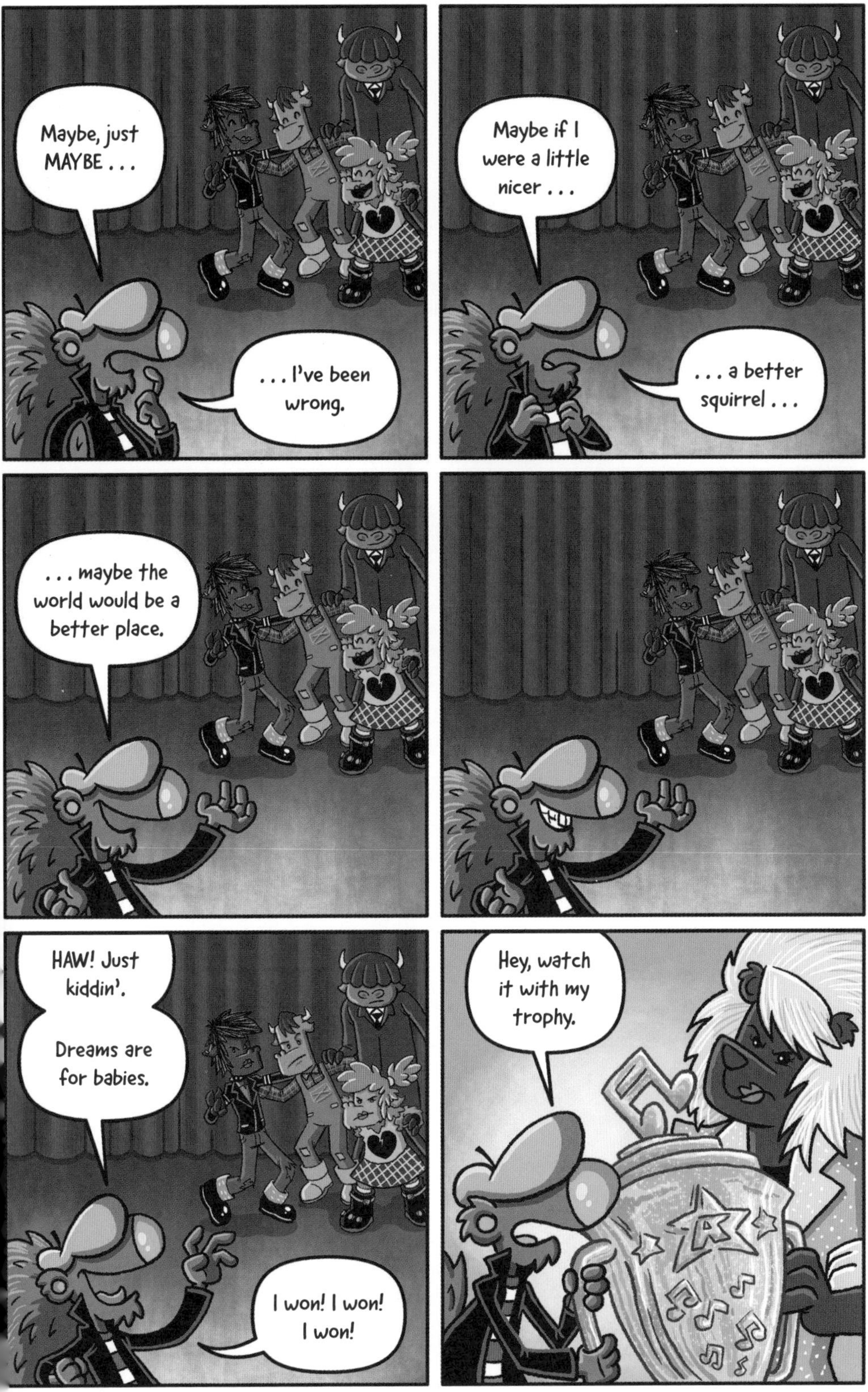

Maybe, just MAYBE . . .
. . . I've been wrong.
Maybe if I were a little nicer . . .
. . . a better squirrel . . .
. . . maybe the world would be a better place.
HAW! Just kiddin'.
Dreams are for babies.
I won! I won! I won!
Hey, watch it with my trophy.

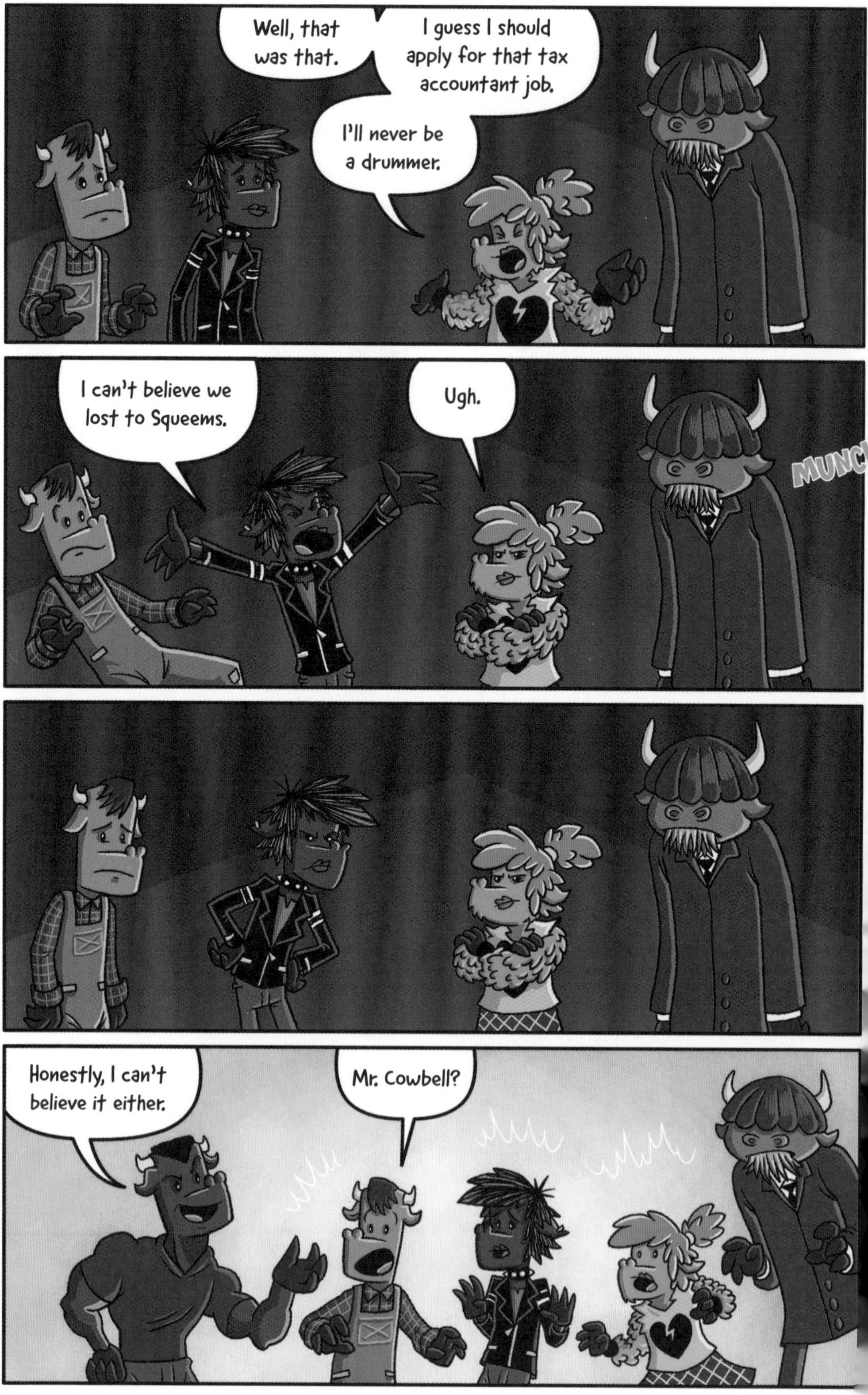
Well, that was that.
I guess I should apply for that tax accountant job.
I'll never be a drummer.
I can't believe we lost to Squeems.
Ugh.
MUNC
Honestly, I can't believe it either.
Mr. Cowbell?

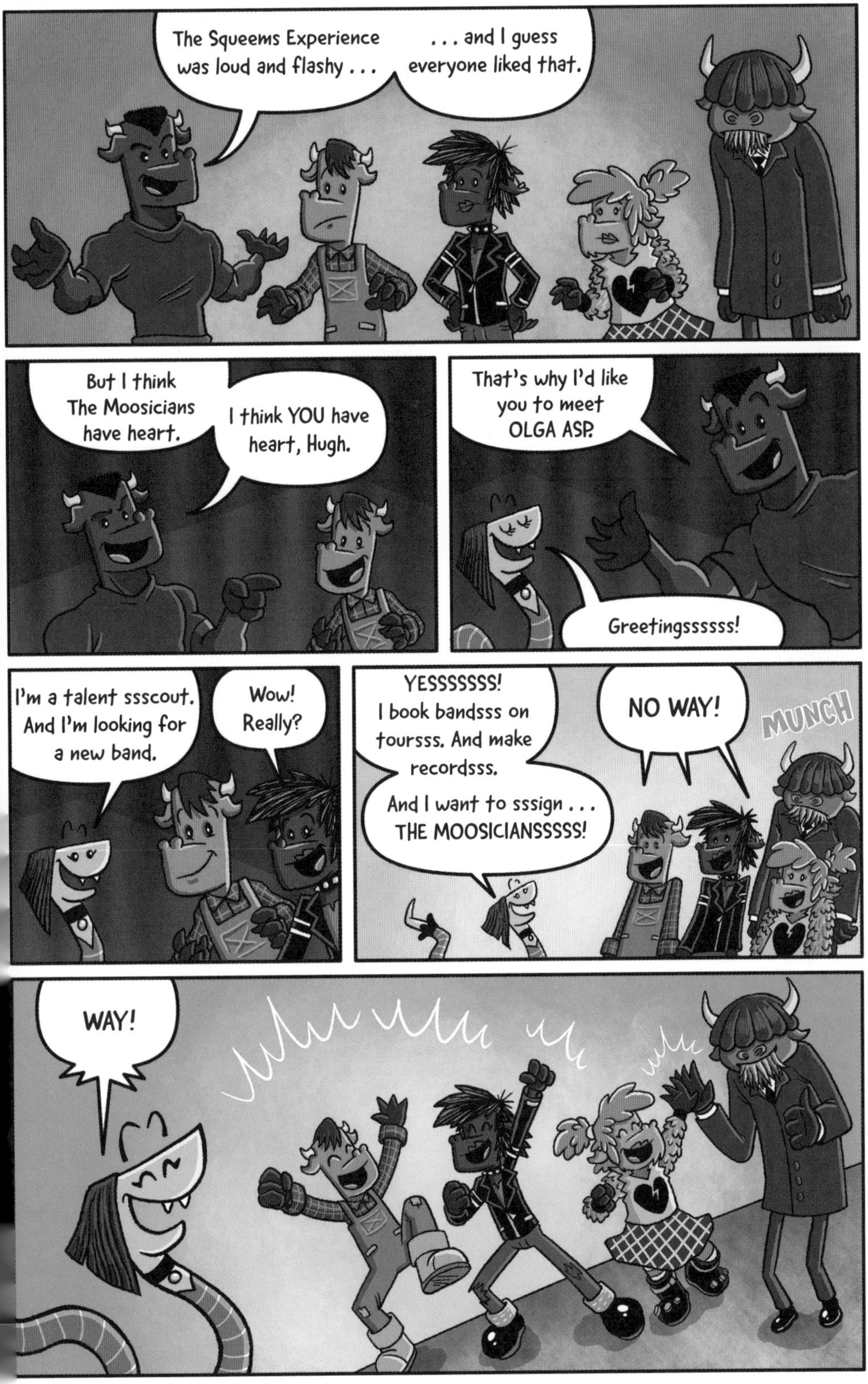
The Squeems Experience was loud and flashy . . .
. . . and I guess everyone liked that.
But I think The Moosicians have heart.
I think YOU have heart, Hugh.
That's why I'd like you to meet OLGA ASP.
Greetingssssss!
I'm a talent ssscout. And I'm looking for a new band.
Wow! Really?
YESSSSSSS! I book bandsss on toursss. And make recordsss.
And I want to sssign . . . THE MOOSICIANSSSSS!
NO WAY!
MUNCH
WAY!

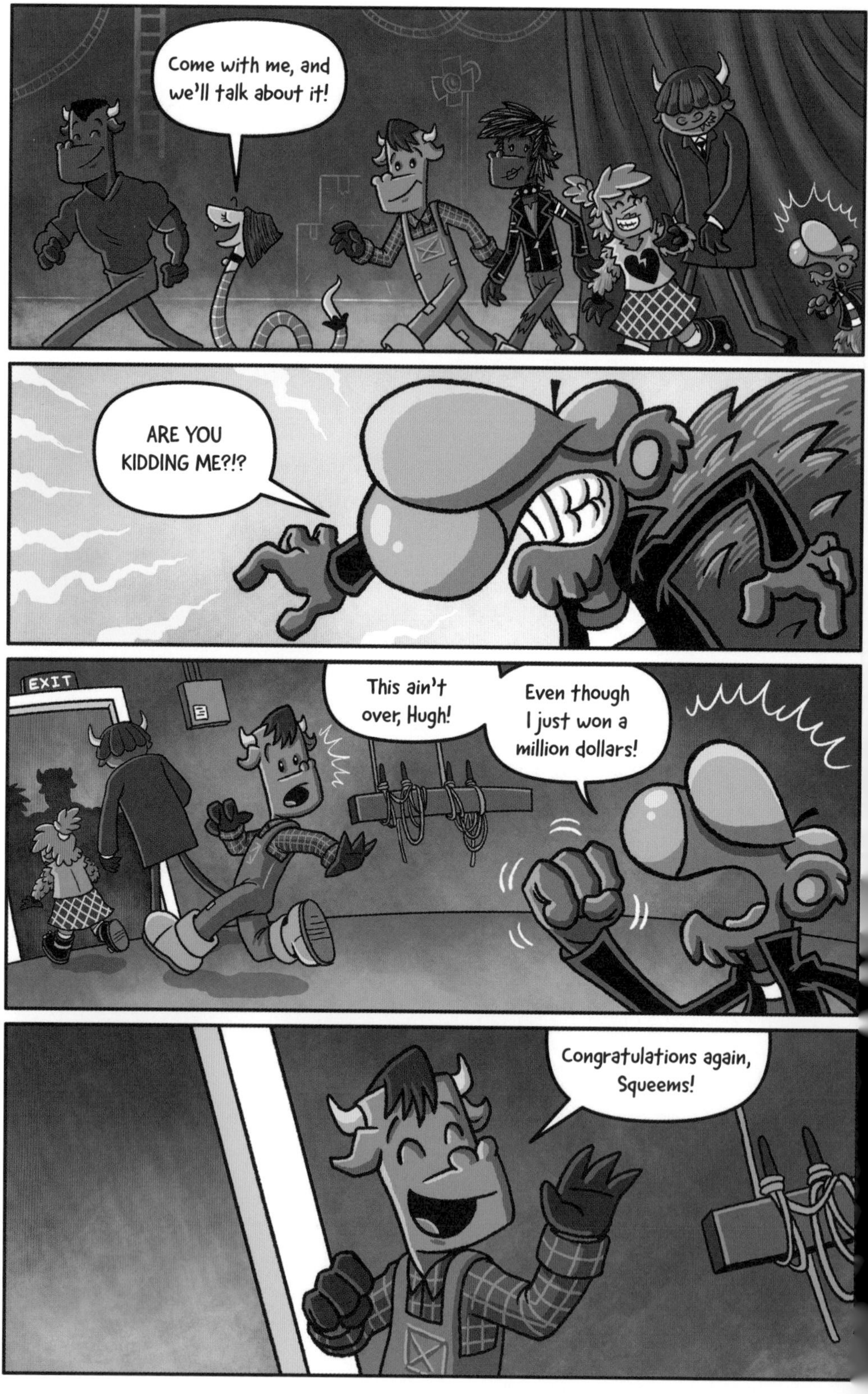
Come with me, and we'll talk about it!
ARE YOU KIDDING ME?!?
This ain't over, Hugh!
Even though I just won a million dollars!
EXIT
Congratulations again, Squeems!

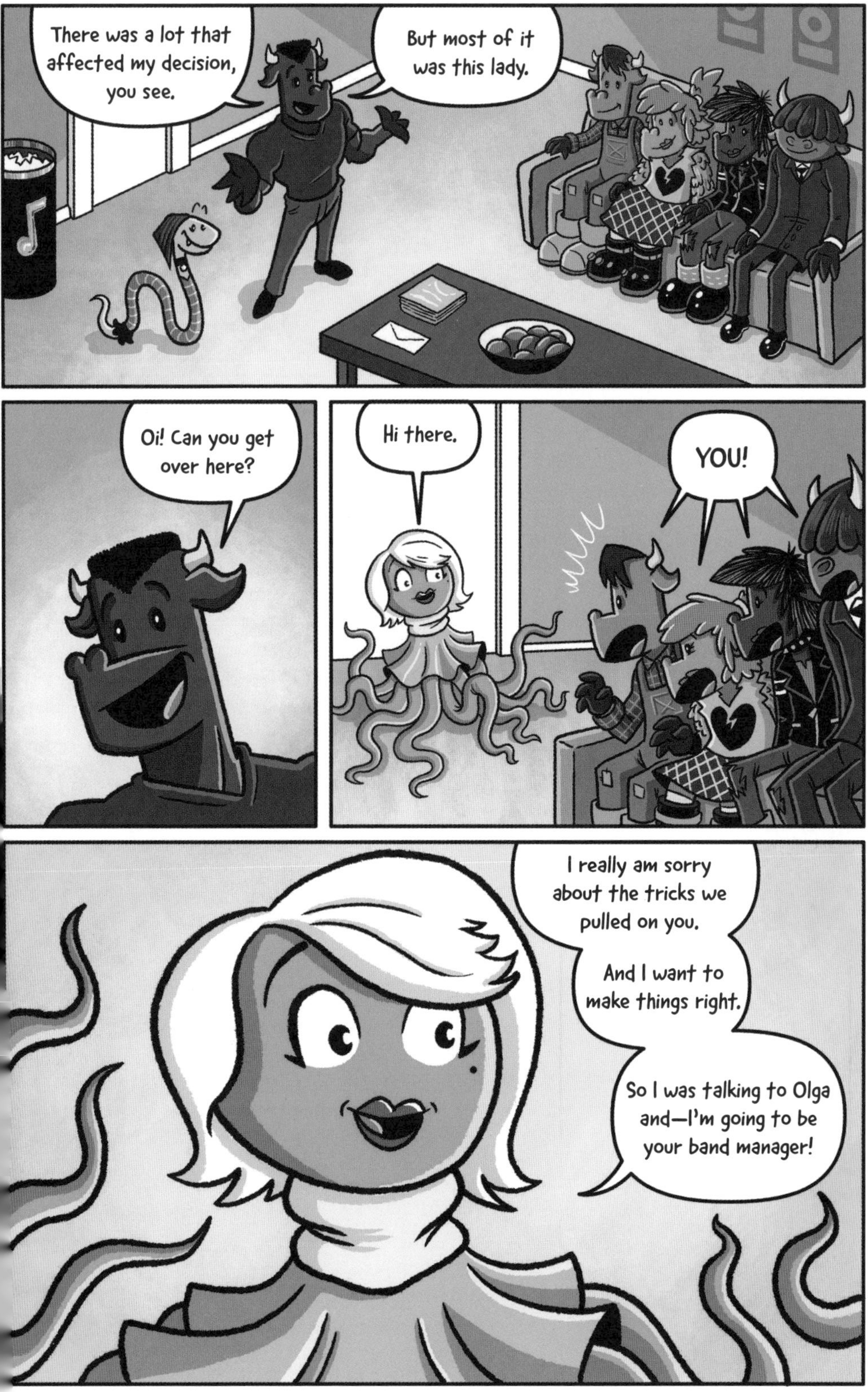
There was a lot that affected my decision, you see.
But most of it was this lady.
Oi! Can you get over here?
Hi there.
YOU!
I really am sorry about the tricks we pulled on you.
And I want to make things right.
So I was talking to Olga and—I'm going to be your band manager!

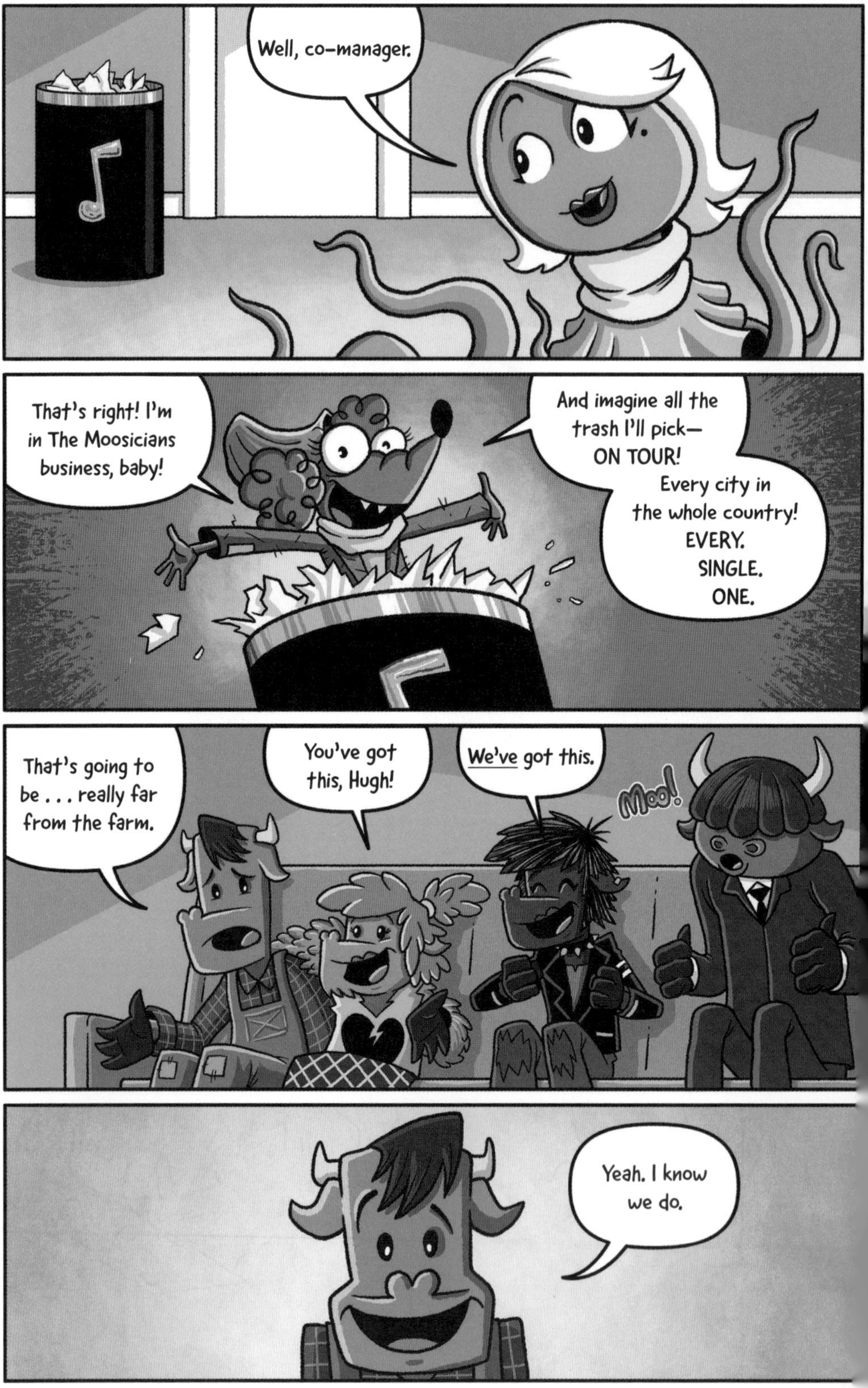

Well, co-manager.
That's right! I'm in The Moosicians business, baby!
And imagine all the trash I'll pick— ON TOUR! Every city in the whole country! EVERY. SINGLE. ONE.
That's going to be . . . really far from the farm.
You've got this, Hugh!
We've got this.
Moo!
Yeah. I know we do.

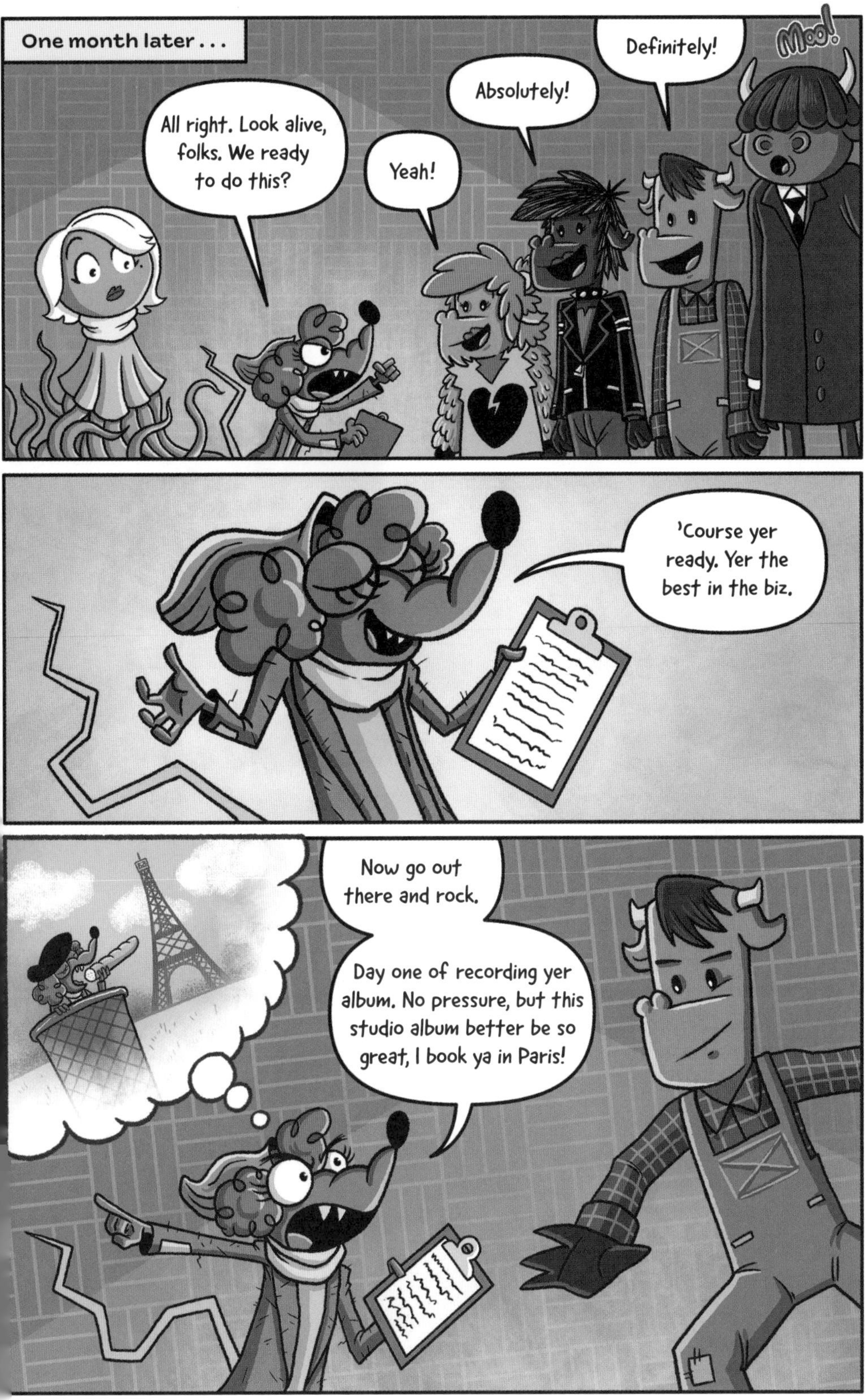
One month later . . .
All right. Look alive, folks. We ready to do this?
Yeah!
Absolutely!
Definitely!
Moo!
'Course yer ready. Yer the best in the biz.
Now go out there and rock.
Day one of recording yer album. No pressure, but this studio album better be so great, I book ya in Paris!

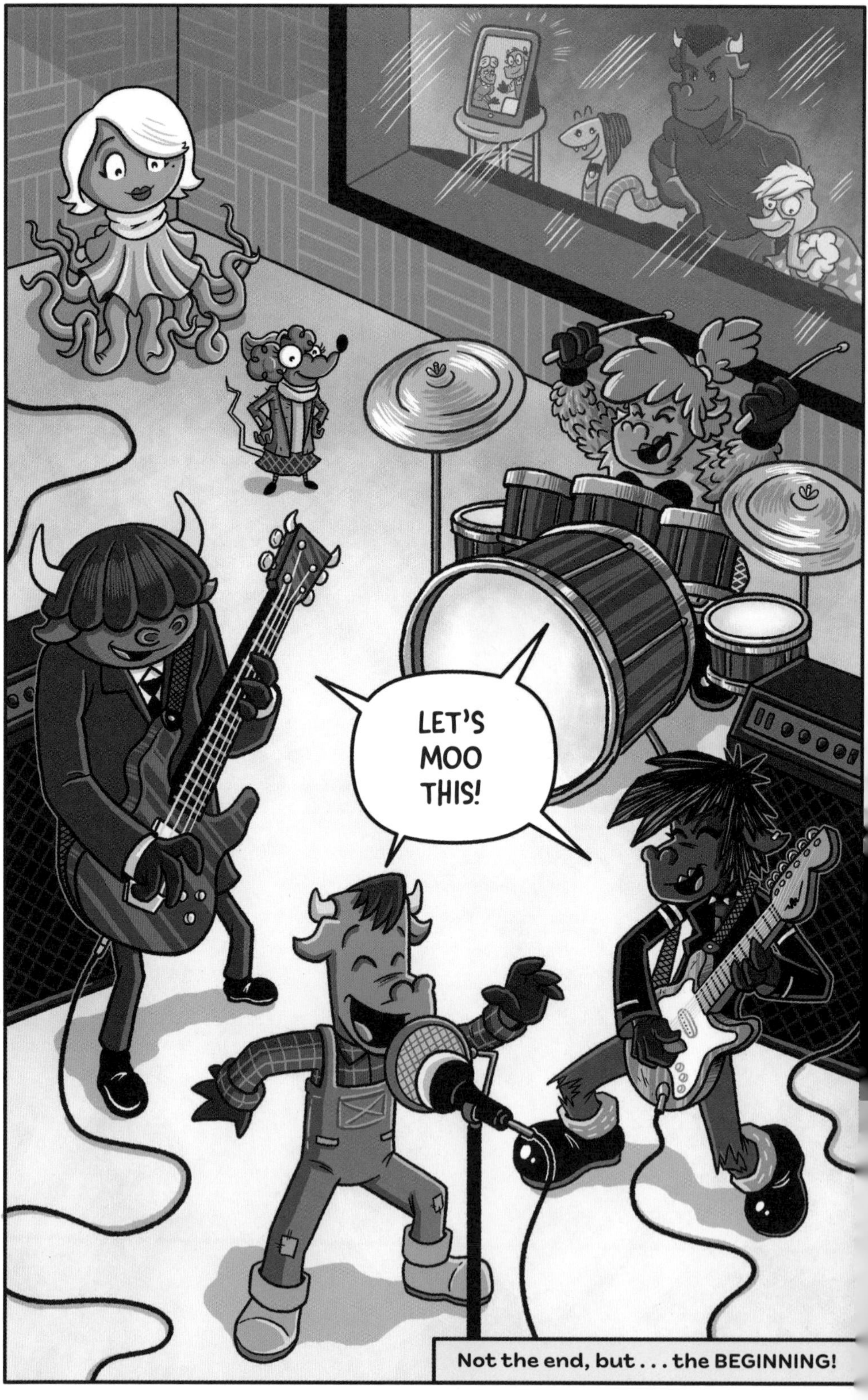
LET'S MOO THIS!
Not the end, but . . . the BEGINNING!